Raves for JAMES KESTREL and FIVE DECEMBERS

"Lyrical, violent, intelligent, breathtaking: this is an unforgettable book."
—*Wall Street Journal*

"One hell of a good story. *Five Decembers* blew me away."
—*Stephen King*

"War, imprisonment, torture, romance…The novel has an almost operatic symmetry, and Kestrel turns a beautiful phrase, too…[He] does this very, very well."
—*New York Times*

"A crime epic for the ages."
—*Dennis Lehane*

"Utterly enthralling. Wildly ambitious and deeply haunting, *Five Decembers* drops you in the middle of a dark noir dream full of heat, loss and memory. Not to be missed."
—*Megan Abbott*

"*Five Decembers* is really excellent. A first-rate book."
—*James Fallows*

"James Kestrel evokes the Hawaii, the Hong Kong and the Tokyo of the 1940s with an urgency, a vividness—a passion—few of us can have met before. Read this book for its palpitating story, its perfect emotional and physical detailing and, most of all, for its unforgettable conjuring of a steamy quicksilver world that will be new to almost every reader."
—*Pico Iyer*

The wind picked up after sunset. The house got cold. They sat next to the fire and looked at a book of photographs her father had brought home from Berlin. She flipped through the pages and described the things she saw. Gothic churches and stone buildings. Subway stations. Flashy nightclubs. She told him about her time in Berlin, living there with her father.

He supposed that most of what they were looking at no longer existed. Whatever she'd seen there was gone. The British and the Americans had seen to it.

They stood up together. She led him down the corridor. The stairs were narrow and steep. She stepped up into the darkness.

"This way," she said. "I'll guide you…"

FIVE
Decembers

by James Kestrel

A HARD CASE CRIME NOVEL

A HARD CASE CRIME BOOK

(HCC-150)

First Hard Case Crime edition: October 2021

Published by

Titan Books
A division of Titan Publishing Group Ltd
144 Southwark Street
London SE1 0UP

in collaboration with Winterfall LLC

Print edition ISBN 978-1-78909-867-9
E-book ISBN 978-1-78909-612-5

Design direction by Max Phillips
www.maxphillips.net

Typeset by Swordsmith Productions

Printed in the United States of America

Visit us on the web at www.HardCaseCrime.com

PART ONE:

Knives and Scars
Honolulu | Wake Island | Hong Kong
November 26, 1941 – December 7, 1941

1

Joe McGrady was looking at a whiskey. It was so new the ice hadn't begun to melt, even in this heat. A cacophony surrounded him. Sailors were ordering beers ten at a go, reaching past each other to light the girls' cigarettes. Someone dropped a nickel in the Wurlitzer, and then there was Jimmy Dorsey and his orchestra. The men compensated for the new noise. They raised their voices. They were shouting at the girls now, and they outnumbered them. The night was just getting started, and so far they weren't drinking anything harder than beer. They wouldn't get to fistfights for another few hours. By the time they did, it would be some other cop's problem. So he picked up his drink, and sniffed it. Forty-five cents per liquid ounce. Worth every penny, even if a three-finger pour took more than an hour to earn.

Before he had a taste of it, the barman was back. Shaved head, swollen eyes. Straight razor scars on both his cheeks. A face that made you want to hurry up and drink. But McGrady set his glass down.

"Joe," Tip said.

"Yeah."

"Telephone—Captain Beamer, I guess. You can take it upstairs."

He knew the way. So he grabbed the drink again, and knocked it back. The whole thing, one gulp. Smooth and smoky. He might as well have it. If Beamer was calling him now, then he was going to be pulling overtime. Which meant tomorrow—Thursday—was going to be a bust. Molly was going to be disappointed. On

the other hand, he'd be drawing extra pay. So he could afford to make it up to her later. He put three half-dollars on the bar, wiped his mouth on his shirtsleeve, and went upstairs.

"This is Detective McGrady."

"Thank Christ."

"Sir?"

"You're not drunk."

"I punched out a half hour ago. If you'd given me a whole hour, maybe I could've done something."

"Some other night. Get back here on the double. I've got the Chief waiting."

"Yes, sir."

He set the receiver back onto its Bakelite cradle and took the other staircase, the one that led directly from the Bowsprit's upstairs office to the street. It was raining, but it wouldn't last. Besides, there were awnings and porticos above most of the Chinatown shops. He had a roof over his head for all but the last minute of the walk back to Merchant Street. He waited on the steps of the Yokohama Specie Bank as a dozen black-jacketed cops roared up and parked their motorbikes stern-to along the curb. Then he crossed Merchant and went into his headquarters.

Captain Beamer's office was in the basement. McGrady came in without knocking and shut the door behind him. He took off his hat and settled it onto his knee when he sat down.

"This just came in," Beamer said. "Not half an hour ago."

"You said the Chief was here?"

"He stepped out a minute."

Beamer pushed up his glasses and swiveled the green shade of his lamp, uncovering the bulb. Now the room was brighter, but just as stifling. Beamer chain smoked with the door closed.

There was no ventilation, and tropical heat seeped through the bedrock. Now he was lighting a new cigarette off the butt of his last. He ground out the old one, the ashtray overflowing to the desk. Even in here, Beamer wouldn't roll up his shirtsleeves. He was that kind of guy. He was wearing a dark uniform jacket and tie, his Sam Browne belt cinched tight around his waist and across his chest. The man was too skinny to sweat.

"We're short. Happens every year, day before Thanksgiving. I'd go up there myself if the Chief could trust someone to sit in this chair all night. He'd rather have you in the field than on the phones. Even if you're a risk. You okay with that?"

"Yes, sir."

"That's what they taught you in the service?" Beamer asked. "No matter what, you say *yes, sir*?"

"Yes, sir," McGrady said. "That's how it goes."

"I'm still getting a feel for you."

"Yes, sir."

"You worked a homicide?"

"Five, on patrol. I was first on the scene—"

"But as a detective?"

"No, sir. You know that."

"I'm making a point. And you're not from here, are you?"

If Beamer had seen the personnel file, then he knew McGrady wasn't from anywhere. He'd seen Chicago, San Francisco, Norfolk, and San Juan before turning six. That was just a warm-up for what came later. His father had given him a good enough taste of the Navy, so he'd tried college instead. Four years later, he was back where he started. Except that he'd joined the Army. His hitch had ended in Honolulu, and he'd stayed on. Beamer might have known plenty about him, but it wasn't a two way street. McGrady wasn't even sure of his new Captain's first name.

"I've been here five years since discharge. Most I've ever lived in one spot. This is home, sir."

"You're either from here, or you're not," Beamer said. "And you're not. You ever walked a dog?"

"Yes, sir."

"If it doesn't know the length of its lead, it's liable to get hurt," Beamer said. He held his hands about six inches apart. "Yours is like this. Run ahead, I'll yank you back so hard your neck snaps."

"All right," McGrady said.

It was just a little thing, dropping *sir*. But it stopped him from reaching across the desk, wrapping Beamer's tie around his fist, and bouncing his pinched face off the desktop. And Beamer didn't even register it. Either you've been in the Army, or you haven't.

"We're absolutely clear on that?"

"Sure thing, Cap."

"Then we'll get along fine."

Beamer's door opened, and Chief Gabrielson stepped in. McGrady began to stand up, but Gabrielson motioned him down. There was one empty chair, but Gabrielson stood with his back against the closed door.

"You tell him yet?" he asked Beamer.

"Just getting there."

"Start with the call," Gabrielson said.

Beamer blew smoke in McGrady's direction. "You know Reginald Faithful?"

"I've heard the name. The dairyman."

"He's got a house around the bend from Kahana Bay. But he runs most of his herd in Kaaawa Valley. He and the Chief are friends, so he called the Chief first. You follow me?"

"No."

"He didn't call the front desk, and tell his story, and get passed around till he got to someone."

"Okay."

"Which means, right now, there are exactly three people in the department who know about this. Which means, I'm not going to open the paper tomorrow and see a story. Am I?"

"I understand."

"Reggie's got this boy," Gabrielson said. "Miguel."

"When you say boy—"

"Not his son. A hired hand."

"Okay."

"So, Miguel came knocking on his door tonight," Gabrielson went on. "He was rattled, had a story to tell. Reggie didn't know whether to believe him or not. But if it's true, you've got a case. Can you handle it, you think?"

"I've just been waiting for the chance."

Beamer blew smoke at the ceiling.

"There's an equipment shed at the back of the valley," Gabrielson said. "Miguel keeps a cot and a blanket in there. Probably a bottle, too. He went in tonight, and got his lantern lit, and the first thing he saw was a guy hanging from the rafters."

"A suicide?"

"You ever heard of someone putting himself upside down on a meat hook?" Beamer asked. He took a long draw on his cigarette. When he spoke again, smoke came spilling out both corners of his mouth. "That'd be a new one to me. In terms of suicide."

"He was hanging from a hook?"

"You better get up there and find out," Beamer said. "Maybe it's nothing but a cowhand with the DT's. But the second you know either way, what do you do?"

Beamer held up his hands again, indicating the length of McGrady's leash.

"Make my report."

"To me."

"Yeah."

"It's your first murder. You've been here five years. I was clearing cases with Apana Chang before you were born. Remember that, and we'll get along."

McGrady took the Pali Road, the lights of Honolulu disappearing behind him as he ascended into the mountains. Then he went over the edge of the cliffs, and the only sign of civilization was the road itself. In full darkness, he came through the switchbacks. He was on the windward side. Jungle shouldered over the road and pushed through the pavement cracks. At stream crossings, waterfalls sprayed the asphalt.

In perfect conditions, it was the better part of an hour to Kahana Bay. Double that at night, then add half an hour for the rain. So it was past ten when he missed the driveway to Reggie Faithful's half-timbered, mock-Tudor house. He found a pull-off, turned back, and skidded to a stop behind three other vehicles.

He switched off the lights and got out of the car, then looked up at the house. The size alone would have impressed him. He lived in a rented room above a chop suey shop on King Street, the smell of onions and oily pork seeping out of the walls. He could reach out from his bed and touch both of his suits, where they hung on the wall.

McGrady shut his door and walked up the stone stairway, and then across a patio. He climbed a second set of stairs to the porch, and there was Reginald Faithful, waiting for him.

"You're McGrady?"

"That's me. You talked to Chief Gabrielson again."

"To find out when you were coming. And that was an hour ago."

"Maybe you've got a faster way over the mountains. Where's Miguel?"

"Inside. My wife's keeping an eye on him."

"He's in shock?"

"You might put it that way."

"How would you put it?"

"The boy's legs were going out from underneath him. Either we gave him the couch, or he'd be on the floor."

"You give him a drink?"

"There was no point. He was drunk when he got here."

"That's his truck down by the road?"

"It's mine—my company's. But he drives it."

"Your wife drives the LaSalle, and you've got the Cadillac."

"Yes."

"Anyone else in the house?"

"No."

The dairyman set his hand on the porch rail and faced down the slope toward his driveway. He was wearing a wash-worn white shirt. Black suspenders kept up his khaki pants. He'd loosened his tie. He looked at the line of four cars, then back at McGrady.

"And what about you?" he asked. "No partner. You didn't bring backup?"

"It's just me."

Faithful tapped his cigar on the rail.

"If you're all I've got, I guess I ought to show you Miguel."

"I'd rather get to the body—if there is one. Can Miguel walk?"

"It'll take both of us to get him down the stairs."

"That's fine. You're coming, too."

Miguel Silva, Reggie Faithful's cowhand, must have been older than Reggie Faithful's father. He had creased, sun-darkened skin, the color of scorched mahogany. His hair was silver-black,

and clipped short. He was sprawled on the couch, face up, his eyes covered with a rolled towel.

"Really? You're taking him?"

That was Mrs. Faithful, kneeling on the floor next to her husband's employee. She was in a gingham housedress, a loose button at the top. Wavy dark hair, eyes to match it.

"Can't he stay with me?" she asked. "Look at the poor man."

"Until I figure out what's going on, you shouldn't be alone with him."

"He's been with us forever. I trust him."

"Then I shouldn't have any trouble with him, either."

Miguel's clothes were soaked through with sweat. There was a strong odor of liquor coming off him. Otherwise, there was nothing wrong with him. He didn't need Mrs. Faithful's tender ministrations. He could sleep it off in a concrete cell, wake up with a bucket of water, and talk.

McGrady leaned down, pulled away the towel, and slapped the old man's left cheek. He could have been rougher. It would have sped the process of rousting the guy, but there was Mrs. Faithful to consider. He wanted her on his side. Someone ought to be.

The old man opened one eye.

"You a cop?"

McGrady had one of those faces. Everything squared off and somehow unfinished, as though his sculptor had snapped a chisel on unexpectedly hard stone.

He nodded, and the man began to sit up.

"You'll be coming with us."

"Not going back in there."

"All the same."

He took Miguel's wrist and hoisted him to his feet. After that, they went three abreast, McGrady on one side and Reggie

Faithful on the other, Miguel's arms over their shoulders for balance. Across the porch, and down the steps, and to the car. They left him sprawled across the back seat. McGrady shut the door on him and looked back at the house. Mrs. Faithful stood at the top of the steps, just the silhouette of her, the house all lit up behind.

2

The pavement ended as soon as he turned off the coast road and into Kaaawa Valley. At the beginning, the valley was broad and there were fields on either side of the stream. He caught scents of wet grass and cattle, of jungle water running down out of the mountains. But the valley narrowed as he drove up it, the fields shrinking as the cliff walls came in toward the stream. They went under a stand of mango trees and then came into a sodden meadow where nothing grew but ginger.

"It's just around the bend," Faithful said. "A quarter mile."

McGrady glanced behind him. Miguel was asleep again.

"Where's he live when he's not sleeping in the shed?"

"His whole family's out in Nanakuli."

"That far?"

"He gets out there once or twice a month."

"So he lives in the shed."

Faithful shrugged.

"It's got what he needs."

McGrady rounded the last bend and saw the shed. It was backed up against the cliffs, a low waterfall off to the right where the stream broke out of the mountains. It was made of unpainted hardwood lumber. It was rotting from the outside in, but the boards were so thick it probably had a hundred years to go.

"I'm going in," McGrady said. "Stay here with Silva. Shout out if he wakes up. Or makes a run for it. Or comes after you."

He pulled the keys from the ignition, got out of the car, and slammed the door. Faithful jumped out and spoke to him over the roof.

"If he comes after me?"

"Half the time, the guy who finds the body is the one who put it there. So if he comes at you, do whatever you have to do. And shout for me. I'll come running."

McGrady went to the back of the car and used his keys to open the trunk. He found his flashlight. A big six-cell rolled-steel job, heavy as a truncheon. He thumbed the switch. Nothing happened. He gave it a hard slap against his left palm. The trunk flooded with yellow light. There was a black leather satchel with the tools of the trade. He opened it and dug past the extra cuffs and the booklets of blank forms and the teak billy-club. He took out his backup piece, which was a .45 ACP automatic. An unauthorized holdover from his Army days, and not the kind of thing he wanted unattended in a car with his chief's friend and a possible murder suspect. He chambered a round, tucked it behind his belt, and slammed the trunk lid.

Reginald Faithful was a foot away from him, blinking against the light and swatting mosquitoes away from his face.

"You got one of those for me?"

"No."

"How about a light?"

"You've got the car lights."

"You're leaving me out here?"

"It's your land."

He walked across the hoof-trodden dirt, pushed the door open with his shoulder, and stepped inside. Before he even brought the light around, he knew the old man hadn't lied about everything. There was death here. If the smell hadn't given it away, the flies would have.

The day had topped out at eighty-five degrees. It was cooler now, with the rain blowing in and out. But the shed had been sealed tight, and was holding onto the day's heat. When the

door cracked open, McGrady recognized the stench right away. There was a slaughterhouse on the west side of the island, and his business had taken him there twice in the last six months. So he knew the smell of pooled blood and piled entrails, and that at least prepared him for what he saw when his eyes focused.

The dead man hung upside down from the rafters, his ankles impaled on either side of an iron spreader bar. There was no question but that he was dead. He'd been split nearly in half, and most of his guts were on the dirt floor. McGrady covered his nose and mouth with the crook of his left arm, and stepped the rest of the way into the shed.

A fly rose up from the floor and settled on the lens of his light. He waved it away, then crouched to look at the man's face. He was young, maybe eighteen or twenty. It was hard to say, because his eyes were gone and his tongue may have been missing. McGrady wasn't about to dig around in his wrecked mouth to find out for sure.

He got to his feet and turned slowly, casting around with the light. He saw Miguel's camp stove and coffeepot. There was a wooden bucket with water and a bamboo ladle. There were shovels and pickaxes, and bits of nameless tackle and gear hanging from wall hooks. There was a cot along the far wall, piled high with a jumble of sheets and old canvas tarpaulins and Miguel's other clothes.

He turned the light up, and saw the rafters and the underside of the tin roof. The spreader bar hung from a rope, which was looped through a pulley. Someone had hoisted the man up, his whole weight on hooks sunk deep into his ankles.

If he'd been alive for that part, the screams would have carried a mile. McGrady figured he'd been alive. His legs and back were slick with blood that had run down from his ankles.

Impossible if he'd been dead. So he would have screamed, long and hard. But there was no one within screaming distance. This far back in the valley, only the cows would have heard him.

McGrady backed out of the shed. He wiped his mouth with the back of his hand and went over to the car. Miguel was motionless in the back. Reginald Faithful came out of the shadows.

"It's true?"

"I need your telephone," McGrady said. "Unless there's another one closer."

"We leave all this here?"

"The sooner we go, the sooner I can come back. But I've got to talk to my captain, and call in the meat wagon."

The Faithfuls left him alone in the house. He decided to call Molly first. One of her roommates answered. The new girl, from California. He couldn't remember her name.

"It's Joe," he said. "Can you put Molly on?"

"She's been asleep an hour. Since she got back from the library. You want me to wake her up?"

"Can you leave her a note?"

"What note?"

"I caught a big case. I'll make it for dinner tomorrow if I can. If I don't, tell her I'm sorry."

The California girl muttered something and hung up. McGrady called the operator again, and got himself transferred to the downtown police station, detective bureau. He had Captain Beamer on the line inside of a minute.

"McGrady?"

"Yeah."

"I was starting to wonder if I could trust you. What've we got up there?"

"It's what the man said. A body, hanging from the rafters. But he's cut up bad."

"It's a man?"

"Yeah."

"You're sure about that?"

"He's naked."

McGrady paused, waiting for his Captain to cut in. But the man said nothing, so McGrady went on.

"I think what killed him was the disemboweling."

Beamer was rubbing the telephone's receiver against his chin. It had been a while since he'd shaved.

"Other marks?"

The truth was McGrady had looked at the body for maybe ten seconds, holding a shaking flashlight against the dark. The guy could have had words carved into his back, entire paragraphs with names and addresses, and he wouldn't have seen it. He'd just seen the one angle.

He said, "Maybe when the coroner washes him off, we'll know more."

"Anyone we know?"

"Hard to say," McGrady said. "He's covered with blood and his face is a mess. I don't think he's anyone I know. I don't know who you know."

"Race?"

"He's got white skin—I can say that for sure. Take out a guy's eyes and it's hard to rule some things out."

"He could be a Jap, is what you're saying. What color is his hair?"

"Bloody," McGrady said. He pictured the body again. "But if I had to guess, I'd say he's Caucasian. He's too tall. Shoulders are broader than mine."

"All right," Beamer said. "Get back out there and sit tight.

I'll round up some help and send it your way. And put Reggie on. I want to talk to him."

McGrady set the phone on the table and walked out of the house. He found the Faithfuls on the porch. Reggie was leaning against the rail, watching the road down below. His wife was on a rocking chair thirty feet away, at the opposite end. Just a shadow, and the lit tip of a cigarette. He hadn't figured her for a smoker. Maybe she dealt herself an exception on nights when corpses turned up on their land. He could relate.

Reggie heard the door close, and turned at the sound.

"Yes?"

"Beamer wants you," McGrady said. He put his hat back on, and nodded toward Mrs. Faithful. Then he hurried down the steps to his car. Miguel was asleep in the back. That was fine. He could hand him off to the patrolmen when they arrived, or he could bring him to town himself.

3

He was on the last bend before the shack, so he took his foot off the gas, letting the rutted road slow the car. There was a noise from the back. A shuffling thump. Then a moan. He turned to check Miguel. One second of inattention, and it almost cost McGrady his life.

Miguel had fallen off the back seat and was now sprawled over the carpeted hump that housed the rear wheel drive train. He hadn't woken up. So it was no big deal. McGrady looked ahead again, and this time he slammed on the brakes.

Fifty feet in front of him, all lit up in the headlights, was the shed. Ten feet closer than that was a pale yellow Packard coupe. In between the car and the shed, there was a man. He was wearing green mechanic's coveralls. He had on a black watch cap that hid all of his hair. He had a scar on the left side of his face that ran from his ear to the corner of his mouth. He was darkly tanned, but the scar was bone white and almost glistening in the headlights' glare. In his left hand, he held a wood-frame bucksaw. By his right foot, a five-gallon gas can. He was squinting into the headlights, blocking the glare with his free hand. He was trying to identify either the car or its driver. And then he dropped the saw, and reached inside his coveralls.

McGrady went for his gun, but the man outside had started earlier. McGrady was still yanking his service piece from its holster when the man came out with a big revolver. He took a two-handed stance with his feet planted and his knees bent, and he started pulling the trigger.

McGrady saw the muzzle flashes—one, two, three—but he never remembered hearing the blasts. A hole the size of his fist appeared in the windshield. Dagger-sharp glass dust peppered his forehead and forearm. A bullet sang past his right ear. He jammed his foot on the gas as the windshield exploded, bullets punching through in a horizontal line as the man outside corrected his aim. The last bullet would have taken his head clean off his neck, but by then he'd drawn his .38, and had his door open, and he was on his way out. He hit the ground shoulder-first, the car still moving. He rolled away from it, got to his knees, and fired twice.

Fast and wild shots, no attempt at aiming. One of them might have hit his own car, but by then it hardly mattered. The thing was shot up anyway. It was still moving, but its momentum was just about gone. It spent the last of its energy ramming the side of the shed. Its motor died, but its headlights stayed on. There was enough light to see the man. He'd run for cover behind the yellow coupe, and now he was aiming over its roof.

He fired three more times, and McGrady felt the slugs burn past. All misses, and now the shooter's gun was probably empty. McGrady stood and fired twice more, going for the coupe's windows, hoping to plug the guy through two sets of glass. The man fell out of sight, but McGrady didn't think he'd been that lucky. He dropped to his knees, then fell on his side, and fired two shots beneath the car's undercarriage. He pocketed the .38, stood up, and pulled his Army sidearm from his waistband. He kept it low down and halfway behind him.

He took a couple of steps toward the car.

"You're all out," he shouted. "And so am I. Six each, right?"

No answer. Maybe the guy couldn't even hear him. Six rounds from a big revolver would do that.

"Come out, and we'll talk. Just a couple of men."

He covered the rest of the distance to the coupe. The driver's window sported a pair of bullet holes a hand's width apart. The rest of the glass was opaque, held up only by the laminate safety film. He couldn't tell if his shots had gone through the passenger window or not. There was no sound at all, except for the ringing in his ears. He tracked around toward the hood. When he was even with the front bumper, he caught motion to his left. He spun that way. Miguel Silva was stumbling out of the stalled-out city car. So disoriented he could barely stand.

McGrady turned back to the coupe, where the danger lay. He was in time to see the man flying at him. He'd coiled himself up like a spring to launch himself over the Packard's hood. He was holding his big revolver by the barrel like a club. McGrady took two steps backwards, lost his footing in a muddy wheel rut, and fell. He got off five shots on the way down.

The powder flashes gave him a stop motion film. Like something from the old penny arcades. The man's arms flew out like wings. He spun, he twitched. The empty revolver was out of his hands and spinning backwards, toward the coupe.

Then McGrady was down in the mud and banyan roots, and the only sound was the ringing in his ears.

McGrady got up. The other man didn't. He was laid out in front of the Packard, face down and arms flung in front of him. McGrady went to his car for his flashlight. He slapped it until it came on, then passed the light over the man. There were big exit wounds in the side of his head and between his shoulder blades. His coveralls were torn open and stained black. There was no point in kneeling and checking for a pulse.

There was something going on behind him. A voice, maybe. He couldn't make it out. His ears were ringing to the point that he was dizzy. When he turned around, Miguel was there. His

mouth was moving, but McGrady still couldn't hear it. He stepped closer.

"What?" Even his own voice was all wrong. He sounded like he was talking from somewhere deep underground. "You gotta speak up."

Miguel was steadying himself against the city car's open door. He looked like he might fall down on his face. But, with effort, he lifted his head and spoke up.

"You a cop?"

"We already talked."

"Inside—it's for real?"

McGrady didn't answer. The way he figured it right then, he was going to be up for at least another forty-eight hours. No use wasting his energy. Instead, he cuffed Miguel's wrist to the car door. Better not to have him wandering around again. Then he took the light and went back to the man he'd shot. The frame saw and the gas can were on the ground a few paces away. After he'd sliced up the boy inside and left the shack, he must have started getting doubts. He must have been worried about what he'd left behind. So he'd gotten the saw and the gas and had come back to finish it. That seemed mostly right, but there was something missing.

McGrady knelt by the dead man and patted him down. No wallet. Nothing in his pockets but a folding knife and a Ronson lighter. No car key. McGrady rolled the man over. His face was a wreck. What wasn't covered in blood was plastered with mud and dead leaves. There were pockets all over the front of his coveralls. He patted them down and found nothing. Not even a gum wrapper.

McGrady went over to the coupe and opened it up. The inside light came on. The stitched leather seats glittered with fine shards of glass from the bullets. There was no key in the

ignition and no key anywhere else McGrady could see. But the
wiring harness had been yanked out from behind the dash and
was hanging beneath the steering column. There were strips of
rubber insulation down in the foot well, probably peeled off
the ignition wires with the folding knife McGrady had found.

He sat in the driver's seat and leaned across to open the
glove box. It was empty. The guy must have tossed the registration out the window after taking off with the car. McGrady got
out and walked around the back to check the plate. It was gone,
too. The threading inside the screw holes was bright. The plate
had been taken off that day. Any earlier, and the metal would
be grimed over with road dust.

He checked Miguel once more, and then walked down past the
deep shadows of the mango trees. The rain had blown off, so
he stood under the stars at the edge of the pastureland, where
he could see the dark outlines of cattle sleeping on their feet.
He leaned against a section of the split-rail fence, and took
inventory.

He had two John Doe stiffs. A young guy who'd been killed
like an animal in an abattoir, and the scar-faced man who'd
come back to tidy up. A mop-job would've been a fine idea.
Except he'd shown up in a stolen car just in time for McGrady
to shoot him down. Bad timing, but dead men weren't known
for their luck. Not that McGrady felt especially lucky himself. If
anyone could have explained the scene in the shed, it would've
been Scarface. Now they could scratch that out.

McGrady looked up, and out.

Approaching headlights lit the mouth of the valley. He
pushed off the fence and started walking down the road to
meet the cavalry. He met them on a wooden bridge a quarter
mile from the shed. Three city patrol cars, plus a meat wagon

bringing up the rear. He stood on the middle of the bridge, his badge outstretched. The lead car came to a stop ten feet from him. Bugs buzzed through the headlights. The driver jacked his window down, then cracked the door, so the dome light came on.

A face McGrady knew, back from his first year on patrol. An old sergeant named Kondo. Good in a street fight, but not limited to that. All the bottles and bricks broken on the crown of his head hadn't done anything lasting.

"Where's the guy?" Kondo asked. "Beamer said there was a shed."

"It's down the road a piece."

"You want to get in?"

"I want you to get out. Pull to the side and let the meat wagon through. It needs to be closer, but the rest can stay down here."

"What's going on?"

"I had to put a guy down."

"You what?"

"He was all set to torch the place. I came up on him. It happened fast."

"Surprise asshole. HPD's here."

"Like that. And he pulled a piece on me."

"He's dead?"

"Clean head shot. The whole thing outside the shed's a mess. We're going to need a couple tow trucks, too. My car, his. Who've you got with you?"

"Everybody Beamer could spare."

"You the senior guy?"

"Yeah."

McGrady chewed on that for a second, but couldn't draw any conclusions. Either Beamer couldn't find another detective to

take the case, or he was trusting McGrady to run with it. It probably didn't matter which, because they both came out to the same thing. McGrady was going to run with it.

"Pull to the side and get your guys. Let's huddle up. I want to do this right."

4

They huddled in front of Kondo's car. Six patrol cops, two men from the coroner's office, and McGrady. He didn't know anyone but the old sergeant, and that was fine with him. They wouldn't start second-guessing his experience. Which was essentially zero, for a thing like this. He gave them the score. He was going to play it safe and slow. Two of the patrolmen were going to uncuff Miguel from the back of McGrady's car, and take him downtown to sleep it off in a cell. Two more were going to drive down to the end of the valley. One guy would get out and stand guard at the valley entrance, and the second would drive up to Faithful's house to borrow the phone. They needed tow trucks. That would leave McGrady and Kondo and the coroner's men on the scene.

The meat wagon had more than one body bag, and that was good. It also had camera gear, which was even better. But they didn't have big stand lights or the right kind of film to shoot anything in the dark, so photos would have to wait until sunrise. Which wasn't all that far off.

The coroner's men could stand off in the shed's yard and wait it out. Animal duty. If a sounder of feral pigs got the scent of blood and came out of the undergrowth, the corpse had to stay intact. Meanwhile, McGrady and Kondo would be in the shed. There was plenty left to look at in there.

They left the door open for air, and stood just inside the threshold with their lights on the hanging body. McGrady's batteries were dying and his light was getting weak and yellow.

"You seen one like this before?"

Kondo grunted. Shook his head.

"Not even close," he said. "Guy must've rubbed someone the wrong way."

"You think?"

"Different if it was a girl. Then it could be someone having fun. Like a sex-fiend thing. But with a man—not the same. How long you think he's been up there?"

"I'll ask the coroner."

"Best guess?"

"A day or two."

"No more, though," Kondo said. "The blood's not dry enough."

McGrady went to the shelf in the back and found a box of matches. Then he went around the room and lit all three lanterns. He pumped them up and got the mantles glowing bright white, and then the little shed was full of hot light and strange shadows.

"What do you want me to do?" Kondo asked. "We could lift the kid down."

"Leave him. Just watch me."

"Watch you do what?"

"If I find something, you can say I didn't plant it."

Kondo made a sour face. The skin on his forehead bunched together over the ridge of bone. McGrady had just trampled some point of honor.

"I could be home asleep right now, and I'd say that anyway. Hand on a bible."

"The jury would give it more credit if you're here."

"What jury?" Kondo said. "You plugged the guy. Case closed."

"I think he had some help."

"Why?"

"Just a feeling."

"You got a feeling about that cot?"

McGrady looked at the cot. Now both their lights were on it. It was piled high with dirty blankets and old clothes.

"What about it?"

"It's bleeding."

Kondo was right. There was a pool of blood on the floor underneath it. The thin mattress was soaked through. The blood had dripped down, had ponded on the packed dirt. Black ants had found it and were lined up along the edges.

"Shit."

"You didn't look under there before?"

"I missed it."

He'd been in too much of a hurry to get out. To get Beamer on the phone, and get backup. He went up to the cot. He picked up a pair of threadbare denim pants and set them aside. Then a checkered cowboy shirt, and a yellowed undershirt. An old sheet. A busted pillow. The last thing was a thin cotton blanket. It was soaked with blood in places. It had gotten wet enough that it clung to the form beneath it. Now it had started to dry, and it would stick when he lifted it. By the shape, McGrady knew what he was going to find, what the blood was adhered to. He found a dry corner and pulled.

"Oh goddamn," Kondo said. "I hate to see that."

She'd been pretty, is what Kondo meant. Probably she'd been pretty. It was hard to say for sure, now. She had dark hair that was long and straight and lustrous. That was easy enough to see. She was naked and bound up with her wrists tied behind her bent knees. The man must have liked his knife. He'd left her body intact, and had focused his energies on her throat and her face.

"Both naked and all torn up," Kondo said. "You think she was his girlfriend? Maybe her old boyfriend didn't like it."

"It's possible."

"Oriental girl, white kid," Kondo said. "If they were seeing each other, they might've had reasons to keep it a secret. Daddy walks in on them, and—"

"Nobody's dad did this," McGrady said. "And if they were lovers, it started somewhere else. They're both undressed, but their clothes aren't here."

"The guy left once, then came back. Maybe he already dumped the clothes."

"They thought this thing through," McGrady said. "They boosted a car, and had a kill spot picked out ahead of time."

"You keep saying they."

"The guy I put down, he had help. He didn't do this by himself. And I don't think he's the one who planned it. His partner's sitting easy, not taking the big risks. Scarface out there—he's the one who got sent back to clean the mess."

McGrady knelt down and looked at what was left of the girl's face. They hadn't taken her eyes. They'd wanted her to see. They'd arranged her to face the kid. They'd made her watch as they worked on him. Cut by cut. It might have lasted hours. And then they'd started in on her.

"What do you want to do?" Kondo asked.

"Let's check his car again," McGrady said. "I could use some fresh air."

It was a Packard coupe, maybe a '37 or a '38. A long hood encased a big eight-cylinder block. Spare tires were enclosed in housings between the front fenders and the foreshortened cab. Inside, there was one generous leather bench seat up front and a tiny perch in the back. The sharply sloped trunk led to the curved bumper. Stem to stern, it was a lot of car. Chrome everywhere, high-end paint. It was probably worth three times

McGrady's city-issue Ford. McGrady opened the door. The dome light came on, but his flashlight was dead. He switched with Kondo, and knelt down. There was nothing under the seats. He'd already checked the glove box.

"How about the trunk?" Kondo asked.

The lid was unlocked. They lifted it and shined the light inside. The felt liner was dark brown, but had darker spots in it.

"Is that blood?" Kondo asked.

McGrady touched one of the spots. His fingertip came back stained red.

"Got to be."

He leaned further into the trunk with the light. Then he backed out and stood up. He showed Kondo what he'd found, aiming the light to illuminate what he'd plucked from the back. It was a long black hair.

"It started somewhere else," McGrady said. "They grabbed them, stripped them."

"Unless they were already naked."

"Either way. They got them into the trunk and brought them here."

"Could you get the two of them in there?"

"The girl was pretty small," McGrady said.

"It'd be tight. Not much air."

"Whoever did this didn't care."

"What now?"

McGrady looked around. The coroner's boys were waiting under the trees upwind of the shed. The man he'd shot was still on the ground, open-mouthed and drawing flies.

"Pop the hood," McGrady said. He got out his notebook and pencil. "I want to get the number off that engine block."

5

Ten o'clock, and McGrady was riding shotgun in Kondo's patrol car as they went back up the Nuuanu Pali switchbacks. Up ahead was the meat wagon. Three stiffs, no IDs. They hit the high point, where tangled ground ferns clung to the mountain-sides. Saw-toothed peaks disappeared into the clouds.

"What do you think?" Kondo asked.

McGrady shook his head.

"Beamer won't be happy. I told him one body. Now we've got three."

"He'll like the third body. You got the guy good."

"He ran out of bullets. I didn't."

"You seem pretty cool about it."

McGrady didn't answer.

"You done it before," Kondo said.

"A couple times."

"Not here, or I'd have heard."

"Not here."

"But you were in the Army."

McGrady nodded.

"Philippines?"

"Outside Foochow. 1934."

"Foochow—where's that?"

"China. Across the strait from Formosa."

Kondo slowed to get through a rough section of road. There was a waterfall here. It misted the pavement, then the car.

"We were in China in '34?"

"I was. I was in the Army, but I'd gotten attached to a company of Marines. We were protecting a consulate."

"You got a story?"

"Nothing worth telling," McGrady said. "Besides, what happened over there—I had a Model 1903."

"I don't get it."

"It's different, with a rifle. Prone position, under a bush. Looking down iron sights and thinking what the wind might do. The guys were a quarter mile away. I never saw their faces."

He was looking at Captain Beamer's face from a distance of five feet. There was a desk between them, and that was it. His skin was smoke-yellow and stretched tight over his bones. He hadn't shaved. He'd been at his desk all night and half the morning. McGrady had finished his report a minute ago, and Beamer still hadn't spoken. He finally broke eye contact when he took a last drag on his cigarette and tamped it out in the tray. He didn't light a new one. It was the first time McGrady had ever seen him without a cigarette.

"You called from Faithful's house and said it was just the one. The male."

"I hadn't found the other, yet."

"I told you to go see what we had, and report. Which part didn't make sense?"

"I went up there on a short leash," McGrady said. He held his hands a few inches apart. "I saw we had a murder. So I went back and called it in. I didn't think you wanted me to take the place apart before I called."

Beamer looked at his pack of smokes, but didn't reach for it.

"This changes everything," Beamer said. "You know that, don't you?"

"Does it?"

Beamer shook his head and reached for the pack. He shook out a cigarette.

"Where was she, anyway?"

"On a cot, under a pile of dirty laundry," McGrady said. "Tied up in a ball so tight, you could've packed her in a suitcase."

"Same wounds?"

"The knife, yes. She wasn't disemboweled. They did things to her they probably didn't do to him."

"And she was a Jap?"

"It's what I thought. Kondo, too."

"I trust Kondo more than you."

"When it comes to that. He's from here."

"When it comes to anything," Beamer said. "Plus he's half Jap. It takes one to know one. What about Faithful's boy? Miguel."

"I'd rather sweat him. Talk to him after the autopsies when I know a little more. Besides, he's too drunk right now to put three words together."

Beamer had to nod. It made sense to do it that way.

"When are the autopsies?"

"Eleven," McGrady said. "I should leave soon. I need to find some wheels."

"It's just down the block. We can walk."

"No—it's in Fort Shafter. The compressor blew out on the coroner's reefer. No place to keep them cool. So he told his boys to take them to Tripler."

Beamer sucked his cigarette down to the last half-inch.

"The Army's doing my autopsies?"

"It's still our case. They're just doing us a favor," McGrady said. "Kondo's already out there, keeping an eye. This was the coroner's call. Not mine."

Beamer breathed smoke through his nose. He used a fingertip to swipe a flake of tobacco from his teeth.

"You can ride with me," he said. He looked at his watch. "We'll go to Pearl first. Kimmel's man wants his daily report, and won't wait."

"The Navy's into this?"

"No, and be glad it isn't. You don't want to answer to them. Sonsofbitches dressed up like waiters, pushing toy boats around on a map."

"This is just about the morning list."

"The arrest list. That's all."

"They always make you do that, face to face?"

Beamer shook his head. "What I hear is the Admiral's taken a keen interest. This particular morning."

"We grab anyone special last night?"

Beamer cocked his head. His eyebrows squeezed together. Maybe McGrady had a brain somewhere between his ears. If Beamer had one too, he would've figured it out six months back.

"I asked myself the same thing. I walked the cells an hour ago. Nobody stuck out. I looked at the list. There wasn't any name that popped. And I know a lot of names. Besides, these guys were all enlisted men."

"What about the ones in civvies, no ID?"

There were always a couple like that. Men who slipped from the line, changed out of their Navy whites, and tore through Chinatown like a case of the clap.

"There were civilians," Beamer said. "Japs and bums. Nobody to get Kimmel all stirred up."

Beamer opened his pencil drawer and took out a metal tube. A Benzedrine inhaler. Ten cents at the Benson Smith Drug Store. He unscrewed the cap and took three hits up each nostril. Then he lit another cigarette. No wonder the skinny old bastard had ground his teeth down to brown nubs.

Beamer drove a city car. He smoked Luckies and sucked his inhaler. He had coffee in a tin cup. The only thing McGrady had ever seen him eat was a hardboiled egg. McGrady swiveled his wind-wing and leaned close for fresh air.

They came down the Kamehameha Highway, past the bars

and the pawnshops and the lunch stands, and reached Pearl Harbor. The carriers were in. *Lexington* and *Enterprise* loomed over the docks, taller than anything downtown. Navy-blue Wildcats lined the flat tops, wingtip to wingtip. Next to Ford Island, battleship row was packed. Gray steel and long guns. Armor reaching for the sky.

Chinatown would go wild tonight. As it did every night.

The Navy set the prices. HPD enforced them. Sailors queued up on Hotel Street, two abreast and a quarter mile long. Buy a token, go upstairs. Three dollars for three minutes. The clock started running when the girl closed the curtain. No exceptions. There was a line to move. There was a dammed-up river of want. Afterward, a spillway of spent and spat desire. And every morning, HPD handed an arrest list to the Pacific Command. This morning's list was in Beamer's briefcase.

Beamer turned to the left. He nudged into the line of cars waiting to enter Pearl Harbor's east gate. McGrady watched ahead. The Waianae Mountains were blue-green in a haze of cane field smoke. A squadron of planes came in low through the gap in the ridgeline, their props catching the sun and tracing gold circles as they banked in unison.

Beamer stopped at the gate and flashed his gold star. The gate lifted and Beamer drove on. Ahead of them, the submarine escape training tower rose ten stories high, rusted spiral stairs wrapping the water tank all the way to the top. COMSUBPAC headquarters stretched in a long concrete U. A green lawn lay between it and the docks. Past it, McGrady counted six subs.

Beamer double-parked behind a flag officer's Lincoln-Zephyr. "Wait for me."

"Okay."

Beamer grabbed a pressboard briefcase. He'd put on his dress cap and uniform jacket. He was reed thin. His most

prominent feature was his Adam's apple, which reached forward as far as his nose. He'd left his Luckies and his inhaler on the front seat.

McGrady pulled one of Beamer's cigarettes and patted his pockets. He found the dead man's Ronson. He lit up and stepped out of the car. The last time he'd had a cigarette, he'd been standing on the bank of the Min River, dead dogs and bloated cows floating past. Now he smoked and leaned on Beamer's car and watched the sky. He stretched and tried to stay awake. He smoked the cigarette, then leaned against the car some more.

Beamer was in and out in fourteen minutes. He swung behind the wheel, lit up, and cranked the ignition.

6

Tripler Hospital was a quarter mile past the Fort Shafter gate. Flowerbeds and more green lawns. Low clapboard buildings, whitewashed and bright. They came up the wooden steps and across a deep porch. There was a man in a wheelchair with a poultice on the left side of his face. He had casts on both legs and his left arm. Pilot wings were pinned to his shirt. Only his right arm was unscathed. He was using that hand to balance a sweaty bottle of Coke on his thigh.

They went into the hospital, and McGrady found the duty desk. A nurse sat there. Beamer hung back and let McGrady badge her.

"Autopsy?" she asked.

"Yeah."

"The morgue's in the T-6 building—back outside, across the quad."

"Okay."

They went out the way they'd come, followed a pathway around the building, and cut across the quad lawn. Midway across, Beamer stopped.

"This is your first autopsy?"

McGrady shook his head. "I saw one at the Presidio."

"Tell me."

"This nineteen-year-old private didn't show up at reveille. We found him in his rack. Blanket over his head."

"Why'd they send you?"

"I sent myself. I was his CO. So I wanted to know."

"And?"

"Someone had come up while he was asleep and put an icepick into his ear."

"You catch him?"

"I had orders to ship to China a couple days later. So I never heard."

Beamer considered that.

"What was your rank?"

"Then, or at discharge?"

"Discharge."

It was right there, in his personnel file. Maybe Beamer had just skimmed the thing. Maybe he'd had the Benzedrine jitters, and was itching on something else.

"I was a captain," McGrady said. "Same as you."

He walked the rest of the way to T-6. Its slatted jalousie windows were open. The trade winds were blowing steadily enough that there'd be a breeze through the place. Which was good. What was better was that every window, and the front door, was fit with a screen. He'd swatted enough flies that morning.

The doctor outranked them both. He was a colonel, and his nameplate said Underhill. The room was fit out with black and white octagonal tiles, and had all the accouterments McGrady expected: drains on the floor, guttered steel tables, a reefer with a dozen square doors and slide-out trays. There were three tables and three sheeted bodies. A dark-haired corporal came in. He was carrying a clipboard. He put on a pair of reading glasses and took a pen from his pocket. Underhill's scribe.

Kondo got up from a chair in the corner and came over. He shook McGrady's hand and nodded to Beamer. The coroner's men were there, too. They'd put new film in their camera, had swapped out the flash box batteries.

"I'll start with the girl," Colonel Underhill said. He'd put on a butcher's apron and was pulling cutting instruments from a wooden drawer.

"Doesn't matter," Beamer said. He lit a Lucky.

The Colonel went to the middle table and used a scalpel to slit the bag end to end. He yanked the bag and spilled the girl onto the table. She was still bound up. McGrady had told the coroner's men to lift her into the bag the way they'd found her.

"Oriental female," Underhill said. "Maybe twenty years old. Healthy until this."

He walked around the table. He bent to look at her wrists where they were tied up behind her knees. Her hands were purple-black.

"She's bound up with half-inch hemp rope. Bowline on her left ankle. Clove hitches around her wrists and he finished up with another bowline on her right ankle."

Beamer shuffled. "Okay," he said. "Cut her loose and get started."

"There's a process to this."

Beamer pulled on his Lucky.

"Get a shot of the knots," McGrady said. He nudged the coroner's guy forward.

The Colonel stepped out of the way and let him shoot three frames. Then he knelt again and looked at the girl's backside. He used the flat of his palms to spread her buttocks apart. Beamer looked away. Underhill remarked on the presence of dried semen. He noted the bruises, the bleeding.

Then he came around the table and looked at her face. He tilted her chin, to see her throat.

"There was a lot of blood at the scene?"

"Pooled up under her head," McGrady said. "It soaked through a cotton mattress, made a puddle on the floor."

"Then the slit throat's probably the cause of death," Underhill said. "We'll see. I'm going to clean her up a bit. You've already got a shot of her face?"

"Yes."

Underhill went to a sink and came back with a basin of water and a round sponge. He began to work gently at her face. Then he rinsed her hair, loosening the thickened blood with his fingertips. The water in the basin turned pink-brown, then darkened until it was opaque.

When he was done, Underhill traced his bare finger along her cheek. There was a linear dark bruise there, dotted with four evenly spaced puncture marks. Directly above the bruise, a blade had slashed a straight cut from her temple to her scalp. None of it had been visible before.

"Sergeant Kondo told me you were in the Army," Underhill said to McGrady.

"Yes, sir."

"Then you should know what made these wounds."

McGrady came a little closer. He looked at the linear bruise, the four puncture marks. The bruise and the punctures lined up with the knife slash. He made the obvious conclusion. They had all been made by the same weapon, at the same time. McGrady scrolled a mental catalogue of arms.

"That's a Mark I trench knife," McGrady said. He turned to Beamer and Kondo. "A double-edged dagger blade, with a set of spiked brass knuckles for a handle. Supposed to be good in close combat. I never had one. They didn't issue them anymore. You saw them around, though. The older officers used them for paperweights."

Underhill nodded.

"He was beating her in the face with the brass knuckles. Some of the knife wounds were probably inadvertent. Just the

blade nicking her on the follow through. I'm sure it's a Mark I.
I used to have one."

"Are there a lot of them?" Kondo asked.

"Plenty. I got mine on the boat to France. Our sergeant was
scooping them out of a crate and tossing them."

"You ever hit someone in the face with one?" Kondo asked.

"The war ended before I got the chance."

"Are they still around?" McGrady asked.

"I could call up the Quartermaster here, get one in ten minutes."

"Can you?" McGrady asked. "We should hold it up against
her. Confirm the match. And maybe then I can borrow it."

Underhill nodded to the corporal, who left the room. He
came back thirty seconds later.

"There's a runner on his way, sir."

Underhill took his scalpel from the table's gutter, and used
the thin blade to slice through the knots. Rigor mortis kept the
girl in place, curled in on herself.

"Let's lay her flat," Underhill said. He looked at McGrady.
"Give me a hand—you take her legs. We'll see if she'll let us do
it without breaking any bones."

McGrady stepped up. He took hold of her ankles. They were
slim and pale. The bottoms of her feet were clean. Whatever
else had happened to her, she hadn't been made to walk outside in her bare feet.

"Let's get her on her back, first."

Underhill was standing behind her head, and had a grip
under her shoulders. They lifted her onto her back. McGrady
clenched his jaw tight, but not from the weight. There was
hardly any weight. His kid brother had weighed about the same,
when he was eight. Then they pulled her straight. McGrady
tugged backwards on her ankles. Underhill went in the opposite

direction, pulling by her armpits. She came up off the table and straightened out with a *crack*. McGrady wasn't sure what they'd dislocated or broken.

As they put her back on the table, there was a thud from behind him. McGrady turned around. Beamer had dropped to the ground. A dead faint. The sound had been the side of his head hitting the tile floor.

7

They put Beamer in a wheelchair, and a nurse used gauze strips to affix an ice bag to his head. Then she pushed him down through the quad to the main building. He could sit on the broad porch next to the convalescent pilot. When he woke up, he could feel the trade wind breeze and look at the flowerbeds and sip a cold Coke. If he drank Coke. It might not have enough kick for his liking.

McGrady turned to go back into the morgue, and saw a private running up the narrow lane behind the hospital. He was clutching a slim cardboard box. He came trotting up the morgue steps, passed McGrady without acknowledging him, and went inside. The screen door slammed.

McGrady heard: "Sir? I got it."

He heard: "Thanks, son. That's all."

The kid came out and caught his breath, hands on his knees. McGrady went back into the morgue and found Underhill holding a Mark I trench knife. He held it by the blade and passed it to McGrady, who took it the way it was meant to be held. Four fingers through the bronze guard holes. It was heavy, all metal. Bronze and high carbon steel. It was a knuckle-duster. It was a spiked mace. It was a dagger. He scraped the pad of his thumb on the blade. It wasn't that sharp. It had been sitting in a warehouse since 1918. But it was good steel. It would take a fine edge. Give it a few minutes with a whetstone and a leather strop, and it could stand in for a straight razor.

*

Underhill was also a man who appreciated a well-honed blade. He made his incisions look easy and clean. Like he was pulling a zipper and opening a bag. He weighed organs. He pointed out the swelling in her brain. He speculated to a near certainty: they'd beaten her for an hour or two before they'd slit her throat.

Underhill went to the sink and began washing his hands. He dictated over his shoulder to his corporal, who scribbled on his clipboard and used the back of his hand to wipe sweat off his forehead. McGrady pulled out his notebook and took it down as well.

"Cause of death—blood loss. Severed internal and exterior carotid arteries, plus the jugular vein. Which injuries were accomplished with a U.S. Army Mark I trench knife. Verified by comparison. You got that?"

The corporal answered without looking up.

"Yes, sir."

"Pre-mortem rape to completion. Last meal was short-grained rice and fish. Likely tuna."

"Can you estimate a time?" McGrady asked. It was the first thing he'd said since the autopsy started. He had to let up on his jaw to get the words out. His teeth sang with relief.

"The last forty-eight to seventy-two hours."

"Based on?"

"Degree of rigor, spread of livor mortis. State of stomach contents."

Then Underhill dropped the girl's organs back into her chest cavity, and slid a tray under her. He and his corporal pushed her into an empty reefer slot and latched the door.

Underhill used a handkerchief to wipe his brow and he looked at McGrady.

"Check on your captain, or proceed?"

"Proceed."

"Good man," Underhill said. "Who's on first?"

"Second victim," Kondo said. "The kid. The other guy's in no hurry."

"That okay with you, Detective?"

"Yes, sir," McGrady said.

Underhill took a new scalpel and slit the kid's bag down the side. This body was heavier. The corporal stepped in to help spill the kid onto the autopsy table. A flap of stiff legs, ropes of entrails. Everyone took a step away, then crept back closer.

"Guy did about half my work for me," Underhill said.

"Those holes in his ankles were from hooks," McGrady said. "A spreader bar. For butchering hogs."

"Looks like your guy's done it before. A time or two. He had some experience. These aren't hesitant cuts." Underhill came another step closer and touched open wounds on the kid's thighs and ribcage. "Same knife. And see how the blade marks are pointing up, toward his toes?"

"Yeah."

"Means he strung the kid up first," Underhill said. "Then went in on him with the knuckles. Kid was already upside down. Like a punching bag."

"Shit," Kondo said.

Underhill went to the sink and filled another basin. He got the same sponge he'd used on the girl. He came back and began washing the kid's face. The water in the basin darkened. The kid's face was slowly revealed from beneath a mask of blood and trapped insects. McGrady didn't recognize him. Kondo didn't seem to. But Colonel Underhill obviously did. He dropped the sponge in the basin, almost spilling it.

"I'll be right back," he said. "I need to go check something."

He turned and walked out. Through the double doors and then he was gone. McGrady could hear his footsteps on the tiled floor in the next room. There was a moment of silence and then the footsteps came back. Underhill pushed through the doors and came back up to the autopsy table.

He spoke to his corporal without taking his eyes from the kid's ruined face.

"Call Fleet Headquarters. Get Admiral Kimmel on the line."

"Sir?"

"Now, son."

"His staff secretary—won't he ask why?"

"Tell him the Admiral can call off the search. And that he should get up here as fast as he can."

The corporal didn't move. He looked past Underhill, to McGrady. But McGrady was no help. He didn't know what was going on either. So the young man turned and went to the far end of the morgue's long room. There was a desk there, and a black Bakelite phone. He picked it up, got a base switchboard operator, and asked to make a station-to-station call.

"What is this?" McGrady asked. "What's going on?"

"This is your case getting a hundred times more complicated. You think your Captain rides you too rough? Wait till everyone else climbs on."

"Who else? And who is this kid?"

"Maybe I'm wrong," Underhill said. "All I've seen is a picture. Kimmel's the one who can make the ID. If I'm right, you landed the biggest case in the Territory. If I'm wrong, I shouldn't tell you the name I was thinking."

"He's not supposed to be missing?"

"Exactly."

"How long is this going to take?"

Underhill looked down the room, at the corporal. He had

the receiver to his ear and was cupping his hand over his mouth. He looked at them and held up one finger. Then he turned away, hunching toward the phone. He'd sweated through his khakis.

"Yes sir," he said. "Yes sir, that's right."

He listened a moment. He glanced toward his Colonel, then turned away again. He held the phone and cupped the mouthpiece one-handed, and jammed a finger in his other ear. McGrady could sympathize. The operators only gave you a good line if it was a call that didn't matter.

"No sir—not there, sir. We're at Fort Shafter. At the morgue."

He nodded. He listened some more.

"Yes, sir. I'll tell him, sir."

He hung up.

"He's on his way."

"How many coming with him?"

"It's just the Admiral."

"Then we've got about fifteen minutes. Let's get this place squared away."

He glanced at the steel table where he'd cut up the girl. It needed a wash down. The slit-open body bag was on the floor, and there was a centipede crawling around inside of it. As long as a new pencil, but twice as thick. It must have been hiding in the girl's hair, or inside her mouth, when McGrady and the coroner's boys had lifted her off the cot and into the bag.

The corporal got the drift, and got to work. Underhill turned to McGrady.

"You'll want to go check on your Captain. If he's come to, he'll need to be here."

8

McGrady crossed the quad. There were tiny birds in the grass. Waxbills, maybe. A whole flock foraging. They fled at his approach, a beat of wings and then silence as they resettled ten feet ahead. If he kept his course, he'd flush them up again. He might chase them all the way across the quad that way. Instead he detoured, to let them be.

He was in no kind of hurry to see Beamer.

The pilot was gone. A nurse must have wheeled him back inside. Beamer was alone on the porch. He was awake now, busy unwrapping the gauze dressing. The ice bag fell off and hit the wooden porch. It exposed a big purple-black knot above Beamer's temple. He heard McGrady and turned.

"Hadn't slept in two nights," he said. "Didn't get anything to eat since yesterday morning. That's all it was."

"I figured."

"I know how stories start."

"Not with me," McGrady said. "And we can worry about it later. There's a problem with the kid."

"It looked to me like all his problems are over."

"The doc recognized him. He put the brakes on the autopsy and had his man call Admiral Kimmel—who's on his way here."

"Kimmel's coming?"

McGrady nodded.

"I think we found whoever it was they were looking for."

Beamer stared out. Glassy, unfocused eyes. His thin chest rattled when he breathed.

"The kid from the shed?" Beamer said. "He's the one Kimmel wanted?"

"Looks like."

Beamer started patting his pockets. He couldn't find his cigarettes, but he found his Benzedrine inhaler. He jammed it up his nose and took a snort. Then he was blinking and coughing, waiting for the stuff to hit his brain.

"You want me to push your chair?" McGrady asked. "You're still shaking."

"Shitcan it, McGrady. I'll walk."

He walked. It wasn't steady. One of his pupils was twice the size of the other. His gait was uneven and he pulled to the right. Turn him loose in an empty field, and he might wander in circles. McGrady had to nudge his shoulder every ten paces to keep him going straight. He wasn't about to take his arm. They went back across the quad and up the morgue steps.

Kimmel wasn't there yet. The corporal was still sweeping the floor. He looked up when McGrady hit the porch. The breeze blew through the building and wafted the dead smell out. Beamer caught it and stopped. He dug in his pockets again, and still came up empty.

"Who's got my smokes?"

The corporal leaned the broom against the wall and found Beamer's pack on a shelf.

"You dropped it," he said.

He tossed the pack to McGrady, who caught it one-handed. He checked it. The lighter was stuffed inside. He handed it to Beamer, who lit up right there. He sucked in and puffed out, and came into the morgue inside a protective cloud. Shuffling steps. That blown pupil, the eye around it blood red. The corporal watched. He went off and found a rolling chair. It was

painted battleship gray. Its cushion was molded into the shape of some file clerk's ass. He rolled it over.

"You want to sit, sir?"

"No."

The corporal left the chair and got the broom again.

"Where's Colonel Underhill?" McGrady asked.

"Behind you."

The Colonel was stepping in from his adjacent office. He'd changed into a crisper shirt. He had on a bright white butcher's apron, never worn until now. He looked like he was working hard at one task. Holding down his breakfast. No one gets out of the service without a few scrapes, but McGrady had dodged one particular burden. He'd never had to give bad news to a flag officer. He knew how it would work. Blame would spread as far as it would go. Like pouring a can of paint down a hill. Most of it would end up at the bottom, but it would stain everything it touched on the way down.

In the corner, the telephone rang. The corporal went to answer it. He listened, then hung up. He turned to Underhill.

"The Admiral just came through the gate."

"Five minutes," Underhill said. "Or less. Then he'll be here."

McGrady went to the autopsy table. Underhill or the corporal had covered the kid with a white sheet. He lifted a corner and looked at the kid's face. They'd rolled up a white cloth and laid it across his eyes, to hide their gouged-out emptiness. They'd clamped a hand under his chin and forced his jaw shut, to hide his missing tongue. Underhill was going to lift this sheet and show the kid's face to the Admiral. He was afraid of what that might do to the man. McGrady dropped the sheet and turned to the Colonel.

"This is Kimmel's kin, isn't it?" he asked.

Underhill didn't answer. He didn't move a muscle. But he didn't deny it.

"His son?"

"Not his son, thank Christ."

"What, then?"

"Nephew. His favorite sister's son. Twenty-one years old."

"He was Navy?"

Underhill shook his head.

"What I heard, he was planning on it. But he was finishing college, first. And he liked his uncle. So he wanted to be close."

"So he was here?"

"At the university."

"Living on base, with the Admiral?"

"On his own somewhere. Near campus. In Manoa, I expect."

"When'd he go missing?"

"Three days ago. He was supposed to meet the Admiral for dinner, and didn't show."

"Kimmel would've sent someone to his house to check on him. M.P.s, or a staff officer he trusted. Don't you think?"

"I'm sure. I would've."

"What'd they find?"

"I don't know."

"How'd you hear about this?"

"The Admiral's staff put the word out. Then an ensign came by, and gave me a photo."

"They showed you in particular, because you work in a morgue?"

"I run the whole hospital, son. And it wasn't just me they came to. They showed all the officers they could find."

"But they didn't get it out in the community. Outside the bases, no one was looking."

Behind him, Beamer cleared his throat. McGrady turned. His captain had taken the chair after all.

"You knew about it?"

"Some."

"Which parts?"

"Just that they were looking for a kid. They gave his name. Henry K. Willard. They gave me a description. But no photograph. And they didn't tell me whose nephew he was."

"His middle name's Kimmel," Underhill said. "They didn't tell you that?"

"They didn't."

Beamer finished his cigarette. He licked his thumb and forefinger, extinguished it with a pinch, and dropped it in his shirt pocket. Then he lit another.

"Did they make a formal missing-persons report?" McGrady asked him.

"Not to me."

"Sirs?" the corporal said. Everyone turned to him. He was standing by the screen door. "He's coming."

"I'll go meet him," Colonel Underhill said.

McGrady straightened his shirt.

"I'll come with you."

They went out onto the porch and down the steps, side by side. Beamer and the corporal stayed put. Beamer in the chair, the corporal standing next to the Admiral's sheet-draped kin.

The Admiral came toward them. White hair, cap off and under his arm. White jacket, white pants. His black shoulder boards carried four stars. They all three saluted simultaneously. Backs coming straight, heels clicking together.

Kimmel looked right at him.

"Who are you?"

"Detective Joe McGrady," he said. "HPD."

"You're the one who found him?"

"Yes, sir."

"Would you like to get out of the sun, sir?" Underhill asked.

The Admiral ignored him.

"Where'd you find him, Joe?"

"On the windward side, near Kahana Bay. In a tackle shed on the back side of Reggie Faithful's dairy farm."

"Condition?"

McGrady glanced at Underhill. The colonel nodded. *Go ahead*, he was saying. *Better you than me.*

"He was dead, sir."

"An accident?"

"Homicide, sir."

"You're certain?"

"There's no doubt, sir. I'm sorry, sir."

Admiral Kimmel nodded. He looked across the lawn. It was shaded with monkeypod trees, each one with the size and spread of a New Orleans live oak. The lawn should have been littered with their seedpods. But this was an Army base. There was nothing beneath the trees but regulation-length grass.

"Why is he here?"

"Our coroner asked Fort Shafter for a favor. The city's got some equipment problems."

"And you're the lead investigator?"

"Yes, sir."

"Then let's go see him. And if it's really Henry, you and I should sit down. We'll need to talk."

Admiral Kimmel stood next to the autopsy table and waited for
Colonel Underhill to raise the sheet.

"It's bad, sir."

"Go ahead."

Underhill pulled the corner back. Kimmel looked down. He
stared for what seemed like a full minute. Then he did something McGrady didn't expect. He reached out and caressed the
boy's cheek. He stepped back. Underhill replaced the sheet.

"It's him."

"I'm sorry, sir."

"I know you'll do your best work. I won't stay to watch."

"It's the right call. You shouldn't watch. But we'll do right by
him."

Kimmel turned to McGrady. His back was rigid, his uniform
crisp. His eyes were the only tell. He'd loved the boy. There
was no doubting that.

"Let's go for a walk, Detective. You and me."

McGrady glanced at the shrouded body. Kimmel read the
conflict on his face.

"Your captain has it covered. And your sergeant. They'll give
you a report. You're the lead man. I want to talk to you alone."

"Go on," Beamer said. He reached into his pocket and
squeezed his inhaler.

Kimmel looked at him, checked the nameplate on his breast
pocket.

"Captain Beamer, with your permission, I'd like to have

McGrady keep me abreast on this. If he's the man in the field, then I want to get my reports directly from him."

Beamer looked like he was trying to swallow a mouthful of dry sand. But he nodded. McGrady caught Kondo's eye and tilted his head toward the sheeted body. He mimed scribbling notes. Kondo dug a notebook from his hip pocket. The nub of a pencil was jammed inside. Kimmel put his hand on the small of McGrady's back, and led him out of the morgue. They went down the steps, side by side.

"It's a bad time for it, McGrady."

"Name a better one."

"Point."

"The Colonel said you were close to him."

"That's right."

"He came here for school?"

"He was starting in January. He had time to settle in."

"Settle where?"

"Manoa."

McGrady already had his notebook out. They were walking across the quad, back toward the hospital's main building. No real pace. Captain Beamer had walked faster when he was punch drunk from bouncing his head off the floor.

"Give me the address."

"Pamoa Street—you know it?"

"Near St. Francis School."

It was tucked up in Manoa Valley, behind the university. It rained all the time there. The roofs grew moss. McGrady knew the neighborhood well. Molly lived a bit further up the valley.

"St. Francis," Kimmel said. "That's right. He's at 2526. It's a white bungalow."

"Who owns it?"

"It's rented."

"Who's on the lease?"

"Me."

"You'll let me search it?"

"Obviously."

"After he went missing, did you go in?"

"I would have."

"But?"

"I told you already—it's a bad time. You read the papers. I had to send other men."

"Military police?"

"I wanted to keep it close. I picked two staff officers."

"They did more than knock on the door," McGrady said. "They would've gone in."

"I gave them the key."

"They searched top to bottom? Or just checked to make sure he wasn't there?"

"They were in and out. Two minutes."

"You still got the key?"

"In my glove box," Kimmel said. "We'll walk down there and I'll get you the key. We can sit inside and talk."

They walked to the Admiral's Lincoln. The doors were unlocked. McGrady got in on the passenger side. He shut the door, then cranked down his window. Kimmel leaned across and opened the glove box. The house key was in an unmarked envelope. Kimmel handed it to him.

"I talked to the nurse in the main building before I came back to the morgue," he said. "They told me Henry came in with two other bodies."

"That's right."

"Explain."

"We found Henry in a shed. There was a young woman in there with him. Also dead. Killed the same way."

"Which was what, exactly? What would I have seen if that Colonel had pulled the sheet all the way off?"

"Are you asking me to be frank, sir?"

"I am."

So McGrady told him what he'd found inside the shed. The Admiral took it straight up, without blinking. When McGrady was done, the Admiral nodded.

"And the third body?"

"After I found your nephew, I went to Reggie Faithful's place to use the telephone. I didn't have anyone I trusted to leave behind. I didn't like leaving the scene unattended, but there wasn't much choice. When I got back, there was a man about to go inside. He drew on me, and I shot him."

"What man?"

"I never saw him before. And I would've remembered. Big guy, knife scar on his face. He'd come back to torch the place."

"He was the one who did it?"

"One of them."

"You're thinking it was more than one?"

An Army major parked next to them. He saw the Admiral's four-star shoulder boards and did a double take. Then he snapped-to, and saluted. Kimmel gave him a nod.

"A hunch says two, at least."

"Hunches don't come out of nowhere. They're based on something."

"Right now it's just a hunch, sir," McGrady said. It was more than that and he could list out his reasoning, no problem. He wasn't ready to share it with anyone yet. He dodged with a question. "Tell me about Henry. Was he seeing a girl?"

"He had a sweetheart back in Norfolk. I don't know how serious. They hadn't seen each other since high school."

"What about here?"

"No one I knew of."

"If he went out with a girl, what are the chances she'd be Japanese?"

Kimmel began to glance at him, but he caught himself. He looked back toward the lawn. The engine wasn't on and the parking brake was engaged, but he had his hands ready on the wheel at ten and two.

"The girl in the shed was Japanese?"

"Does that surprise you?"

Another pause, Kimmel weighing his response.

"I suppose not," he said. "That might not look so good these days. But it wasn't that way."

"Why's that?"

"Henry was studying the language. He could already speak it. He was learning to read it. That's what he was going to be doing, at the university."

"And afterward, when he joined the Navy, he'd work for the Office of Naval Intelligence?"

"They're hurting for men like Henry. We need more of them than we could ever get."

"Who else knew what he was planning?"

"He didn't talk about it. For a boy his age, he understood discretion."

"But?"

"But it wouldn't be terribly hard to guess, if you knew his language skills and his family. You figured it out, just now."

"True."

"You think all this is connected?"

"Right now, I can't rule anything out."

"It was some kind of interrogation?"

"Like I said—everything's on the table," McGrady said. "When did he go missing?"

"Three days ago."

"You're talking about Sunday. The twenty-third."

"He was supposed to come to our house for dinner. He didn't show. He didn't answer the telephone. I sent my men around midnight."

"How was he supposed to get to your place?"

"He was going to drive."

"He had a car?"

Kimmel nodded.

"A Ford. He bought it when he got here."

"You know the model and the plate?"

"No."

"But it was registered to him?"

"It had to be. He'd driven it onto the base. They check that at the gate."

"All right, sir," McGrady said. He opened his door. "Was there anything else?"

Kimmel shook his head.

"Keep in touch, Detective. I want to stay abreast. If you don't find me, I'll find you."

The Colonel was almost finished with Henry Kimmel Willard's autopsy when McGrady got back. It was bound to be a quick one. There weren't many incisions for him to make. They'd been done already, back in the shed.

The man McGrady shot was next up. There was no mystery about how he'd died. McGrady told the corporal, and the corporal wrote it down. The mystery was the man himself. He was big and well-built. Colonel Underhill pegged his age between forty and fifty. He had blue-green eyes and, in spite of McGrady's head shot, all his teeth. He had the scar on his face. It was a long, twisting road. It wasn't particularly well stitched together.

Colonel Underhill used his scalpel and cut away the man's coveralls, then his underclothes. He tossed it all in a heap on the floor. Now the man lay naked. There were five recent bullet holes in him. Four in his chest, and one midway between his left eye and left ear. That one had come out the back of his head. A big, messy exit.

"What kind of gun were you using?" the Colonel asked.

"A forty-five ACP."

"I thought HPD was packing thirty-eights."

"I shot that dry and didn't hit him. I put out his car's windows, and that was about it. I got him with my backup."

"It's a better gun," the corporal said. "More accurate."

"It wasn't like that. I baited him out of his hiding spot, and shot him close to point blank."

"Look at this," the Colonel said.

Everyone crowded in but Beamer. The Colonel was pointing at the man's hip. There was a misshapen, dime-sized scar there.

"You weren't the first man to shoot him," the Colonel said.

He used both hands to roll the man onto his side. He checked his backside. He set him back down, without comment. He picked up his scalpel.

"Let's dig around and have a look."

"A look for what?" Beamer asked.

"There was no exit wound. The bullet didn't go clean through. It might've gotten caught in his pelvis. But the entry scar isn't so big. I bet the medics left it in place. They didn't want to cut him up to go after it."

"It could be anywhere," McGrady said. "Bullets go all over. You might have to cut him into little pieces."

"He won't mind."

Colonel Underhill cut a large X over the top of the scar. He folded the skin flaps back and then worked his way down

through the muscle. It was easier for him than it would have been for a surgeon. He didn't have to worry what he was doing to the patient. He went to a drawer and got a pair of thin rubber gloves, came back, and began probing into his excavation with his fingers. Evidently, he'd done this a few times. He knew what he was doing. In less than a minute, he came out with the bullet.

He washed it at a sink and then set it on a white cloth for them to look at. It was a jacketed round, and it was largely intact. It was a little flattened on the nose, but that was it. Then he turned to McGrady.

"You correctly ID'd the knife," he said. "Now tell me what you see here."

McGrady picked it up and turned it over in his hand. He didn't have to think long. He knew small arms.

"It's a full metal jacket ball round, from a rifle. Surprising it didn't go all the way through him. Maybe it went through someone else, first. Slow it down a little."

"What kind of rifle?"

"I can't just eyeball the caliber."

"We'll measure it."

The Colonel turned to his corporal, who went to the drawers. He came back with a metal caliper. McGrady took it and looked it over. It was a fine instrument, capable of measuring to the tenth of a millimeter. He fit the jaws around the bullet just ahead of the cannelure groove where the brass casing had been crimped on. He bent down to read the marked lines.

"Call it seven-point-seven millimeters. Maybe the rifling shaved it down from seven-point-eight."

"Which means?"

"It's probably a thirty-aught-six."

"And?"

"It's got a flat tail, and the jacket's made of nickel."

"Which you've seen where?"

"Practice rounds. The M1906 ball. They were surplus. We used them on the range, and saved the better ones for combat."

"Surplus from what?"

"The Great War."

"And so," the Colonel said. "We've got a man between forty and fifty years old. He's got a thirty-aught-six cupronickel bullet in his hip—the standard issue ammo for the Springfield rifle the last time our boys went off to France. And he's got an old knife scar on his face. Conclusions?"

"No conclusions possible," McGrady said. "Just guesses."

"I'll say it if you won't," the Colonel said. "He's got a U.S. Army bullet in him. If it was a Mauser, it wouldn't be silver and you'd have measured more than eight millimeters. So he got shot by one of our doughboys when he was in his early twenties. And if he was standing in a trench, fending off a bayonet charge, more likely than not, he'd get it in the face."

"He's German, is what you're saying," Kondo said.

"He's got that Kraut look," the Colonel said. "But McGrady's right. It's just a guess. This scar might be twenty-three, twenty-four years old. It might only be five. No way to tell. And like McGrady said, there were a lot of surplus M1906 rounds. They got around. He could be anyone. He could've been shot by anyone."

"But we've already got the old knife," Kondo said. "He was in the war. On one side or the other. If he's German, maybe he picked it up. Like a trophy."

Beamer drove back to the station. He rolled his window down and flicked the butt of his Lucky out. It bounced off the windshield of an ice truck heading the other way. The guy swerved and honked. Beamer allowed himself half a smile. The lump on his forehead was black and purple.

"I want you to pair up with Fred Ball for the rest of this," Beamer said. "He should be in a room with the kid from the liquor store thing. That won't take him long."

"All right."

"What's your next step?"

"Pull some records. Send out some feelers. Then search the kid's house. Kimmel gave me the address and the key."

"Wrong," Beamer said. He spat out the window and lit another Lucky. "Your next step is you go and find Fred Ball. Then you bring him current. Then you ask him what to do."

"Captain—"

"That's how it is," Beamer said. "If Kimmel wants to see your face out front, then you're who he'll see. I'm calling the shots. Then Detective Ball."

McGrady nodded. There was nothing else Beamer wanted to talk about, apparently. He didn't say another word, and neither did McGrady.

As soon as Beamer shut his office door, McGrady set about ignoring his orders. He went and found Marcia Lee, in the secretarial pool. She was alphabetizing a stack of folders. She was

wearing a brown skirt and an ink-stained white blouse. A thin strand of freshwater pearls lay around her neck. When she saw him, she took off her reading glasses.

"Detective—happy Thanksgiving."

"I forgot. You too."

"Don't you have anywhere to go?"

"I've got a place. We'll see if I ever get there."

She looked down. He'd probably just missed a dinner invitation at her parents' place. If his circumstances had been any different, he wouldn't have minded that at all.

"Can you do three quick things before you get out of here?" he asked.

"Of course."

He took out his notebook.

"I want you to send a cable to Packard Motors, in Detroit. Copy this down." He read the serial number he'd taken from the Packard's engine block, and she transcribed it. "See if the factory's got any information on where that car went."

"Okay."

"Next, pull records on auto thefts. I want every car stolen in the last year and not recovered."

"That couldn't be more than one or two."

"Probably not."

"And the third?"

"Dig up a car registration. The name's Henry Kimmel Willard. He had some kind of Ford. Once you get all the details, put them on my chair. Then type up an item about Henry's car and stick it in tomorrow's roll-call bulletin. I want patrol to find it."

"All right," she said. "Happy Thanksgiving."

"You already said that. But, you too."

He left before she started to blush. It would spare both of them the embarrassment. He went down to the holding cells

and looked in on Miguel. He was asleep on the concrete floor.
No blanket, no pillow. It'd be another few hours before he'd be
able to string a sentence together.

After that, he toed Beamer's line. He asked around and got the
word on Fred Ball's whereabouts. He found him in a basement
interrogation room. The perp was gone. Back in a holding cell,
nursing his wounds. Fred Ball was sitting alone at the wooden
table. A single overhead bulb cast a cone of light around him.
He had a glass of ice water. He'd dipped his handkerchief in it,
had wrapped the wet cloth around the knuckles of his left
hand. The story around the station was that Ball had gotten
meaner after his wife took off.

He was writing on a mostly blank piece of paper. It was
already signed at the bottom. On the top, in big letters, it said:
Confession.

Detective Ball looked up. He and McGrady were the same
age, but Ball had nearly ten years of seniority. He hadn't wasted
time going to college, going to China with a bunch of Marines.
He'd joined HPD straight out of Roosevelt High. He was still
built like the lineman he'd been back then. A tall stack of fat-
clad muscle with a buzz cut.

"McGrady, right?"

"That's right."

"You need something?"

"I was just seeing how it's done."

"And I was born yesterday." He clenched his hurt hand and
squeezed water out of the handkerchief. "What do you want?"

"Beamer made us a team."

"That right?"

"I'll buy you lunch at the Royal and tell you about it," McGrady
said. He hadn't eaten since lunch yesterday. Last night he'd

ordered his whiskey and was thinking about Molly and dinner, and then he'd gotten the call.

"The Royal. I'll meet you there. I need to finish writing this up."

The Royal Saloon was closed. Even though Marcia Lee had reminded him twice, McGrady had already forgotten what day it was. So he stood on the corner of Merchant and Nuuanu and waited for Ball to come along from the station. It wasn't long. He looked at the dark window and the handwritten sign.

"You like chop suey?" McGrady asked.

"I got a choice?"

"Probably not."

They walked into Chinatown. Hotel Street went dark for nothing. Any day of the year, any time of the day, it had all the same things on offer. Brick buildings and painted shutters and dark enticements spelled out in lights.

They ended up on the second floor of Wo Fat.

It was packed. They had to wait in line for a table. The chatter was in Mandarin and Cantonese. It put Ball on edge. McGrady didn't mind. He'd liked it in China. Aside from a few skirmishes, it had been a fine time. Good billets in the consulate, plenty of food. Friendly locals. A waiter led them to a table. It was next to a window. They overlooked a line of sailors. They were waiting to get into Annie's and the Black Cat Lounge. The Hula Girl, with its chasing lights and grass-skirted, bare-breasted neon nymph.

"You'd hate to be the guy at the end of that line," Ball said.

"It moves quick enough."

"There's probably less than fifty whores on the clock. A thousand men waiting. Do the math, and picture it."

"I'll pass."

They watched out the window. The men clutched their tokens

and shuffled forward. The line snaked inside. The waiter came back. He wore a black vest over a crisp white shirt. He set down a pot of loose-leaf tea and took out a pad and pencil. McGrady poured tea for both of them, and picked up his cup. "You want me to order?"

"Fine."

He ordered in Mandarin. His accent was a mess, but the waiter understood him. Hot and sour soup. Salt and pepper pork chops. A big plate of chow mein.

"How long were you over there?"

"Less than a year."

"You picked it up that quick?"

He shook his head.

"I learned more in San Francisco. I was there longer."

When the food came, he laid the case out. Ball warmed up a little when he saw the pork chops. He warmed up a lot more when McGrady told him he'd shot a man dead that morning. Apparently that made up for speaking some Mandarin. They talked about the autopsies, and then Ball circled back to the question everyone else had asked.

"What makes you think he wasn't the only guy?"

"A couple things," McGrady said. "It would've been hard for one man to do it. They got grabbed from somewhere else. They were stripped—"

"Unless they were already naked."

McGrady nodded.

"But then he got them into the trunk of a car. Which he'd stolen ahead of time. He drove them up to the shed, which he'd scouted. He got them out, hauled them in. Strung up the boy. He kept control of both of them the whole time, even though there'd have been times when just one of them would keep his hands full."

"That's what ropes and guns are for," Ball said. "Plus, the guy was a real specimen."

"He was big. I'm not saying he couldn't have done it by himself. It would've been easier with a partner," McGrady said. "And there's what he did when I drove up on him."

"Which was?"

"He was right in my headlights. He put his hand up, to block the glare. He was trying to see who I was."

"So?"

"If he'd been working alone, he would've started shooting the second he saw me. He had two dead bodies in a shed. He was standing there with a frame saw and a gas can. It wouldn't have made any difference who I was. He'd just want me dead."

Fred Ball bit into a pork chop. He thought it through. He spat a wad of gristle into his hand and nudged it under his plate.

"That makes some sense."

"It makes plenty of sense. He hesitated, because he wasn't sure. He thought maybe I was his partner."

"What's our next move?"

"I'm supposed to ask you."

Ball picked up his bowl and sipped his soup. He looked into it and made a sour face. He set it down.

"Beamer doesn't care for you."

"I've figured that out."

"Why should he? You went to college. You were a captain in the Army. Same rank as him, but let's face it—the Army's a different ballgame. It's the majors, and HPD's not even a farm team. People don't like what they don't understand. This soup, for instance. The hell's in it?"

"Congealed duck's blood. You get so you like it."

"You're serious."

"Also, as for Beamer—I'm not from here," McGrady said.

"Don't forget that. That's his real beef. What's your call? What's our move?"

"Same thing you would've said. We search the kid's house. We come back to the station and brace Miguel. Then we call it a day. You got family here?"

"I've been seeing a girl. If I can make it to her place by dinner, she'd like that. You?"

"You must be the last guy who hasn't heard the story. My wife got on the *Lurline* with a sonofabitch she met at the Royal Hawaiian. Last I heard, she was in Utah with him. You ever tried divorcing a woman you can't find?"

"I never even tried getting married."

They walked back to the station. Fred went to get his car, and McGrady jogged inside to the equipment room and signed out a camera. He checked that it was loaded with fresh film. Then they rolled to Manoa. Fred drove down King Street, between the Iolani Palace and the Supreme Court. The street was empty. There was only one car parked in front of the Federal Building. Ball nodded at it with his chin.

"You know who that is?"

"Some FBI man. Why, do you recognize it?"

"That's Bob Shivers' car. Guess G-men are just like the rest of us. They don't get Thanksgiving, either."

"They're worried. Kimmel, too. And not just about his nephew. He said it's a bad time."

"You don't need him telling you," Ball said. He'd stopped at Punchbowl to let a line of canvas-topped Army trucks go past. "You just have to open your eyes."

That was no joke. The signs were everywhere, and not just the trucks. New ships, daily. They unloaded men and materiel. Different ships picked up the same and steamed out, past

Barber's Point and the western horizon. They'd built a picket line out there. Frontier outposts. Log forts on the plains, blue-jacketed cavalrymen peering over the walls. Names like Midway and Johnston Atoll. Palmyra and Wake. Flights of bombers came in from California. B-17s, loaded with nothing but fuel. They spent the night, and took off at first light. Hopping islands westward, all the way to MacArthur in Manila.

"What do you think?" Ball asked. "You were in the Army."

"I went where they told me. Same as these guys."

"But you were an officer."

"I never had to negotiate with Hirohito."

"I can tell you right now," Ball said. "It's a waste of time to even try. They're just yanking our chain."

Ball's knuckles had started to bleed again. He pulled out his damp handkerchief and wrapped it around his fist. The convoy passed, and he drove the rest of the way up to Manoa. On the way, McGrady took out his .38. He popped the cylinder and dumped the six empty brass cases into his hand. He dropped them out the window. Then he reloaded with new bullets from a box he'd grabbed off his desk in the station.

They parked opposite Henry Kimmel Willard's rented digs. The place was a craftsman bungalow dug into a hillside behind the University of Hawaii. There was a one-car garage at the street level and a long set of red-painted concrete steps that went up the slope to the house. Fred Ball shut off the engine. He got out, slammed the door, and went over to the garage. He put his hands around his eyes and peered through a dusty window.

"No car."

McGrady came up alongside him. He wiped the glass with the side of his hand and looked in. The garage was empty. Bare shelves. An empty workbench. A pegboard with no tools. There were oil stains on the concrete floor. Someone had been parking a car in there, but it was hard to say how recently. They took the steps up to the house. The way was lined with banana trees. A couple of them were heavy with bunches of fruit that needed to be picked soon. Columns of ants were on the march up the green stalks. McGrady took the key from his pocket and was about to unlock the door. Before he could, Ball rang the doorbell. They heard the two-toned chime. A dog started to bark in the house next door. Good ears, McGrady thought. It probably knew everything, start to finish. If only Detective Ball could cuff it to a chair in an interrogation room. Beat the story out of it.

"You going to open up?"

"Sure."

McGrady slid the key into the lock and turned it. They stepped inside and left the door standing open. There were some letters on the floor. McGrady picked them up. A bill from the Mutual Telephone Company, postmarked November 24. Another bill from the electric company. McGrady dropped the electric bill and had a look at the telephone bill. It was the size of a post-card, printed on heavy stock. He turned it over. The kid hadn't used his phone at all. Then they went room to room. There was a bathroom just off the entry hall. Next to the sink was a Miracle Tuft toothbrush, a safety razor, and a bar of soap. There were two towels on the floor. McGrady knelt and ran his finger inside the bathtub's drain. He came out with a long black hair. He held it up for Ball to see.

"Hers was the same length?"

"Yeah."

The living room was mostly empty. There were a couple of wooden chairs. A beat-up Philco table radio sat on the floor. Henry hadn't bought a table yet. In the bedroom, there was a mattress on the floor. Clean white sheets, two pillows. Ball knelt next to it.

"You can smell her perfume," Ball said.

"Kid had only been here a couple weeks. I guess he got right down to business."

In a chest of drawers under the window, McGrady found Henry's clothes, neatly folded. He opened the closet and pulled the cord to turn on the overhead light. Shirts on hangers, a three-piece suit purchased for another climate. A straw hat upside down on a shelf.

They went upstairs. There were two bedrooms and another bathroom. All three rooms were completely empty.

They checked the kitchen last. Ball opened the Frigidaire and had a look inside. There was a glass bottle of milk, uncapped.

A pound of hamburger wrapped in brown paper. A dozen eggs, a jar of pickles. Ball grabbed two bottles of Primo lager.

"You want one?"

"Why not."

McGrady found a bottle opener in a drawer. They popped the caps and leaned against the countertops.

"You know what's missing?" McGrady asked.

"What?"

"Books. The kid was learning Japanese, right? And he was serious about it. So there should be at least a couple hundred books in here. And his journals, and whatever else he practiced with."

"You think?"

"I can find out for sure," McGrady said.

He set his beer on the counter. There was a telephone on the kitchen wall. He picked it up and listened for a tone, then dialed the operator. He asked for the Pearl Harbor exchange, waited for the base operator to come on the line, and then asked for Admiral Kimmel. He gave his name and waited. In two minutes, Kimmel was there.

"Detective McGrady?"

"Yes sir," he said. "I'm standing in Henry's house. Were you ever inside it?"

"Two or three times."

"Did he own books?"

"What books?"

"Any sort of books. Textbooks, dictionaries. Pulp novels. Anything."

"Of course he had books. He had a couple footlockers full of them."

"Footlockers."

"That's right."

"Did your men see them, when they went in?"

"They didn't say."

"Go ask them."

"It's urgent?"

"Yes, sir."

Kimmel set the phone down. McGrady heard static. He picked up his beer and finished it off. Then Kimmel was back.

"Detective?"

"Still here. Go ahead, sir."

"They said there were books in the bedroom. Books and papers. All lined up along the walls. He hadn't bought shelves yet."

"Thank you, sir."

"I take it they're missing?"

"Yes, sir."

"Someone broke into the house after my men searched it?"

"There wasn't a break-in. But they would've had his key."

Kimmel thought about that for a couple of seconds. He muffled his end of the line and spoke to someone else. Then he came back on.

"I have to go. Let me know when you have more."

"I will, sir."

Kimmel hung up. McGrady set his bottle in the sink.

"What do you think?" Ball asked.

"I want to go talk to Miguel Silva, if he's up."

"We can get him up."

He finished his beer and put the bottle in the sink next to McGrady's. Then he turned on the faucet and ran the tap over his raw knuckles.

They crossed the station's basement, went down the corridor to the holding cells, and stood looking at Silva's cell. It was empty. The floor was wet from a recent mop. The air still smelled of vomit.

"You looking for your drunk?"

McGrady turned. The officer from the booking desk had followed them.

"Yeah," Ball said. "Silva. Old guy."

"Chief Gabrielson cut him loose."

"When?" McGrady asked.

"An hour ago."

"Gabrielson did that himself?"

The officer nodded. "Opened the door, walked him outside. Put him in a patrol car."

Ball looked at McGrady, then glanced at the stairs.

"Damn it," McGrady said. "What's he doing?"

They took the stairs side by side. The chief's office was on the top floor, in the corner. His secretary played gatekeeper. Her desk blocked his door. But she was gone.

McGrady opened the door without knocking. Ball followed him in. The Chief began to stand up, then changed his mind.

"Sit down, gentlemen."

Ball sat. McGrady stayed put.

"Sir—"

"Don't worry about it, McGrady," the Chief said. "Faithful needed him back on the job. You can't keep a dairy cow waiting."

"This is a double murder."

"And I talked to him myself," Gabrielson said. "His story's just fine. He's got a dozen witnesses in Nanakuli. He was out there until sundown on Wednesday. Drinking with the boys."

"He's got a dozen drinking buddies to back him up," McGrady said. "That's good enough?"

"Reggie Faithful vouches for him," Gabrielson said. "That's good enough. If you want to go talk to him again, try next week. He'll have time then."

Gabrielson's telephone rang. He looked at it. Neither McGrady nor Ball moved. The Chief answered.

"This is Chief Gabrielson."

He listened. Then he palmed the receiver and pointed at the door.

"Shut it on your way out, would you?"

McGrady walked out. Ball followed, and closed the door. They didn't speak until they were back at McGrady's desk. Ball rolled a chair over. They huddled up, kept their voices low. There were twenty cops in earshot.

"What's your take?" McGrady asked. "You know him better than me."

"Not by much. He and Faithful go back. I know that."

"So that's just how it's going to be," McGrady said. "That's what you're saying."

"We don't have to keep him in the loop," Ball said. "From here on."

"Fine with me."

McGrady and Ball walked out of the station's basement door and came up the ramp to the sidewalk on Bethel Street. A man in a rumpled tan suit came up to them. Another man shadowed behind him.

"Joe McGrady?"

Ball turned and saw the man's face. He put his hand on McGrady's shoulder and started to pull him back. But by then, McGrady was already answering.

"Who's asking?"

The second man stepped out from behind the first. He had a Clipper Special camera, with a mounted flash bulb. He snapped two shots, fast.

"Is it true Admiral Kimmel's nephew was murdered alongside a Jap girl in a North Shore lovers' nest?" the tan-suited man asked. He got it out so fast, it sounded like one word. "And you shot down the killer last night?"

"I've got no comment."

"I got a couple," Ball said. "Number one, you got it all wrong. Number two—"

Ball swung at the photographer. He held back, slowing his fist on its arc, giving the man just enough time to stumble backwards. The reporter caught him before he spilled onto the sidewalk.

"Get out of here," Ball said.

The men retreated past Ball's swinging range. The photographer got his camera up again.

"Detective Fred Ball, right?" the reporter said. "I remember you. Port police arrested you dockside. Trying to drag a man off the *Lurline*'s gangway."

"What's it to you?"

"Almost nothing," the man said. "A column inch. Maybe two."

Ball was turning red. The back of his neck, his ears. He weighed as much as the reporter and the photographer put together. He was armed with a .38, and likely had a lead sap and a switchblade tucked in his jacket pockets.

"Let's go," McGrady said.

He steered Ball away. Ball came willingly enough. He just needed a little direction. They went down Merchant, towards the closed-up Royal Saloon. Ball's car was parked at the curb. McGrady opened the driver's door, and Ball got in.

McGrady shut the door. Ball sat a while, then rolled down the window.

"You need a ride somewhere?"

"Manoa, if you're headed that way."

"I'm not headed anywhere," Ball said. He was still red. He wasn't shaking yet, but he looked about one drink away from it. "Probably nothing open but Chinese joints."

"Then come with me," McGrady said. "Molly likes to make a big thing out of a dinner."

"You're serious."

"She ordered a turkey last week, in Kaimuki. Plus, she's got three roommates. Single girls, from California and New York."

"You're inviting me?"

"We're partners."

"Says Beamer."

"Still."

"Get in."

They were rolling down King Street again. It shouldn't have been dark yet, but with the rain blowing in over the Ko'olau Mountains, it was. Ball hit the wipers and pulled the knob for his headlights.

"That guy, John Carroll—he had it right."

"Which part?"

"I got arrested. Outside the *Lurline*."

"Okay."

"I had the guy's arm, and hoisted him over the gangplank rail. I got him good. I think I broke all his fingers. Maybe his elbow."

"He press charges?"

"You gotta be kidding. He wanted to get aboard and clear out. He probably would've cast off the lines himself, but his hands worked for shit."

"How'd Carroll find out?"

"He hangs around the station. It's his beat. You haven't run into him?"

"I learned how to keep my head down," McGrady said. "Standard Army procedure. What paper's he with?"

"The *Advertiser*. But he's thinking big. He wants to get his stories out on the wire services."

"Beamer won't be happy."

"He'll just have to suffer. You didn't leak it. And you can't keep something like this a secret. It's going to come out. It's too big a deal."

Molly's rented house was on the west side of Manoa, ten minutes' walking distance from Henry Kimmel Willard's place. It was a white Greek Revival, four bedrooms and a hedge wall around the property. She shared it with three other girls, all graduate students. Molly said there was safety in numbers. She made it a joke, but McGrady knew it was true. She'd spent a good part of her life in places she wasn't welcome. It was how he'd met her in the first place—she'd come into the downtown police station, talked her way past the duty officer and then the

chief, who'd finally given in and brought her to McGrady.

The first thing she did was invite him to dinner. Before he could ask, she told him why. She'd found his name in a Schofield Barracks archive, and wanted a firsthand account of the Fujian Rebellion. She was writing a paper. He was an eyewitness. A living source. He agreed to do it, so long as he could pick the place and pay the bill.

Their first date was that evening. He took her to Wo Fat. He ordered five courses and told her everything he knew, including how he'd crawled along the river bank and taken a position inside a bramble of dead vines, sighting across the water at a group of men who'd kidnapped a consular officer's wife the week before. Three shots, three kills. He'd picked the shell casings out of the mud and pocketed them. At Wo Fat that night, he took one of them out, now clean and polished. He gave it to her.

She ate it up, all of it.

She wanted to hear more. For once, he wanted to tell it. They closed the place down, then went walking to an all-night bar on Smith Street where they could get brandy and coffee and continue a conversation that stretched until dawn.

It was dusk when they arrived at Molly's place. No one came when he rang the bell, so McGrady tried the door. It was unlocked. He stuck his head in and called down the hallway.

"Hello?"

There was no answer.

The house smelled like she'd been hard at work. Roasted turkey and sage stuffing. Sweet potatoes and pies. He could hear music coming from the back. He opened the door the rest of the way, stepped in, and nodded for Ball to follow him. They found the girls in the backyard. They'd gone native. They had bamboo torches in the lawn and flower leis around the neck of

the hardwood tiki statue McGrady had hauled back from the North Shore on the roof of his car. The girls had dragged their table outside, laid it with candles and cut orchids, and an end-to-end spread of food.

The music was coming from a radio they'd brought out. Lil Green was asking her man why he couldn't do right. Molly and her roommates were dancing on the lawn. Barefooted, natural. They wore hibiscus print dresses and had tucked plumeria blossoms behind their ears. They had their own house and a tall hedgerow and they didn't know they were being watched. If they did, they didn't give a damn. They held slender-stemmed cocktail coupes. They raised them up above their heads and they moved their hips to the bass line, and they sang along with Lil Green.

McGrady saw the makeshift bar they'd set up on a side table. A bottle of Havana Club rum. A cutting board of quartered limes, a box of sugar, a bowl of crushed ice. Molly had learned to make daiquiris. She'd taken a fancy to them.

"Is this what you do every night?" Ball asked.

"No."

"There ought to be a couple dozen men trying to get in here. Pounding on the door and climbing the hedges."

"They keep to themselves. They're studying, most of the time."

He stepped out the back door and went down the steps. Molly saw him and turned.

"Joe!"

She brushed her dark hair away from her face, knocking her plumeria blossom loose. She caught it, replaced it, and came up to him.

He brought her in close, and kissed her. Her hair was perfumed and her lips were as sweet as the drink in her hand.

"Sorry I'm late."

"We ate without you. Now we're having fun."

"This is my new partner, Fred."

She let go of Joe's waist and stepped back to look at them both. She was only a little bit drunk. He could see the flush on her cheeks and her throat.

"Hi, Fred," Molly said. "Make up a plate. Joe can get you a drink. And Joe can get me one."

She finished hers and rattled the bit of crushed ice in the empty glass before handing it to him.

There was a ring of rattan chairs in a corner of the yard. A rain-warped low table sat in the middle. McGrady and Ball went there with their plates, and Molly joined them. Her roommates slipped off inside, taking the bottle of Havana Club with them.

Ball drank half his daiquiri and then attacked his turkey. He hadn't eaten much of lunch. He swallowed and looked up.

"I'm sorry, ma'am," he said. "Here I am, crashing your Thanksgiving."

"Joe called ahead and made sure it was okay," Molly said. She kicked McGrady's leg under the table. "And I told him, of course!"

"Well, thanks."

"So you're a detective."

"Yes, ma'am."

"Are you really Joe's partner? I thought he didn't have one."

"He does today."

"Just for this case," McGrady said. "I think."

"It's a big one?"

"Too big for me on my own."

"But the two of you together, you can handle it?"

"I don't know." He looked at Fred Ball. "What do you think?"

Molly's roommates came back out of the house, and started dancing again. They had the uncorked bottle of rum and passed it back and forth between them.

"I think that's not going to end well," Ball said.

Molly looked over her shoulder to see what Ball was talking about. McGrady could see the line of her neck, the shape of her jaw. She was lovely.

"I'll deal with them in a minute—but what about the case?"

"I think by Sunday, our friend Bob Shivers is going to come nosing around. He'll want a piece. And then the Navy will get in on it, too. M.P.'s, or whoever it is they have. By Monday, we'll be lucky if we're even allowed to look at the reports."

"Can you tell me about it?" Molly asked.

"Not really," Fred Ball said.

"It's a murder case," McGrady said.

"A double."

"Is there a man on the loose?"

Ball looked at McGrady. McGrady shook his head, but Ball either didn't get it, or didn't care.

"Joe took care of him last night. One of them."

"It's all right," McGrady said. "It was one of those things."

"What things?"

"I came out okay."

"You're really all right?"

She put down her drink and took a good look at him. It was dark in the backyard. Torchlight, and whatever spilled from the kitchen windows. She touched his forehead, found some of the tiny cuts left by shards of his windshield. He'd picked most of the glass out already, but her fingers were more delicate. She found a sliver as thin as a human hair and pulled it out. She held it on the pad of her forefinger and brought it up to the firelight.

"That's part of his windshield," Ball said. "Joe needs a new car."

"Not a new one. It just needs some new glass," McGrady said. "Anyway, I can walk home from here."

Molly touched his cheek. He wasn't going to tell her how lucky he'd been. The man had missed him by less than an inch. And it wasn't that he was afraid of telling her he'd shot a man. That had been the subject of their first conversation, and it hadn't put her off of him. But it wasn't the kind of thing he wanted to tell her in front of Ball. He hadn't told Ball everything. He'd held back on things that didn't matter to the case.

"I'm just tired, is all. I've been up since yesterday morning. Let's talk about something else. It's Thanksgiving."

She backed off. The radio went to a Woolworth's advertisement. Without music to dance to, her roommates came over to say hello. They were beyond tipsy. McGrady knew it for sure when they began to fawn over Fred Ball. They asked to see his gun, his badge. When the music came on, they asked him to dance with them, three on one. They were too drunk to keep to their feet. One stumbled into his arms. Molly got up then, and led them away, upstairs. She was the grown-up one. The leader of this little pack. She was twenty-nine.

Ball came back and sat down. Molly was gone a while.

"Looks like we got here a couple hours too late for you," Joe said.

"The redhead almost puked on me."

"She likes you, then."

They finished their plates and got slices of pie. They hauled everything in from the outdoor table and washed the dishes. Then Molly came down and found another bottle of Havana Club in a cabinet. They took it back outside. The roommates were nowhere in sight. Molly must have gotten them all tucked in.

She made another round of daiquiris. They had a toast. She scooted her chair up against McGrady's and put her head on his shoulder and her arm around his waist. Her whispered breath was warm on his ear.

"You'll be busy on the case?"

"Looks like."

"Will I see you again before Christmas?"

He turned to her, and she gave him her ear to whisper into.

"Absolutely," he said. "I want that."

She answered, her lips against his ear.

"I want more than that."

It was one of the last private conversations they would ever have.

Fred Ball was under his chin, driving him... McGrady was seated her chair sideways, McGrady had placed his hand on his shoulder and her arm around his waist. He could feel his breath on her neck.

"You'll be sorry about this—" Something something and something about one thing.

13

After Fred Ball called it a night, they stood on the front porch together and watched him go to his car. He gave a salute from his open window, knocked over the trashcans across the street while backing out, and headed off down the valley to the sound of dogs howling. McGrady was ready to walk back to his place on King Street. It was only two miles. He turned to Molly to say goodbye.

But she took his hand and pulled him back into the house. She closed the front door, and locked it. She set the chain. Then she touched her finger to his lips. She pointed at the ceiling. She shook her head.

McGrady nodded. He understood. He wasn't at all sure what she had in mind, but she didn't want her roommates to hear. All at once, he wasn't drunk anymore. There was just Molly, holding his hand and drawing him down the hallway in her bare feet. There was the warm thrill of being alive, and free, and vital.

All four bedrooms were upstairs.

She led him up, slowly. One hand holding the rail, one hand clutching his. She stopped where the stairs made a dogleg turn. The steps were larger here. They could stand on the same level. She brought his hand up, and bit his finger.

He didn't make a sound. She kissed his knuckles, and led him on.

She paused near the top, and checked. There was no light. All three of her roommates were in their rooms, doors closed. She continued upward. They turned at the landing and went

down a hallway. He'd never been up here. He didn't know which room was hers. She went all the way to the end of the hall and opened the door. She led him in and shut the door, but didn't turn on the light.

He could see well enough by the moonlight coming through her street-facing window. There was a four-poster bed with white sheets. A dresser. An oval standing mirror. He knew she had some family money. She was on a scholarship at the University, and she worked at the library. However she was paying for it, her place was a lot nicer than his. He was suddenly ashamed of his room. She hadn't seen it yet. But if they'd reached the point where she was sneaking him into her bedroom, then she'd be coming to his place soon enough.

She led him across the room and opened another door. It was a bathroom. Steam wafted out. It smelled of jasmine. She had a claw-foot tub. It was full of water. She reached down and swished her fingers through it, and he did the same. The water was hot. While they'd still been in the backyard, she'd excused herself to go upstairs. She'd come up here to run this bath. She'd planned this while they'd been sitting outside, getting Fred Ball drunk and keeping his mind off his ex-wife.

And now she was turning to him. She put her hands on the back of his neck and laced her fingers together. She pulled him close and kissed him. Then she was sliding his suit jacket off, and pulling the knot out of his tie, and unbuttoning his shirt. She ran her fingers up his chest.

"Shhh," she said.

She moved back. She pulled her dress over her head in one smooth motion and tossed it on the floor. She was naked beneath it. Her skin was pale white in the darkened room. He had seen her in a swimsuit, just once, on a picnic at the beach. Before tonight, he had kissed her four times. Now she was kneeling

down and untying his shoes. He put his hands in her hair. She got his shoes off, and then straightened up to work on his belt.

He moved to help her and she pushed his hands away. She wanted to do this herself, and so he let her.

She led him into the tub, and got in behind him. There was a folded washcloth on the soap dish. She used it to wash his back, then his chest. Then her hands were underwater. He turned his head, and kissed her over his right shoulder. She must have sensed he was going to whisper something. She pulled back and put her finger against his lips.

He still understood. The rules remained in place. He let her know with a nod. No one could hear a thing. No one could know he was here, that they were doing this. They were complicit.

She turned him around, shifting so that his legs went underneath her. Then she was sitting on him. She wrapped her bare legs around his waist. The tub was just wide enough to fit them that way. He hadn't expected any of this. He hadn't been looking for Molly. She'd found him. Now she had three fingers pressed hard against his lips. Her eyes were an inch from his, and they were open. He wanted to thrust up, into her. But he stayed still. He let her lead, and she did. She guided him. She moved him against her, back and forth and back again. Then she settled down. She began to open her mouth, just enough that he could see her teeth. But she closed it quickly, clamping her lips before she could make a sound.

She didn't shut her eyes until very near the end. When that moment came, she leaned in and bit his neck. It was the only way she could stifle her cry.

They stayed together in the bath until the water lost its heat. She didn't take her hand from his mouth until she got out and put on a robe that was hanging on the back of the door. He climbed out and stood dripping on the tiles. She gave him

a towel. It smelled like her. Like jasmine and plumeria. He dressed. Everything but his shoes.

Neither of them had breathed a word since they were outside.

She led him across the bedroom again, to the door. She kissed him there, long and deeply. He thought again of whispering something to her. There was plenty he could have said. But their silence was just as valuable. It had gone on for so long it would be a shame to break it. It would violate the rules she had laid down. It would break the spell. He had questions. They'd have to wait. Maybe it was better that way. Maybe there was nothing to ask, because all the answers were right there, in what they'd just done. She'd laid bare all that was between them.

He woke before dawn in his rented room on King Street. He could barely remember the walk home. Maybe it had rained. Maybe he had sat on a bench at a bus stop to get his breath back. It was unimportant.

Downstairs, the chop suey shop was gearing up. Banging pans, frying garlic. The kitchen staff began yelling in Cantonese. He got up and went to the other end of the room. He lit the stove, started the percolator.

He was only thinking of Molly while he sat at the table and waited for the first cup of coffee. And the same as he shaved and dressed in his other suit and poured the rest of the coffee into a flask to take with him. He was thinking of her finger on his lips as he went down the stairs and through the street door and as he walked through the gray morning to catch the Beretania Street trolley that would take him downtown.

A paperboy spotted him.

A ten-year-old kid. Tousled black hair, no shoes. A fat stack

of papers in an *Advertiser* shoulder bag. McGrady was the only other person on the street. The boy jaywalked McCully to intercept him. The kid maneuvered to cut McGrady off. He held up the morning paper, and McGrady saw it.

He and Ball had made the front page.

14

A manapua man was coming out of Chinatown, bent under the weight of the dozen steaming lunch pails hanging from each end of the yoke he wore over his shoulders. McGrady flagged him down. The man set down the buckets and opened them up to show his goods. McGrady pointed at what he wanted, and fished a coin from his pocket. The manapua man put a handful of dumplings and a *char siu* pork bun in a piece of newspaper. McGrady gave him a nickel, and walked the rest of the way to the station, eating his breakfast as he went.

He went to his desk first. There was a slip of paper on the message spike. He pulled it off and read it.

See me. –JHB

That would be Captain Beamer. Now at least he knew the man's initials, but he still had no idea what the J and the H stood for. Jittery Hands—that would fit. He tossed the message slip in the wastebasket and pulled out his chair. Marcia Lee had left a thin stack of paper there.

First, she'd run down Henry Kimmel Willard's Ford.

It was a Model 48. It had rolled off the assembly line in '35. Maroon paint job, a flathead V-8. HPD had already found it for him. There was a carbon copy of the report. Last night, patrol officer John Kaiwi was coming around the bend near the Makapuu lighthouse and had spotted a break in the guardrail. He put on his flashers, parked, and got out with a light. It took him a while, scrambling down the rocky slope, but he eventually spotted the car. It had gone all the way down, and was hanging

backwards off a rock. Kaiwi got close enough to get the plate number, and to shine his light inside. No bodies. The car was still there, unless a wave had knocked it off its perch and into the ocean.

Next up, Marcia had pulled the stolen car reports. There were only two from the last year that were still open files. One Chevy, one Ford. No one had reported a missing Packard. That worried McGrady. He tucked the reports under his arm and went off to search for his partner.

He found Ball in the basement, two-finger typing on an Underwood. He was squinting, biting the tip of his tongue in concentration.

"Beamer's looking for us," Ball said, without looking up.

McGrady leaned to look at what Ball was typing. It was a write-up of the liquor store kid's interrogation and subsequent confession.

"I know," McGrady said. "I had a message on my desk. You see the paper?"

"I saw it. Want to go now?"

"Might as well."

Ball finished up. He yanked the sheet from the typewriter, signed the bottom, and tossed it in a secretary's in-tray. They crossed the basement, to Beamer's office.

Ball knocked, and opened the door. Smoke wafted out. They went in and shut the door behind them, and sat opposite Beamer. His desk lamp was lighting up his ashtray, which was over-flowing. There was a pack of Luckies, a Benzedrine inhaler, and a flask of coffee on the desk. There was also a copy of the morning's *Advertiser*. When they sat down, he turned it around.

McGrady looked at the photograph again. He looked ambushed and surprised. Ball looked like he was about to knock the photographer's teeth out.

"Wednesday night, I brought you in here. I gave you your marching orders. You agreed I wasn't going to open the paper and see a story."

"We didn't leak it," Ball said.

"I'm not asking you."

Beamer sucked on his cigarette. He leaned forward, into the light. He was sporting a huge purple knot on his forehead.

"Ball's right," McGrady said. "Those reporters ambushed us on the curb. The only thing they got from us was our picture."

"You can tell it wasn't us," Ball said. "If we'd been feeding Carroll, he'd have gotten something right."

"He got the kid's name," McGrady said. "He got some of the autopsy details—"

"Except for that bit about you fainting," Ball said. "That was just horseshit, plain and simple."

Beamer breathed smoke through his nostrils. He didn't take his eyes off McGrady.

"He was way off the mark when it came to the scene, and everything else," McGrady said. "So he didn't get it from HPD, because HPD was on the scene. He got it from the Army, or the Navy."

Beamer unclenched his jaw. He picked up the paper and dumped it in the wastebasket next to his desk.

"I didn't want this thing getting out of hand, but it has," Beamer said. "Everybody's trying to get in on it. John Kincaid called the Chief. He'd already talked to Governor Poindexter and Kimmel. He's trying to put something together."

"Who's John Kincaid?" McGrady asked.

Beamer shook his head.

"John Francis Kincaid. He's a director of Alexander & Baldwin."

"Rich as a Rockefeller," Ball said.

"Good for him," McGrady said. "What's he got to do with us?"

"He saw the paper and saw an opening."

"I don't get it."

"You would if you were from here."

"Educate me."

"Alexander & Baldwin is in the business of owning things. Mostly land. Sugarcane and pineapples. And it owns most of the Matson Navigation Company, which wants contracts to haul Navy materiel. So add that up and tell me why Kincaid might want to spend a little money and throw his weight around to do Admiral Kimmel a favor."

"Got it."

"I hope you do," Beamer said. "Right now we've got jack shit to bring to the table."

McGrady stood up. He put on his hat, and showed himself out.

They were driving again, in Ball's car. Down King Street towards Diamond Head, then onto Waialae Avenue. They passed the hog farms in Kahala, and then the Kuapa fishponds on the one-lane road toward Makapuu Point and the lighthouse that warned ships off the eastern cliffs.

"If Beamer didn't faint, how come he's got a lump on his head the size of a lemon?" Ball asked.

"I've sworn silence."

"He fainted. Jesus. The guy's losing it."

"I'm not saying anything."

"Silence is an admission. You know that."

"You say that to perps when you've got them in the room?"

"I don't have to. They just start talking. Happens every time."

"For some reason."

"There it is," Ball said. He pointed ahead. "That's gotta be it, right?"

A quarter mile out, where the road took a sharp left turn around the point and toward the village of Waimanalo, there was a missing section of guardrail. They rolled up on it, and Ball slowed the car. The guardrail boards were splintered and snapped. Sharp, recent breaks.

Ball pulled to the side and shut off the engine. He set the parking brake. They got out and walked over. It was a long way down to the ocean. Two hundred, three hundred feet. The slope was steep, but just short of vertical. Henry Kimmel Willard's maroon Ford was still hanging onto a rock. It looked like a light push would send it over. The water was dark blue. The same color as the open ocean. When the car finally slipped off the rock and sank, it would be gone for good.

McGrady went back to Ball's car. He opened the back door and lifted out a canvas bag. It held a camera and a fingerprint kit. He went back to where Ball was standing.

Ball looked at his leather-soled wingtips, then at the rocky pitch in front of them.

They picked their way down the slope. There were bushes to hang onto. Thorny, wind-shaped kiawe trees—what McGrady used to call mesquite. They went side by side so that they wouldn't send tumbling rocks into each other. It took about five minutes to reach the bottom.

"Now what?" Ball asked.

"I'll go," McGrady said. "You take pictures."

"You fall in, don't panic. I'll go for help."

"That's swell of you."

McGrady took off his jacket and tie, and then his shoes. He rolled up his pants. The waves were washing past the rear tires. He took the fingerprint kit from the bag, and then crawled

down onto the boulder where the car had come to rest. The rock was huge, and flat on top. It slanted into the water at a thirty-degree grade. The car was facing uphill, and its rear bumper had probably been submerged at high tide. Now it was hanging in the air.

The downward journey hadn't been kind on the Ford. It couldn't have rolled on its tires. The slope was too rocky for that. It must have tumbled end over end. All the window glass was missing. Walking down, they'd passed its muffler and one of the doors.

McGrady came up to the driver's side. That door was intact. It had a chrome twist handle, and would likely have had some prints on it. But the car had been hit repeatedly by spray from the breaking waves, the water baking off in the sun. The handle was crusted with salt. Pulling latent prints would be impossible. He opened the door and looked inside. There was no key in the ignition. The gearshift was in the central position, and the parking brake was off.

He stood up, so he could see Ball.

"It didn't go through the guardrail on its own power," he said. "No key, and the transmission's in neutral."

"They pushed it with the Packard?"

"What I'm thinking."

"Anything inside?"

"Not in plain sight."

He shut the driver's door and came around to the other side. He wanted to look in the glove box, but didn't want to get inside the car. Any added weight could send it over the edge. There was no passenger door. It had ripped clean off during the tumble down from the road. He opened the glove box, but it was empty.

The gearshift knob was made of polished wood. It was still clean enough that he might be able to work with it. He set his

fingerprint kit on the seat and opened it up. He chose a dark aluminum powder and used a fine bristled brush to dust the knob. A whorled thumbprint appeared. He got it off with a strip of lifting tape and stuck it onto a transfer card. If the print didn't belong to Henry Kimmel Willard or the scar-faced man, then his second man theory would have some real legs.

Now he went to the back of the car. To get there, he had to climb down onto a ledge of rock, his back to the ocean. The trunk was locked. The last thing he wanted to do was start yanking on it.

The first wave that came wet his feet, and the spray splashed the backs of his legs. Some of the waves were bigger than others. He expected to get soaked, if not swept away, if he hung around too long.

"Trunk's locked," he called over to Ball.

Ball was photographing the car. He'd shot the last frame and was winding up the film so that he could load the camera with fresh stock.

"What are you gonna do?"

"Shoot it," McGrady said. "Stand off a bit."

"Sure."

Ball backed up, still winding the film. McGrady drew his .38 and fired into the trunk's lock, point blank. He tried the lid and it began to come up easily. A bigger wave hit just then, and he closed it just in time. He was soaked from his shoulders to his feet. While the water and foam were still running off the rock, he lifted the lid the rest of the way.

"I think we got their clothes," McGrady said. "His and hers."

"We better get a picture, before you get them out of there."

McGrady shut the trunk lid, so a wave wouldn't wash everything away. He climbed off the little ledge and stood in the sun while Ball finished changing the film. Then he took the camera,

timed the waves, and got back into position. He lifted the lid with one hand and shot a frame. A jumble of clothes—khaki pants, a man's white undershorts. A checkered shirt. A dark purple skirt. Feminine underthings. Most everything was speckled with blood. He closed the trunk and wound the camera, lifted the lid and shot another frame. Three more like that. Then he handed the camera back up to Ball, gathered the clothes from the trunk and held them in a wad under one arm as he climbed out from behind the car.

He paused on the way back up to the road and looked down on Henry Kimmel Willard's crushed Ford. They'd photographed it, dusted it, and taken what they could. It had better be enough. He was pretty sure it would be gone by sunset.

Ball double-parked in front of the chop suey shop, and waited while McGrady ran upstairs to put on fresh clothes. He put on the pants from last night, because at least they were dry.

On the way to the door, he changed course. He sat on his bed and picked up his phone. Ball could wait another minute. Molly hadn't spoken a word to him last night and now he felt like he could have an entire conversation with her if he just heard her breath on the end of the line. That would be enough. The phone rang, but there was no answer. Not even a stray roommate to take a message. He hung up and went downstairs. He'd never lived in a place long enough to feel homesick when he left. Now he had an idea what that was like. It wasn't as bad as he'd imagined. Missing her was its own peculiar satisfaction. It was proof he belonged somewhere.

They drove to Fort Shafter, through the gate and up the hill to Tripler Hospital. Ball parked where Beamer had parked the day before. McGrady led them on the path around the main building, and across the quad. Colonel Underhill wasn't around, but they found his corporal and told him what they needed. He ran off, and came back in a moment with the fingerprint cards from yesterday's stiffs.

McGrady laid them on an autopsy table, and took out the transfer card with the print he'd pulled from the Ford. He'd done an all right job getting it. The top and bottom were smudged out, but in the center, the pattern was clear.

"Got a magnifying glass?"

"Sure."

The corporal went to a drawer and came back with a small glass. McGrady took it and leaned close to make the comparisons. He held the transfer card alongside each of their thumbprints. It was easy to rule them all out. The thumbprint was a concentric whorl. Henry and the scar-faced man had arched prints. The girl had right-leaning loops.

"Not a match?" Ball asked.

McGrady shook his head. He stepped back and gave the magnifying glass to Ball.

"See for yourself."

They didn't get back to the station until nearly two o'clock. There was an empty interrogation room. Concrete floor, brick walls. It smelled of smoke and sweat. They shut the door, and spread the victims' clothes out on the wooden table. There was blood on the khaki pants and on the girl's white blouse. Small spots of it. Nothing like what had been in the shack. The girl's skirt was torn in the back. McGrady could picture it. Big hands on either side of the seam. Flex and rip. Her silk hose were shredded. McGrady found one of the girl's long dark hairs on the boy's shirt. There was nothing else to find. He folded the clothes and put them in a cardboard box.

"What do you think?" Ball asked.

"I'm wondering about that Packard, up at the shack. It'd been stolen, so I had Marcia Lee check the reports."

"Nothing?"

"Nothing. And it's a nice set of wheels. Low miles. Good leather on the inside."

"If it was yours, and it got stolen, you'd report it," Ball said. "That's what you're saying."

"But not if I were dead," McGrady answered. "There could be another victim somewhere."

"Maybe it was the girl's car."

"If it was hers, why'd they hotwire it? They had her, so they would've had the key. I cabled Detroit with the engine block number, but we haven't heard back yet. Even if Packard sends us something, I don't know if it'll do any good."

"There's no Packard dealer here," Ball said. "You know that, right?"

"I didn't."

"You got to ship them in from California, special." He rubbed his thumb against the pads of his fingers. "Which costs big money. There can't be more than ten here, any color. Get a list of them, and then go knock on every door."

"That would work if we can get the list," McGrady said. "There's no easy way to check. It'd have to be a hand search. They don't index by make and model. Somebody would have to pull every registration and read it."

"Send Marcia Lee down," Ball said. "The car's a '38, so it wouldn't have been registered any earlier. Tell her to start there and work up to '41."

"That could take a while."

"You got a better idea?"

"I'll do it myself. Why don't you and Marcia see if anyone's reported a missing Japanese girl?"

He was thinking the paper might have actually done some good. A fair number of Japanese girls came in from the plantations and the outer islands, and took domestic positions in the big houses around Manoa and Diamond Head. They cooked and cleaned and watched babies. In exchange they got room and board, and their parents received a remittance. After this morning's paper, Japanese families all over the Territory were probably making calls, checking in on their daughters.

Ball was nodding.

"We need a handle on her," Ball said. "I'll call all the sub-stations and see if they've gotten anything that hasn't been routed through here."

"There might be a few. We can make the rounds tomorrow, talk to the families and see if their stories match our girl."

They sealed the box of bloody clothes, and put it in the evidence room. Ball went upstairs to find Marcia Lee, and McGrady took a walk over to King Street. He cut across the palace grounds for the shade of the coconut grove, then jaywalked Punchbowl to reach City Hall. The motor vehicle records were in a basement room. Rusting steel file cabinets were lined up like the stack room in a library. He found the records clerk, showed his badge, and told him what he wanted to do.

The man just laughed at him.

"That's gonna be about a hundred thousand registrations," the man said. "You know where to get coffee?"

"Sure."

"Have fun."

McGrady had never worried too much about getting ink on his hands. He liked fieldwork, but more often than not, cases got solved in rooms like this. It was part of the job. He got the first drawer full of 1938 vehicle registrations, and carried it over to the reading table. He took out a stack as thick as a dictionary, and scanned the first one. A Chevy. Next up, a Ford.

"Make sure those go back in the same order."

"You bet."

"Might be easier with the light."

The clerk had crossed the room from his little desk. He hit a switch. A series of bulbs clinked on, one after another, illuminating the length of the room. The bulb directly over McGrady was burned out.

                         o

By dinnertime, he'd reached some conclusions. The people of Honolulu liked their Ford automobiles. They also liked Chevrolets and Buicks. Packards were a rare breed. He made it all the way through the first half of 1938 and only found five, but none of them were coupes. His hands were black from handling carbon copies. He went to the washroom and cleaned them as best he could. Afterward, he hunted up the clerk and made him hand over the building keys. He promised to lock up when he was finished. If he finished. He took a break. When he came up out of the basement and stepped outside, he was surprised it was dark.

He walked to the station and called Molly. There were other cops in the room, behind him and next to him. They were banging on typewriters and talking on phones and booking drunks.

She picked up on the third ring.

"Molly?"

"Joe!" she said, but it was a whisper.

"You're not alone."

"Neither are you," she said. "You're downtown?"

"And I've got to work late. I'll be all night, digging up records. I wish I could see you."

"I wish you could, too."

"Well."

"I've got an idea," she whispered. "Where will you be in an hour?"

"City Hall."

"Have you eaten?"

"Not since breakfast."

"Don't eat. I'll bring you something."

"Molly, last night—"

"Hush," she said. "That's for later. I'll be there at seven. Out front."

"Okay."

She hung up, and he walked back to City Hall. He wasn't sure how Molly planned to get here from Manoa in half an hour. She didn't have a car. She had a bicycle from Woolworth's.

The bell at Kawaiahao Church tolled seven o'clock. McGrady corrected his watch, and wound it. Two minutes after that, a taxi pulled to a stop on King Street. Molly got out of the back, and left the door open. She was holding an enamel lunch pail. She handed it to him and then folded herself around him. She was wearing a gingham dress, and had put her hair up above her left ear with a barrette.

They kissed, and she let that linger long enough for him know that it was all right. That nothing had changed. Now he understood what had been eating him all day. He was depending on something that itself depended on another person's free will. And he couldn't watch her all day, and head off second thoughts before she had them. They just had to trust each other. Which was exactly as it should be, but it was dangerous all the same.

"Let me give you cab fare, at least," he said.

"No sir," she said. She kissed him once more. "Girls who take cab fare—you never know what they'll do next."

She pressed three fingers against his lips.

"See me tomorrow?" she asked. She pulled her fingers away, so he could answer.

"You bet."

She trotted back to the cab, and got in. He watched it roll away. Then he let himself back into City Hall, went down the basement stairs, and ate Thanksgiving leftovers alone at the reading table while he plowed through the rest of the 1938 records.

He worked fast. He had a system down. The forms were all identical, and he learned how to fan out a stack of them like a deck of cards and scan for the make and model. In 1940, some pencil pusher in the motor vehicle department changed the form. He developed a new system, but the old forms kept showing up into early 1941. So he went back to reading them one at a time, to be sure he wasn't missing anything. He'd never realized what a hundred thousand of anything looked like. He'd never realized there were so many cars on this island.

Ford won out from midnight to two A.M.

Chevy squeaked into the lead at three, and held onto it for half an hour. Then it was Ford again. Popular car. McGrady had owned three of them, and had probably driven hundreds. He remembered the first. It was in Virginia. He had to start it with a crank. His father had warned him. If you're not careful, it'll jerk back and break your arm. He and his brother drove it up into the Shenandoah Mountains. He'd been fifteen years old. Tom was fourteen. They fished for brook trout. They'd cooked their catches over campfires. Joe had taught Tom which woods to burn, and which to avoid. A good time. Their last good time. Three weeks later, Tom came down with the Spanish Influenza. Joe had it too. Two brothers went together to the hospital. One came home and one didn't.

Tom had wanted to join the Army. Joe had wanted to go to college. Tom died, so Joe did both. He had to live for both of them. He looked up from a stack of registration forms and

squinted at the burned-out bulb above him. He'd never strung it all the way together until just now. Four A.M. in a basement, covered in black carbon powder, and he finally understood the last twenty-three years. He was half dead. A ghost. He'd have to tell Molly.

He found a Packard. A coupe. It was light yellow. He copied all the information into his notebook, and kept going.

He jerked awake when he heard a door shut. He looked around. He was still in the records room. The last drawer was in front of him. He'd fallen asleep with his notebook as a pillow.

"You left the whole building unlocked."

He turned around. The clerk had come in and was setting his things down on his desk.

"Anyone could've come in. Someone could've walked right into the Mayor's office."

"Anything missing?"

"Who knows? I want my keys back."

McGrady stood up and stretched. He took the keys from his pocket and tossed them to the man. He dumped the last of the 1941 files back into the drawer and carried it over to the right filing cabinet. Then he pocketed his notebook and walked out, carrying Molly's lunch pail by its handle. It was nine A.M., and hot. He crossed King Street and waited for the trolley.

When he got back to his room, he showered and then shaved at the sink. He had one shirt left that was clean and ironed. He pressed his pants and put them back on. As he was buttoning his shirt, the phone rang.

He was hoping for Molly, but it was Ball.

"You ready to go?"

"Sure," McGrady said. "Where?"

"Ewa. The Okinawan Village, out in the sugarcane."

"You've got a lead on the girl?"

"It's solid—I'll fill you in when I get there."

"Where are you?"

"Home. Kaimuki. Give me twenty minutes."

Ball hung up, and McGrady made coffee. By the time he was done drinking it, Ball was downstairs, tapping the horn.

The Okinawan Village was on the west side of the island, on the high end of the Ewa Plantation. They'd have to skirt all the way around Pearl Harbor, then push out into the cane fields that ran up to the slopes of the Waianae Range. Ball gave him the rundown.

"The parents are Hideki and Aiko Yamashiro. They went into the Ewa sub-station yesterday to make the report. Their daughter's Harue. Eighteen, nineteen years old."

"She lived with them, or on her own?"

"It's like you figured. She was a maid for a family. The parents hadn't heard from her for about a month. But that wasn't unusual—they don't have a telephone. The father reads English. He saw yesterday's paper. He and the wife got scared. They went and found a phone. They called the girl's employer. He said she took off a week ago."

"Who's the employer?"

"Get this—it's the best part. He's the dean at Mid-Pac. So he lives in Manoa. About four houses down from our boy Henry. Same street."

"No kidding."

"Right?"

"We'll have to go see him after this. What's his name?"

"Reed. Elijah Reed, I think."

It was getting hotter, and now there was dust blowing in through the open windows. They stopped in Aiea and bought

cold Coca-Colas at a gas station, popped the caps and took the bottles with them in the car.

They went on, and up. Red dirt and sugarcane baking in the sun. Pearl Harbor lay spread out behind them. Carriers, battleships. A fleet so large that to fit it in one harbor, the Navy had to raft the ships together, rail to rail. Ball braked hard, to miss a stray dog that had darted across the road in front of them.

"You been up here before?" Ball asked.

"Not since my last year in the Army. '36. We were surveying some of this."

It took another forty-five minutes to reach the village, the last bit on dirt roads. It was built on the rockiest, most uneven ground. The least suitable for cane. There were mango trees and groves of papayas planted around the encampment as windbreaks. There were about fifty identical houses. Double-peaked tin roofs, wood slat sides. They were all painted green, with white trim. There were women and children tending to gardens and chasing chickens. There was a shrine in the central courtyard.

McGrady had seen towns in the Virginia hills that were ten times worse.

Ball parked and they got out. They'd brought the whole camp to a standstill. Everyone was looking at them. McGrady walked up to the nearest woman.

"Hideki Yamashiro?" he said.

The woman pointed at a hut on the other side of the camp. Before they reached the steps, a man opened the door and beckoned them up. They climbed up to the little porch. McGrady saw two pairs of shoes outside the door. He leaned against the porch rail, and took off his shoes. Ball frowned, but did the same. They went into the two-room house. There was a low table with cushions on the floor. There was a stove in the corner. Aiko

Yamashiro was there. She turned around and bowed to them. She was wearing a simple white yukata. Hideki's was dark gray.

"Please," Hideki said. "Sit."

They sat cross-legged on the floor. Aiko brought them cups of green tea.

"You were expecting us," Ball said.

"Yes."

"Your daughter is Harue Yamashiro?"

The man nodded. He was sitting opposite them. His wife joined him, kneeling at his side. Ball paused and touched the lapel of his jacket. McGrady shook his head, and Ball took his hand away. Neither of them wanted to show the picture.

"Do you know if she had a boyfriend?" Ball asked. "Was she seeing somebody?"

The Yamashiros looked at each other, and spoke in Japanese. Then Hideki turned back. Aiko was shaking her head.

"No boyfriends," Hideki said. "No boyfriends. Harue is a good girl."

"Okay."

"Did she ever talk about leaving? Going to another family, or maybe back to Japan?"

Hideki shook his head.

"How long was she with the Reed family?" Ball asked.

"Two years."

"Any problems?"

Again, the Yamashiros spoke to each other, and Hideki answered for them.

"No problem," he said. "Harue is a good girl. A hard worker."

"Was Mr. Reed surprised when she took off?"

"I don't know."

Ball touched his jacket pocket again. He looked at McGrady, and McGrady nodded. They could go on like this forever, and

no matter what Hideki Yamashiro said, they'd still have to show it to him. There was no way around it.

"I got a picture of the girl we found," Ball said. "I'll show it to you. But your wife shouldn't look."

"She can't look?"

"It'd be better if she didn't," McGrady said. "Maybe she should go in the other room."

The man told his wife. She said something to him, and he turned back to McGrady.

"Is it bad?" he asked. "The picture is bad?"

"It's bad."

The man explained, again, to Aiko. They negotiated back and forth. Finally he turned to them.

"She will stay," he said. "She is the mother. So she will stay."

"Okay," Ball said. "It's her choice."

He reached in his pocket and brought out the photograph. It was printed on a three-by-five matte card. He laid it on the table. It was the best shot they had of her face, and it was cropped well enough that her slit throat was out of the frame. Her face was bad enough, though. It had been pummeled to a pulp with brass knuckles, and there was no way to hide that.

Aiko saw it and screamed. Her hands flew into her hair, fingers twisting and pulling. Hideki slapped his hand over the photograph, hiding it. Then he slid it closer to him, and lifted one side of his hand so he could view it again while shielding it from his wife. He looked closer. He shook his head.

He turned to Aiko. She was turning white. Her eyes were rolling back. Hideki grabbed her by the shoulders. He started talking, fast. He grabbed the photograph and showed it to her again. He thrust it in her face and made her look.

Then he turned back to McGrady and Ball.

"It is not her," he said. "It's not Harue. Not Harue."

He handed the photograph back to Ball.

"Are you sure?"

"Not Harue."

"Is she sure?" Ball asked. "Ma'am, are you sure?"

Aiko nodded. She wiped her eyes.

"Okay."

They stood up and went to the door, then out onto the little porch. A crowd had gathered at the base of the steps. Hideki Yamashiro came outside to talk to them. He didn't look any happier than when they first saw him. His situation was unchanged. If anything, it was worse. Now he knew the full range of possibilities.

McGrady and Ball put on their shoes and walked back to the car.

"I guess we can scratch Elijah Reed off our list," McGrady said. "No point visiting him now."

"How many Packards did you find?"

"Six."

"That many?" Ball asked. "You want to knock on doors today?"

"Probably no time for all of them," McGrady said. "There was one in Wahiawa, and one on the North Shore. We could hit those first, then do the ones in town tomorrow."

"Sounds good."

They spent the afternoon driving, and found both Packards parked safe in their owners' garages. Ball elected to take the long way back to town. Along the coast, past Reggie Faithful's house, past the road that led to the kill shed, then over the Pali Road and down again. He dropped McGrady at the station. It was five o'clock. Molly would be working in the student library until eight. McGrady sat at his desk and handwrote notes from the day.

At seven o'clock, he caught the King Street trolley and rode it all the way down to University Avenue. Then he walked to the library and was waiting outside it at five after eight, when Molly stepped out and locked the building.

She saw him as she was turning around, putting the key ring into her purse. They had the campus to themselves. She came over and took both his hands.

"Sweetheart," she said.

"Molly."

"I've got good news and bad news."

She saw his face and laughed.

"The good news is you don't have anything to worry about," she said. "The bad news is we can't do anything like that again for about a week."

She put her hand up and touched his cheek. She was waiting to see whether he got it. Ten years ago, he would have been hopeless.

"Do you understand?"

"Sure."

She pulled him to her by his lapels, and kissed him.

"I'm tired and I don't feel so great. Will you walk me home, though?"

"You didn't ride your bicycle?"

"You can push it for me."

"Okay."

They got her bicycle from the rack by the library, and they walked together. McGrady pushed the bike along beside him with one hand. He held Molly's hand in the other. They talked about their days. They stood close together under a monkey-pod tree while a brief rain shower passed down the valley. He saw her home and kissed her at the door, and walked the two miles back to his room.

He went to bed, content.

At nine o'clock the next morning, he found another note on his message spike: *See me*. He turned around, and there was Ball. He had an identical paper slip in his hand. They crumpled them and overhand tossed them to a distant wastebasket. They went to the basement corner and knocked. Ball opened Beamer's door. The old man was on the telephone. He waved Ball off, and turned away from the door. So they sat in chairs in the hallway outside his office.

Eventually, he came out. He hitched up his pants, tightened his tie's knot, and nodded for them to follow him. On the way up the steps to the Bethel Street exit, he spoke to them over his shoulder.

"Kincaid and Kimmel have gone off the rails. We're being summoned."

"Summoned where?"

"Kincaid's office. And he's got his little club there with him."

They walked down Merchant Street toward Bishop. The Alexander & Baldwin Building was a block ahead. Before they reached it, Beamer ducked into the shade of a small courtyard.

"Tell me what you've got."

They brought him up to date. It took long enough for him to smoke one cigarette all the way down. When they were finished, he dropped the butt and twisted it out with his heel.

"The print means nothing," Beamer said. "It could be a year old. It could be anybody's."

"Sure," McGrady said. "But more likely than not, it came off whoever put the car in gear and sent it through the rail."

"Look—we go in there and start talking about a second man, Kincaid's going to whip them up into a froth. More than he has already."

"What if there's a second man?" Ball said.

"Christ. You, too?"

"McGrady's made some good points, sir."

"You're persuaded?"

Ball paused to consider it. A panel truck rattled past, ferrying empty bottles from Chinatown bars to the brewery on Queen Street. There were a couple motorcycle cops stuck behind it, their exhaust pipes machine-gunning.

When it was quiet again, Ball nodded.

"I'm persuaded," he said.

Beamer started walking.

"Neither of you open your mouths unless somebody asks you a specific question," he said. "I don't want to give Kincaid an opening. He'll have us chasing shadows for ten years if it makes him look good."

They walked the rest of the way to the Alexander & Baldwin Building and climbed the steps to its Bishop Street entrance. They came through the doors into the broad travertine lobby. Ball stood with his hat in his hand, looking at the tile mosaics spread around the walls. A woman crossed the lobby and met them.

"Captain Beamer, and Detectives McGrady and Ball?"

"Yeah," Beamer said. "Are we the last ones?"

"They're waiting for you."

There was an elevator. She got in and rode with them up to the fourth floor, then ushered them down a hallway to a great room that took up the entire south end of the building. She opened the double doors and showed them into Kincaid's office.

If not for the fact that there was a wraparound balcony, with broad, open doorways on three sides, the room would have been thick with cigar smoke. Governor Poindexter was in a chair by the window, and was the first person McGrady saw as he entered. The Governor had a cigar in one hand and an ashtray on his knee. He was wearing a dark suit and his tie was held in place with a gold chain. He brushed the side of his finger down his mustache and stood when they entered.

Bob Shivers and Chief Gabrielson were together by the window. The chief was lighting his cigar with a cedar stick. Kimmel was on the couch. His cigar was smoldering in an ashtray on the low table in front of him. The last man, facing away from McGrady, in a wingback chair, had to be Kincaid.

He stood up and turned around. He was younger than McGrady had expected. Late thirties or early forties, with no gray at all in his collar-length hair.

"Take a seat," he said. "We'll get down to business."

The chairs were spread around the room. McGrady ended up close to Poindexter, who turned to him.

"You're McGrady."

"Yes, sir. I guess you saw the paper."

"Rumor has it you're a good shot."

"Spectacular," said Kincaid. "In fact."

"There's more to do," McGrady said.

Beamer cut in before McGrady could get any further.

"He did an excellent job. We've found the boy's car, and we've found a few other leads that might bear fruit. But the most important thing is that McGrady put the man down. As for the update, I've heard the reports of everyone on the case and can give it to you now—"

Chief Gabrielson cleared his throat.

"We're not here for an update," he said. "The purpose of this meeting has changed. Admiral?"

Admiral Kimmel nodded. He unbuttoned the breast pocket of his jacket and took out a sheet of typewriter paper. He read it to himself, folded it, and replaced it.

"I got this an hour and a half ago. A coded message from Wake Island."

Beamer was about to ask something, and the Chief cut in again.

"They've got a forward air station there, John. Four or five hundred Marines."

"This relates to the case?" McGrady asked.

"Yes," Kimmel said. "It does."

"Probably," said the Chief.

"There was an incident on the twenty-eighth of November," Kimmel said.

"The twenty-ninth on Wake," Kincaid added. "It's on the other side of the international date line. I'm sorry, Admiral—go ahead."

"They've got one Marine dead, and no suspect."

"Okay," McGrady said.

He caught Ball's eye. Ball shook his head. At least they were both lost.

"There's a surgeon on Wake," Kimmel said. "Lieutenant Kahn. He did the autopsy."

Kimmel was looking directly at McGrady now. Maybe he felt a certain connection. The two of them had stood together over the mutilated body of his kin.

"It was Kahn's opinion," Kimmel went on, "that the boy was tortured with a knife, that he died from blood loss after being disemboweled."

"Is that all he said?" McGrady asked.

"In the first message, yes," Kimmel answered. "You know how it goes on coded radio. We keep it terse. It gives the Jap codebreakers less to work with. But I replied, and asked for more details. And it was what I feared."

"Details like—"

"Bruise patterns," Kimmel said. "Puncture marks. What you'd expect to see if someone was using a Mark I trench knife."

"Was the Mark I issued to that battalion?" McGrady asked.

"No, detective," Kimmel said. "It wasn't. They've got knives, but not the Mark I."

Now Kincaid jumped in. He was leaning back in his big chair, one ankle resting on his knee. Cigar smoke drifted around him.

"We understand McGrady had a theory about a second man," he said. "An accomplice. There was some internal debate about

that. Admiral Kimmel's new information should put that to rest."

Bob Shivers cleared his throat. McGrady knew him by sight, but had never spoken to him. He was a tall man, with a face so clean-shaven he looked like a boy. His dark hair was parted down the middle and shiny with pomade.

"The Bureau's stretched thin here. I don't have a big operation. When the Admiral called me, I checked. There was one military flight from Honolulu to Wake that fits the timeframe. We're assuming the murder took place no later than Monday—the twenty-fourth. Six B-17s took off from Wheeler Field on Tuesday. They refueled on Midway, stopped over on Wake, and went to Guam the next morning. So he could've been part of a bomber crew."

"But not likely," Kimmel said. "When those boys make a refueling stop, they're busy the whole time they're on the ground. Then they go."

"What about civilian planes?" McGrady asked.

"Pan Am has its Clippers," Shivers said. "The flying boats. One flight fits the window. It stopped over in Wake. It was in Guam on Friday," he said. He looked at his watch. "It landed in Manila yesterday."

"That's the end of the line?"

"For that aircraft," Shivers said, "But Pan Am runs other flights out of Manila. Once you're there, you can fly anywhere. Hong Kong, Macau. Singapore."

"Do we know anything about the passengers?" McGrady asked.

"The ticket office isn't open yet," Shivers said.

"Ball and I can go. It'll be open by the time we get there. They'll have the passenger list."

"Get it," Governor Poindexter said. "Bring it back. We'll meet here at noon, to decide."

"Decide what?" McGrady asked.

"Depending on what we find, someone has to go out there," Poindexter said. "Bob's men are all tied up. And the Admiral can't send Navy men off to a foreign country. It's a sensitive time. We don't want to spark an incident."

Shivers cleared his throat again, his baby-smooth hand over his mouth.

"Do you have a passport, McGrady?"

"Yes, sir."

"I don't," Ball said. The room ignored him.

"McGrady's a civilian," Kimmel said. "But he knows how the military operates. He can investigate on Wake and then go on to wherever our man went. He's seen action in the Orient. He knows how to handle himself over there."

"Who's paying for this?" Beamer asked. "Pan Am's not going to let him on a Clipper for free."

"Let's find out where he's going, first," Kincaid said. "And then I'll make the arrangements."

18

Pan Am didn't have a ticket office in Honolulu. It used Inter-Island Airways as its agent. When McGrady and Ball rolled up to the hangar at Rodgers Airport, they saw the airline's name written across the length of the white building. Block letters eight feet high. Workmen on a hanging platform were pulling the old letters off. The new letters were leaning against the building, waiting to go up. Inter-Island was becoming Hawaiian.

They stepped out. The ticket office was over on the right-hand side, in a squat addition to the hangar. The office's flat roof supported a radio antenna that reached a hundred feet upward. There was a windsock at the top, whipping in the strong breeze. Propellers buzzed against the air. The sky was so bright everything was washed out.

They walked over and found the doorway and went inside. The office smelled of freshly laid linoleum. There was a waiting area. Doorways led into the hangar and out onto the flight tarmac. They crossed to the counter and McGrady hit the call button. They heard a buzzer on the other side of the wall, in the hangar.

They waited, and then a young woman came out. She wore the gray skirt and matching jacket of a flight attendant. There was a hibiscus in her dark hair.

"Yes?"

McGrady badged her.

"This is about the Pan Am Clipper flight on the twenty-fifth. The San Francisco-to-Manila run. We need to see the passenger list. We need to know if anyone boarded in Honolulu."

She swallowed.

"I can get that."

She knelt behind the counter, and they waited. In a moment she came back up. She had a ledger embossed with Pan Am's winged-globe logo. There was a stack of carbon-copied forms. She flipped through the book and sorted through the forms, and then she looked up.

"There was one man who boarded in Honolulu, yes."

"You got his name?"

"Mr. John Smith."

Ball coughed, to cover a laugh.

"Before you let a John Smith on a flight to China, do you check his passport?" McGrady asked.

"All that's right here," she said.

She showed McGrady a carbon copy of another form. Presumably, he was looking at John Smith's own handwriting. He'd written down a home address in San Francisco. 713 Kearny Street. He had a U.S. passport with a 1939 issue date. He'd written down the number.

"Where was he going?" Ball asked.

"Hong Kong," she said. "See?"

She gave them carbon copies of his tickets.

"One way," she said.

McGrady took the ticket and the receipt. John Smith had paid over five hundred dollars in cash, the same morning the flight left. Ball was looking at it too. He patted McGrady on the back.

"Looks like you're gonna get more of that blood clot soup," he said. "And I'm not jealous one bit."

By noon they were back in Kincaid's office. The Governor and the Chief were gone. Kimmel was still on the couch. Beamer was in the chair the Governor had vacated, scowling at an unlit

cigarette. McGrady spread the documents on Kincaid's desk, and everyone gathered to look at them.

"His address," Beamer said. "His passport. Jesus."

"John Smith," Ball said. "A dollar says it's phony."

Shivers picked up Kincaid's brass telephone and dialed. He spoke in a low whisper. McGrady heard *cable* and *Washington*, and then Shivers was reading out the address and the passport information. When he put down the phone, Kincaid picked it up.

"Are we decided?" he asked.

"Yes," Kimmel said. "McGrady goes."

Kincaid began to dial.

"The next flight is the day after tomorrow," Shivers said. "Which means John Smith is one week ahead of you."

"If we don't get word back from Washington before you leave, we'll wire you," Kimmel said. "There's a cable office on Midway, and another on Guam. Wake is radio only, and we try to keep that channel clear."

"Understood."

"And I'd like a word in private, Captain," Kimmel said. He glanced at Beamer, who'd begun to step forward. "I'm sorry—I mean McGrady. Not you."

The Admiral walked away from the desk. McGrady followed him. They went onto the balcony overlooking Bishop Street and Kimmel shut the doors. They looked down at the traffic.

"There are a couple of ways you could play it, once you get there."

"Yes sir."

"You could go to the Hong Kong police station, tell them who you are, and make a formal request for assistance."

McGrady had never gone to a foreign country on police work. But he had a general understanding of how it was supposed to

work. You didn't get off an airplane in another land, and start kicking in doors and arresting people.

"That's by the book, sir."

"Or you could take a more quiet approach."

"I could."

"Did you ever have a commander who gave you operational discretion?"

"Yes sir."

"Did you understand why?"

"He trusted me to read the situation, then get the job done. However I saw fit."

"I trust you, Captain McGrady."

"Thank you, sir."

Kimmel opened the doors and led them back into Kincaid's office. Kincaid was on the phone. Beamer was staring at his cigarette, and Shivers was still studying the Pan Am documents.

"We're all sorted out here," Kimmel said. "McGrady has a long trip in front of him. He needs some time to get ready."

Beamer shrugged.

"Fine by me," he said. "Detective Ball can handle what needs handling until McGrady gets back."

Kincaid had been speaking into the receiver in a low voice, but now he put his hand over the phone's mouthpiece and looked at McGrady.

"They say it'll be easier getting you there than getting you back. I'm booking a round trip, open return. I can get you perfectly fine accommodations on the outbound leg, but the return flights are bought up."

"Nobody's going to Manila or Hong Kong just now," Kimmel said. "Everyone with any sense is getting out."

"Great," McGrady said.

"On the return trip, you might not have a seat with the other

passengers," Kincaid said. "You might have to sit on the upper deck, with the navigator and the radioman. But we'll get you on the plane."

"Okay."

"You know where the Clippers dock?"

"West Loch. Pearl City."

Kincaid clipped the end off a new cigar.

"Be there, Tuesday morning at five thirty A.M. I'll have a girl meet you with an envelope."

He went home and took stock. He found his passport. It wouldn't expire for another two years. He'd gotten it in the Army, to travel on leave. Thinking about dates—tomorrow was the first day of December. He figured he'd be gone around two weeks. Five days out, five days on the ground in Hong Kong, five days back. He guessed he ought to pay his rent before he left, so he didn't come back to find his place cleaned out and let to someone else.

He wrote a check and put it in an envelope, walked it downstairs and gave it to the old man behind the register in the chop suey shop. He wanted to see Molly, but she was tied up until eight. He was at loose ends. He started walking. Down McCully Street and into Waikiki. Down Kalakaua Boulevard, with the beach on his right and Diamond Head in front of him. He took off his shoes and walked down to the water. He could see whales spouting, a mile or two offshore.

After a while he sat on a bench and wiped his feet clean, and when he had his shoes back on he walked into the Royal Hawaiian Hotel. The Pink Palace, Molly called it. They'd gone there a few times for drinks on the verandah. On an impulse, he went up to the registration desk. The man behind it was reading a ledger, but when McGrady approached he pushed his glasses onto his head.

"Yes sir?"

"You got any vacancies around Christmas?" he asked. He knew she wasn't doing anything for Christmas. Her family was in Berkeley. She was on her own. "Maybe the twenty-fourth to the twenty-sixth. For two."

"Let me check," he said. He got out a different ledger. The reading glasses came back down to his nose. "Yes sir. I can give you a suite."

"That'd be fine."

"And your names?"

"Mr. and Mrs. Joe McGrady," he said.

He paid twenty percent down to hold the room, and then he walked to the bar wondering what he'd just done. It was presumptuous. But she'd been just as forward that night. In the hotel they would be discreet enough. They wouldn't see anyone they knew. They could wear rings, if she wanted. Maybe she'd want a real one. Maybe she wouldn't want anything to do with it. Maybe he'd lose his nerve, and not even tell her. In which case, he'd just thrown away five dollars. He ordered a beer and thought about the way she'd looked at him, those two or three seconds before she'd reached up to pull off her dress.

He couldn't believe he was going to have to leave the day after tomorrow.

McGrady stepped off the Clipper and stood on the dock under the motherly shade of the plane's wing. He'd gone from Honolulu to Midway, and from Midway to Wake Island. Kincaid hadn't been kidding about the outbound flight. His accommodations were better than fine. On the airplane, he had the bridal suite. The entire back of the plane. A bed, a desk, a reclining chair. The steward brought him three-course meals on bone china plates. Cream of celery soup and Beef Wellington and little platters of fruit and cheese to go with his Bordeaux.

Wake Island was low and sandy. The afternoon sunlight was like the inside of a whitewashed kiln. He could hear the surf booming onto the reef a mile away. He followed the other passengers along the path to the low-slung hotel. Maybe Frank Lloyd Wright drew it up, but no-frills contractors had built it. They'd hauled kit pieces off ships, then bolted them together. He crossed the breezy verandah and stood in line to get his key.

When he got to his room, he pulled back the curtains and slid the window up. The place got used once a week, if that. The air buzzed with the scent of flowers and a rich woman's perfume. A champagne cork was balanced on the sill. The housekeepers must have missed it. He popped the window screen and stuck his head out. There was the turquoise lagoon, dotted with darker patches of coral. A long path of clean sand bottom lay down the middle. Pan Am had dynamited the coral to clear a landing strip for its Clippers. Across the lagoon, he could see the khaki-colored buildings and white tents of the Marine base.

It was all very fine. It should have been a big thrill. He was rubbing elbows with Carnegies and Rockefellers. He didn't want any of it. He wanted Molly. There was so much they hadn't said to each other yet. So much they didn't even need to say.

He pulled off his jacket and laid it on the bed. He took off his tie. He washed his face at the sink and dried it on a Pan Am towel. He took the envelope Kincaid's girl had given him, and hid it under his mattress. It had five hundred dollars in cash for his incidental expenses. It also held his open return tickets to Honolulu, and the name of his hotel in Kowloon. Altogether, the envelope was worth half his annual salary.

He left his gun in his briefcase, but got his wallet and his passport. Then he went back to the lobby and found his Wake Island hosts. Major Devereux was the CO. Lieutenant Kahn was the sawbones.

"Feel better?" Kahn asked.

"Much."

"We'll take you over to the site," Devereux said. "And then we'll show you the body."

"You still have it?"

Kahn nodded.

"There's a cold storage room in Camp Two—the civilian quarters. He's in there."

"How much did you hear about why I'm here?"

"Almost nothing," Devereux said. "They told us to meet you. You're a Honolulu detective. Provide all reasonable assistance."

"Okay."

They had come out of the hotel, and were walking down the steps. Their truck was parked out front. They climbed in, the three of them together on the bench seat. Kahn drove, and Devereux took the middle. He was a small man, wiry and hard-looking. Like most of the Marines McGrady had known.

"What can you tell us?" Devereux asked.

"Officially, almost nothing."

"Then let's go off the record."

"We had a double murder in Honolulu. Happened a week ago Monday. I can't tell you the victims' names. One of them had an important uncle—leave it at that."

"What's the Wake connection?"

"The kids in Honolulu were killed with a Mark I trench knife. Same as your guy. They were tortured first—beatings, little cuts. The boy was disemboweled."

"I see."

"The next morning, a man walked into the Inter-Island Airways ticket office and paid cash for a one-way trip to Hong Kong. He landed here last Thursday afternoon, and when he took off the next morning, your man was dead. Disemboweled with a Mark I."

"That's fairly damning," Devereux said.

They came through a grove of ironwood trees and Kahn stopped the truck. Ahead of them was a wooden bridge that led a few hundred yards across a shallow channel. Kahn opened his door and got out. McGrady followed.

They jumped off the embankment and down onto the hard-scrabble beach. Kahn and Devereux walked away from the bridge. They came to a well-trodden piece of sand and stopped.

"It was right here," Devereux said. "For whatever that's worth now. The man's name was Russo. Private First Class Vincent Russo. From Los Angeles. Nice kid. Friends with everyone."

"You combed the area?"

"Everything we found is in a box in my CP."

"Except my good shoes," Kahn said. "I took those back."

"What?"

"We found my wingtips on the beach. Russo had been in the sickbay that day. He had a day's leave on account of someone

dropped a block of concrete on his foot. We figure when he was unattended, he broke into my footlocker and stole my shoes. He was also wearing my pants and shirt when he was killed."

"That's bizarre," McGrady said.

"It's so strange," Devereux said. "The bartender at your hotel described him. Russo was there that night. Drinking in civilian clothes. He talked to one of the passengers for a bit."

"So he faked his way into the sickbay, then snuck out to get drunk," McGrady said. "He found the only civilian bar in two thousand miles and did what he could to fit in. Old story, right?"

"That's how we figured it."

"But somewhere along the way, he ran into someone he shouldn't have—I should go talk to the bartender."

"You want to see the body first?" Devereux asked. "Take a look at the things from the beach?"

"Sure."

Private Russo was every bit as bad as McGrady expected. He'd been in cold storage for a week. Not frozen, but at forty degrees. He was wrapped in a tarpaulin and that was it. His skin didn't contain him. He was stored in between sides of beef and cases of Lucky Lager. The stench met them at the sliding door.

"I cut off the clothes to do the autopsy," Kahn said. "Which is why I'm sure they were mine."

"You still have them?"

"We burned them."

"I would've, too," McGrady said.

"The kids in Honolulu—they looked like this?"

"Close enough. I've seen about all I need here."

"Good."

They drove to Devereux's command post. It was a framed tent full of desks and telephones and filing cabinets. Devereux

sent his only staff officer off to get the box. McGrady assumed that somewhere in the brush, the Marines had a bunker. A real combat CP. You wouldn't want to fight off a Jap invasion from inside a tent. And that was what they were preparing for. All the signs pointed to it. The coastal artillery. The airfield. The black mines he'd seen in the harbor entrance, as the Clipper came in for its final approach. The staff officer came back.

"Here you go, sir."

The man lifted the lid from a wooden box the size of a milk crate. There was a pair of pants and a matching suit jacket.

"Whose clothes were these?" McGrady asked. "You burned what you cut off him."

"We don't know," Devereux said. "We were figuring it was whoever killed Russo. Maybe he ditched the clothes because they were bloody."

"Then what? He was walking around in his skivvies?"

"Middle of the night on an island like this, you can do anything you want. Including kill a Marine."

McGrady held up the jacket. It was like a pup tent.

"Big guy," McGrady said. "Got to have a foot on me."

Devereux invited McGrady to dinner in the officer's mess. It probably wasn't as good as the food at the hotel, but it was food he was used to. These were artillerymen. They manned antiaircraft batteries and shore defense positions. Not something McGrady knew a lot about, but he liked being with the officers. A few of them had been in China. All of them had been in Nicaragua. They swapped stories. They were expecting a squadron of F4F Wildcats to arrive any day now. Then they'd have their own fighter wing. They sounded like they were ready. Like they knew they were going to fight. Not if, but when. He was happy to hear all of it, only because it took his mind off things.

After sundown, Devereux drove him back to the hotel. He went to the bar. It was nearly empty. He pulled out a stool and ordered a whiskey, then got to work on the bartender. The man remembered it well. He'd already been grilled by the Marines, which tends to cement a person's recollection.

"The Italian guy was a talker," the bartender said. He looked like a Wake Island lifer. "Russo, right? He was a big spender. He had a wad."

"What about the passenger he was talking to?"

"I got his tab somewhere. Let me see."

The bartender went back into the supply room and sorted around. He came back with a clipboard.

"If you're not a Pan Am passenger, I charge for the drinks. You see? So I charged Russo. He said he was a civilian contractor. A Morrison–Knudsen guy."

"But if you're a passenger?"

"Then I book it different. I look up your room number and I note your tab down on this sheet, and you settle up at the end of the line. Like I'm doing with you."

The bartender slid the clipboard across the bar, and McGrady turned it to face him.

"Who was he talking to?"

The bartender jabbed with a cigar-thick finger.

"This one. John Smith. Room 109. See here—he was drinking rum."

"What'd they talk about?"

"I couldn't say. I don't snoop any more than I have to."

"Did Smith talk to anyone else?"

"Not Smith. But Russo did."

"Who?"

"He had eyes on a girl. She was traveling with her father. I noticed them coming off the plane. Russo did, too."

"Noticed how?"

"This big, slow double take. Probably every man who laid eyes on her did the same thing."

"And you saw him talk to her?"

"He came back late at night, bought a bottle of bubbly. I was sure what he was all about."

"He meant to drink with her?"

"He got a couple of glasses, took the bottle and went outside."

"You're talking good champagne?"

"Brut. Close to twenty a bottle."

"And?"

"I don't know. I didn't see him again after that. He left the glasses on the steps. I found them in the morning."

"What was the girl's name?"

"No idea. She didn't come into the bar."

"Tell me about her."

"Pretty thing, early twenties. Half Chinese. The father was white. British, I guess. She spent some time by herself, sitting on the dock in the afternoon. Everyone in the bar could see her out that window. A lot of sidelong glances, if you know what I mean. She had a sketch pad. Maybe she was drawing the Clipper and the lagoon."

"You have everyone's name on that list. With their room numbers."

"Yeah."

"Who stayed in room 102 that night?"

McGrady was thinking of the champagne cork he'd seen on his windowsill. The bartender studied his clipboard, and looked back up.

"Emily Kam, is what it says. That must be her. It's the right kind of name."

McGrady went back to his room after that, but he couldn't sleep. He turned off his light and looked out the window. It was a full moon tonight. He could see the Boeing glowing silvery white as it pulled against its dock lines. He went out and walked in his bare feet down the path, so that he could sit next to the plane. Maybe this same ship would carry him home next week. He wanted to picture that.

20

The sunrise was slow in coming. The sky overhead was clear, but there were clouds far away to the east and they lit up pink and orange. Just before daybreak, the Clipper's crew came down to the dock and began preparing the plane. The pilots were up in the cockpit, flipping switches and checking instrument readings. He watched them a while, and then he walked back to the hotel. He packed what he had, which wasn't much, and carried his suitcase down to the lagoon. A crewman ushered him to his suite in the Clipper's tail section. McGrady closed the door and got into the bed, and didn't wake up until they were airborne.

It rained the entire time he was in Guam. The approach had been rough, and the landing chaotic as the plane's hull set down in the choppy harbor. There was a covered walkway from the dock to the shore, and cars to take the passengers to the hotel. McGrady came last, and let everyone else check in.

Guam was different than Midway and Wake. People actually lived here. There were towns and villages. Women worked in the hotel. The clerk who checked him in was a dark-haired Chamorro woman. He showed her his badge.

"You were on duty last time the Clipper came through?"

"Yes."

"I'm trying to find out about a passenger. His name was John Smith."

"I don't remember him."

"Big guy. Tall."

"There was a tall man."

"Yeah?"

"He had a broken arm. He asked for a doctor to come to his room. The porter had to drive out and find one."

"He say anything about how he broke it?"

She shook her head.

"Do you know if he talked to any of the other staff?"

"I didn't see."

He laid a dollar on the desk.

"Do me a favor and ask around."

She took the dollar and tucked it inside her dress. She went to get his room key, and when she came back, she was holding an envelope as well.

"These came for you."

He went to his room and opened the envelope. It held two postcards, both from the Commercial Pacific Cable Company. The first was from the FBI. The message itself was typed on thin strips of teleprinter paper, hand-cut and glued to the card:

BE ADVISED DC CONFIRMS JOHN SMITH PASSPORT INFO
FALSE STOP SAN FRANCISCO STATES 713 KEARNY IS
VACANT LOT

R SHIVERS

Ball would be getting his dollar, if anyone had bet against him. Probably no one had. McGrady looked at the second message.

ON YOUR RETURN SURPRISE AWAITS DO NOT FORGET
TO MISS ME

LOVE M

He tossed the cable from Shivers into his suitcase, then carefully folded Molly's into his wallet. As he was doing that, a

telephone rang. He hadn't even noticed there was one in the room. He went to the desk and picked it up.

"Detective McGrady?"

"Yes."

"This is Maria, at the front desk. I did what you said."

"Yes?"

"I didn't find anyone else the tall man talked to. But one of the other guests talked about him."

"I don't understand."

"A lady called the front desk and left a message with the night clerk."

"Which was what?"

"If John Smith should ask for her room number, that it not be given to him."

"That's it?"

"Yes."

"What was her name?"

"Emily Kam."

"What do you know about her?"

The woman paused. She must have been shuffling through a Pan Am ledger. The airline was dropping carbon copies of its forms all across the Pacific.

"She was traveling to Hong Kong, on a Hong Kong passport."

"That's it?"

"She had dinner brought up to her room. She didn't eat downstairs with the other guests."

"Can I send a cable from the hotel?"

"The forms are in your desk. Bring it up front when you're finished."

He thanked her and hung up. Then he went to the desk and found the cable message slips in the drawer. He sat down with a pen and wrote two messages.

REQUEST ASSISTANCE OBTAIN HONG KONG ADDRESS
OF CLIPPER PASSENGER EMILY KAM MUST HAVE ON
ARRIVAL AS SHE IS WITNESS

MCGRADY

He labored far longer over his reply to Molly. He had Kincaid's expense money, and could afford to wire her an entire book. He could tell her every time he'd thought about her since leaving her at her front door. But in the end, he kept it short.

I HAVE NOT FORGOTTEN A SINGLE THING AND NEVER
WILL I HAVE A SURPRISE AS WELL BUT YOU HAVE TO
WAIT UNTIL THE TWENTY FOURTH

LOVE J

Because of the weather, the plane was late reaching Manila. It cut a zigzag course across the Philippine Sea, adding five hundred miles to the route. It landed in the dark, far from shore, and took a long while taxiing to the dock. He could see the waves outside his window. Froth and spray. Passengers in the forward compartments were heaving sick.

He'd been in Manila in '29, then again on the way back from Fujian in '34. It was bigger now. It had grown to accommodate the troops. There were neon signs, and bars, and girls in low-cut dresses. He checked into the Manila Hotel and asked about messages. There were none. His room was hot and dark. It reeked of pipe smoke. He opened the window and then spent time pulling up the leather liner inside his shoe and digging at the sole with his pocket knife. He needed to hide Kincaid's five hundred dollars. He couldn't leave that kind of money in the room, and knew enough about Manila pickpockets not to even consider carrying a wallet.

✿

In the morning, he took a taxi back to the harbor, and boarded his final flight. It was less than seven hundred miles to Hong Kong. The plane was smaller than the one that had brought him from Honolulu. He didn't have a private suite or a bed. He sat in a window seat for five hours watching the ocean.

Before the plane set down in Victoria Harbor, the pilot had to circle twice to wait for red-sailed junks to get out of the way. They taxied up to the Kowloon side, and the men on the dock shouted in Cantonese as they used boathooks to catch hold of the mooring lines.

He looked at his watch. He'd reset it for local time, and it took him a while to reorient himself. He'd traveled so far that to piece together his place in the world he had to work it out backwards. It was 1:30 P.M. in Hong Kong. Sunday, December 7, 1941. He did the math. Back home it was Saturday evening. The sixth of December. Molly would be in the library for the next hour and a half. Tomorrow would be her day off. She could sleep in. He liked that thought. It made a peaceful picture. A good way to start this day.

He gathered his things and stood in the aisle, waiting his turn to shuffle off the plane.

PART TWO:

Chakken
Hong Kong | Tokyo
December 7, 1941 – January 6, 1942

The funicular tram led through a long tunnel of banyans and vine-wrapped incense trees, and there were only glimpses now and then of the city and the harbor falling away as the car climbed the slope. Emily Kam's house was near the top of the Peak, and he rode the tram through all five stops to the end of the line. The passengers filed off the car and followed the railings to get outside. He came out of the station and stood in the sunlight, trying to get his bearings on the map he'd bought.

"Detective McGrady?"

He turned. A young woman was coming out of the station. She hadn't been on the tram. He'd have noticed her. She was wearing a tailored blue dress and had a matching bow in her dark hair. Her accent was British.

"Miss Kam."

"My father's house can be difficult to find. I thought it would be better if I waited for you here."

"I'm sorry—I didn't mean to inconvenience you."

"I had no other plans for the day. After you called, I walked over."

He put the map under his arm, reached into his pocket, and came out with his detective's gold star.

"I'm out of my jurisdiction. By a long stretch. You don't have to talk to me. But I was hoping you might want to."

"And why is that?"

"I'd like to know about a man on your flight last week."

"There were a lot of men on that flight."

"I think you met this one, and didn't like him. You asked the hotel staff in Guam to keep him away from you."

"You seem well suited for your line of work."

"How's that?"

"You're good at it."

"That's kind," McGrady said. "I'd also like to ask you about Vincent Russo. A U.S. Marine. I think you drank some champagne with him, on Wake Island."

She looked at him a moment, then looked back toward the tram station. There was a little café across from it.

"I'd rather we have this conversation somewhere else. Not in my father's house."

"All right."

She pointed to the café, and they walked there.

"You must have just arrived from Manila," she said. "You've only been here two hours, and you're already getting to work."

"I'm in a hurry—I'd like to catch up to him, if he's still here."

"Catch up to John Smith?"

"Yes."

"Am I the only person you came to talk to?"

"I came to find Smith. As soon as I got to the hotel, I put out some feelers, trying to get a line on him. Then I called you and came up here."

"How does one put out feelers?"

"Mostly by greasing palms—a half-dollar for porters hanging around the seaplane dock. A dollar for bellhops and desk clerks at the nearest hotels. Then I got all the rickshaw men loitering by the ferry terminals."

"That must have cost a fair amount of money."

"Enough."

"But it can't be how you got my address."

"For that, I cabled the FBI when I was in Guam. The field

office in San Francisco sent an agent to the Pan Am ticket office. They cabled it back to the Peninsula, so it was waiting for me when I checked in."

"The FBI," she said.

"The federal police."

"I know what it is," she said. "John Edgar Hoover and his men from Washington. Your Mr. Smith must be important."

"You could put it that way."

They went into the café, and then through it, to a table under an awning in the rear garden. He pulled out her chair and waited until she sat, and then he sat down across from her. She ordered a bottle of mineral water. He did the same. When it came, he poured a bit into the glass, and drank it.

"You first noticed him when you were boarding in Honolulu?"

"That's correct."

"What stood out?"

"He stood out in general. He was very tall—taller than you by a head, probably. Big across the shoulders as well."

"When did you first talk to him?"

"On the flight from Wake to Guam. After I'd spoken with Vincent."

"Can we back up?" McGrady asked.

"All right. Back up to where?"

"What were you doing on the Clipper to begin with?"

"It's a long story."

"I've got all day."

"It's sordid."

"I'm a detective. You won't shock me."

"There's a diverse cast of characters."

"What characters?"

She took another sip of her water. He understood several

things at once. She was rich. She was bored. She was going to draw this out because he couldn't stop her.

"There's the prominent Hong Kong barrister—and later judge—who had an affair with a tea shop hostess. Which congress produced an illegitimate daughter. There's the daughter, who at the age of six was hired as a maidservant in that same man's house."

"I see."

"This little girl, she served the Lord and his barren wife until she was fifteen. Then one day—the wife was out, of course—the Lord called the girl into his study and mentioned in an off-hand way that he was her father."

"Where's it go from there?"

"I'll skip ahead a bit. There's a happy twist toward the end, in which His Honor's long-suffering English wife catches a fever and dies."

"That's a happy twist?"

"Because you see, overjoyed at his luck, the Lord marries the tea shop hostess and adopts his own half-breed daughter. They all moved into his mansion and lived happily ever after."

"I asked what you were doing on the flight."

"Oh yes, well—some years passed. The Lord began to worry he had no connection to his daughter. That matters. Connection. And so, as a gift for her twenty-second birthday, which incidentally was last week—"

"Happy birthday."

"—the man took his daughter on a tour of the American West."

"So you were coming back from that trip."

"I could tell you the whole story, but it's very long," she said. "And it's funny—I had this same conversation with Vincent Russo on Wake Island. Because everyone always has the same question. They always ask—"

"What's a girl like you doing in a place like this?"

"Or some variation."

"How'd you wind up talking to Vincent Russo?"

"He came knocking on my hotel window with a bottle of French champagne and hopes of being invited inside. He said he'd seen me getting off the plane. He'd made up his mind on the spot that he'd get to know me. It was quite endearing."

"Did you invite him inside?"

"Certainly not. I stood on one side of the window, and he stood on the other. We drank champagne and talked."

"That's it?"

She blushed. She picked at the condensation on her glass.

"I did kiss him goodnight. He asked, and I obliged. He was charming. But what does he have to do with John Smith? And what does John Smith have to do with anything?"

"What time was that, when he left?"

"A few hours after sunset. I'm not sure, exactly. You didn't answer my questions. Allow me to redirect. Is Vincent Russo in trouble?"

"No, Miss Kam. He's not in trouble."

"But you're being less than forthright."

"I'm sorry to break it to you. It sounds like you liked him."

"Sorry to break what?"

"John Smith killed Vincent Russo."

She stared at him, her mouth open. It took her a long moment to recover. He sat and waited it out.

"But why?" she asked.

"I don't know."

"Where did they find him?"

"On the beach. Between Wake and Peale. By the bridge."

"When we landed on Wake, the hotel staff told us not to walk over there," Emily said. "The Marine base—it was off limits."

"Maybe when Vincent was walking back to the base, he bumped into Smith doing something he wasn't supposed to be doing. Taking photographs. Mapping gun positions. That kind of thing."

"Are you suggesting John Smith was a spy?"

"Before he got to Wake, he killed two kids in Honolulu," McGrady said. "One of them was an admiral's nephew. So tell me—why did you ask the hotel staff in Guam to keep Smith away from you?"

She looked at the tabletop and spoke quietly.

"The first time I spoke to John Smith was on the flight from Wake to Guam. It was after breakfast. My father was asleep. I went back into the cocktail lounge because I was bored. I saw John Smith there. He was trying to tie a magazine around his arm. Like this, with a piece of twine in his teeth."

She mimed the action, and he nodded.

"So I came and sat down opposite him. He told me he'd sprained his arm, but when I looked at it, it was quite obviously broken."

"Did he have a German accent?"

"You think he's German?"

"I'm just asking."

"He had no accent at all."

"And when he boarded in Honolulu, was his arm broken?"

"No—I'm certain I would have noticed," she said. "I helped him tie the magazine on. We spoke for a minute or two. He ordered a scotch and soda from the steward, and then he told the man to get Miss Kam whatever she preferred."

"He knew your name."

"He said he'd learned it from my luggage tags."

"So he'd been watching you."

"Which happens, with men," she said. "From time to time. It

didn't surprise me at all. What surprised me is how he reacted when I asked him why he'd been out so late—"

"He'd been out late?"

She nodded.

"I woke in the middle of the night. I'd heard something. I don't know what. I went to the window and saw him coming back to the hotel. He was dripping wet, in swimming trunks. And holding his arm."

"You told him you saw that? How'd he react?"

"His eyes—he was intense. That's not it. He was angry. Just a flash of that. Then he got control of himself. He asked again if he could buy me a drink. But I saw what I saw. And I thought he was dangerous."

"He is dangerous."

"My instinct was to get away from him, Mr. McGrady. Which would be difficult, of course. We were both on an airplane. I left the lounge and went back to the forward compartment."

He poured some more of his mineral water into his glass. He swirled it around and looked at it. She asked him a question.

"It was Vincent who broke his arm, wasn't it?" she asked.

"Vincent was a Marine. They can fight."

"And I saw John Smith coming back to the hotel after he'd killed him."

"If you'd told him the wrong thing, I'd be looking at four murders instead of three. He'd have gotten you in Guam."

"That makes me feel cold all over."

He could see it on her skin. The prickle of goosebumps.

"You were smart to keep clear of him," he said. "When you got to Hong Kong, did you happen to see where he went?"

She shook her head.

"My father and I were the first off. We took a rickshaw to the Peak tram. Our luggage came later, by porter. In fact, the last

time I saw John Smith was when we were getting onto the plane in Manila."

McGrady just nodded. He wasn't disappointed. He'd never thought this would be easy.

"Can you do your best to tell me what he looks like? I already know he's big. What about his face?"

"Wouldn't it be better if I drew him for you?"

"You draw?"

He already knew she drew. But he wanted her to tell him. She lifted her purse off the floor, and took a sketchbook out of it. She handed it across to him, and watched as he flipped through the pages. She'd done pencil sketches of her trip through the West. He saw the Grand Canyon. A hotel in the desert. A man who must have been her father, sitting on a train. She was rich, and at loose ends. She needed something to fill her days when Marines and detectives weren't calling on her. So she'd turned to this. But it wasn't just an idle hobby.

"You're damned good at this."

"Thank you."

He flipped to one of the last pages. There was a handsome young man with a shy smile, leaning on a windowsill. He was pouring a glass of champagne.

"Is this Vincent Russo?"

"Yes."

"And you drew that later, from memory? He wasn't posing for this?"

"I started it in the hotel in Guam and finished it in Manila. I wanted to remember him."

"How long would it take you to draw John Smith?"

"You mentioned the Peninsula—is that where you're staying?"

"Yes."

"We'll meet in the lobby, tomorrow morning at eight," she

said. "We'll have tea. They have a fine Darjeeling and a passable curry. I'll give you the drawing."

"Thank you, Miss Kam," he said. "This will help a lot."

"Now you're going to go back down and check the feelers you put out."

"I am."

He took a handful of coins from his pocket, and started to sort through them, flipping them with his index finger so he could read the denominations.

"Here," she said. "Let me."

She leaned across, took his hand and plucked twenty cents from his palm. She laid the four coins on the table.

"That covers both of us, and a tip?"

She gestured for him to bring his hand back. She took another coin and put it down.

"I'll see you tomorrow, Joe McGrady," she said.

22

He came out of the Garden Street tram station and waved off the rickshaw pullers who were hustling for riders outside the gates. On the way to the ferry pier he passed a pub. Dark wood, polished brass, and Union Jacks. Off-duty policemen were gathered by the taps. He looked at them as he walked past, and then he stopped and checked his map. He'd marked the Central Police Station earlier. It wasn't far. A ten-minute walk to the west, on the corner of Hollywood Road and Old Bailey. Kimmel had given him freedom of action. He could do this formally and officially, or he could keep it off the books. His discretion.

When he got to the point where he'd need to turn left to walk up to the police station, he went straight on to the ferry. He'd greased plenty of palms after getting off the flight from Manila. If that went nowhere, then after his meeting with Emily Kam tomorrow, he'd go over to the station and make a formal request for help. By then he'd have a good sketch of John Smith. With the assistance of the Hong Kong Police, he might get somewhere. He could take the sketch around to all the same men he'd seen this afternoon. The local police could spread it even further.

He paid his fare and boarded the ferry, then went out to the bow to watch. The harbor was busy with vessels of every description. Sailing junks and rich men's pleasure yachts. There was a Royal Navy destroyer anchored in the center of the harbor, launches shuttling back and forth between the ship

and the shore. He watched a bird of prey swoop low over the water. A kite, he thought. It didn't belong in the city any more than McGrady did, but it was still in its element. It was hunting.

He went into the Peninsula and the man behind the desk told him there were no messages yet. He took a cable form and a pen and wrote a few lines for Molly. He'd arrived. He was safe. He missed her. He tried to think of what else to say and came up empty. He was too tired. He hadn't eaten since Manila. He handed in the form and waited while the clerk counted the words to calculate the fee. After he paid, he left the hotel and wandered.

Behind the hotel was a labyrinth of alleyways. Everything was on offer. All of it was cheap. Food and liquor. One-room brothels. Girls waited by their staircases if they didn't have a john. Other stairways led up into darkness. The rafters groaned. He took a meal of dumplings and noodles and ate at a low wooden table in the middle of a covered alley that was choked with steam and noise. The woman who owned the shop poured him a cup of clear baijiu liquor that he hadn't asked for. He paid for it anyway, and drank it.

When he was done, he walked back to the hotel. His suite looked over Salisbury Road to the harbor. Across the way, he could see Hong Kong Island and Victoria Peak, where he'd spoken with Emily Kam. It was getting dark. The sky was going pink and purple. The telephone in his room rang. He jerked around, and spotted it on the desk in the other room. His first thought was Molly. But of course, there was no telephone that could connect him to her.

He snatched the receiver off its cradle.

"Yes?"

"Mr. McGrady, sir. This is Ian. Front desk."

"Go ahead."

"A man's asking for you."

"What's his name?"

"Mr. Li."

"What's he want?"

The desk clerk muffled the phone and spoke in Cantonese. The conversation went back and forth for a while. Then the clerk was back on.

"I'm sorry, sir. He says you gave his friend a dollar this afternoon. He says his friend can't help you—wait."

The clerk and the man spoke again, more briefly this time.

"But he can help you if you pay him a dollar, too, he says. I'm very sorry about this, sir. It was wrong to bother you. Shall I send him on his way?"

"No—tell him to wait. I'll be right down."

Mr. Li was sixty or seventy years old. He was lean and wiry. Bone and muscle. He wore the plain, dark-colored clothes of a peasant. He was waiting with his arms across his chest, as though he were cold. McGrady figured he was just uncomfortable in here. They'd probably been trying to toss him out since before he made it up the front steps.

"Mr. McGrady?"

The desk clerk was Chinese. His accent was so crisp that on the phone McGrady assumed he was talking to a London-bred Brit.

"That's me," McGrady said. "Mr. Li doesn't speak English or Mandarin?"

"No sir. Only Cantonese."

"Can you translate for us?"

"Yes, sir."

"Ask him how he can help me."

The clerk spoke with Mr. Li. Then he turned back to McGrady.

"He'd like his dollar first, sir."

"Sure."

McGrady took a coin from his pocket and handed it to Li. The old man slipped it up his sleeve, and began to talk to the clerk, who stood there nodding as he listened. When Li was done, the clerk faced McGrady.

"You're looking for a tall American man who arrived on the Pan American Manila route last Sunday. Mr. Li pulls a rickshaw on the Hong Kong side. He picked up the tall man at the Star Ferry terminal half an hour after the airplane arrived. He took him, and two suitcases, up to the Empire Hotel."

"Ask him how he remembers so well."

The clerk nodded, and asked. Li answered, gesturing with his hands as he spoke. McGrady had a pretty good idea what the clerk was going to say when he said it.

"He remembers because the American was like a giant. His suitcases were heavy. Mr. Li had a hard time of it."

"Okay," McGrady said. This could still be a scam. There was an inherent problem with paying witnesses. It was almost the same as beating them. They'd say anything. "Tell him I'll give him another two dollars if he can tell me what was wrong with the tall man."

"What was wrong with him, sir?"

"He was hurt. If Li really saw him, he'd remember how."

The clerk translated. Li nodded right away. He grabbed his left arm and held it up to his chest as if it were in a sling. He spoke to the clerk, but this time McGrady didn't need the translation.

"He had a broken arm," the clerk said. "It was in a plaster cast."

"Where's the Empire Hotel?"

"Are you asking me, or him?"

"I don't care. Whoever knows."

"It's in Sheung Wan. Near the Western Market, on Connaught Road. A bit of a walk, once you get off the ferry."

"What kind of place is it?"

"It's not like the Peninsula. It draws a different clientele."

"Could you write the name down in Chinese?"

"Of course."

Li said something to the clerk, who translated for McGrady as he was scribbling the Empire's name in Chinese characters.

"He'd like his other two dollars."

"Sure."

He wanted to leave right away, but first he went back to his room. He put his suitcase on the bed and opened it up. He hadn't been sure if his luggage would be searched on arrival in Hong Kong, so he'd come off the plane with his .38 tucked in the back of his pants. It turned out to be an unnecessary precaution. A red-faced Brit had stamped his passport on the dock without even glancing at the suitcase. He'd been carrying the gun like that all day, but now he wanted his underarm holster. Considering the man he was hunting, he took the trench knife, too.

He went on foot to the ferry terminal and crossed the harbor once more from Kowloon to Hong Kong. Then he turned right and followed the waterfront, now and then pausing to stand in the open doorways of shops or near enough to the red lanterns of vendors that he could check his map. He came into Sheung Wan, and found the red brick pile that was the Western Market. He was about to walk in and ask around for the Empire Hotel, but then he spotted it himself. It was on the other side of the

street. It had a wooden sign above the door. Weather-faded script, both English and Chinese. It was a narrow tenement, four stories high, in a tightly packed block. He had a cop's eye for vice. It didn't matter which country he was in. He guessed half the businesses on the block were brothels. The other half depended on them.

It was raining, and cooler than he'd expected. He spent ten minutes standing under an awning, hands in his pockets. He watched the Empire Hotel. Then he crossed the street, dodging rickshaws and motor coaches and the deepest pools of water. He went up the steps and through the door. Across a narrow lobby was an empty reception desk. There was an office in the back. To the right, a wooden staircase went upward. He went to the desk and rang the bell.

A sallow-looking man came out of the office. He wore a dull red shirt with a black silk vest over it. He laid his hands on the desktop. McGrady counted four rings and nine fingers.

"Yes?"

"I'll make it quick, and worth the trouble," McGrady said. "How many rooms have you got?"

"Fifteen."

"How many are occupied?"

"Fifteen."

"You keep a registration book?"

The man studied him a while before answering. McGrady reached into his pocket and felt for his wad of bills. He brought a handful of them out.

"A registration book—yes."

"This is yours if I can look at it for a couple of minutes."

"What do you want to see?" the man said. "I can read it to you."

"No. I want to see it myself."

He spread the bills out and showed the man. A single U.S. dollar would stretch a long way on this block. With five, a man could go absolutely crazy. They both knew it.

"All right," the man said. "But do it fast."

He took the money, and gave McGrady the registration book. McGrady stood back and opened it. He scanned the most recent entries and got the hang of it. It was written in English and Chinese but there was nothing he couldn't understand. He flipped back a week. November 30, 1941. The day the Pan Am flight had come from Manila carrying Emily Kam and John Smith.

And there he was. John Smith, of San Francisco. He'd paid for ten nights. Which meant that unless he'd left early, he was still here. In room 401.

McGrady heard footsteps coming down the stairs. Heavy, slow steps. A big man.

McGrady closed the book and handed it back across the desk. He unbuttoned his coat, and stepped to the side. Now he could see the desk clerk and the stairs in one glance. He saw a pair of black shoes on the stairs. A pair of brown trousers. The full man came into view. He was a Sikh, wearing a turban.

McGrady nodded to the clerk and followed the Sikh out the door.

Back under the awning on the other side of Connaught Road, he stood with his hands in his pockets and watched the building again. On the one hand, he couldn't believe his good luck. On the other, he wasn't sure what to do with it. If he'd been in Honolulu, he'd have gotten Fred Ball and Sergeant Kondo, and anyone else they could round up. They'd have made the clerk go upstairs and knock on the door to 401 with some petty question about noisy pipes. If he came back and gave them the nod that

Smith was in, they'd have charged upstairs with guns drawn. They'd have kicked in his door and shot him dead if he did anything more than raise his hands.

None of that was on the table right now. He needed the Hong Kong police. He needed to make this an official, sanctioned visit. And for that he needed to go back to his hotel and drop off his gun and his knife, and pick up the file he'd brought with him. Autopsy shots. Miguel's statement. Photos of John Smith's Pan Am tickets, and Agent Shiver's telegram confirming that Smith's passport was a fraud. They wouldn't be able to turn him down.

That meant two more ferry rides, and an hour's worth of walking. The best time to hit Smith would be four or five in the morning, when even the worst brothel crawler had made it home to bed. So he had time if he hurried. He rushed back the way he'd come. He jumped aboard the ferry as its gangplank was lifting, drawing shouts from the line handlers down below. On the Kowloon side, he jogged back to the Peninsula, and went to the elevator without stopping at the desk to see if there were messages.

Because of that, he never got to find out if Molly had answered him.

When the elevator doors opened, he trotted down the hallway to his room. He opened the door, shut it behind him and fumbled for the light switch. When the light clicked on, there were three men around him. Hong Kong policemen, in their dark blue uniforms. They had round English faces. They smelled of whiskey. They were holding wooden batons, their arms cocked and ready.

Before McGrady could get out a word, all three of them started swinging. They had him surrounded. He got his hands

up, his face tucked into his forearms. A boxer on the ropes. The only way out was to go down. He collapsed to the floor. Fast, no warning. Then he lunged into the front man's knees and tackled him. They crashed into the console table in the hallway. A falling lamp bounced off the back of McGrady's head. He pulled his .38 and cocked the hammer. He was going to put a warning shot into the floor, next to the lead man's ear.

The two cops still on their feet finally got clear truncheon shots at his skull. Everything went sideways. The room flashed bright, and then went dim.

He fell off the lead man. He dropped the gun. He didn't black out. He was still struggling. The gun was right there. An inch from his face, hammer cocked. A cop put a foot on his back and pressed. Another knelt next to him and snatched up his hands. He'd never been cuffed. He'd never been pulled to his feet by a set of handcuffs, either. His shoulders and elbows popped. It hurt so much he gasped. They spun him around and leaned his back against the wall. One of the cops patted him, and found the knife.

"Joe McGrady?"

He didn't answer. His passport was in his jacket pocket, with his badge. They found it and passed it around.

"It's him."

"Look here. He's a policeman. Honolulu."

The lead man was getting up off the floor. His knees weren't broken but he didn't seem too sure of it.

"Doesn't mean he isn't the man," he said. "You already found the gun and the knife."

"Let's go."

"Get his things," the lead man said. "He's not coming back here."

They pushed him out into the hallway. They went away from

the main elevator bank and into a maid's closet. There was a service elevator here. When the car came, they shoved him in. On the ground floor, they shoved him out again. He was in a laundry. A couple of shirtless men looked up from a sheet mangle and watched.

They brought him out the back door, where they had a paddy wagon waiting. They muscled him into the back and slammed the doors, and he'd only just managed to find a way to sit when they started the engine and took off.

The paddy wagon was in motion for less than a minute. When the doors opened, only two of the men were there this time. They got him out, down onto the ground. He was standing on the quay. There was a police launch tied up to the bollards in front of them. They shut the paddy wagon doors and slapped their palms on the black steel. The truck drove away.

"Get on with it," one of the men said. "Aboard."

The launch had a diesel engine, and it was running. Its crew was ready to go. They got McGrady across the gap between the quay and the gunwale, and put him on a bench on the foredeck. They cast off and then he was crossing Victoria Harbor once again, the lights of Hong Kong Island blurry on the oily water in front of him.

He guessed he was going to make it to the Central Police Station tonight after all.

There was a rap on the holding cell door around eleven P.M. A wooden baton hitting plate iron. He stood up and went to the back wall. He leaned against the yellow-painted bricks. They'd taken his handcuffs off when they'd put him in the cell. That had been more than two hours ago, and he was still rubbing at his wrists.

The door swung open. Two policemen were standing there, batons in their hands. One Chinese, one British. He hadn't seen either one of them before, and bore them no grudge. They'd have to earn that.

"Where we going?"

It was the first time he'd spoken since greeting the doorman at the Peninsula.

"Identity parade," the Chinese cop said.

"Face the wall, hands behind your back."

He did it. No choice, unless he wanted another crack in his skull. The cops came into the cell and cuffed him. He was trying to figure out what an identity parade was. They led him down a hall and around two corners, and then through a door marked with nothing but a number. They opened the door and escorted him through. As soon as he saw the setup, he understood.

There were eight other men in the room. He saw various states of dress, hygiene and sobriety. The greatest common denominators were that they were all white and they were all holding numbered cards. A camera was set up on a tripod, aimed at a blank white wall.

An identity parade was a lineup.

A second door opened. A plainclothes Chinese inspector came in, followed by a blonde. Two steps in, and every eye in the room was on her. She couldn't have been more than twenty-five. She had white tape on her nose, and her eyes were swelling up. They weren't black yet. By morning she'd be lucky if she could see at all. Her red dress was ripped at the neckline. There was a handprint on her throat. Some policeman had put his uniform jacket around her shoulders like a blanket.

The inspector saw McGrady and frowned. He nodded with his chin. The cops uncuffed him quickly. They pressed a number card into his hands. Intentionally or not, they'd just accomplished what Fred Ball would have called an Oklahoma Show-up. A favorite tactic of Fred's. They'd let the woman see him in handcuffs. They'd signaled who they wanted her to pick. Chances were all but certain she was going to make them happy.

"All right," the inspector said. "Line up, backs to the wall."

The men with number cards shambled into position. They weren't in any sort of order. McGrady was the last to the wall. He pressed into the middle of the line and held his number card out.

"Hold still," the inspector said. "Let us get the shot."

The camera flashed and clicked. The cop behind the tripod wound it up and took another frame.

"Is he in here?" the inspector asked.

The woman looked at them.

"Number four," she said.

"You're certain?"

She nodded.

"I'm certain," she said. Her accent wasn't British. It was nothing at all. "That's him."

She touched her throat and turned away. McGrady glanced down to look at his card. Of course it was number four.

✿

It wasn't until they brought him back to the station's cell block, uncuffed him once more, and locked the door behind him that he started thinking about his situation. No one had told him what he was being charged with. After the lineup, he could guess.

John Smith had to be behind it. He must have paid the blonde well. She'd let him beat her up. The only question was how he'd found out about McGrady. Or maybe the better question was who had betrayed him. A porter. A desk clerk. He'd handed his calling card and a half-dollar to upwards of twenty men. Maybe one of them had decided to negotiate a higher price from John Smith.

He sat down on the brick bench. He realized he was on the wrong path. Right now it didn't matter how he'd wound up in here. The question was how he was going to get out. It might be easier in the morning. Daylight would bring a shift change. Higher-ranking men would be in the building. If he could talk his way out of this, it'd be by talking to them. Not tonight's crew. Not while the men who'd arrested him and botched his lineup were still in the building.

It was close to midnight. He took stock. They'd taken his passport, but he still had his watch. They'd taken his belt, but not his shoes or the shoelaces, which meant that he still had Kincaid's wad of cash. He had a sink and a toilet. He had the brick bench. High up on the back wall, a good ten feet past the highest point he could possibly reach, was a barred window the size of a piece of paper. The door was a solid slab of iron.

He lay down on the bench and tried to work out what time it was in Honolulu.

It was a struggle, running the numbers. The lumps on his head jumped with each heartbeat. It was like getting beaten all

over again. He had to count the hours backwards on his watch face. Finally he had it. It was almost five A.M. at home. Molly would still be sleeping. It was Sunday morning for her. He closed his eyes and tried to will himself there. Or if God wouldn't let him have that, maybe he could just send her a thought. One thought, his mind to hers. It wasn't asking much. Three words would do.

24

At six A.M., while he'd been half asleep on the bench, someone opened the slot on the bottom of his door and slid a metal tray into his cell. The slot closed. Footsteps moved off. Wheels bumped and axles squeaked. A food cart of some kind. He got up from the bench and went to inspect the tray. There was a tin bowl of lukewarm congee. A cup of weak tea. He drank the tea first, and then the congee. The food slot couldn't be opened from the inside. He'd have to keep his bowl until someone came and demanded it from him. He washed it in the sink to give the cockroaches less incentive. Then he lay back down, his jacket as a pillow.

He waited.

At eight thirty, he sat up again. He wasn't sure what he'd heard until the sound came a second time. He was inside a thick-walled fortress. But for the tiny window high above him, the walls might have kept out every sound. Because of that opening, he could hear well enough. He sat listening to the explosions. Now and then he caught the roar of propellers and snatches of machine gun fire. A little while later came the deep, evenly spaced booms of heavy artillery. Big coastal defense guns, probably. He could feel the concussions in his stomach. If he leaned against the wall, he could feel them even more. Century-old dust came loose from the ceiling and upper walls. It drifted downward. A descending fog. He watched it swirl in the shaft of sunlight.

There were voices now, too. Coming from the inside. Since last night, he'd known there were other cells around him. He

hadn't known whether any of them were occupied. His fellow prisoners had been silent all night, and all morning. But now the jailed men were shouting back and forth in Cantonese.

He couldn't understand a word of it. But he didn't need to. His imagination was as good as anyone's. He also had a more recent view of the facts than any man on the cell block. He'd hopped islands from Honolulu to Hong Kong. He'd started at one American military base and had passed through four others on the way. At every stop, there'd been airfields lined with bombers. There'd been torpedo boats and massive earthworks around shore batteries. All of it had been built or moved, at great expense, to counter one threat. Everyone had known this storm was coming.

Now the war was here. The only thing he could do about it was sit and wait.

No one brought lunch. No one came to drag him in chains to an arraignment, or to tell him it had been a mistake and he was free to go. No one came at all. He listened to the thundering artillery. The other men around him were doing the same. The guns were firing from within the city, but he never heard the shells land. Likewise, he never heard explosions from incoming rounds. He drew conclusions. The Brits must have had bigger guns than the Japs. They were engaging the enemy somewhere over the horizon. If the Japs fought to within their mobile guns' range, they'd start shooting back. That probably meant the Japs were fifteen miles away, and would start shooting when they'd closed it to five. He looked around again. Thick walls, arched ceiling. He was on the ground floor, and there were several floors above him. If he had to sit in a building during a shelling, he could do worse.

By six thirty, it was dark outside and even darker in his cell.

There'd been a light all last night but tonight it hadn't come on. Either the Japs had bombed the power plant, or the city had blacked itself out intentionally. It didn't really make a difference to McGrady. He was glad he'd washed his bowl. The roaches would be out in force. They'd been waiting ten million years for this moment.

He couldn't see his watch anymore, and had lost track of the time. He was just sitting in the dark, letting his mind freewheel on the case. Better that than to get started on anything else. Molly, for instance. He thought about John Smith and how close he'd come at the Empire Hotel. Because he'd missed meeting Emily Kam, he didn't even have a face to put to the fake name. He'd been beaten by a shadow. He should have just gone upstairs, kicked in the door, and shot him. Worst-case scenario, he'd have been arrested right away. Then he'd be sitting on the same cell block. At least he'd know what he was charged with. Things would make sense.

A door opened. Footsteps advanced across the brick floor. Someone rapped twice on his door with something hard. A baton, probably.

He stood and went to the front of his cell. A postcard size panel slid open. Eye level, if he stooped. He squinted at the lantern light.

"McGrady?"

"Yeah."

"You've a visitor."

McGrady looked through the slot. A uniformed police officer stepped away. He handed his lantern to the man behind him. McGrady had never seen him before. He had messy brown hair, and a decent tan suit. He was younger than McGrady, but not by much. He stepped forward.

"I'm Nathan De Vries," he said. He had an East Coast accent. Boston, maybe. "I'm from the consulate."

"Who sent you?"

"We got a call last night—an American in lockup. I hear you're a detective."

"Honolulu P.D.," McGrady said. "Why would they call you?"

De Vries was patting down his pockets. Jacket, then pants.

"We've got an understanding—any American who gets locked up, we get a call."

"That's why they brought me to Central, and not the Kowloon precinct?"

"Maybe," De Vries said. He'd found a cigarette case and was looking for a light. "Or it could be the charge against you. You're in Hong Kong now. Aggravated rape is a capital crime. So they'd want to bring you downtown. To the big boys."

"That's how they're charging me—aggravated rape?"

"You didn't hear?"

"I didn't hear anything."

De Vries found a box of matches. He lit his cigarette. He pulled a second one from the case and offered it to McGrady through the slot. McGrady shook his head. If he'd shot Smith last night, he'd have taken it. He'd have earned it.

"A lot's gone on today," De Vries said.

"I heard."

"What'd you hear?"

"Artillery. Aerial bombs. Machine guns. The Japs made their move."

"Everybody thought they saw it coming," De Vries said. "But no one saw this."

"I need to cable Honolulu."

"Not possible."

"What?"

"The cable's down. We don't know where along the line it got cut."

"Where else could it be but here?"

"You don't understand. The Japs hit Pearl. They got Wake. Then Guam and Manila the same time they were hitting Hong Kong. It's a fifty-five hundred mile front."

McGrady grabbed onto the door, fingers through the slot so he could pull his face close.

"What do you mean, they hit Pearl?"

"They hit it. Same as here, same as everywhere else."

"Troops? An invasion?"

De Vries took a long pull on his cigarette and breathed out. Then he shook his head.

"All we've heard is planes. Carrier based, you'd suppose. Two waves in the morning. They sunk the *Arizona*. Some others. I don't remember—it's been a long day."

"How are you getting all this?"

"Wireless."

"Did they bomb the city?"

"Which city?"

"Honolulu. Jesus."

"All I heard was they hit Pearl."

McGrady studied his visitor. The man was green. He looked like he'd gone to college, and then gotten a job involving a typewriter.

"Do you have the pull to get me out of here?"

"Not a chance. Not for aggravated rape."

"I didn't do it. It's a setup. Call in some favors."

"This is a crown colony. It's not Nicaragua. They have a process."

"I've been listening to their process go to shit all day."

"I can't do it, McGrady. I can get you a lawyer, but I don't

know when. I don't even know when they'll be able to arraign you. The men who arrested you—the whole force has been pressed into coast patrols."

"Can you reach Honolulu on wireless?" he asked.

"We don't have a transmitter at the consulate. We used coded cables," De Vries said. "What good would it do if I could talk to Honolulu?"

"Admiral Kimmel can vouch for me. Governor Poindexter, too. I'm here on their business."

"You didn't go through the formal channels."

"I didn't get the chance. I was on the ground about eight hours, and busy the whole time."

"Busy doing what?"

"Chasing a murderer."

"What murderer?"

"He strung up Kimmel's nephew. He made a Japanese girl watch, and then did her. He came here on the Pan Am Clipper, one week ahead of me. On the way, he left a dead Marine on Wake."

"You're saying it was him who set you up?"

Hong Kong's artillery let loose another salvo. The iron door between them vibrated.

"Who else would've?"

"You never saw that woman?"

"First time was at the lineup. You know her name? If you followed her, she'd take you straight to him."

"I couldn't do that. We're diplomats, not police. Even if I had authority—which I don't—there's no time right now."

"The man's traveling on a sham U.S. passport. He's getting all kinds of help. We've got reasons to think he's a German."

"And?"

"Connect the dots, De Vries," McGrady said. "There's a war now. This man's an enemy. Your rules have changed."

De Vries smoked his cigarette and looked at the ceiling. Fine particles of sand were falling from the arched brickwork above him, shaken loose by the latest blasts.

"This war might not be such a bad thing for you," De Vries said. "It'll change a lot of people's priorities. If the Crown Counsel can't find his complaining witness, he'll have to cut you loose."

"So all I have to worry about is what the Japs do between now and whenever that happens."

"We'll just have to wait and see about the Japs."

"Easy for you to say," McGrady said.

"I'll try to come see you tomorrow."

"Don't work too hard."

Ten minutes after De Vries left, the food slot on the bottom of his door slid open. A tray appeared. On it was a cup of tea. American power on full display. De Vries had thrown his weight around. McGrady sat on his bench and drank it. He didn't get his hopes up for anything else. That way, when the clock ran out on December 8th, and he never got dinner, he wasn't terribly disappointed.

Dawn brought three hours of air raids, and another bowl of congee. The man who shoved the tray through the food slot was jumpy. He pushed it too hard. The tea spilled. McGrady drank what he could off the tray, and the little bit that was left in the cup. Most of it was on the floor. He had the congee and went through his routine again. He washed the bowl. He put it with the other, from yesterday's breakfast. It troubled him that no one had come to pick up his dish. There was a breakdown. The station was coming apart under pressure. He was locked in the middle.

❖

De Vries came near sunset. Same routine. Someone knocked and said McGrady's name. The slot opened. The officer walked off and left De Vries in front of the door. He patted his pockets and got a cigarette lit, and put everything away without offering one to McGrady.

"They let me bring you something," De Vries said.

He knelt and opened the lower slot. He pushed a paper parcel through. Then he rolled in a liter-sized glass bottle.

"What's this?"

"Dumplings," De Vries said. "Beer. And Halazone tablets, to treat water."

"Can you unlock that door from out there?"

"I'd need a key."

"If you had it, would you do it?"

"I don't know. The British are our allies."

"And we're theirs."

"We're evacuating the consulate."

"How?"

"China National Aviation—American pilots, flying for the Nationalists. They're coming in and out of Kai Tak Airport at night."

"When do you leave?"

"Ten o'clock."

"Did you talk to anyone for me?"

"I did what I could."

"What now?"

"We'll fly to Chungking, then on over the Himalayas. We'll make our way to Delhi however we can and regroup there."

"Not you, you fool. What happens to me?"

If De Vries felt at all chastised, McGrady couldn't tell it from his face. His expression was dull and his eyes were bloodshot. He must have been drinking gin since lunch.

"When we get to India, we'll write a letter on your behalf."

"A letter. Where would you even send it?"

"We can take it to the British, in Delhi. Make a formal protest."

"I've got a better idea," McGrady said. "Go down the hall, and find the guy who let you in here."

"And do what?"

"Give him five hundred dollars for the key and tell him to go get a drink."

"Who's got five hundred dollars?"

"Would you do it?"

De Vries looked around. Furtive. Guilty, before he'd even done anything. He'd last about a minute on the streets.

"I couldn't. He'd arrest me and put me in the cell across the hall."

"Three hundred for you, and two hundred for him."

"I can't do it, McGrady."

"Change your mind, I'll be here. Waiting for the Japs."

"The Brits won't surrender."

"I'm not worried they'll surrender. I'm worried the Japs will mop the floor with them."

"I've done all I can."

McGrady stepped away from the door. Then he turned back and punched it with his right hand, hard enough to peel the skin off his knuckles. He grabbed his hand and squeezed it, to stop the bleeding. Fred Ball wouldn't have wasted energy hurting himself. He'd have reached through the slot and grabbed De Vries by the neck.

"Think about me when Hong Kong falls," McGrady said, "You could've done something, but didn't. Catch your goddamned plane."

He turned away from the slot and nearly tripped over the

package of dumplings. He stopped himself from kicking it against the wall, from stomping it flat. He'd regret that, later. He was hungry enough already to see that. Instead, he sat on the bench and listened to De Vries walk away. When all the doors were shut and the block was dead dark, and silent, he found another thing to regret.

If he'd kept calm, he could've asked De Vries to get word to Molly. The man almost certainly could have done it, eventually. But now that door was closed, just like all the others.

The hours went past, and nothing happened. No one came. De Vries must have been gone, his plane lifting up through the dark. Carrying him away to the subcontinent and safety. Outside, the artillery blasts went on and on. The cell had been warm during the day, but the temperature dropped throughout the night. He knew dawn was coming, because he was hunched on the bench and shivering. Then there was something new. He could hear the explosions of incoming rounds. They were too far off to be landing in the city. They were probably falling north of Kowloon. The Japs had moved the lines. They were close enough now to have begun a barrage of their own.

He ate the dumplings to keep the cockroaches from having them. Then he opened the beer by prying its cap off against the edge of the iron door. He sat on the bench and drank it as dawn lit his tiny window. He thought it would be the most miserable drink of his life.

The years ahead would prove him wrong.

Six days ago, the Japanese had pulled their artillery within range. From then on, the shelling was constant. And as far as McGrady could tell, it was indiscriminate. There were times when they'd slow down, maybe waiting for more ordnance to come up from the rear. Then they'd just toss a few shells an hour, usually after midnight. A sound enough strategy to demoralize an entire city. You could only go so long without sleep. You could only hold your breath for so long.

Four days back, while there was still some semblance of order in the station, McGrady had managed a few words with the man who brought the day's congee. The Brits had evacuated the New Territories and Kowloon. They'd ceded everything but Hong Kong Island.

Starting three days ago, there'd been no news at all. No congee in the morning. No tea. The other jailed men banged on their cell doors for a while, then quit. The power was out. The water still worked. McGrady had his beer bottle. He filled it with tap water from the sink, and treated it with Halazone tablets from De Vries. He sat on his brick bench and looked at the door. He listened to the shelling.

Two days ago, he heard street fighting. Machine guns and bolt-action rifles. Grenades. Over the next forty-eight hours, the sound grew steadily louder. The Brits were contesting every block. A losing fight. They weren't pushing the Japs into the sea. They were ceding ground. The battle engulfed the Central Police Station on the morning of the twenty-first. Now he was lying on his bench, listening to it. It was right outside. He could

smell cordite. He could hear officers from both sides. They were shouting at their men, at each other. There was shattering glass. A machine gun opened up, from inside the building. One side or the other had come in and set up a position in a high corner.

The fighting went into the afternoon. Then it moved on. The silence stretched an hour. It ended all at once when the cell block's steel door slammed open. Laughter bounced down the corridor. Footsteps. A whisper. When they were right outside his door, a man barked something. An order.

"Chakken!"

"Hai!"

McGrady stood up. He shook out his folded jacket, and put it on. Outside the door, he heard hands slapping wood. Metal clicking against metal. Then a key in a lock. Not his lock, not his door.

Hinges creaked.

A man started speaking rapid Cantonese. Then he screamed. The Japanese soldiers screamed back. They were so loud, they drowned out everything else. Then it was quiet. They went to the next cell.

The key, the latches, the rusted hinges.

The next prisoner never spoke any words. He screamed, and was cut off. McGrady heard the blows fall this time. He knew what order the commander had given, what he was doing to save bullets.

The third prisoner knew it too. McGrady heard the locks turn and the bolts slide back. But this time, there was no sound of the door opening. There was shouting in two languages. A struggle over the door. The man in the cell was trying to hold it closed. If it was anything like McGrady's, there was only a small handle on the inside. Nothing to get a grip on. The man must

have changed his plan. He stopped resisting, and pushed the door open. It took the Japs by surprise. McGrady heard men falling over each other. Running footsteps. Then a rifle shot. A body hitting stone.

Footsteps.

McGrady heard the key in his lock.

Staying in the cell meant death. Running out meant death. There was nothing to do. He buttoned his jacket. He stood straight in the center of his cell. The iron door swung open. There were three Japanese soldiers blocking the entryway. They had their rifles leveled at him. Their bayonets were fixed. Long, thin blades. They were dripping with blood.

The soldiers looked at McGrady. He had his hands at his sides, fists clenched in anticipation. He looked through the soldiers' faces. Through the wall behind them. He looked all the way to Molly, in Honolulu. He kept his eyes open. He wouldn't close his eyes for them. He saw Molly. He told her what he should have said a hundred times before he left.

One of the soldiers leaned out of the cell and looked down the hallway. He shouted to someone McGrady couldn't see.

"*Amerikajin!*"

"*Nani?*"

"*Amerikajin ka igirisujin da—*"

"*Yamero!*"

"*Hai!*"

All three soldiers lowered their blades. McGrady's eyes refocused. The soldiers parted as their commanding officer came into the cell. McGrady figured him for a second lieutenant. He had a single star on a red and yellow device attached to his collar. Knee-high boots, all scuffed up. A sheathed sword on his hip. His khakis were soaked with sweat.

The officer stepped up to McGrady.

"USA, or British?"

"USA."

The officer put both his hands in front of him. He was holding a pistol. He touched his wrists together.

"You," he said. "Turn."

The officer demonstrated. Hands behind his back, wrists together. He didn't mind turning his back on McGrady. His men had him covered. McGrady turned and faced the back wall. He put his hands behind him. One of the soldiers set his rifle on the ground next to McGrady's feet. Another saw him notice it, and put the flat blade of his bayonet against the side of McGrady's neck. It was warm with someone else's blood. The other soldiers quickly bound up McGrady's hands. Thin cord cut deep into his wrists.

One soldier led him out of the cell block. He saw dead men in two cells. A third body lay on the floor. Blood was fanned out in front of him. They'd shot him in the back of the head. Behind McGrady, the officer and his two remaining soldiers went back to work. They opened another cell. McGrady listened to a man die. Caught, caged, and bayonetted. He didn't scream. Neither did the soldiers. It was a quiet death. Scuffling feet, hard breathing. McGrady was still walking. Through the iron cage door and back into the police station. Down a hallway. There was shattered glass. Bullet holes dotted the walls. They passed a policeman who'd been shot in the face. They went down a flight of stairs and through the entry hall. Outside the building, down the steps. There was a dead Sikh soldier on Hollywood Road. Face down, stripped of his weapons. A little way beyond him was a shell crater.

"*Migi ni magare!*"

The soldier gave him a jab with the bayonet. Hard enough to

feel its tip through his jacket. Then a rightward shove. McGrady turned right. They walked up Hollywood Road. The shelling had blown the façades off half the buildings. He could see into kitchens and bedrooms and shrapnel-blasted tailors' shops. The streets were littered with mounds of brick and glass. Abandoned vehicles choked the intersections, shot full of holes and still burning.

After a block, the soldier shouted at him again. The same routine as before. Command, jab, shove. This command was different than the last. The soldier wanted to turn left. They crossed the road between shell holes, stepped up and went into a half-demolished building. Until this morning it had been a bank. The wooden teller booths were blasted to bits. There was no ceiling and no roof. The marble floor was cratered from a shell or an aerial bomb. They stepped around caved ceiling timbers. There were a couple of Japanese soldiers sitting on the ground, flanking the circular vault door. They stood up when they saw McGrady and his escort. One of them started spinning the wheels to open the door.

He pulled it, and it came open slowly. It probably weighed more than a tank. Now McGrady could see inside. The vault had been cleaned, and then refilled. The Japanese had carried out all the cash and valuables. Then they'd packed it wall to wall with civilians. A couple of dozen of them stood blinking at the light. Men, women, and children. They were all Brits. There were no Chinese faces. He'd seen how they were dealing with the Chinese. The soldier prodded him over the high threshold. Then the soldiers closed the door. A slow swing, a solid boom, and complete darkness.

One of the Brits had a flashlight. He switched it on and aimed it up at the ceiling.

"Welcome to the Banker's Club."

"Thanks."

"You're American."

"From Honolulu."

"Pearl Harbor got hit, too."

"I heard."

"Where'd they find you?"

"Near the police station. I was trying to keep my head down."

McGrady looked around the vault. Every man was over sixty. None of them were giants. There were some injuries, but he didn't spot any broken arms. John Smith wasn't here. Neither was the blonde from the lineup. The man with the flashlight was probably the youngest of the men. He had a grey-brown mustache. He wore a bloodied pinstriped shirt. It was missing a sleeve. McGrady spotted it tied around the arm of a little girl next to him.

"How long have you been here?" McGrady asked.

"Since morning."

"Anybody speak Japanese?"

He saw people shake their heads.

"One of the officers had some English," the flashlight man said. "He said they're going to move us, once the battle's over."

"Where?"

"Stanley Prison—it's to the south," the man said. "Are you injured? We've got a nurse in here."

"That's me," said a woman's voice. McGrady searched the dark and found her. She was wearing a nightgown, and had a man's suit jacket around her shoulders. "I can have a look at you, if you'd like."

"I'm all right."

"Then I'll save our battery," the flashlight man said. "Is everyone ready?"

There were sounds of assent from around the room. McGrady

found a place to sit, his back against the wall. The light went out. They sat in the pitch black together. The near silence lasted less than a moment. Then a child began to whimper. His mother hushed him by singing. She sang a Christmas hymn. In the dark, her voice was the only thing. Confident and sure, and beautiful. He imagined it was Molly's voice. McGrady hunched into himself, and held on.

26

The Japs had been pulling the men out of the vault, one at a time. The first to be taken was the man with the flashlight, who managed to slip it to the nurse as he passed her. The soldiers shut the vault door and left everyone in darkness again. The door and the walls were too thick to hear anything from outside.

They sat and waited. McGrady kept track of the time by counting seconds. Forty-five minutes passed. Then the cogs and wheels in the vault door began to creak. The door opened. A Japanese officer stood in the opening, one booted foot up on the threshold. The Brit who'd welcomed McGrady to the Banker's Club wasn't with him. The officer pointed to the man next to McGrady.

"You," he said. "Come."

The man looked around. There weren't any good choices. He stood up. He had three or four days of beard growth, and blood on his shirt. He looked as thirsty as the rest of them.

"Where's Clive?" he asked.

"Come," the officer said. His hand went to his sword's hilt.

The man obeyed. He stepped to the threshold. The officer took him by the upper arm and pulled him out of the vault. The door swung shut. It was dark again, but not quiet. This time the room was full of whispers. Everyone had questions. No one had answers. The children had stopped crying. They were too thirsty for tears. McGrady closed his eyes. It made the dark less dizzying. He started to count again. He took off his shoe and pulled out the insole. He still had John Kincaid's five hundred dollars. The wad was untouched. He'd spent only his own money

up to now. But to do him any good, he'd need to be able to grab
it fast. He put his shoes back on. Then he folded the bills and
put them inside his right sock.

The gears spun and the door opened.

McGrady stood up. The officer was back. The light was soft
and unsteady. It came from a kerosene lantern in a soldier's
hand.

"I'll go," McGrady said.

The officer looked at him, and nodded.

"These people need water," McGrady said. "Food, and water.
A chance to relieve themselves. We haven't had anything in a
day and a half."

"Come."

"Will you get them water?"

The officer said something in Japanese. He gestured with
his hand.

"Come," he said.

The man must have reached the limits of his English. So
McGrady raised his hands to his mouth and mimed drinking.
He pointed to the room. The officer nodded. He understood.
Whether he cared and whether he could do anything about it
were separate issues. And undetermined. The only thing left to
do was go with him.

As soon as they'd shut the vault door behind McGrady, a pair
of soldiers took hold of him. They strong-armed him across the
bank lobby. Night had fallen. The officer led the way. The
streets were empty, the buildings dark. The Japs had cleared
the intersections of shot-up cars. They'd filled the bomb
craters with rubble from the buildings.

He could see it all just fine. He'd been in mineshaft black-
ness for days. If they'd pulled him out into the afternoon sun,
he might have gone blind. They walked up the middle of the

street. He heard no gunfire. Not even artillery in the distance. They went up the steps to the Central Police Station. Japanese flags flanked the doorway. That was as good as a headline or a radio bulletin. The Brits were finished here.

The power was still out. The station was lit by candles and lanterns. A Japanese officer sat at the duty desk, facing ten British civilians crammed on a wooden bench. Leg irons bound them into a human chain. They watched McGrady as he went past. No one spoke. No one made any kind of gesture at all.

McGrady's escort led him through the building. He saw a squad room. It had been ripped apart. There were papers everywhere. The lockers had been tipped over, their contents searched for information or souvenirs.

They took him to the back, and put him in a small stone room. There was a battle-scarred table. There were two wobbly chairs. There was a caged light bulb high on the wall, but it was dark. He knew the drill. He sat down on the chair that faced the door. He kept his hands on the table, expecting to be cuffed. Or at the very least, frisked. Instead, the two soldiers and their officer walked out. When they left, he was in the dark again.

He sat a long time. He waited. He lost his edge and put his face on the table and slept. Some time after that, the door opened. A new officer walked in and set a lantern on the desk. It hissed and spat out white light and made the room hotter still. McGrady blinked. He got himself focused. The officer was older. Maybe a colonel. A brigadier general. He sat across from McGrady. He had a pistol in his right hand. He set it on the table, his finger on the trigger. He stared at McGrady, and said nothing. A more junior officer stepped in. He had a writing pad and a pen.

"Do you have any documents?" the maybe-colonel said.

"No."

"You have no wallet?"

"No."

"Why not?"

"Ask the men who grabbed me. They took it, and never gave it back."

"Are you accusing a Japanese soldier of theft?"

If the officer had walked to this room by the same path McGrady had taken, he'd have seen a couple dozen uniformed thieves going about their work. If what had happened to the Chinese prisoners in the jail had been widespread, he'd have seen a lot worse than thievery since the city fell.

"I'm sure it was a misunderstanding," McGrady said.

"Stand up and turn out your pockets."

McGrady did. His pockets were empty.

"Take off your jacket. Give it to me."

He shrugged out of it, and handed it across. The officer made a face. McGrady had been using the jacket as pillow, blanket and hand towel for almost two weeks. The man went through the jacket's pockets. When he was finished, he tossed it on the table. McGrady put it back on. He sat. A third soldier came into the room. He was sweaty, red-eyed, and built like a fireplug. He said nothing as he crossed around the table and took up a position behind McGrady.

The officer smiled.

"What's your name?"

"Joe McGrady."

"You aren't British."

"American."

"Where do you live in Hong Kong?"

"I don't live in Hong Kong. I came here a couple weeks ago. Less than a day before you guys showed up."

"How did you come here?"

"On an airplane."

"From where?"

"Honolulu."

If the colonel gave a signal, McGrady didn't catch it. But the man behind him went into action. He punched McGrady in the back of the head, then locked his right arm around McGrady's neck, closing down his throat by flexing his bicep. McGrady tried to stand up, but the man had all the power. All McGrady could do was scrabble around with his feet and claw at the man's arm.

Just before he blacked out, the man let go. McGrady fell forward into the table. He held onto its edge, gasping and gagging.

"I was saying—you're lying. You didn't come from Honolulu."

The officer waited until McGrady could whisper a response.

"Not much I can do, if that's what you think."

"I studied English in Honolulu, in 1934," the officer said. "What color is the Royal Hawaiian Hotel?"

"Pink."

"What street is it on?"

"Kalakaua," McGrady said. He sat up again. He touched his throat, and tugged at his collar. "Did you enjoy Hawaii?"

"I didn't care for it—too hot, and too many Chinese."

"If that's how you feel, maybe you shouldn't have invaded Hong Kong."

"Tokyo establishes the policy. The Army implements the policy. What is your job?"

"I'm in the hotel business."

"Then why are you here?"

"Looking at hotels."

"Lying—again."

"I wasn't lying the first time."

This time, McGrady expected it. The man behind him grabbed

him by the neck. His hands were like plate iron. He was good at his work. He brought McGrady right up to the edge of darkness, and then let go. Again, the officer waited. Arms crossed, leaning back in his chair. Relaxed, patient.

"What hotel business?"

It was nearly a minute before McGrady had the breath to answer.

"I work for a company. Alexander & Baldwin. It owns a lot of land. It wants to build hotels on some of that land. Like the Peninsula, in Kowloon."

"You were staying there?"

"To study it."

"How did you find it?"

"I thought it was just fine."

"Which department of the United States government sent you to Hong Kong as a spy?"

"I'm not a spy."

"You've been lying since you sat down."

"If you don't believe me, that's your problem."

McGrady tensed up, ready to be choked out. Ready for anything. Nothing came.

"In fact, it is your problem," the officer said. "If I thought you were a civilian, you could stay here, in a camp with other civilians. We both know you don't belong there."

"I'm a civilian."

"You will be transported tomorrow."

"Transported where?"

"Is your jacket warm?"

He was alone in the interrogation room for an hour. Then a soldier came in and sat across from him. He had the look and bearing of a file clerk. He slid a piece of paper across the table.

McGrady looked at it. The only thing he understood was his name, which had been typed. The rest was handwritten in Japanese. There was a formal seal at the bottom. A name chop, in red ink.

"I'm not signing anything," McGrady said.

"You keep," the clerk soldier said. "You lose, you die."

McGrady took it. He folded it and put it away.

He spent the night on a bench, one leg shackled to an eyebolt in the wall. He kept touching at his throat, trying to gauge the size of the spreading bruise. The duty desk was across from him. The ten men who'd been on this bench when he entered the station were gone. He was almost delirious with thirst and hunger. The soldier at the duty desk was drinking tea, pouring it into a small cup from a flask. McGrady couldn't stop himself from watching. He felt like a dog.

The soldier behind the duty desk saw it. He took pity. He gave McGrady hot tea in a tin cup. He refilled it for him twice. Then he shared half a ball of rice. There were flakes of dried fish in it. Bits of seaweed. It had been the man's own dinner. McGrady gagged on the first bite. Not because of the taste, but because it hurt to swallow. The desk soldier was watching him. McGrady touched his throat. He knew a single phrase in Japanese. He mouthed it now.

"Domo arigato."

The man nodded.

In the morning, the Japanese put him into a column with a hundred other prisoners. They were all men, and all white. Brits, Australians. At an officer's whistle, they set off marching. Down Hollywood Road, down the narrow Pottinger Street steps, and then through a maze of streets until they reached the harbor. Here, the Japanese had built an enclosure. A holding pen. They spent the morning standing there, getting rained on. Their guards lounged beneath an awning on the other side of the dock.

A few nervous-looking Chinese were out and about on the street. They must have spread the word: there were men in a cage. Gawkers came. Chinese wives and girlfriends began to show up. They reached through the wire to hold onto their men one last time. They were crying and passing things. The soldiers didn't care at all.

McGrady sat alone. He wasn't scanning the small crowd outside.

"Joe?"

He looked up. A young woman was pressed close to the wire. It took him a moment to recognize her. She wasn't a wealthy heiress anymore. She wore the clothes of a peasant. A conical straw hat. Her face and hands were streaked with mud, as though she'd spent the night digging with her hands. He got up and came to the wire.

"Miss Kam."

"The soldiers murdered my father."

"What—"

"I saw it from the forest," she whispered. "John Smith was there."

"You saw him?"

She nodded.

"He speaks Japanese. I thought you should know."

"Emily."

"They're going to put you on a ship," she said.

"I know."

"What do you want me to do?"

"Hang onto your drawing."

"It's in my father's house," she said. She was crying now. "I can't go there—they've put soldiers in it. He—he wouldn't—and they—"

He reached through the wire and took her left hand. She held on tight.

"Where are you staying?" he asked her.

"My grandmother's apartment," she whispered. "I don't know how long we'll last."

He turned her hand up and looked at it. Her fingernails were torn and bloody. Her skin was covered in grime. He could only imagine what had happened to her. And this was just the beginning. It would get worse from here.

"You need money," he said.

"What—Joe—"

He still had Kincaid's wad. Five hundred American dollars. He let go of her hand and got the bills, then pushed them into her palm. He didn't know if they'd do her any good or not. But he guessed where he was going, they'd be worth less than nothing.

"Joe, you can't."

"I just did."

She began to cry even harder. She hid the money up her sleeve. She wiped her nose with her forearm.

"I'll get the drawing. I'll—I'll just get it."

"Don't. Draw it again."

She'd been holding her right hand close to her body. Now she brought it up and showed him the broken knuckles.

"I can't."

"Then forget it. If there are soldiers in the house, it's not worth it."

"I'll get it. But how will I find you?"

"Stay alive. Try to get to Macau if you can. The Portuguese are neutral. Then we'll just figure it out. You should go now."

He held her hand once more. She bowed her head. When she turned away, he could tell from the slope of her shoulders that she was still crying.

In the evening, a ship arrived. A rusty tramp steamer, like a thousand others in Hong Kong harbor. But this one was flying a Japanese flag. The soldiers who had been lounging on the dock got up. They opened the holding pen and used their bayonets to goad the prisoners up the ship's boarding plank. Up on the deck, the crew had formed into a gauntlet. They were holding sticks. They welcomed the prisoners aboard with beatings. McGrady put his hands up to protect his face, so they beat him in the chest and on the legs. He crossed the deck and followed the line of men into the ship.

For eight days, they steamed north. He was sure of the heading. Every day was colder than the one before it. He was sure of the duration, although a crewman had taken his watch. He'd been packed with the other prisoners into an oily cargo hold. But he could count the days. Light filtered through a ventilation funnel. So he'd known day from night. In the daytime they fed the men twice. A morning meal, and an evening meal. Always the same thing. A soup of rice and fish. It was more than he'd had in a while.

There were a hundred and thirty nine men in the compartment with him. His best guess was that they all spoke English. But no one had said a word, after the first day. On the first day, the ship's captain came in. He read them the rules. Talking was strictly forbidden. Infractions would be dealt with severely.

A few hours later, the guards caught two men whispering. They dragged them to the front of the compartment and beat them with their rifle butts. No one got up to defend them. They all just watched. McGrady watched. When the guards were tired of beating the men, they yanked them into the corridor and slammed the door.

They never came back, and the lesson was learned.

They sat in silence. They ate in silence. They were escorted one at a time to the head. They sat on straw ticks and nursed the wounds they'd received while running the gauntlet. On the third day, when the ship got into a big cross-sea, they clung to their mats and felt the deck tilt side to side as the ship rolled. The men who were seasick were the only ones to make noise.

McGrady thought about submarines. Black hulls. American

skippers just below the waves, tracking like wolves. Or air-planes, diving from above. He wanted his country to strike back. He wanted vengeance and victory. Just not until this ship got through.

There was one sound. One constant, from below. The engine, churning away. It brought a steady sense of motion. He relied on the sound, and the motion. He relied on the two meals a day and his trip to the head. It all ended without warning. The for-ward momentum bled away. The engine revved once, in reverse, and stopped the ship altogether. Then the engine shut off.

The silence was broken earlier than he'd have liked. Above, a flurry began. Footsteps on the deck. Shouting. McGrady closed his eyes. It was getting harder to see Molly's face. It was better with his eyes closed. Then he could find her. Draw her close.

Soldiers brought the men up onto the deck and lined them against the ship's fantail. The wind was freezing. A city was spread in front of him. Mostly low brick and wooden buildings, but a few standouts. Banks or government buildings with clock towers. An enormous bay lay behind them. White gulls pin-wheeled above a fishing boat. The sky was gray and the air was hazy. He smelled seaweed and smoke.

He had no idea where he was. The prisoner beside him saw him looking. The nearest Japanese crewman was far away. The man risked a whisper.

"Yokohama. I was here in '32," the man said. He was an Irishman. He nodded his head toward the starboard rail. "Tokyo's over there."

McGrady looked that way. He'd have to take the man's word for it. He saw nothing but gray haze.

❊

He stood with his back to the rail and felt the wind go straight through his clothes. The crew faced them, clubs in their hands. The tramp steamer's captain came out. He had a logbook. He stood in front of the first prisoner and held out his hand.

"Paper."

The man dug it out. A card like the one McGrady had been given. The captain inspected it. He checked something off in his book. He gave it back to the man and moved to the next prisoner. It began to grow dark. A civilian newspaperman and his accompanying photographer came up the gangplank. They spoke with the crew and the captain. They walked around the deck and shot photographs of the prisoners shivering in their tropical wool suits. By then it was raining. The crewmen and the newspapermen were wearing black oilskin jackets and good hats.

When the captain was finally finished checking their papers, three squads of new soldiers came aboard. They had white armbands on their uniforms. Military police, McGrady supposed. They were in a hurry. Their CO didn't want to stand in the rain any longer than he had to. They barked in Japanese and marched the prisoners down the gangway. The pier was long, and busy. Ships were tied up on both sides. The pier ended at a locked and guarded gate. They went through it, and then along the Yokohama waterfront. Citizens stopped in their tracks. Men on bicycles. Rickshaw pullers. Women carrying babies and small children wrapped in cloth and tied to their backs. Most only watched. Others jeered. A boy threw a lump of cooking charcoal. It bounced off the side of a prisoner's head. The man kept walking as though nothing had happened.

They went past warehouses near the docks. They saw war materiel being loaded into cargo nets and hoisted aboard transport ships. Munitions and machine parts. Bomber engines. Little

trucks loaded with sacks of rice and cloth-wrapped barrels of rice wine. They came to a complex of high brick warehouses built on reclaimed land jutting into the bay. There was a fence, topped with five strands of barbed wire. Soldiers huddled in their guard booths to stay out of the rain. They were armed with carbines and sidearms.

The parade of freezing men went in through the gate. There was a sign above it, but it was in a Japanese script McGrady couldn't read. They crossed an asphalt staging area and then went through a door that seemed tiny compared to the size of the building.

Inside were hundreds of bunks, but no prisoners. Maybe they were just going to spend the night here, before being shipped out by rail to work camps. At least there was a coal stove. The air was ten degrees warmer than outside. Which made it about forty degrees. It was better than standing in the freezing rain.

An officer was waiting in the middle of the giant space. He was flanked by military police. The line of prisoners marched across the room. The guards fanned them out for review. The officer must have been the warden. The camp commandant. He wore a khaki uniform and a black leather jacket, and he had a white scarf loose around his neck. McGrady expected a speech. Some kind of recitation of the rules.

Instead, the officer pointed to one of his men, who went to the end of the line and spoke to the first prisoner.

"Paper."

Everyone knew the drill.

The men dug into their pockets and brought out their cards. They stood waiting. The soldier went down the line. He wasn't taking notes or marking anything in a ledger. He was looking for something in particular and he'd know when he found it.

When he got to McGrady, he looked at the writing a little longer. His eyes moved from the card to McGrady's unshaven face. Then he turned and walked back over to his commander. They studied the card together.

The commander nodded. He gestured toward the far side of the building. A metal staircase rose up to a lofted office. The soldier came back over. He gave McGrady the card and then pulled him out of the line. They walked across the warehouse. The men behind were silent. McGrady and the guard went up the stairs, footsteps ringing out on the welded steel. At the top was a closed door.

They reached the top and the soldier opened the door. He pushed McGrady in, a hand at the small of his back. It wasn't a rough shove. The soldier came in behind him and shut the door.

In the center of the room was a desk. Behind the desk was a man. He wore a black overcoat with a double-breasted suit beneath it. His top hat sat brim-down on the desk. He had round spectacles and a trim black mustache, and he was looking at McGrady with a mixture of curiosity and concern.

He stood up, and crossed the room. He reached into his pocket and took out a black cloth bag. He passed it to the soldier, who pocketed it. The soldier and the man bowed to each other, and then the soldier left.

The man waited until the soldier was gone, and until his footsteps had made it all the way down the stairs.

"Please," the man said. "Let's sit. Let's talk, just the two of us."

"Okay."

McGrady sat in one of the two straight-backed chairs facing the desk. He'd sat in a hundred chairs just like it, facing as many identical desks. He had an idea he was about to have a conversation unlike any he'd had before.

"You're Joe McGrady, from Honolulu."

It wasn't a question. It also wasn't anything he hadn't already admitted. It was probably written on his card. McGrady nodded.

"You flew from Honolulu to Hong Kong, and when the war started, you got caught up there. You told an officer of the Imperial Japanese Army that you were in the employ of Alexander & Baldwin. That you were in Hong Kong to evaluate luxury hotels."

His English was immaculate. If McGrady had been listening to him over the telephone, he'd have guessed he was talking to a Connecticut Yankee.

"However, that was not true," the man said. "You are a detective in the Honolulu Police Department. You came to Hong Kong as part of a murder investigation."

McGrady stared at him. He'd been too tired to have anticipated a confrontation like this. He had no response.

"It's all right," the man said. "I'm on your side."

McGrady said that to people sometimes, too. If they were tired enough to think it was true, they might start talking.

"It's really no use denying it," the man said. "I'm quite sure of my facts. You and your partner, Fred Ball, were investigating the deaths of Henry Kimmel Willard and a young Japanese woman. You shot a man dead on November 26, but you believe he was not the only man responsible."

McGrady couldn't help it. He nodded. The man was right. There was no point denying it.

"How do you know all this?"

The man leaned down and brought up a briefcase. Then he opened it up and brought out a newspaper. He set it on the desk between them.

It was a copy of the *Honolulu Advertiser*. The November 28, 1941 edition. He and Fred Ball were there on the front page,

above the fold. He stared at the paper and tried to imagine how it had made its way here. There was really only one option. It had to have been in a mailbag on the same Clipper flight that carried McGrady to the Orient.

"Why do you have this?"

"I wired friends in Honolulu and asked them to send me the papers. By airmail."

"What friends?"

"It doesn't matter."

"Who are you?"

"My name is Takahashi Kansei," he said. "Takahashi is my surname, and—"

"I know how Japanese names work."

"I work in the Ministry of Foreign Affairs. I'm the first deputy to Togo Shigenori. Do you know of him?"

"I know about Tojo."

"Not Tojo. He is the Prime Minister. I'm discussing Minister Togo—the Foreign Minister. He would be the equivalent to Mr. Roosevelt's Cordell Hull. Or Mr. Stalin's Vyacheslav Molotov. Do you understand?"

"You work for the Foreign Minister. What's that got to do with me?"

"This isn't official government business," Takahashi said. "This is personal. This is about my family."

"Now I'm really lost."

"You see—I know who the murdered girl was. She was family. My niece. And I know why she was killed."

"What?"

"We've already spoken more than I'd like to here."

"What do you suggest?" McGrady asked. "We can't just walk out."

"I paid the soldier," Takahashi said. "I also paid his commander.

And if you'll agree to come with me, I can take you out of here. Tonight."

"Why?"

"I'd prefer you survived this war. If you do, you could finish what you started and catch the man who killed my niece. And may I be frank?"

"You can say anything you want."

"I'm not at all sure I can protect you if you stay here."

"You're offering what?"

"Safety."

"But this isn't official?"

"Not at all. This is entirely personal," Takahashi said. "And I can promise you, you'll be safer with me than if you stay here. Do you have any things? Bags or personal items?"

"Are you joking?"

"Then we can leave immediately," Takahashi said. He pointed to a door on the back wall. "All you have to do is follow me. We'll go outside. We'll walk down a stairway. My car is at the bottom."

McGrady stood up. He walked to the window overlooking the warehouse, and peeked through the blinds. The military police had stripped the prisoners. The Englishmen stood naked and shivering while men in white coats doused them with pump-sprayers of liquid disinfectant. The commandant was shouting into a metal megaphone. McGrady turned around.

"You're going to get me shot, aren't you?"

"No, Joe McGrady," Takahashi said. "I'm going to keep you alive. When you get home, you can repay the debt."

29

Takahashi's car might have been an antique. It was a black sedan, with raised chrome headlights and a boxy hood. It looked like a Ford Model T. But everything was a little bit smaller, and it could have come off an assembly line yesterday instead of 1925. Takahashi led him over to the left side of the car. For a second McGrady thought he was supposed to drive. But then he looked through the window and saw the steering wheel was on the right. He got in, and closed the door.

Takahashi came around. He put his top hat on his lap. He started the engine, and fiddled with the heater knobs. Then he dropped the car into gear and drove toward the gate. He tapped his horn twice, and a guard trotted out of his booth. His carbine was slung over his shoulder. If he came over to the car, and looked in the windows, McGrady figured he'd have about a second to make a decision. But the soldier didn't even glance at the car. He opened the gate. Maybe Takahashi had already paid him off, too.

"There is a privacy curtain to your left," Takahashi said. "Close it, if you please."

McGrady looked. There was a felt curtain bunched up behind him. He pulled it shut, closing off the side window. He could still see out the windshield. The rain had turned to snow. It spattered on the glass. The wipers scraped it up into lines of slush.

"It's good to do this in the dark," Takahashi said.

"Because I'm a foreigner?"

"Precisely," Takahashi said. "They gave you an identity card?"

"Yes."

"Give it to me."

McGrady handed it to him. Takahashi held it near the top of the steering wheel, and ripped it to small pieces. He rolled down his window and let them fly out into the wind.

"The man in Hong Kong said if I lost that, I'd die."

"In a sense, you already have. Because I have a better one for you."

"Yeah?"

"Your name is Hans Schmidt. You are a German. A Lutheran pastor."

"I don't speak any German."

"Neither do most Japanese. Say something in German. You must know a few words."

"Mein Fuhrer."

"That's it?"

"That's all I've got."

"Das ist nicht gut."

"You speak German?"

Takahashi nodded, and pushed up his round glasses.

"Before he was the Foreign Minister, Togo Shigenori was the Ambassador to Germany. I was with him, in Berlin. I had Ribbentrop and Hitler for conversation partners. It makes one wish to study, carefully, at home."

"You must've had a ball."

"At a state dinner, a diplomat swallows any dish. Without choking."

"I bet," McGrady said. "Does Minister Togo know what you're up to?"

"Not as such," Takahashi said. "He doesn't need the burden. But please understand—we see eye to eye on several topics. The wisdom of this war, for instance. Though perhaps I go a bit farther than him, on that subject."

"How's that?"

"There is the wisdom. Which is merely another way of asking, can we win it? And then there is the morality. Which poses the question of whether we even have the right to try."

"You're a pacifist?"

"Would that surprise you?"

"A bit."

"There are plenty of us. Our voices weren't heard. We were speaking reasonably. They were waving swords and shouting. It wasn't an even contest."

"Everyone makes mistakes. Next time around, you'll do better."

"There won't be a second chance. And now it's not even safe to whisper."

They were rolling slowly away from the waterfront. The streets were narrow, and mostly empty. People were huddling inside, but only to stay out of the snow. There was no fear of an attack. That was plain. The lights were on. He saw electric bulbs. Strange scripts traced out in neon. Candlelight filtered through rice paper screens. There were rickshaws parked under awnings. Near-empty trolleys traced clean tracks through the fresh-fallen snow.

The heater was working now. McGrady held his fingers down near his feet, where the warm air was coming out. Even though he was warming up, he couldn't stop shivering. He bit his lips and tensed his muscles, and got himself under control.

"How'd you know I was coming today?"

"When the Army ships suspected spies to Japan, the names are sent along ahead. There's a list. It gets passed through the various departments."

"Because if I'd really been a spy, a guy like you might have met me somewhere. Berlin, say."

"Correct," Takahashi said. "And then I could contribute whatever information I happened to have. They would build a file. It's useful, isn't it?"

"What is?"

"To have a file, before you begin an interrogation."

"It is."

"But I saw your name, and I knew it from somewhere else."

"The *Advertiser*," McGrady said. "Who was she? Your niece, I mean."

"Her name was Miyako. Takahashi Miyako. She was my brother's only child. You must understand—my brother and his wife died in 1923, in the earthquake. Miyako came to live with us. She became like a daughter. She was a sister to my own daughter."

"Why are you sure it was her?" McGrady asked. "The newspaper didn't have a name, and it didn't run a picture."

"It published the story on November 28," Takahashi said. "I didn't get a copy of it until December 9. But I was worried about her a long time before that."

"Why?"

"On the 24th, my friends were supposed to meet her. They couldn't find her. They cabled me. They said her rooms were empty. They asked whether she'd been sent home."

"Sent home?"

"She was working in the consulate. The Japanese consulate, in Honolulu. She was a translator."

"She learned English, from you."

"Certainly."

"So she went missing a couple of days before the newspaper story came out. Other girls did, too. I met some parents. It doesn't mean she's the one."

"Tell me about the man you shot. *Er war deutsch, ja?*"

"You're asking me if he was German?"

"Yes."

"He could've been."

"Tell me."

"He had a U.S. Army M1906 ball round in his hip. The kind of load we were shooting in the Great War. He and his buddy were using a trench knife from the same period."

"They used it on Miyako?"

"They did," McGrady said.

He watched Takahashi for a reaction. He saw a slight deflation. A slump in his shoulders, a bend in his neck. It looked genuine. The normal thing to do would be to offer some condolences to the next of kin.

McGrady said, "We thought they might have picked it up off one of our men, back in the war. Like a trophy."

"As men do."

"Sure."

"We have some understandings with the Germans."

"Everyone knows that."

"There are agreements beyond what everyone knows."

"For example?"

"When the Germans need something done inside our sphere of influence, we supply an asset. And vice versa. It's easier to run operations with people who look the part."

"You're talking about assassinations."

"I'm talking about spy craft, of all descriptions."

"Including murder."

"Of course murder."

They were on a somewhat larger road now. It ran parallel to a pair of train tracks. There were few cars on the road, but the trains were almost constant. They left clouds of black coal smoke. Where the land was uneven, brick and mortar archways carried the tracks across the hollows. The road stuck to the ground.

McGrady saw houses built beneath the archways. He saw
hand-painted signs. There was enough Chinese script that he
could get the gist. The signs advertised noodles. A dozen vari-
eties. Men stood over small charcoal fires, hawking skewered
chicken and roasted pork. There was lantern light, and firelight. People were trekking through the snow, heading toward
the light and shelter and companionship beneath the tracks.

"Why would someone in your government want a couple of
Germans to take out your niece?"

"Do you know the name Yamamoto Isoroku?"

"No."

"I'm talking about Admiral Yamamoto."

"I haven't heard of him."

"By now, most of your country has."

"He's a big deal?"

"He planned the attack on Pearl Harbor."

"I haven't been keeping up with the news since then."

"Before she went to Honolulu, Miyako was in Admiral Yamamoto's secretarial pool."

"Okay."

"She typed handwritten notes. Do you see?"

He didn't see. Or he didn't want to see. He watched the
snow in the headlights. It swirled and spun and made him
dizzy. He thought about opening the door and jumping out. As
far as he could tell, Takahashi wasn't armed, and wouldn't try to
stop him. But there was nowhere to go. Japan itself was a
prison. If Takahashi wasn't who he claimed, or couldn't deliver
what he'd promised, leaving with him had been a terrible mistake. At least in the prison camps, he could follow the rules,
and keep his head down, and suffer the system. Now he was
entirely beyond the protection of any rules.

"I'm tired, Mr. Takahashi," he said. "On top of that, I'm
starving. My skull's cracked. I've got a broken bone in my wrist.

I'm worried about a thousand things besides this case. The only thing I see is I'm an American in Japan and I'm liable to have my head chopped off."

"Let's fix one thing at a time," Takahashi said. "If you're hungry, we can eat."

He pulled the car toward the side of the road. He put two wheels up on the low stone curb. He killed the engine and doused the lights. The elevated train tracks loomed above. Up ahead, a hundred feet through the falling snow, was a glowing archway.

"Stay here," Takahashi said.

"Wait a sec—"

"I won't be long."

Takahashi got out of the car. There was a blast of cold air, and then he slammed the door. McGrady sank low in his seat. He watched Takahashi settle his top hat on his head, and trudge off toward the lighted archway. Families and couples walked past. McGrady put his hand over his eyes, and turned his face toward the curtain.

He waited. The car grew colder. Trains rumbled past on the overhead tracks. Their whistles shrieked. He began to wonder whether Takahashi had been playing an elaborate and deadly joke. Then the door opened, and he was back. He handed McGrady a piece of newspaper folded into a cone. Then a green glass bottle. The newspaper was rolled around a handful of grilled sardines. There was a thick skewer of chicken. He sniffed the open bottle, then tasted it. It was sweet and citrusy. Some kind of soft drink.

It was a feast. More food than he'd have gotten in five days aboard the ship. He looked at Takahashi. The man had started the engine, for the heat, but he hadn't begun to drive.

"Eat," he said. "Take your time. There's no need to hurry. We have a long drive."

McGrady ate the fish first. Heads, tails, bones and all. Then the chicken, which was grilled over charcoal and slathered in a salty sauce. He finished it, and wiped his fingers clean on the newspaper.

"Thank you, Mr. Takahashi," he said.

"Do you feel better?"

"Yes."

They were driving again. It was still snowing, but the flakes were melting as soon as they hit the road. The street glistened in the headlights. They were passing dark buildings. Factories, maybe. Granaries or breweries. It was hard to tell.

"If your niece was in the Admiral's planning meetings, someone suspected she knew the details of the attack."

"That is my fear."

"Did she know?"

"I have no idea," Takahashi said. "But beginning in September, she was clamoring for change. She asked me to pull strings. To speed up her posting as a translator. Unfortunately, I obliged."

"What happened in the beginning of September?"

"I don't know."

"She wanted a job in Honolulu, specifically?"

"Anywhere in the United States, she said. Honolulu was her preference."

"When did she arrive?"

"The first week of November. She went by ship—Yokohama to San Francisco, then westbound to Honolulu on an American liner."

"What makes you think anyone was worried about what she knew?"

"The Kenpeitai came to my house and searched it while I was gone."

"The what?"

"Kenpeitai," Takahashi said, pronouncing each syllable slowly. "The military police—the men who led you off the ship today. But the Kenpeitai also have a branch of secret police. The Tokko."

"If you were gone, how do you know they searched the house?"

"My daughter happened to come home early. She saw them from the end of the street. They came out of the front gate carrying Miyako's things."

"Is that normal, the secret police searching a house?"

"They keep themselves busy. But perhaps it's not so normal when it happens to someone like me."

"A high government official."

"High enough," Takahashi said. "In any case, they came back a few days later, while I was home. They wanted to know—had Miyako talked about her work for the Navy? Was she loyal to Japan? Did she have foreign friends?"

"Here's another one," McGrady said. "Was she a pacifist?"

"Everyone in my family is a pacifist."

"Did they know that?"

"Of course not."

"They must believe you're loyal."

"They should believe that. I've served a long time."

"So if Miyako planned to pass secrets to the Americans, she might not have told you."

"She might not have. It's true."

"When did the secret police come and talk to you?"

"The twenty-second of November."

"The twenty-first, in Honolulu," McGrady said. "A few days before she and Henry went missing. Did you send a cable, to try and warn her?"

"Of course," Takahashi said. "But I didn't have the chance for two days. I was afraid they were following me."

"When you finally got it out, how much did you say? The consulate might have been reading her cables."

"What I said was hidden inside other meanings."

"Like a code."

"A code, yes," Takahashi said. "Also, I didn't cable her directly. I sought out my friend."

"Who is this person, exactly?" McGrady asked. "How do you know he didn't sell Miyako out?"

"That wouldn't have happened."

"How can you know?"

"I'm sorry to give you so much family history."

"You warned me. You said this was all about your family."

"My wife and I separated, some time ago," Takahashi said. "It was by mutual agreement. There was no animosity between us. She remarried an American businessman. Her name is Henderson, now. Kumi Henderson. For all purposes, she's an American. She has no loyalty to Japan. She despises the militarists."

"That's why she left you?"

"One of many reasons."

"And she's your friend in Honolulu?"

"Yes."

"Did Miyako know her aunt was in Hawaii?"

"Nobody knows where Kumi went," Takahashi said. "Not Miyako, not the Kenpeitai. Not even Sachi—my own daughter."

"What was the plan, if Kumi had found Miyako?"

"She and her husband were going to hide her. In their house."

"But Kumi never found her."

"She didn't."

"Do you have a photograph of Miyako?"

"I do," Takahashi said. "In my house."

"Is that where we're going?"

"It's the only safe place for you."

﹡

Tokyo spread and sprawled. It was as though someone had built a medieval village on a New York scale. They passed through vast wards of low wooden houses. He saw women drawing water into buckets from public wells. He saw men struggling against the wind, pushing wood-wheeled carts. Miles like that. Then they entered richer neighborhoods. Western influences. Stone and brick buildings many stories tall. A train station that might have been plucked from central London. Intricate brickwork topped with bronze domes. Its hotel blazed with electric light. Past the station was a castle, surrounded by a moat. Its outer wall was made of hewn stones the size of boulders. Ancient willow trees dangled their winter-bare branches toward the frozen water.

The engine purred. It pumped out heat. McGrady's suit had been wet from rain and snow. Now, as it dried, it began to stink. He didn't care. Not even when Takahashi discreetly cracked his window a quarter of an inch and tilted his face toward the icy new air. He didn't care because his stomach was full for the first time in over a month. He wasn't thirsty. He wasn't sitting on bricks or in a black vault or in the hold of a ship.

He leaned back against the seat and watched outside. He tried to think how he would explain it to Molly. It was like sitting in a theater, and watching a dark film. Like being carried through a black-and-white dream, tugged along on a subconscious current. He had control over exactly nothing. He could watch, or he could close his eyes. Those were the only choices. And if he closed his eyes, it would all happen anyway.

Takahashi drove onward. He took what seemed like random turns. McGrady saw tiny bars lit with paper lanterns. He saw soldiers lined up outside a run of brothels. He was lost ten times over. They came to a darker part of the city. There were

wooded parks. Far back in the trees, moving lanterns cast roving shadows.

A many-tiered pagoda rose ahead of them. Its silhouette was black against the snow-gray sky. If he'd looked overhead to find two moons, he wouldn't have felt any farther from home. He closed his eyes. It was his only reliable trick for finding Molly. Takahashi tapped his shoulder.

"Ueno," he said, pointing toward the pagoda. "The zoological garden. We're close. When we're in Tokyo, we live in Yanaka. Behind the university."

"You mean to have me stay with you?"

"Yes."

"For how long?"

"Until the war's done."

"You got an idea how long that might be?"

"Sooner, if there could be a diplomatic resolution."

"You see that happening?" McGrady asked. "I saw them preparing in Honolulu, and I'll tell you what. They weren't looking to settle their differences with a piece of paper. I don't see that here, either. Maybe you know more than me."

"I see what you see. But I must hope—because a military solution would be catastrophic. If the war comes to Tokyo, I'll send Sachi to our family home. It's in the mountains outside Nozawaonsen. But you and I would have to stay here."

"I hope you don't get sick of me. I could be on your couch a long time."

30

Takahashi turned onto progressively narrower streets. Now the lane was hardly wider than the car. There were walls on each side of the road. They were eight or nine feet high and peaked with curved roofing tiles. As far as he could guess, the walls enclosed small estates, and temples, and cemeteries. He saw cypress trees and pagodas. Takahashi came to the end of the lane. In front of them was a wall made of stone and earth. A wooden gate stood in their headlights. Solid double doors. Takahashi put the car in neutral and set the parking brake. He stepped out, went to the gate, and pushed the two doors open. Then he got back into the car, and drove through. He killed the engine and got out again.

McGrady waited until the gate was closed. He pulled his privacy curtain aside, and looked out. He couldn't see anything but a garden. Bamboo and bare trees. He opened his door and stepped out.

"Come," Takahashi whispered. "This is home."

"Okay."

He looked at it. It was two stories tall, and made of unpainted wood. The roof was steeply pitched, and the eaves were slightly upturned. It had the same kind of heavy tiles on the roof that he'd seen on the walls. If he'd seen it in San Francisco, he might have mistaken it for a temple.

"Sachi may be asleep," Takahashi said. "I'll wake her."

"Did she know I was coming?"

"We discussed it, last night. The list with your name came several days ago."

"She knows what happened to her cousin?"

"She knows what I know. From the paper."

"Because she read it, or because you read it to her?"

"If the question is whether she speaks English, she speaks it very well. In fact, she was born in San Francisco. I was posted there for a time. Her English is as good as her Japanese, and a little better than her German and her French."

"How old is she?"

"The same as Miyako. Twenty-five."

"She lives here?"

"Yes," Takahashi said. He studied McGrady, and frowned. "You have some concern?"

"If she should go out, and talk about me—"

"You needn't worry," Takahashi said. "Sachi is in the mold of her parents. Very much so."

"How's that?"

"She's a pacifist. She's a cosmopolitan. She is a product of a worldly upbringing. But mostly, what I mean is that she is not stupid."

A light came on in one of the upper rooms. The window was made of small panes of smoky glass. McGrady saw a flash of white skin. A sweep of long, dark hair. He looked away immediately, but he wasn't fast enough. He knew what he'd seen. A young woman, rising naked from a bed and pulling a robe around her. Takahashi glanced up, and only saw the light.

"Well," he said. "She must have heard us. Quickly, please— let us go inside before you freeze. Should you fall ill, a doctor would be complicated."

McGrady hadn't even thought of that. It was an entirely new thing to worry about. He followed Takahashi up the house's broad wooden steps. He took off his shoes at the doorway, and carried them inside with him. Takahashi pointed to a shelf just

past the door, and he set them down next to other shoes. They walked down a corridor. It was framed with thick wooden posts, and the walls on each side were made of sliding rice paper screens. The floor was padded bamboo matting.

They came into the main room. In the center was a square pit lined with stones. The hearth. Sachi Takahashi was kneeling there, her back to the door. She was wearing a printed robe. She'd put her hair into a bun at the back of her head, held in place with a pair of sticks. She was blowing on the coals in the bottom of the hearth.

Takahashi spoke to her in Japanese. She answered, but didn't rise up. She was still breathing the fire back to life. McGrady couldn't see the flames, but knew it had lit when the rising curls of smoke suddenly disappeared. She straightened up and turned around, without getting off her knees.

"Detective McGrady," she said.

He bowed to her, bending at the waist and keeping his eyes on her, the way he'd seen Takahashi and the soldier greet each other in the Yokohama commandant's office. He couldn't quite believe the night bookended by those two bows.

"It's good she has rekindled the fire," Takahashi said. "We can have tea. And while we drink it, we can heat a large kettle. I'm sure you'd like to bathe."

"I'd like that," he said. "Very much."

"Sachi tried to think of what we would need for an American guest. If we were successful in convincing you to stay with us. She went out over the last few days, and bought you some things."

"Thank you."

Takahashi nodded. Then he spoke to Sachi in Japanese. She stood up, went away down the corridor, and opened one of the sliding doors. She came back a moment later carrying a bamboo tray. She bowed to McGrady, and held it out to him. There was

a bar of hard white soap. An American safety razor, a box of blades, and a boar bristle brush. There was a nylon toothbrush, and a tube of British toothpaste. A comb. A bottle of after-shave. Everything was new and unopened. It all lay atop a folded, dark blue kimono, an inner robe to wear beneath it, and a pair of slippers.

McGrady took the tray. After a month of starvation, and darkness, and murder, he wasn't prepared for such kindness. He didn't know how to respond.

"How did you find all this?"

Sachi looked at her father. He spoke for her.

"We know diplomats. She went to Roppongi. Most of this came from the Swiss."

As Sachi set about making the tea, Takahashi showed McGrady to his room. It was down the corridor, behind a sliding screen. There was a futon mattress raised above the floor. It had heavy blankets. A firm-looking, round pillow lay at the top. There was an electric lamp, set into the wall. There was a small wardrobe, where he could hang his filthy suit and where he could set down his small tray of new possessions.

"Is there a bathroom?"

"It's outside. Most houses in this neighborhood still use what you'd call an outhouse."

"That's fine with me."

"I didn't like most of what I saw in Berlin, you understand."

"You mentioned."

"I did come to appreciate a German bathroom," Takahashi said. "It's hard to reproduce here. I tried my best. Let me show you."

They went back through the house. There were more sliding doors in the back. Some of them opened directly out into the

garden. Takahashi led the way across the frozen ground. He was barefooted, following a trail of stepping-stones. They went to what looked like a large garden shed. It was surrounded by bamboo. The hollow stalks rattled in the wind.

"Never stand there," Takahashi said. He pointed at a round wooden lid on the ground. "The old privy hole. You wouldn't want to fall in."

Takahashi opened the shed's door, and turned on a light. There was an iron grate in one corner. Embers of a fire gave out a bit of heat. There was a porcelain toilet, with a high overhead tank. There was a deep cedar tub. A cast iron pitcher pump to fill it.

They went back to the house. Takahashi sat on the floor at the head of a low table and motioned McGrady to sit across from him. They waited for Sachi to serve them. She moved from hearth to table on her knees. She knelt by the fire while they drank.

The tea was hot. It was dark green, and good. Sachi refilled McGrady's cup. She knee-walked off, and came back with a small tray of sweets. McGrady couldn't identify any of them. He ate one, and couldn't say what it was.

Takahashi spoke to his daughter again, in Japanese. She answered. She stood up and went away, and when she came back this time, she was holding a framed photograph. She set it on the table, propped up and facing McGrady.

He put down his tea, and picked up the photograph. He studied it. It showed a young woman from the waist up. She was beautiful, the same way that Sachi was beautiful. She had delicate features. A fine small nose. A dimple in her chin. She'd turned her head to the side, to give the camera her profile. There was a small dark mole at her hairline. He pictured what she'd look like after John Smith and his friend did their work.

"Yes," he said. "Miyako is the woman we found."

Takahashi bowed his head. He nodded. Sachi had folded her hands together. She pressed her thumbs against her forehead.

"We knew," Takahashi said. "The moment the Kenpeitai came and took her things, we knew."

Later on, McGrady went barefooted across the yard carrying his bamboo tray of gifts. In his other hand, he had an iron kettle filled with boiling water. He bathed, crouching in the cedar tub and trying to make his hot water last as long as he could. He used his soap, and his razor, and shaved. It had been more than a month, and it destroyed the blade. There had been fifty in the box. He had no illusions. He'd have to ration them. He put on the two robes, and went back to the house before he froze.

Sachi had gone upstairs to bed. Her father was still by the hearth. The fire was burning low. There were only a few lights on. The room smelled of tea and fresh bamboo. The house was silent and cold, except for a small ring of warmth close to the fire. It was like being in a forest. Takahashi lifted a brown bottle from the table. He tilted its neck toward McGrady's empty teacup.

"What is that?"

"Sake," Takahashi said. "Very good sake."

"All right."

Takahashi poured for them. McGrady sat back down.

He lifted his cup, and raised it to Takahashi. The man represented a government that had caused all of his problems. The man's personal intervention might well have saved his life. So McGrady was torn as to whether and how completely he should express his thanks. He settled on a nod.

"Mr. Takahashi."

"Detective McGrady."

They drank. Takahashi wasn't kidding. It was very good sake. It was ice cold, from sitting outside. It was dry and sharp.

"What are we going to do?" McGrady asked.

"I've given this some thought. I've discussed it with Sachi."

"And?"

"Obviously, I will be at the Ministry much of the time. You can't risk going out."

"I'd thought at least that far."

"You can't sit and be idle," Takahashi said. "I propose a regimen."

"Of what?"

"Study," Takahashi said. "Sachi will teach you Japanese."

"You'd leave me alone with your daughter?"

Takahashi looked at him, and then nodded.

"I would," he said. "I believe that, like Sachi, you are not stupid. It's occurred to you that if you dishonored her, I would turn you out. Which would be the end of you."

"Fair enough."

"In any case, the studying will help her, as well. She will perfect her English. One of you will benefit at the end of the war. The other will possess an amusing parlor trick."

"You got an idea which way that's going to go?"

"The best Japan can hope for is a stalemate in the Pacific, and a truce."

Takahashi refilled their cups. They drank.

"You're scared for Sachi," McGrady said. "You're hiding her. Same as me."

Takahashi had been about to drink. But he set his cup down.

"It's not just because my wife left us. It's not just because of what happened when Miyako left. But those, of course, are considerations."

"I understand."

"I would feel better if you found the man who killed Miyako."

"And when I do?"

"I recognize that when you find him, you'll likely be outside of your jurisdiction. Don't you think?"

"That's probably true."

"Then you should be prepared to do whatever is necessary."

"You're the second uncle who's asked me to kill him."

"The other was Admiral Kimmel."

"That's right."

"There is an irony," Takahashi said. He poured more sake into their cups. "He and I have a brotherhood. We have a common cause."

"Right now, he's just trying to sink your ships before they get any more of his. I doubt he even remembers he sent me out here."

He wondered who else was thinking of him. And how long that might last. He set his cup down, and fumbled it. It rolled across the table and fell to the bamboo floor. He leaned to pick it up and got dizzy doing it. He nearly tipped over. The sake hadn't been a good idea. He put his palms on the table and stood up slowly.

"I'm going to bed, Mr. Takahashi."

The first morning of his imprisonment in Takahashi's house, he woke and stared at the sliding paper door. It took a long moment until he remembered all the pieces of the journey that had brought him here. He saw them in reverse. The nighttime drive. The ship. The black vault and the jail cell in Hong Kong. The Clipper flight. Standing at the end was Molly. Every moment took him farther from her. She was receding. Getting smaller and darker. It was like watching a candle flame die beneath an upturned glass.

Then he was empty again, and cold. The only sound was rain outside. He got out of bed and put on the robe.

He went down the corridor to the front door. He opened it a crack and peeked out. Takahashi's black car was gone. The street gate was closed. The sky and the houses across the street were the color of wet ash. He went back to the main room. There was a bit of fire in the hearth. He sat on the floor next to it, and listened to the rain.

Sachi slept somewhere upstairs. She must not be in the house. The morning was too far along. The house was too quiet. Still, he wasn't about to go upstairs to find out. He went back to his room. There was a low desk. It was about a foot off the floor. He supposed the idea was to kneel in front of it. Sachi had supplied him with blank paper. A fountain pen. He took that and went back to the hearth, where it was slightly warmer.

Takahashi was right about one thing. He needed a regimen. He needed to work. It would give him an identity and a

purpose. He would still be somebody when he got back.

He began to write down what he knew. He'd lost his file in Hong Kong. All his notes. All his thoughts for follow-up inquiries. The photographs. The autopsy reports. He'd spent days on the ship trying to keep everything alive in his mind, so that he could set it back down.

Now he had new information. The girl wasn't a mystery anymore. She had a name. She wasn't a bystander. She'd been the target. Henry Kimmel Willard was the unlucky one. He was like a man who walks into a bank, mid-robbery, and gets shot in the face. He wondered what the Admiral would think about that.

He pictured the scene. He sketched it out. The boy was hanging upside down. Tortured, gutted. The girl tied up. He remembered thinking: *they made her watch*. Now he understood. It wasn't just a revenge hit. They had a more practical purpose. They were trying to keep a lid on something big. Maybe she'd told people already. Maybe she hadn't. Either way, they needed to know. How far had the secret spread? Could it be contained, or should the whole enterprise be called off?

They couldn't just ask. They wanted to make sure she told them the truth. So they strung up the boy and started in with the knife. Then they asked her the questions.

He heard footsteps outside. The front door opened and closed.

He folded his new notes in between his robes and stood up as Sachi entered. She was wearing a more formal kimono than she'd had on last night. It was tied up in the back with an elaborate, wide sash. Her hair was misted with rain. She was flushed. She'd been out in the icy wind, struggling down the street with an umbrella.

She set an enameled tin lunch pail on the table, and put her umbrella away into a closet. Then she bowed to him.

"*Ohayou gozaimasu*," she said. "Good morning, Joe-san."

"Good morning."

She said something else, a much longer phrase. Then she translated it for him.

"How do you feel today?"

"Better. Thanks."

"Are you ready to begin?"

"All right."

"*O suwari ni natte*," she said.

She gestured to the cushion where he'd been sitting. He sat. She nodded, and knelt opposite him.

"You don't mind your father's plan?" he asked.

"I don't mind."

"It seems like you'd have something better to do than teach me."

She shook her head.

"I was a clerk, until December. The same as Miyako. After the American newspaper came, my father asked me to stay home. Now I have nothing to do."

"Where were you clerking?"

"In the Ministry of Foreign Affairs. I worked in the cable coding room."

"You worked with codes?"

"Nothing secret," she said. "Just *Wabun*—Japanese Morse code. Dots and dashes."

"You don't really need English lessons, do you?"

"It's good to practice," she said.

Last night, she hadn't spoken a word except to say his name. She'd deferred to her father. She'd let him speak for her. That wasn't so odd. He'd seen plenty of people who had one face for strangers, and a second for their families. Everyone had many roles to play. She could be the obedient daughter, serving tea on

her knees. That might truly be her. She might be many other things at different times.

"What will we do if the Kenpeitai come knocking while we're sitting here?"

She turned to look at the front door, as though the secret police were already marching in. She shook her head.

"We must hope they don't."

"They've come twice already."

"Then I'll delay them."

"How?"

"I'll stand behind the door. I'll—I can tell them I'm undressed. That they must wait until I have a robe. You can hide in the garden."

"Sounds like a plan."

Last night, he'd seen Sachi take charcoal from a wooden box near the door. Now he got up and walked over to it.

"May I?"

"Please," she said. "I'll make tea."

"I'd like that a lot."

He brought a few handfuls of the charcoal back. They were broken oak sticks, baked in a kiln and carbonized. They burned with no smoke and hardly any smell.

"Would you really like to learn Japanese? While I was walking this morning, I thought of some lessons. It will be difficult, since we can't go out. You'll be more domestic than a housewife. I'll have to find ways to bring the world to you."

"You're kind," McGrady said. "You and your father."

She turned her face away, and said something in Japanese he didn't understand. Then she said something else, in English.

"Would you like to begin?"

"We can start in a minute," McGrady said. "I'd like to ask a few questions."

"About Miyako?"

"The two of you were close?"

"We grew up as sisters," Sachi said. "Her parents were killed in the Kanto earthquake. We were both young."

"So it's possible you knew her better than anyone."

"Of course I did."

"Before she left for San Francisco, did you and she have a chance to talk alone?"

"We did," Sachi said. "Right here."

"Did she say what she was going to do?"

She looked at her hands, which were folded on top of her knees. She'd begun to cry. She didn't wipe the tears away, but let them run down her cheeks. She made no noise, and didn't move. She looked back up at him.

"Did my father tell you what he suspects?"

"He did."

"He's right, of course."

"What did she tell you?"

"Everything."

"What happened at the beginning of September?"

"The Prime Minister approved Admiral Yamamoto's war plans. The Admiral obtained the Emperor's blessing. From then on, the course was set. They did not tell the Ministry of Foreign Affairs. Which means that my father's work to avoid a war had no meaning. The diplomats they sent to Washington were buying time to prepare the fleet."

"She knew all of that? Down to what the Emperor blessed?"

"Yes."

"I thought she was a clerk who typed notes."

"She learned a lot from the notes."

"Tell me what you're leaving out."

Sachi looked down again.

"She had become friendly with one of the Admiral's staff officers."

"When you say friendly—"

"You understand what I mean. And this man, when he was at his most comfortable—he liked to boast."

"Did either of you tell your father what she knew?"

"How could we?" she asked. "And not just because of how she'd learned it. If we told him, what good would it have done? He couldn't act on information he wasn't supposed to have. It would be too dangerous."

"So Miyako leaned on your father for help getting a job, but didn't tell him why."

Sachi nodded. McGrady thought of something else.

"If she wanted to pass something to the Americans, why not just walk into the embassy in Tokyo? It was still open."

"Because she'd have to walk back out again," Sachi said. "And it was watched. We didn't realize they'd be watching her in Honolulu, too. That was our mistake."

"Did the Kenpeitai talk to you when they came here?"

"Just my father."

"And your father doesn't know what you know."

"He doesn't."

"Then they made a mistake too."

"Do you think they'll be back?"

"I don't know how they work," McGrady said. "They might be too busy. They might have decided it doesn't matter anymore."

"But they could come back."

"They could always come back. If it were my case, I'd be back."

She had no response to that. He looked at her, until she looked away. She finally wiped her eyes with the back of her

hand. The rain shushed against the roof. A motorbike went down the street outside, its exhaust pipes echoing off the walls. Sachi moved, on her knees. She came around to his side of the table. Not so that she could be closer to him, but so that she could watch the front door.

PART THREE:

Meetinghouse
Tokyo | Honolulu | Hong Kong
November 23, 1944 – December 31, 1945

32

He watched the gray light of dawn spreading through the rice paper door. He listened to the world waking up outside. Bicycle bells. Birdsong. He was waiting for one particular sound. He'd heard it every morning for a week, and had deduced what it was. As quietly as he could, he got out of bed. He put on his robe. His clothes from Honolulu were in the wardrobe, on a hanger. Takahashi had taken the suit to a cleaner two years ago. McGrady hadn't worn it since. He took the jacket now, and folded it over his arm.

He did the math again. He'd spent one thousand fifty three days living in Takahashi's house. He hadn't spoken to Molly since December 2, 1941. The last he'd heard from her had been a cable, on Guam. That had been December 5, 1941. He struggled to keep her alive in his mind. He knelt at his desk, every night, and wrote to her.

He was running out of things he could tell her. He was spending eight or more hours a day with Sachi Takahashi. Sitting by the table during the day, or walking in the garden after dark, when it was safer for him to step outside. There was a cherry tree that blossomed in the springtime. There were dwarf maples that turned blood red in the fall. In the winter, bright orange fruit clung to the naked limbs of the persimmon trees. They were best after they'd frozen on the branch, and then been brought in to thaw. The ice changed them into something tender and delicate. Sachi showed him how to split them with a knife and eat them with a spoon.

They hadn't run out of things to say to each other. Not in a

thousand days of conversation. If he didn't know the words in Japanese, she taught him. Because he couldn't go out, she'd go for him. She'd bring things back. Artifacts for discussion. Maps and books of photographs. A bag of seeds and a shovel, so that they could plant a vegetable patch. A small vase, so that they could bring flowers into the house. A piece of chocolate, to share.

He'd lost so much hope that there were times he would forget what had been taken from him. They would be digging weeds in the garden by the light of a lantern, or sitting by the hearth with dinner, and he'd catch himself wanting nothing beyond what he already had. He'd catch himself feeling content. Then he would go back to his room and write to Molly, and hold onto his memories until they were in tatters.

He heard the sound he'd been waiting for.

It was outside, on the garden wall. A soft cluck, and a dusty flutter of wings. A chicken had made a habit of foraging in the garden every morning. It would pace on the wall a while, and then hop down. He didn't know where it came from, or where it went when it left. He knew where it was going today.

He tiptoed out of his room. He went down the corridor, and carefully opened the front door. He scanned the neighboring houses. There was one window that overlooked the garden from this angle. Its curtains were closed. Takahashi's car was gone. He'd lost some standing at the Ministry after Togo Shigenori had resigned in despair. So now Takahashi compensated by coming in hours before dawn. He had to prove his loyalty. His dedication, to a cause he privately detested. It was wearing him thin. His mustache had gone gray. He took no pleasures but two: talking to Sachi, and drinking with McGrady until one or the other of them fell asleep.

McGrady stepped outside. He was still holding his suit jacket. He spread it out in his hands as he went down the steps. At the

corner, he leaned and peered. The bird was there, scratching at the ground by the wall of the house. It was a big rooster. He wondered how it had survived this long. Inside of a five-mile radius were six million people who'd be happy to eat everything but its beak and its claws. He was one of them.

He crept up, the coat out and ready. The rooster was focused on the ground. It didn't notice McGrady until he was already coming down. He popped the coat over it, and pinned it. Then he reached under, and got it by the head. One hand, then the other. He wrung its neck, fast and hard. Like twisting water from a washcloth. He heard a bone snap. He felt a bit of blood on his palm. The rooster was still.

He picked up his coat and walked around to the back of the house. He dropped the rooster on the step. He went inside and was washing his hands at the basin when Sachi came down. He addressed her in her own tongue.

Good morning, Sachi.

Are you all right? Are you bleeding?

I am very well. I've killed a rooster.

You've done what?

A rooster, in the garden. I caught it and broke its neck. If it had been a hen, we could have kept it for the eggs.

Wasn't it somebody's?

It didn't seem to think so.

Will you show me?

"Sure," he said. "It's out back."

They went out. She looked at the bird. When it came to food, they were doing better than most of Tokyo. Her father could skirt the rationing system. He could bring things home from the Ministry. On the return legs of his trips, he could smuggle whatever would fit in his suitcase. But any kind of meat was hard to come by. A whole chicken was unheard of.

"How shall we cook it?" she asked.

"I'll pluck it, and we can hang it. When your father comes home, I'll roast it whole. Do you know what day today is?"

"Thursday."

"It's Thanksgiving," he said. "Normally, we'd have a turkey. This will do just fine."

She went back to Japanese. It had gotten so he hardly noticed the transition. They wove back and forth, switching by whim or for convenience.

What else should we do for your holiday?

Nothing—a meal, all of us together. That's all.

Do you know how to pluck a fowl?

I don't understand.

I'll teach you some new words.

All right.

Should we go inside? It's cold.

It's better if we do this outside. It could make a mess.

"*Hai*, Joe-san," she said.

He roasted the chicken in the hearth. He rubbed its skin with sea salt and *shoyu*, and put it in a cast iron pot with hot coals piled around it and on the lid. They ate it with rice and pickled radishes. They picked the bones clean, and then Takahashi went outside to get another bottle of sake from the racks underneath the house.

When he'd refilled their cups, McGrady raised his.

I have never been properly thankful, and I regret that.

McGrady-san—

I would like to thank you for the kindness you have shown me. I've been a guest in your house close to three years. I know what it's cost you to keep me.

It has been our honor.

I will repay you. I will find the man.

That chance might come sooner than you know.

There's news?

Good for you, not so good for us. The Americans took Tinian and Saipan. They are building air bases.

I've never heard of Tinian.

It's close enough for your heavy bombers. That's all that matters.

I'm sorry. And not sorry. I don't know what to say.

Then drink. It's all anyone can do about it. And the one thing we'll never run out of is sake. I made sure of it.

McGrady drank. Takahashi did as well. Sachi took the bottle and refilled both their cups. She was drinking tea.

"I almost didn't come with you," McGrady said. "I'm talking about the night we first met. I thought it was a trick."

"It was, in fact. But it was them I tricked. I was worried, you see. If they should come looking for you, it would be hard to keep you hidden. The better alternative was to make sure they never looked."

"What did you do?"

"I paid the commandant to change his records."

Takahashi laughed and shook his head. He was pleased, to finally divulge his secret. He splashed more sake into their cups. They drank.

"On your first night in Yokohama, you struck an officer of the Kenpeitai. Of course, you were executed on the spot. With a sword, as tends to happen. It served as a demonstration for the other men."

"What do you mean, I was executed?"

"You're dead, McGrady-san. Don't you see? In the records. In all the reports that go to the Army, and the Navy, and the Ministry, and the International Society of the Red Cross—"

"The Red Cross thinks I'm dead?"

"It was the only way to keep you safe. No one would care about a dead man."

"I see."

He studied his cup of sake. Takahashi had filled it past the brim. A clear meniscus rose above the cup's rim and trembled each time the breeze moved through the house. McGrady looked back up at his host. He switched to Japanese. Not for a whim, but for a purpose. It was easier to hide his emotions in his hosts' language. Its formality could flatten anything.

Thank you, Takahashi-san. You have cared for me so thoughtfully. I am in your debt.

It was the most practical way to do it. And you are entirely welcome.

McGrady drank his sake. He reached for the bottle and refilled their cups. He finished his dinner, and he helped Sachi wash up. He waited for his hosts to go to bed, and he bade them goodnight. Then he went into his room with the half-finished bottle of sake and he knelt down at the desk. He reached up underneath it, and took out the roll of pages he'd wedged there. This was the only thing he'd hidden from either of them. He'd written something to Molly every night for a thousand days. Sometimes just a few sentences, sometimes entire pages. It was a book-length manuscript of his longing.

And now he knew how pointless it had been. For all the time he'd been writing it, she'd believed him dead. Someone at HPD would have gotten the Red Cross list. Someone would have told Fred Ball. Fred would have gone and told Molly.

It was that simple.

She wasn't waiting. She hadn't built a widow's walk on top of her roof. She wasn't scanning the horizon for a sign of the ship bringing him home. Takahashi had it right. Nobody cares about

a dead man. Not after three years. He took the roll of pages and went back to the main room. He opened the sliding doors to the outside. Cold air blew in. He didn't want to fill the house with smoke when he sat down by the hearth and fed his letters to the fire.

In the morning, the Americans came.

He couldn't see them. They were above the clouds. There were so many bombers that in spite of the air raid sirens, he could hear the roar of their propellers.

He was standing in the garden, looking up. Sachi came to him. She was barefooted. Her hair was down. Her father was gone. The bombs started to land. They were far away. Five miles, at least. There were so many. It wasn't a rainfall. It wasn't a downpour. They were falling so closely together that one explosion began before the last ended. A continuous, rising thunder.

The antiaircraft fire was much nearer. There must have been batteries across the city. They'd all opened up. He couldn't imagine what good it would do to shoot at invisible planes. But the gunners blasted away. Their fragmentation shells streaked upwards and disappeared into the low gray cover. The clouds flashed from the inside. Pulses, like lightning. Flocks of panicked birds raced in all directions. At every shell burst, they startled off on different courses.

Sachi turned to him. She took his hand. She held it with both of hers, and clutched it against her breastbone. They stood facing one another. As close as they'd ever been. In fact, before this moment, they had never even touched. Now they were pressed up close. Yet they weren't looking at each other. They were each staring at different swaths of the sky.

33

The American noose was tightening. Takahashi's ministry was looking for air. So for weeks, Takahashi had been warning them that he would have to take a journey. They should be prepared for his absence. He came home on the evening of March 8, and announced it with certainty. He'd be leaving in the morning. It was dangerous, of course. This was no time to travel. He would be going by train to Aomori, in the north of Honshu. Then by ferry, to Hakodate, on the south end of Hokkaido. From there, he'd go to the Sapporo airfield by Army car. An unmarked transport plane would fly him to Khaborovsk, which lay near the Soviet-Chinese border. He'd be vulnerable until his plane crossed into Soviet territory.

Takahashi waited until Sachi had gone outside for her bath. He motioned McGrady to the table.

The radio doesn't say it, but I will. Your submarines torpedo any ship they see. And they come in close enough to mine the harbors. Your carrier fighters can show up anywhere. Only Mr. Roosevelt can predict them. Meaning that to them, I'm fair game.

I understand.

So you know what I am going to say.

I probably do. But say it anyway.

Should I fail to return, Sachi will take care of you. But I would ask that you also take care of her. She has no one else.

I give you my word. But please be careful, Takahashi-san.

Some things are beyond my control. Do you understand? I've been speaking quickly.

I understand. Sachi is a very good teacher.

She is remarkable.

The Ministry wants you to get reassurances from the Russians.
Takahashi had nodded. His eyes were red. Sake and exhaustion.
The Allies are already contemplating how to divide their spoils.
It would be better if the Soviets kept their focus on Germany.
How long will you be gone?
Five days.
We will wait for you.

When he woke in the morning, Takahashi was gone. It was just past seven. He ran the numbers. He calculated his days. By now it was pure habit. There was no reason to count. He had nothing to go back to. Everything he had was here.

He went out to the main room. Sachi was waiting for him by the hearth. She poured him a cup of tea and he sat down opposite her.

"What would you like to do today?" she asked.

"It looks nice out."

"It's springtime."

"Let's pretend we're taking a walk," he said. "Are there still parks?"

"Many."

"Movie theaters?"

"Of course."

"If I could walk through that gate, I'd go to a park. I'd walk in the sunshine. Then I'd take you to a see a movie."

She touched his wrist, then pulled her hand back. She spoke with her face turned away from his.

If you could walk out, then you could also go home.

Then I could take you wherever you wanted to go.

It's more than I can bear, Joe-san. You talk about what could be. I think about what is not.

He put his hand on her shoulder and turned her back to him. She looked up.

"Then let me tell you what I want for today, Sachi."

"All right."

"Do you have a favorite park?"

"Yoyogi Park, around the Meiji shrine. It's a forest."

"Walk there. Then go and watch a movie."

"What good would that be for you?"

"When you come back, you can tell me about it. I want to hear the whole story. Scene by scene."

"What kind of movie?"

"You pick. Whatever looks good."

He spent the rest of the day in a corner of the garden. He was wearing a hat, and keeping his head down. The one house that overlooked Takahashi's garden wall had installed heavy blackout curtains. The rest of the land around them belonged to a temple, and was used as a graveyard. So he felt reasonably sure no one would spot him and call the Kenpeitai.

It was worth the risk to be out there. He was digging their bomb shelter. The plan was straightforward. He'd make a square hole in the ground, six feet deep. Takahashi had found some heavy timbers to put over the top. Once those were secure, he intended to pile the excavated earth back on top of it. He'd dig a trench, later, to get in and out. After that, he could worry about lining the walls and floor with wood planks and bamboo matting.

He'd kept himself in shape. He did pushups in his room. Sit-ups, on his futon. There was a low beam in the outdoor bathroom, and he did chin-ups there. Digging this hole was a different kind of work. The ground was hard. There were many roots and stones. It felt just fine to work until he hurt. He worked all day, with no breaks.

He stopped when he worried Sachi might come back. The hole was finished. He could top it off and cover it with earth tomorrow. He went inside and built up the fire, to heat the kettle for his bath.

34

Later on, he'd remember this day down to its tiniest details. He'd match his memory against the accounts in books and newspapers. He'd work out the timing. He'd understand that while he was getting out of his bath and wondering what time Sachi would return, the bombers were lining up on runways fifteen hundred miles away. They were making full-throttle sprints into the wind. Their wings were polished silver. Their noses were hand painted with taunts and slurs and busty centerfold girls. There were so many, it would take three and a half hours for all of them to rise aloft and turn toward the north.

Three hundred thirty four crews. Three hundred thirty four planes. Between them, they were carrying close to three and a half million pounds of napalm.

35

Sachi had done more than walk through Yoyogi Park and visit a movie theater. She'd visited markets. She'd fought through the lines, and made purchases. She had a few handfuls of finger-length squid wrapped up in a sheet of newspaper. She had an onion and some tiny mushrooms. She went outside to the garden and came back with a couple of slate gray river stones from the rock beds around the cherry trees. Disk-shaped stones, the size of his hands. She put them into the hot coals. She took up a knife and began to slice the onion.

What would you like to hear about my day?

Everything.

I walked in the forest. It was cool in the shadows, and peaceful. I visited the Meiji shrine.

What does it look like?

Like something very old. I will find you a photograph some-time. It's made of cedar and copper. The columns of the torii gate are built from logs six feet thick. To reach it, you walk down a sandy path through the trees. It's too early for blossoms, of course. But there were birds.

What did you do there?

I bought an ema—a piece of wood to write a wish upon. After I wrote my wish, I hung it on the shrine. Then I stood there a while, reading other people's ema.

She used her finger on the table to trace the new word. He watched, then traced it back.

What did they wish for?

That their sons might come home, or that they might die with honor.

What did you wish for?

For the world to be such that you and I might take a walk together.

She opened the sake and poured for both of them.

Afterwards, I went to Asakusa. I watched a movie.

Please tell me about it.

Truly, it was not very good.

But tell me.

She nodded.

"There were women working in a factory. It was an optics factory. They were making lenses. They were having contests with each other, to see who could make the most."

"Make the most lenses?"

"Optical lenses. Yes."

"Why?"

"To please their supervisor. To beat the Americans. Why else?"

"This was really a movie, in a theater? You had to pay to see it?"

"They used to be better," Sachi said. "Now the government censors rewrite the scripts."

"It's no good going out anymore, is it?"

"It's better here."

She raised her cup to his, and they touched the rims together. They drank cold sake. He thought of half a dozen things he might have said to her. He said none of them. He watched her face. She was considering responses to all the things he could have said.

It was a long while before she broke the silence.

"Let me show you something," she said. "It's called *ishiyaki*."

"Stone grill."

"Very good."

"My teacher is remarkable."

She turned her head so that the spill of her hair hid her face. She used a pair of sticks to fetch the river stones from the coals. She set them inside lidless wooden boxes she'd half filled with

coarse salt. She put a box in front of him. He could feel the heat rising from the rock. With chopsticks, she plucked half a squid from the bowl. She set it on his stone. It sizzled and popped. She put onions and mushrooms on next. Then she refilled his cup.

My teacher is remarkable in every way. Her father agrees.

She laughed. This time she looked at him when she spoke.

If I were making optical lenses to win the war, I would make so many. They would pile past the rooftops. And I am enjoying our date very much. You should drink a little more, but not too much.

I'm not sure I follow you.

Take it any way you like.

She tied her hair up into a knot at the top of her head. She rolled up the sleeves of her kimono, and loosened its sash.

"Try the *ishiyaki*, Joseph McGrady."

"Call me Joe."

"Sometimes Joe is too simple. Sometimes I like to hear your whole name."

"But I'm simple."

She reached beneath the table, and took his left hand.

You are not. Nothing is. Nothing ever will be.

Now I truly don't understand.

Look at me.

I am.

You are not looking. Meet my eyes. I've given you ten thousand hours. For that, you can meet my eyes. Here, when we are finally getting to the point.

He looked. She was still holding his hand beneath the table. She reached with her other hand, and put it behind his neck.

Tell me you understand. Tell me you know what we have been doing, all this time.

I know what we have been doing.

Tell me.

Sachi—

Then say it. You must know the words.

You've never taught me.

I've taught you everything you need to know.

Watashi wa—

He stopped. It would be no good to get this wrong. He took a breath, and tried again. He looked her straight in the eyes, and told her.

Aishiteimasu.

She let go of him. She smoothed her kimono and sat up straight.

"Joe—I do, too," she said. "Of course I do. And I have, for so long."

The wind picked up after sunset. The house got cold. Sachi brought the cushions close to the hearth. They sat next to the fire and looked at a book of photographs her father had brought home from Berlin. She leaned against him, the book half on his lap and half on hers. She flipped through the pages and described the things she saw. Gothic churches and stone buildings. Subway stations. Flashy nightclubs. She told him about her time in Berlin, living there with her father.

He supposed that most of what they were looking at no longer existed. Whatever she'd seen there was gone. The British and the Americans had seen to it.

She put her head against his shoulder. He turned, his lips brushing her hair. She smelled like chrysanthemums. She always had. It had taken him well over a year to place the scent. Finally, she'd brought a bunch of them home for their vase. Then he knew.

She was holding his hand. She was using the pad of her forefinger to tap something against his wrists. Taps and strokes.

Dots and dashes. She'd practically run out of things to teach him, and so a few months ago she'd moved to this. It was like she said. He knew what they had been doing. She wasn't just trying to teach him. She wanted a reason to touch him. Now he was trying to follow the code. But he couldn't. She was too much. It was easier when they were sitting across from each other at the table. She turned to him, and looked up.

"How long have you been here now?"

"One thousand, one hundred and fifty nine days."

"You count by the day?"

"You count by the hour."

"Not all of them. Only the ones that mattered," she said. She put her hand against his chest. "Since you've been here, you've never been upstairs."

"I haven't."

If I invited you, would you come?

I would.

But we must turn off the lights.

He nodded. The citywide blackout started at ten o'clock.

They stood up together. She led him down the corridor. The stairs were narrow and steep. They led up to a sliding door. She opened it and stepped up into the darkness. He followed. She closed the door behind him, and took his hand.

"This way," she said. "I'll guide you."

She led him down a much narrower hallway. He could see another rice paper door ahead. The moonlight must have been coming through a window on the other side. The paper glowed a soft white. She opened the door and led him into the room. She had one end of the house to herself. There were three windows in the room, facing three different directions. They went to the west wall, to see the moon. It was a quarter full, and close to setting. Past the garden wall, a graveyard spread out for

acres. The headstones' shadows stretched toward the house.

He hadn't seen past the wall since coming through the gate the first time. He remembered the moment of his arrival. He'd been freezing. He'd been filthy. He had nothing. Now he looked behind him. Her bed was there, as he knew it would be. It was a futon, raised up on a platform of solid wood.

The first time I saw you, I was standing down there. I looked up, and you were getting out of this bed.

You saw me?

I did.

I sleep naked.

I know.

Why did this take so long?

So that it would be right.

It is, isn't it?

"Yes," he said. "It is."

She turned to him and put her hands around his waist. They were both wearing kimonos and underlining robes. The fabric was soft from many washings. They could feel each other perfectly well.

"Have you ever?" she whispered.

He nodded.

"And have you?"

"No," she said. She backed up, so she could look him in the eyes. "But since we are being truthful, the answer could almost have been yes."

She waited to see if he'd take the bait. He did.

"Almost?"

"I was eighteen."

"Then this was in Berlin."

"It was," she said. "The boy was the son of the Russian ambassador."

"Do you speak Russian?"

"I don't. And he didn't speak German, English, French or Japanese."

"Then what language were you speaking?"

Her eyes lit the way her father's did, when he was pleased to share a secret.

"None."

"What stopped you?"

"His father came home. I had to climb out the window," she said. She came back up against him, holding him tight. "He must still have several of my things."

She leaned up and shushed his laughter with her lips. He pulled back after a moment. He was cradling her face in his hands. He wanted to look at her. He wanted to mark this moment.

There can't be another woman like you, Sachi.

I doubt that's true. There are a lot of women. But we can be certain of one thing.

What?

There isn't another American in Japan having a night like this.

Then we should get away from the windows.

There is the bed.

Is that where you'd like to go?

Will you show me what to do?

If you teach me the words.

Maybe there are no words.

They went to her futon. They knelt on it, facing each other. They were used to teaching each other. They knew how to be patient. They knew how to begin with first principles. How to lay a foundation and then build something lasting upon it.

Even if he'd had a watch, he wouldn't have been checking it. Which meant that much later, when he was alone in his own house behind Diamond Head, drinking Tennessee whiskey and going over the records, he could only speculate. He knew from almanacs that the moon had set close to midnight. He knew from memory that when they'd spent themselves the first time, it was very dark. He knew from talking to officers of the XXI Bomber Command that the first observation B-29s arrived high over the city at 12:03 A.M., on March 10. There they began to circle. They had cartographers aboard. The mapmakers had one task. Chart the coming destruction.

The two pathfinder bombers came next, at five thousand feet. They started their runs over Asakusa at 12:08 A.M. They flew at right angles to each other. At their base on Tinian, they'd set their intervalometers to drop incendiaries every fifty feet. They were laying trails of fire on the ground beneath them. Their paths intersected halfway through their runs. When they climbed and banked for the south, they had left behind a cross of fire. A target to mark the center of the Taito Ward. The flames would guide the other bombers in.

He couldn't remember exactly what he and Sachi had been doing then. They might have lit a tiny candle, so they could lie together in her bed and read a journal she'd kept. They might have moved past that, to something else.

He wasn't sure. All he knew for certain was that for whatever reason, neither of them heard the air raid sirens. And in any case, those sirens hadn't gone off in Yanaka until things were well underway.

She was on her stomach beside him. Elbows on the futon, chin propped inside the V of her palms so she could look down at his face. He was tracing her ear with his fingertip. The room was cold. They weren't. They were on top of the covers and didn't need them.

"Wait," she said. "Don't move."

She rolled over and slipped off the futon. She crossed the room and knelt at her desk. He could just see her. It was dark now. The moon was gone. He heard a drawer open. She was taking things out and setting them on the desk. She struck a match, and then he could see her naked silhouette. The knot in her hair had come loose.

He closed his eyes, and felt himself floating. Disembodied. Unconnected. A year ago, he'd begun dreaming in Japanese. Even in his sleep, he never ventured past the garden wall. It wasn't safe in any respect. He couldn't remember his brother's face. He couldn't remember Molly's. His life was gone. It had just started. He was spent. He wanted Sachi again.

His contradictions were holding him together and tearing him to pieces.

"If you were any kind of normal girl, right now, you'd be asking me—what are you thinking, Joe?"

"I know what you're thinking."

She was still kneeling, her back to him. She was either reading or writing. He couldn't tell which.

"Do you really?"

"If I proved it, then you'd be afraid of me," she said. She

stood up and turned around. She was holding a small candle in one hand. In the other, she had a black book and a fountain pen. "You'd think I had a strange gift."

"I already think that."

"Good," she said. She set the candle on a shelf above the bed. Then she climbed next to him and lay down on her stomach again. "Do you know what I'm thinking?"

He shook his head.

"I've got no special talents," he said.

"You have several."

"I know what I hope you're thinking."

"And what's that?"

He put the backs of his fingers against her cheek. She leaned into them while he spoke.

If I bought an ema, and wrote out my wish to hang at the Meiji shrine, I would write—let me live in a world where Takahashi Sachi has no regrets.

You already live in that world.

Do I?

"You do," she said. "You can see for yourself."

She opened the black book. He knew her handwriting well. He'd been studying it for years. She flipped backwards until she found the page she wanted.

"Here," she said. She handed him the book. "I wrote this three days after you arrived."

He got up on his elbow, so he could hold the pages to the candle's light. He read what she'd written. He closed the book and handed it back to her.

Do you see now?

I believe you.

I knew this would happen. I wanted it. I would only have regrets if it had never happened.

He picked up the book again and thumbed the pages. She must not have written in it every day, or she'd have filled it up long ago. But it was clear she'd been writing in it for a long time before he came.

"Was there anything in here you were worried about the Kenpeitai seeing?" he asked. "If they searched the house, they must have found this."

"They didn't."

"How do you know?"

"I was carrying it with me. I almost always do."

"Did they take everything of Miyako's?"

"All we have is the photograph."

"You miss her," he said. "Both of you."

She traced her hand from his chest to his stomach.

Sometimes, he talks to you all night. When I see him in the morning, I know he's been talking about Miyako.

I've made promises to him.

I know what he wants. Will you really do it?

That depends.

On what?

What would you have me do?

If you'd asked me three years ago, I'd have sided with him. Not anymore. We'd be no better for it. We'd be stained with murder. If we want a better world, we should start by being better.

All right.

I could never ask for it. I could never stand to see it done.

Then I won't do it.

She put her lips against his throat.

But would you have, if I'd asked?

I'd do anything you asked.

Truly?

She'd come back up. Her face was above his. He tucked a lock of her hair behind her ear. No part of her was hidden.

Then let me ask for some things. Let me show you what I want.

She took the book from him, and dropped it on the floor. She pushed him down, so that he was on his back again. She got up on her knees, and then straddled him. Her hands were flat against the futon on either side of his head. Her face was a foot above his. He could see her very well now. It wasn't just the candle. There was an orange glow coming from the east window. It softened everything it touched. He'd never seen her in such beautiful light. He put his hands on her hips. He leaned up to kiss her.

He caught motion with one eye. He stopped, and turned. Her bedroom door was sliding open. He saw a hand on the door's frame. Spidery, pale fingers.

Sachi—

If only it had been her father. But he knew it wasn't. The intruder began to shout before McGrady could finish.

There's a blackout! Put that light out! The Americans—

The man wore the khaki uniform of the Kenpeitai. He had black boots and a peaked cap. He wore a bamboo sword and a sidearm. He'd stopped, mid-sentence. His mouth was still open. Sachi was frozen on top of McGrady. The three of them stared at each other. Then Sachi screamed and rolled off. She grabbed at the blankets to cover herself.

The Kenpeitai soldier shrieked a single phrase. One of the first McGrady had learned in his new tongue.

Amerikajin desu!

The soldier fumbled at something tied around his neck. A police whistle. He got it in his mouth and let loose with long, shrill blasts. McGrady sprang off the bed. It took three leaping steps to cross the room. The soldier went gape-mouthed. The

whistle fell from his lips. He tried to unsnap his holster. It took him a second, and that cost him his life. McGrady got there first. He hit the soldier in the jaw, and followed with a punch in the neck. He kneed him in the groin. The soldier doubled over. McGrady spun him around. He brought his left leg around to brace the man's ankles. Then he tackled him to the floor. He pinned him, one knee hard between the man's shoulder blades.

The Kenpeitai soldier screamed. Someone was surely going to hear him. If he had friends, they'd be on their way. It had to stop. It had to end.

McGrady reached forward and put four fingers into each of the man's eyes. He jammed his knee down into the man's spine and pulled his head backwards. McGrady arched his back and flexed. He pulled until the soldier's neck snapped. He didn't hear it. He knew the instant it happened. The man stopped fighting. His body went entirely still. McGrady had severed the nerves. Paralysis. The soldier wasn't dead. His head was still alive. McGrady could feel his jaw working. Eyes darting back and forth. McGrady let go. The soldier's forehead thumped onto the tatami mat.

He took the soldier's pistol from its holster and stood up. He went to the west window. Sachi was sobbing at the foot of the bed. He stepped past her and stood against the wall, where he could peek outside without showing himself. The street was empty. The front gate was open. There was a bicycle leaning against it. He went to the north window. Temples and cypress trees. He went to the east window. He could see the back half of the garden. The sky was blazing orange. It was full of bombers. They were lit from beneath by the fires they'd set. They flashed bright silver. They were coming in groups of three and four.

Clouds of smoke rose beneath them. Searchlight beams stalked through the haze.

There was no squad of Kenpeitai surrounding the house. The soldier had come upstairs without any backup. He'd been riding his bicycle through the neighborhood. He'd seen a light in a window. He'd come upstairs to enforce the blackout.

McGrady went to Sachi and knelt in front of her.

I had no choice.

Stop it.

What would have happened to us if I hadn't?

Don't touch me.

He took his hands from her shoulders. He got back from her.

They would have killed you. They would have killed me. When your father got home, they would have killed him.

No.

I had to.

She cried out as though he'd slapped her. She dug her fists into her eyes. Outside, the Yanaka air raid siren finally wound itself up. Its wail was piercing. The nearest AA batteries began firing. It was a relief. They needed something to mask their shouting.

Sachi—

I knew him.

What?

He was just a boy. He lived down the street.

He was Kenpeitai. He was going to shoot us. You have to be quiet.

I used to watch him for his mother. Before we went to—

Sachi—

No.

I had to. I didn't have—

He wouldn't have said anything. He would have understood. He was just a boy. I could have told him.

Sachi—

No. No. You killed him. You killed a boy in my house. You —

It's a war. Nothing's right anymore. We get through it however we can.

I hate it. I hate all of it.

I need your help.

I hate —

There was an explosion outside. It rocked the house. He ran to the window. A bomber was spinning wingtip over wingtip, a thousand feet above the ground. Its left two engines were on fire. They had traced a flaming spiral in the sky. As he watched, the entire wing ripped off. The wing flipped backwards, and fell on a separate trajectory. The rest of the plane was headed down. It was coming straight at the window. He ran to Sachi and grabbed her. He pulled her out of the room. He dragged her down the corridor, to the stairs. There was no time. He knew that. He knew he had to try.

They were halfway down the stairs when the next explosion came. The house shuddered. Light flashed through the windows. The plane had crashed somewhere else. They got to the bottom of the stairs. He pulled Sachi around and held her close to his face.

"You need to listen to me."

"No."

"Please, Sachi."

She stared at him. He could feel her going limp. He didn't want her to faint. In the movies, he'd slap her. Break her out of a trance. He let go of her. He took a step back.

"I'm going back up. I'll get your robes. You have to stay near the door. If the bombs start falling here—if the fire gets to Yanaka—you run."

She just looked at him. A minute ago he'd seen only horror and disgust on her face. The firelight had let him see it in her

eyes. But now her face was blank. She was looking at a stranger.

He ran back up the stairs. He stepped over the soldier he'd killed. He grabbed her kimono and her under robe, and went down again. She was waiting where he'd left her. She took her kimono and put it on. She went down the corridor to the front of the house.

He went back up. He rolled the dead Kenpeitai soldier over. All he'd seen before was the uniform. The white armband, and the gun. A soldier. A lethal force. But Sachi was right. He was a boy. A boy whose father wasn't a high official. He was underfed. The deprivation showed in his face. In his sunken chest. He couldn't be more than seventeen. No wonder he hadn't been able to pull his gun in time. He'd had no real training. Killing him had been as easy as snapping a pencil.

The boy's bared teeth and bloody eyes said everything. He'd died in terror. He'd died in pain. Now McGrady was taking him by the ankles and dragging him into the hall. Down the stairs. The boy's bamboo sword came off his belt. It clattered down to the entry hall. His head hit every step. Sachi would hear it, and know what he was doing.

McGrady dragged him past the hearth. He went out the back doors. The sky was orange and black. The bombers were still coming. He could hear their engines. He could hear the AA bursts. He didn't hear bombs exploding. This was something new. Some awful innovation. The Americans had learned how to light an entire city on fire. He could smell the burning now. A sickening stench of gasoline and flesh. A roar came from the east. Wind-driven flames. Sirens. Screams.

He dragged the dead boy across the yard, toward the bathroom. Takahashi had built it next to the spot where the outhouse had once stood. There was the heavy wooden cap covering the old hole. He'd been warned. Don't stand there. You might

fall through. McGrady lifted the lid away. An earthy, fecund stink rose up. The hole was a little more than a foot and a half wide. No telling how deep.

He shoved the boy in, head first. He fed him into the ground until his feet were out of sight. He threw in the gun. He went back to the house for the sword, and tossed that in, too. It was no kind of honorable burial. He didn't have time for anything else. He brought shovelfuls of dirt from his bomb shelter excavation, and filled in the top of the hole. He put the wooden lid back in place.

When he'd hidden the bicycle under the house and closed the front gate, he washed his hands. Then he went to find Sachi. She'd fled back upstairs to her bedroom. She was standing at the east window, staring at the firestorm's glow. He took his robe from the floor and put it on. She turned to look at him. She'd come back to herself. Her face shone with tears. He stood next to her. She took his hand and held it tight.

Look at them. Will they ever stop coming?

I don't know. The boy—

You don't have to say anything about it.

You were right.

We were both right. He was a boy. And you didn't have a choice. I hate that they didn't give us a choice.

He looked above the bed. The candle she'd lit was still burning. It probably didn't matter now. The entire eastern half of Tokyo was burning. He went to the bed anyway. He leaned over the flame and blew it out. Then he came back to her.

He stood next to her. She put her arm around his waist, but it was different now.

"Did I tell you that I hated you?"

"I don't know," he said. "You might have."

"I don't hate you. I hate this, and what we've done. But not you."

They watched the planes. The antiaircraft fire had died away. All the batteries within range of the planes must have been overrun by fire. The searchlights were gone. And the bombers were still coming. They flew in and out of smoke. They hit scalding whirlwinds of rising air and got tossed around the sky like toys. McGrady watched one get flipped tail over nose. It plummeted half the distance toward the ground. Then the flame-blasted air forced it up again. The pilot recovered. He banked and went on.

The bombers came for two and a half hours. The fire wasn't a fire anymore. It was beyond a raging storm. There were no words for what it was, because no one had ever seen anything like it. Tornadoes of flame danced toward each other. They met and became swirling columns of fire, a thousand feet high. The house shuddered in the wind. The fire was sucking in air, consuming everything. The wind became a gale, and then a hurricane. They watched. They listened to the roar. They waited to see if they would need to run. It wasn't clear running would do any good.

Seven in the morning looked the same as half past midnight. The sky was a black lid of smoke. The sun may have been above it, somewhere. But there was no good light. It was a lost day. A missing page. Skip this history.

They stood by the window until it was clear the fire wasn't going to reach them. They went downstairs, where the stench of smoke wasn't quite as bad. They went into McGrady's room and shut the door. They took off their robes and got beneath his covers and slept close to one another. She wanted him to hold her through her nightmares. In exchange, she held him through his.

He dreamt of fire and smoke. He dreamt of dragging a

war-stunted boy down the stairs and burying him in a privy hole. He dreamt that the boy was still alive when he went into the ground. McGrady would startle awake. He'd hold onto Sachi, but he knew it was no good. He knew that after this, he'd lost her.

When he woke in the later afternoon, she was gone.

Sachi left two notes on the table. One was for him alone. The other was for her father. He read his. He left her father's unopened.

She stood by what she'd said before the firestorm. She stood by what she'd said afterward. What they had was everything. There was no saving what they had. It had been incinerated along with everything else. They had spent three and a half years circling toward each other inside a walled garden. Outside, the world was burning down. Now the fire had come to them. Where had they thought this path would lead, when they'd set off? Was it foolishness or something worse that had brought them to this point so wholly unprepared? But now they were here, and she had no more options than McGrady had when he'd broken the boy's neck.

Whether she wanted to or not, she had to leave.

There was the old family place in the mountains. He'd seen pictures. She'd told him how the hot springs sent steam through the snow. The forests were foggy in the wintertime. The trees were glazed with sulfurous ice.

She wasn't running from the bombs. She was running from him. She couldn't stay in the house with him. She couldn't sleep knowing he was downstairs, while the boy he'd killed was buried somewhere in the back. One fact or the other would drive her crazy.

She begged him not to tell her father about the boy. She begged him not to tell her father what they'd been doing before the boy walked in. She begged him not to tell any of it.

She begged him to forget her. She promised she would never forget him. It would be her price to pay. For the boy. For the fire.

He burned her note in the hearth. There was no need to open the doors first. Everything already reeked of smoke. The whole world was a funeral pyre. His eyes were burning and his throat was raw. He held the paper until the flames licked his fingers. He dropped it into the ashes. He told himself he should work. He should go outside and finish the bomb shelter. He should dig and build until he couldn't lift his arms. Maybe that would hold him together.

Instead, he knelt down on the floor and cried until it was dark. He cried for Sachi. For the boy he'd killed. For the city that had died. For everything that might have been but would never be. He cried until he choked. Then he went out and got the shovel.

Takahashi came home at midnight, two days later. McGrady was in Sachi's room when he heard the gate open. He got up and went to the window. There was a sliver of moon. It was enough. There was no other light to compete with it. He saw the car drive in. It wasn't black anymore. It was coated with gray ash. Takahashi had driven in without his headlights, but when he opened the door, his dome light came on. He lifted his suitcase from the seat beside him and stepped out. He looked sick to his stomach. Like he could hardly handle the weight of his slim traveling case. He studied the house. The roof, the upstairs windows. The garden walls. McGrady had swept the ash off. He'd cleaned the windows. What Takahashi saw must have reassured him. He got some strength back. He slammed the door.

McGrady beat him to the front door. He opened it for him.

"Takahashi-san."

"Detective McGrady."

They bowed to each other. Takahashi looked past him. He was expecting to see his daughter kneeling by the hearth. Just as he'd been expecting his city to still exist when he returned.

"Sachi wasn't hurt. She was here, with me. She was okay."

"Where is she?"

"She took the Nagano train. The night after. She wanted me to give this to you."

He gave Takahashi the note she'd left. He still didn't know what it said. They went together into the main room. Takahashi knelt by the hearth. McGrady lit a candle. There were blackout curtains downstairs. Things might have been so different if she'd let him install them upstairs, too.

Takahashi read the note. He folded it into his lapel pocket, and stood up.

I would ask you to come with me, McGrady-san.

Where?

We'll go for a drive.

All right.

What happened between you and Sachi?

Nothing happened.

She loves you.

She told you that?

She didn't need to tell me that. I've had three years to watch her with you.

Then you should know I love her too.

You don't need to tell me that, either. What happened?

I don't know what she told you, in her note.

I don't know what she told you, before she left.

She told me there was no way forward.

Takahashi nodded. He picked up his top hat and set it on his

head. He buttoned his coat and took his car keys from his pocket.

"We'll take a drive, McGrady-san," he said. "I want you to see."

He was in no position to refuse. And if he could have refused, he'd have been ashamed to do it. He'd be no kind of man. So he followed Takahashi out the door, and to the car. He didn't bother with the privacy curtain this time. The streets were empty. They circled around the south end of Ueno. McGrady saw the pagoda in the zoo. He remembered it from the night of his arrival. Then they crossed the railroad tracks and there wasn't anything to see at all. They were on a barren plain. The road cut straight ahead, through an ash field.

Takahashi drove without his lights. He rolled down the street at five miles an hour. There were hulks standing above the flat horizon. Melted cars. A few brick walls derelict in fields of slag. It was like driving across a lava flow. Takahashi stopped the car.

"Let me show you something."

He got out. McGrady followed, and walked around the car's hood to join him. They set off together, picking their way through the ash. It had been baked into a hard crust. There was still heat coming off it. It crunched under their feet like half-frozen snow. They went past a melted car. There were four people in it. They were charred black. A breath of wind might blow them to dust. He realized what he had been sweeping from the porch and washing off the windows. He understood what he'd been breathing.

They went onward. They passed a brick and stone building. Its walls still stood. Everything inside it and around it had been incinerated.

"There," Takahashi said. He pointed ahead. "There's one."

McGrady couldn't see what they were walking toward. He

didn't ask. He'd see it soon enough. They crunched forward. They came to a pit. Maybe it had been a cellar. Maybe it had been a bomb shelter. Now it was just an open grave. Ten feet deep, twenty feet long. A hundred bodies inside. They'd been carbonized. They had no faces. He couldn't tell their genders. He guessed the ones holding infants were women.

"This goes on, and on, and on," Takahashi said. "We could walk this way for an hour and a half. We wouldn't get to the end of it."

"Takahashi-san—"

"Don't tell me you're sorry," Takahashi said. "Do you know how many people lived here?"

"I don't."

"No one ever will," Takahashi said. "No one will ever count the dead. For every one of these we see, how many more got baked underground in a bomb shelter? How many got turned to dust?"

McGrady saw a light in the far distance. A red-filtered flashlight. Someone was picking through the rubble. There was nothing to scavenge. There was nothing here at all.

"Do you think I'm angry at you, McGrady?"

"You've got a right to be."

"I'm not angry at you. But do you know what I keep asking myself?"

"I don't."

"If Miyako had lived—if she'd passed what she knew to the Americans, would we be standing here right now?"

"I wouldn't be."

"And neither would I. Our fleet would have sailed, and your submarines would have been waiting. Your bombers could have finished off the stragglers. Miyako could have sent ten thousand men to their deaths. It would have been a kindness to her country."

"You're right."

"Do you know what I want you to do?"

"Sachi made me promise that I wouldn't."

Takahashi reached into his coat pocket. He brought out a gun. The same kind the Kenpeitai boy had been wearing.

"That was before she left you."

"It was."

"She abandoned you, McGrady."

"She did."

He was looking at the gun. Takahashi wasn't pointing it at him. He was holding it at his side.

Have I abandoned you?

You have not.

Have I turned you out of the house?

No.

If I did, you'd beg me to shoot you instead. It'd be better than if the mob found you.

It would be. Surely.

But I am not abandoning you because of this.

I wouldn't hold it against you if you did.

Kill him, or don't. I don't care. But find him. Look at all of this, and remember it. There was one chance to stop it, and he killed her. So make him pay.

I will, Takahashi-sensei.

Let's go back, now. Would you like that?

Please.

It will be the two of us, until it's over.

All right.

Do you know how we are the same?

I don't.

We're in love with women who can't stand us. We drove them away because we showed them what we were willing to do.

So here we are.
I'm just waiting for the end, McGrady-san.
It won't be long, I think.
It won't be easy, either.

39

On August 15, 1945, Takahashi came home in the middle of the day. He left the front gate open. He didn't shut his car door. He found McGrady sitting at the table. McGrady set down his book and looked up.

"What's the matter?"

He couldn't read Takahashi's face. The man was trembling, and that put a jolt of fear into McGrady. The firebombing raids happened at night. Daytime used to be safe. But whatever had happened to Hiroshima and Nagasaki happened in full sunlight.

"Wait here," Takahashi said. "We've got a couple of minutes. I need to get the radio from upstairs."

Takahashi dropped his hat on the table and went up. His bedroom was there, on the other end of the hallway from Sachi's. McGrady waited for him. He looked outside, into the garden. He'd never bothered to finish the bomb shelter. It was clear it would do no good. He didn't want to dig his own grave, and then sit down in it to wait. Takahashi came jogging down the stairs a moment later with a radio. He set it on the table and powered it up. Then he tuned it, and adjusted the volume. There was crackling silence. A clear channel. Takahashi turned to McGrady.

"The Emperor is about to address us."

"To say what?"

"What do you think?"

Before McGrady could answer, the broadcast began. The Emperor's voice was quiet and childlike. He wasn't speaking live into a microphone. It was a prerecorded phonograph, and

not a very good one. It was hard to hear for all the scratches. McGrady could barely understand a word of it. He looked at Takahashi.

"He is speaking classical Japanese," Takahashi said.

"Do you understand it?"

Takahashi nodded.

"Of course." He listened a bit, eyes closed, fingers flat against the table. Then he began to translate. "He has pondered the general trends of the world most deeply. He sees the actual conditions obtaining in the empire today. He's decided to effect a settlement of the present situation by resorting to an extraordinary measure."

They listened to the Emperor for another thirty seconds. McGrady could only understand every fifth word. But he didn't need to understand to know Hirohito wasn't rushing to get to the point.

Takahashi cleared his throat.

"He has ordered his government to communicate to the Allies that Japan accepts the provisions of their last declaration."

"What last declaration?"

"Unconditional surrender," Takahashi said. "In view of what happened the sixth and ninth of August."

McGrady didn't answer. He didn't listen to the rest of the broadcast. He got up and went outside and stood beneath the cherry tree. He got down on his knees and closed his eyes.

He stayed with Takahashi for two more weeks, because there was nowhere else to go. Takahashi was at the ministry, sometimes for days at a stretch. McGrady paced in the house. He waited for Sachi to send word, or to come back. She did neither. He heard on the radio that American ships were gathering in Tokyo Bay. A delegation of Japanese was going out to sign an

instrument of surrender. Still, he waited. By then it was habit. On the third day after the surrender ceremony, Takahashi offered to drive McGrady down to the harbor. McGrady turned him down. It wouldn't do Takahashi any good to be seen doing it. It would raise questions on both sides. So McGrady went into his room and took his suit out of the wardrobe. He put it on. He hadn't worn his shoes since arriving.

He and Takahashi stood on the front steps together.

McGrady didn't know what to say. They shook hands. Then they embraced. They both knew they'd never see each other again. McGrady spoke first.

When you see her, tell her that I love her. Tell her that I'll wait. I will.

And when I catch him, I'll tell him you sent me. I'll get word to you.

They bowed to each other. Then McGrady walked down the steps, and out the gate. He left with nothing in his pockets except for the few pages he'd written about Miyako Takahashi. He had no map. Getting lost didn't concern him. He was lost before he started. Going home was the greater unknown.

He walked down the walled lane, graveyards and temples on either side of him. He passed through the university campus. He walked in front of the Tokyo National Museum. He'd never seen it with his own eyes, but he could have toured its galleries blindfolded. Sachi had taken him through it with her voice.

People stopped and stared at him. He nodded to them. He bowed to a man who bowed to him. There was no angry mob ready to pull him limb from limb. There were no children throwing lumps of charcoal. When he walked through the fire-torn wastelands, he stopped to help a woman draw water from a well. She had burn marks on her face and hands. He asked where to find the Americans. She pointed the way.

°

He found an American landing party in the late afternoon. At first they didn't know what to do with him. This American in a suit and tie, walking out of the rubble with his hands up. Near sunset they put him in a launch and ferried him out to their flagship. The sky was full of low-flying fighters. The bay must have just become the largest American naval base in the world. He'd never seen so many warships in one place. He lost count at a hundred and fifteen. At the end of a long reach of gray and choppy water, Mount Fuji rose in the distance. The launch came up alongside a ship. They brought him up the gangplank. The last step was stenciled with the battleship's name. He'd just stepped aboard the USS *Missouri*.

The next morning, September 6th, he stood on the rail and watched as the *Missouri* weighed anchor. Then he sat on the fantail near the handful of stray Americans who'd made it aboard. To a man, they were in worse shape than him. One was missing an eye. Another had been burned from the waist up. All five of them were emaciated. They watched the shore. The battleship was cruising down Tokyo Bay for the open sea. Yokohama had been flattened. The entire coastline was cratered. They were escorted for the first twenty miles by American minesweepers working to clear American mines.

Missouri was a fast ship. When the minesweepers turned back, she opened up. She steamed at close to thirty knots. Japan was gone in less than two hours.

There was just a long gray cloud on the horizon, and then that disappeared too.

They gave him a cot in a corridor near the enlisted men's mess.

He talked to the crewmen and heard about the war. The men marveled at the atom bomb. They spoke with unreserved joy. Jap cities had been obliterated. Jap women and children

had been vaporized. It was a small price. A bargain basement deal. Who wouldn't grab it up? They could go home. They could call off the invasion of the main islands. They were all going to live to see their twenty-first birthdays.

McGrady listened. He said nothing. He didn't tell them what it looked like from the ground. He didn't tell them what Takahashi had shown him in the pits and the ash fields. Torch a woman and her baby into carbon, and there were no fine points left to distinguish. They might have come from any country.

They didn't need to hear it. They'd had more news than him. They'd seen more than him. They told him about Berlin and Stalingrad. They'd told him about the death camps. They told him about the island campaigns. They'd fought hard, and won. He wasn't going to take it away from them.

The ship called at Guam.

They took on passengers. Troops going home. Liberated POWs. McGrady listened to their stories. He walked around. He moved from one group to the next, so he never had to say anything. There was canned beer. There were endless urns of coffee. The freezers were full of beef. They gave him new socks and underwear. Khaki pants and white t-shirts. A laundry bag, with his name on it.

Now his corridor was crowded. There was a second cot jammed up against his. He moved outdoors. He put his bedding under a gun turret. When he wasn't sleeping, he spent his time on the fantail. He watched the wake. It churned white in the day and glowed green at night. They were burning through the miles. Home was up ahead.

No one knew he was coming.

He saw it the morning of September 20th. He sat on the starboard rail and watched. The mountains were visible first. Wild, emerald green. The ship was headed into the wind. He breathed

it in. He could smell the island from twenty miles out. Flowers and clipped grass and red dirt. They'd crossed the ocean un-escorted. Now an entire fleet raced to see them through the last few miles. Fishing boats. Teak yachts. Little tugboats. Skippers honked their horns. Girls threw flowers and leis.

The water went from deep blue to turquoise. They were at the entrance to Pearl Harbor. A pair of fireboats waited at the mid-channel buoy, spraying water into the air.

A brass band was waiting on the dock. Photographers angled for shots. Everyone wanted to see the *Missouri*. The Japs had come aboard in their funny top hats and signed the surrender while MacArthur stood over them like a khaki-clad skyscraper. Now the boys were home. Now the ship was right back here, where the whole thing started.

He went to his turret and sat on his blanket. He waited aboard until the buzz died and the band went packing. Then he walked down the gangplank and stepped ashore. The base had grown tenfold. The new buildings were made of concrete and steel. There were antennas and radar dishes. Airplanes crossed the sky to land at Rogers and Hickam. There was more of every-thing. It was all bigger and newer.

He walked across the base and went out the main gate. He climbed the hill to Kamehameha Highway and stuck out his thumb. The first driver stopped. An Army lieutenant driving an open-topped vehicle. The man looked absolutely jazzed to be alive.

"Where're you headed?" he asked.

"The police station, downtown. It's still on Merchant?"

"I guess so," the lieutenant said. "Hop in."

The lieutenant drove fast. He wove in and out of traffic. The roads were crowded with cars of all colors. There were no rick-shaws. There were no men pushing wooden carts. The signs were all in English. The bars were pouring American beer and

American bourbon. You could buy a hamburger for a nickel. If you had a nickel. McGrady didn't have a penny.

"Police station, huh?"

"That's right."

"You look like a cop. Are you a cop?"

"I missed some work. Maybe they'll take me back. Maybe they won't."

"How much work?"

"Fourteen hundred days, give or take."

The guy's eyes moved back and forth while he put that figure into years and months. He braked, to miss a delivery truck.

"That's the whole goddamn war."

"Yeah."

"What the hell?"

"I went to Hong Kong on a case. I got there December 8, 1941. You see where this is headed."

"How was it?"

"If I had it to do over, I'd do some things differently."

The lieutenant didn't answer. The wind blew past. The sun was shining. McGrady looked at the vehicle they were racing along in. He'd never been in anything quite like it.

"What is this—a car or a truck?"

"I don't know. It's a Jeep," the lieutenant said. "What if they don't take you back?"

"I don't know."

"What else can you do?"

"I used to be in the Army."

"We're not looking. We're cutting back."

The guy drove. He fiddled a cigarette out of a pack and lit up. He offered one to McGrady, who waved it off. He'd breathed enough smoke.

"Way I see it, HPD's got to take you back."

"How's that?"

"You were on the job the whole time. A soldier goes out there, and the Japs get him—he doesn't need to wonder if he's still got a job. He's got enough to worry about without that."

"Makes sense."

"And you should tell your chief, you want back pay."

"Back pay."

"Back pay," the lieutenant said. "You got a house?"

"You're looking at everything I've got."

He'd put on his suit. He was holding his laundry bag. It had a toothbrush, a razor, and a U.S. Navy blanket.

"You get fourteen hundred days of back pay in one go, you could get a lot of things."

The lieutenant let him out at the corner of Merchant and Nuuanu. They shook hands and then McGrady walked down past the Royal Saloon. The police station was still there. Across the street, the Yokohama Specie Bank had been commandeered by the military police. There were uniformed guards outside, M1 Garands on their shoulders. They were probably the same age as the Kenpeitai boy. But they looked fed and trained.

McGrady went into the station. There was an officer at the duty desk. There were other men milling around. He didn't see anyone he knew. He went to the desk.

"Help you?"

His mind lost traction. He was just looking around the station hall. The old smells of sweat and coffee and ammonia. The dusty light from the high windows.

"I need to see somebody."

"Who?"

"How about Fred Ball? Is he around?"

"Let me check."

McGrady spotted a face he knew.

"Hey—Kondo."

Kondo turned around. He stared at McGrady for ten long seconds.

"Holy shit."

The desk guy looked up.

"What?"

"This guy—this is Joe McGrady."

"The detective? You're talking about that McGrady?"

"Hey," McGrady said. "How've you been?"

"How have I been? How have you been? You're supposed to be dead."

"Yeah."

Kondo came up. He pumped McGrady's hand. He slapped his back. There were other officers gathering now. He didn't know any of them. They'd come when they'd heard his name. He figured how it was—he'd gotten famous around the station. Joe McGrady, the detective who went to Hong Kong and never came back. He was going to lose a lot of luster. The story sounded better if it ended with a sword in Yokohama. Whatever watered-down version he told people wasn't going to come close to the truth.

"What the hell happened?"

"What do you think?"

"We heard you got killed. They took you to Japan, and you got killed."

"I was in Japan all right," McGrady said. "I even made some headway."

"Headway?"

"On the case."

"Jesus Christ, you're still thinking about that?"

"What else would I have been doing?" McGrady asked. "Is Beamer still around? And where's Fred Ball?"

"The old man's too angry to die and too stupid to quit," Kondo said. Then his face flattened. "As for Fred—"

"What?"

"We should sit down. The three of us."

"He's around?"

"I'll go get him. You wait here. You want lunch?"

"If you're buying."

"I'll buy. Or Fred will," Kondo said. He looked at his feet. He patted McGrady's back again. He gave him a bear hug, and then pulled back. "Oh shit, Joe—hold on."

Kondo left. He came back upstairs in ten minutes. He had Fred Ball in tow. He was more or less the same. He'd lost a little weight around the middle. He'd compensated for it in his shoulders. He looked like he could muscle through a brick wall. Kondo had filled him in. He came straight up to McGrady. He shook his hand.

"Joe."

"Hey."

"How about the Royal?"

"If it's open. Last time we tried, it wasn't."

"Sure," Fred said. "Let's go."

"What about Beamer?"

"See him later," Ball said. "I got to talk to you."

Kondo came along behind them. They went to the Royal and got a booth. Kondo sat on the inside, with Ball beside him. They were both looking at McGrady. The waitress came up. She was the same waitress who'd always been at the Royal. She smiled at McGrady like he'd been in there yesterday.

"You want a beer?" Ball asked.

"Sure."

"I need a beer."

"Make it three," Kondo said.

She went away.

"What happened over there?" Ball asked.

McGrady held his thumb and forefinger a half inch apart.

"I got this close," he said. "I tracked John Smith to his hotel. And then I got arrested—"

"You what?"

"Arrested. He set me up for a rape. It was bullshit. He got a woman to point me out in a lineup. You'd have loved their technique. I was in lockup when the attack started."

"Same day we got hit," Kondo said.

"Then I ended up in Japan."

"And?"

"I got a line on the dead girl. I got her name. I know what she was doing here."

"How the hell did you get that?"

"Her uncle came and found me. He'd been following the Honolulu papers," McGrady said. "What about you guys? Did you trace the Packard?"

"What Packard?"

"You don't remember? The guy I shot, he was driving a boosted '38 Packard coupe. We were trying to figure out where he'd gotten it."

"Okay—I remember that," Ball said. "We did trace it. The guy's name was Daniel O'Brian."

"Better known as Danny Boy," Kondo said. "You heard of him?"

"You're talking about the pimp?"

"Ex-pimp. He got stabbed in '43."

"Did you interview him? You got notes?"

Kondo was shaking a toothpick out of the glass jar.

"The case is closed down, Joe," Ball said. "No one's looking at it anymore."

"We've had every other kind of thing to handle," Kondo said.

The waitress came back with three beers in heavy glass mugs. She set them down and went away.

"Then I'll open it up again."

"If Beamer lets you," Ball said.

"Why wouldn't he?"

"He didn't want you on it in the first place," Ball said. "He got outgunned because Kincaid wanted to kiss an admiral's ass."

"Kimmel's history, now," Kondo said. "That changes things."

"He got shitcanned," Ball said. "They stripped his stars and sent him packing. Because of Pearl."

The three of them looked at their beers. They were silent a while. Finally Kondo picked his up and held it out to the middle of the table.

"Take it as it comes, Joe," he said. "Right now, it's just good you're back."

Ball and McGrady took their glasses and clinked them together with Kondo's. Ball and Kondo drank. McGrady set his down without touching it.

"You heard I was dead."

"You were on the list," Ball said.

"I figured."

Kondo looked at Ball. There was some kind of sign language going on between them.

"I need to talk to you about that," Ball said.

"You told Molly."

"I told her, yeah."

"How'd that go?"

"She was pretty broke up about it," Ball said. He swirled the beer around in his mug. "I was too. Just so you know."

"He was," Kondo said. "We talked about it. A bunch of times. Right here."

"Okay."

Ball picked up his beer and drank about half of it.

"Tell him," Kondo said. "Or if you don't want to, I will."

"Jesus Christ, I'm telling him," Ball said. He looked back at McGrady. "At first it was just—you got to understand how it was. I felt bad about everything. She needed some company. She asked me if I could stop by."

"I get it."

"I didn't think I was her kind," Ball said. "I'm not like you. But I kept her company."

Ball laid his hands on the table. McGrady saw the ring.

"So, you know—"

"When did it happen?"

"January, 1944."

McGrady nodded.

"I guess you divorced that other one."

"I did, yeah."

"Congratulations," McGrady said.

He looked at his beer. He looked out the window at the street.

"That's all?"

"Fuck, Fred. What else do you want?"

"I mean—you were dead. It wasn't like you were gone a few days and I moved on her. You were goddamned dead."

"I know."

"We've got a boy. He just turned one."

McGrady wasn't looking anywhere. He was doing the math. He was running the numbers and making the comparison. Molly's life, alongside his. When she'd gotten married, he was still writing her letters every night. When she gave birth, he was still holding on. He was doing everything he could to keep her face from fading.

It wasn't her fault. It wasn't Fred Ball's fault. It was a complete disaster and nobody had done anything wrong.

He slid his beer across the table to Ball.

"That's great," he said. "I'm real happy for you. You got this check, right? Because I got nothing."

"Where you going?"

"To see Beamer. To get my job back."

He got out of the booth and walked. Ball didn't come after him.

He went back into the station through the basement entrance on Bethel Street. He walked to Beamer's office and knocked. There was no answer. He tried the handle and it was locked. He walked back upstairs. He still didn't see anyone he knew. He went up to Chief Gabrielson's office. Maybe it made more sense to start all the way at the top. Gabrielson had been there from the start. And he'd been in the room at the Alexander & Baldwin Company when Kincaid and Kimmel had hatched the plan to pack McGrady off to Hong Kong.

The chief's secretary saw him going to the door and tried to stop him.

"Sir?"

"It's okay. He's been waiting for me."

He opened the door and stepped inside. He closed it before the secretary got there. Gabrielson was behind his desk. He was in uniform, but he'd taken his hat off. He was leaning back and looking at a typed report.

He set it down and looked at McGrady over the top of his reading glasses.

"Yes?"

"How are you, Chief?"

"Do I know you?"

"McGrady, sir. You sent me to Hong Kong in '41. The Henry Kimmel Willard case."

"You said McGrady? Joe McGrady?"

"I got back this morning. I figured you'd want my report."

The secretary opened the door and poked her head inside. The chief waved her off.

"He's fine."

She shut the door. The chief took off his reading glasses and set his report aside.

"What happened out there?"

He finished the day sitting on the sea wall near Aloha Tower, watching ships come in and out of the harbor. He was drinking Kentucky bourbon from a bottle that fit in his lapel pocket. Gabrielson had loaned him ten dollars. He'd told him to report back to the station at eleven in the morning. There'd be a new badge waiting for him. A new gun. A set of city wheels.

Gabrielson hadn't asked McGrady where he was staying. Ten dollars could take care of that, and a lot more. There was the Alexander Young Hotel, on Bishop Street. There was the YMCA. There was Kawaiahao Church, which could be talked into letting him put his blanket on the floor.

He wasn't worried about tonight. He was thinking long term. His old room above the chop suey place was gone. The landlord would have tossed his things years ago. He couldn't remember what he'd had in there. Nothing worth crying over. Nothing he wouldn't throw away himself if he had it right now.

He sipped the bourbon. He let it sit on his tongue.

He'd asked Gabrielson about back pay. It took the old man by surprise. He didn't have an answer. The city's attorney would have to weigh in. The mayor would have to sign off. McGrady figured he'd do some checking, too. He'd found a phone directory. He'd found some lawyers with Bishop Street addresses.

He'd go around in the morning, after he'd shaved and eaten breakfast. He'd see what they had to say about it.

He took another long pull from the bottle. He looked out across the ocean. He watched the sun head down. His thoughts went out past the horizon. All the way to Sachi, in the mountains. It was midday in Japan. Maybe she was walking in the forest. Maybe she was kneeling by the hearth, blowing a pile of charcoal to life. He closed his eyes. She'd promised she wouldn't forget. If she'd given him the chance, he would have told her the same thing.

He finished the bottle. He wondered what the hell he was supposed to do next.

40

It was December 7, 1945. He woke up at dawn to mark the anniversary.

By this time four years ago, he'd been thrown in a Hong Kong jail cell. He was living through his fifth December since he'd gotten on the Clipper in West Loch. Four years ago, and yesterday. He tried to see all the days, strung out one after another. So many of them would be black.

He went outside. His garden was well tended. He walked across the close-cut grass in his bare feet. He opened the wooden gate in the high rock wall. The beach was right there. Fifty feet of sloped sand, and then the Pacific.

He listened to the waves. He listened to the wind move the bamboo and make the stalks rattle. Five Decembers. He had a house and an easy mortgage. He had a job and a city car and an Army surplus Jeep. He had thousands of dollars in his bank account.

Every time he stepped outside, he felt like his pockets were empty. He felt no closer to home. He'd stayed alive for all these days, and he didn't have a thing to show for it. He'd lost Molly. He'd lost Sachi. Beamer had blocked him off, and shut him out of the case, so he'd lost that, too. He had a handful of promises he didn't know how to keep, and that was it. At least other men had scars. Something they could point to. They'd been in battles that had names. They could gather in bars, or toss footballs around in a park, and trade stories.

✿

After he'd had his tea, he went outside again. He'd had the out-door bathroom built the same time he'd put up the wall and planted the garden. He showered and dressed. He put on his gun before he donned his jacket. He put his badge in his lapel pocket. He took his car keys and went around to the carport, and drove down through the long morning shadow of Diamond Head to the station.

He parked on Merchant and saw the old manapua man coming up out of Chinatown under the weight of his lunch buckets. He bought a handful of dumplings, and went to the station to eat them at his desk.

It was quiet, even by Friday morning standards. He opened a binder and started going through autopsy photographs. It was a simple case. An ex-soldier had beaten his three-year-old son to death with a belt. McGrady had arrested him. On the ride downtown, the man explained himself. The boy wet his pants. The kid ought to have known better. The man told the boy, who weighed thirty-two pounds: *put up your fists and fight.*

McGrady found a desk with a typewriter. He started writing up what he'd seen at the autopsy. The station was quiet. There was the snap of hammers hitting the ribbon. The click and recoil as the platen moved a space to the left after each new letter. He stopped. He listened. He heard a bang from downstairs, and a moan.

He typed another sentence. Then he stopped again. This time he heard a shout. More like a growl. He heard rubber-soled shoes scrabbling against slick concrete.

McGrady stood up. He yanked the page out of the typewriter. He walked that back to his desk and dropped his reports. He went downstairs. He went past Beamer's office and past the drunk tank and the individual lockup cells. There were cops here and there, but not many. No one else seemed to hear what he heard.

The interrogation rooms were all the way at the back of the basement. Two of them were dark, and there was a light coming from the window of the last. Ball liked that one the best. It was the smallest. It had the most mold growing on the walls. It was the hottest. He could make a lot of noise in there.

McGrady looked through the window.

Fred Ball had a kid cuffed to the chair. Ball had knocked the table over. He was standing behind the chair. The kid's eyes were closed. He was sobbing soundlessly. Curling down into himself and waiting for whatever was going to come next. Ball reached down and put his hands around the kid's neck.

McGrady opened the door.

"Fred."

Ball looked up. He wiped sweat off his forehead and his upper lip.

"You come down here to see how it's done?"

"I'd like a word."

"I'm busy right now."

"We can talk in there or out here. You pick."

"What's this about?"

"It'll be quick."

Ball leaned down to the kid's ear. He whispered something. Then he straightened his jacket and stepped out. McGrady closed the door. It put him with his back to Ball. McGrady took his time. He turned around slowly.

Then he hammered his fist into Fred Ball's nose. The blow knocked the back of Ball's head into the coral block wall. McGrady followed it up with a jab in the gut. The first punch did real damage. Ball's nose was free-flowing blood. The second did nothing. Ball absorbed it. He was a hunk of gristle stuffed into a suit. He grabbed at McGrady, meaning to get him in a bear hug. That would have been the end of it. Ball could have crushed the air out of him. But McGrady saw it coming. He ducked and

sidestepped. He pushed Ball from behind, and sent him into the other wall.

Ball's face bounced off it. McGrady swept his legs from beneath him. He brought his old partner down face first. He landed with his knee between Ball's shoulder blades.

Ball screamed. He probably thought it hurt. McGrady figured he could show him a thing or two about that. He'd seen pain. He'd dealt it out. He got a grip on Ball's head, using his eye sockets as handholds. He started pulling back. No way he could break Ball's neck. That would be like tying a knot in an elephant's trunk. So he didn't worry about it. He gave it all he could. When he had Ball's face six inches off the floor, he shoved it back down and heard Ball's nose pop like a grape.

McGrady used the back of Ball's jacket to wipe the blood from his fingers. He stood up. He brushed himself off.

"That's not who we are, Fred," he said. "We're better. That's all I wanted to tell you."

Ball was moving, but he wasn't trying to get up. McGrady stepped across him, and looked up. There were a dozen cops gathered at the end of the hall.

A half hour later, he was in Beamer's office. He was looking at his badge and gun on the other side of the desk. Beamer was jiggling his inhaler up and down. There was a Lucky burning in the ashtray and a second one between his fingers.

"You want to know why I'm so happy right now?"

"I hadn't noticed you were."

"I'm happy because I can finally tell you to get the hell out of my station."

"All right."

"You never fit in. You don't belong. You don't have what it takes. You're not a team player. I could go on."

"Sure. Go on."

"You look at this city like it's a meal ticket. You cost us nine thousand dollars just by coming home."

"That didn't include interest. You got a deal."

"I'd ask what's wrong with you, but this time at least, everyone knows," Beamer said. "You think you had something with Fred's wife."

McGrady breathed out slowly. He didn't move. He pictured what it would look like if he did to Beamer what he'd just done to Ball.

"It wasn't about that."

"I talked to him already."

Beamer took a drag on his cigarette. He went to tamp its ash and noticed the other one. He set down the one he was holding and picked the other up. He looked at his inhaler. It was clear he wanted to jam it up his nose and have a good snort. He reached for it, then set it aside.

"He's not going to file a complaint. He's going to let it slide, on account of his wife. I don't care either way."

"All right."

"I want you out of here in thirty seconds. If you've got anything in your desk, get it fast, or I'll put a squad on you."

McGrady stood up. He walked out of Beamer's office and went back upstairs. He went to the squad room. He opened the file closet and knelt in front of the unsolved shelf. He took the bound stack of documents from the Henry Kimmel Willard case, tucked it under his arm, and walked out.

So his anniversary turned into a vacation. It wasn't a windfall. Just like his nine thousand dollar payout wasn't a windfall. He'd earned it. He'd paid for it.

He took a bus to Waikiki and walked the rest of the way down Kalakaua to his house. He got in his Jeep and drove. He

went around past Koko Head to the spot where Henry Kimmel Willard's car had gone through the guardrail. The car was long gone. It was on the bottom somewhere. The war had given it plenty of company. Millions of tons of company. It was all the same story. The car was just a footnote lost in the prologue.

Takahashi was right. It would have all been so different if Miyako had finished what she'd set out to do.

He drove on.

He went up to Kahana and then down Reginald Faithful's dirt road. He parked where he'd parked four years ago. There was nothing left of the kill shed. It had been torn down. Ginger had taken over the soft naked earth beneath it. He walked around. There were cattle lowing in the pasture behind him. The stream trickled beneath a tangle of vines.

Miyako and Sachi had looked a lot alike. They were cousins, after all. He knew how Sachi moved. He knew how she spoke and how she thought. He knew what she sounded like when she was screaming. Now he could picture what it had been like inside the shed. He waded through the ginger and stood on the spot. He sat down on the dirt that had soaked up Miyako's blood.

He went back to the paved road. He wasn't worried about what would come next. Maybe he'd lost the capacity to be worried. Things would work out. Or they wouldn't. It didn't really matter. Everything that mattered was already past.

In the late afternoon, he stopped at Hirata & Sons on King Street and bought sake and groceries. While Mr. Hirata rang it up, McGrady spoke with him, in English. He hadn't used Japanese since his last moments in Tokyo. He wasn't worried about losing what Sachi had given him. He was still dreaming in her tongue. Her voice narrated his days. He figured as long as he had that, he was okay.

When he got home, he parked the Jeep in the carport and walked around to the gate. The garden wall was high, and the house was set so far back that only the peak of its roof was visible. He closed the gate behind him and walked down the stepping stone path to his front door. He took off his shoes on the porch and went inside. He had only just finished putting his groceries away in the refrigerator when the doorbell rang.

There was no peephole. No window next to the door. He opened it, and stood staring at the woman on his step. She wasn't crying yet, but he could tell all she needed was a little nudge.

"Joe," she said.

He waited a moment, so that when he spoke his voice would be his own.

"I guess I should invite you in."

"All right."

She slipped off her shoes and stepped inside. He closed the door after her. She smelled the same. Jasmine and plumeria. She looked the same. Maybe it was that she was wearing a dress he recognized. It was the one she'd worn on their last full day together. She could have stepped straight from that day into this one.

He walked ahead of her through the house. He hadn't bought much furniture yet. Most of what he had was low to the ground. There was a table in the main room. Six cushions around it. The room smelled of clean, fresh bamboo. He'd had the floors ripped out and replaced with tatami mats just a month ago.

She sat down. He sat on the far side.

"I wish that hadn't happened today," she said.

"Is he okay?"

"He'll get better. They took him to Queen's. They reset his nose. He's lying down at home now. I put an ice bag on his eyes."

"Nothing permanent?"

She shook her head.

"You shouldn't be angry at him," Molly said. "If you want to be angry—"

"I'm not angry at you, Molly."

"Joe—"

"This wasn't about you."

"So you just—" she stopped and looked at her lap. She was holding a small purse. She set it on the table. "All right. If that's what you say, then I believe you."

"Do you know why he comes home and puts cold towels on his knuckles?"

"I haven't asked."

"Does he hit you, too?"

"Joe—no. He's never laid a hand on me."

"Well at least there's that."

"Or our son," she said. She looked up at him. Now she was crying. "He's great with him."

"I'm glad."

"Did he tell you what I named him?"

"No."

"He wanted it to be Fred," Molly said. "I put my foot down."

"Okay."

"His name's Joe."

McGrady nodded. He had no response. She didn't seem to expect one.

"He saw you the first day you got back," she said.

"We had a beer."

"He kept it from me," Molly said. "I didn't find out until later, that you were back. I'd have found out from the newspaper. That article. But he must have known the story was coming out. He got it off our lawn and threw it away. I'd have never known,

except a friend mentioned it. She'd saved the clipping. She showed it to me. That was two weeks ago."

"Molly—"

"I didn't know what to do. I didn't know if I should find you and explain myself. If I should leave you alone—"

"You don't have to explain yourself."

"But I do."

"You don't," McGrady said. "I'm not angry. I don't blame you. I'm sorry it happened. But there's not a lot to do about it."

"What if—"

"Molly, stop. There aren't any what ifs."

She put her hand on the table, palm up. She was reaching across to him.

"But would you?" she asked. She wasn't looking at him. She was looking at her hand. Waiting for him to take it. To lace his fingers into hers. "If I left him, would you?"

The windows were open. He could hear birds in the garden and the surf on the other side of his wall.

"You married him," he said. "You've got a son. It's what you've got. You can't undo it."

"I could."

"You wouldn't want to."

"You're saying no."

He nodded.

"I'm saying no. I wouldn't."

She wiped her tears with the back of her hand. She wiped her nose. She looked around the house while she dealt with the blow. He watched her take the place in, watched her swallow down a bitter mouthful.

"It's nice," she said. "This place. It's peaceful."

"I needed something. I'm still working on it. I'm not sure what I'm trying to do."

He got up and went to the kitchen. He knew exactly what he was trying to do with the house. He just didn't like to think about it. He found a soft linen hand towel and brought it back. He handed it to her. She wiped her face with it.

"It's my fault you lost everything," she said. "When January came, I knew you hadn't paid rent past December. So I went and talked to your landlord. I got all your things out. I put them in my place."

"You shouldn't—"

"I held onto them, and held onto them. I had to move—my roommates had left, and things were getting tight—I brought everything with me. I was going to keep it. I was going to have all of it for you, when you got back. I was going to be the good girlfriend. The one who waited. Who saved everything. Then Fred came and showed me your name on the list."

"I'm so sorry, Molly."

"I gave everything away—"

"That's okay."

"—except what I could fit in a hat box."

"You didn't have to save anything."

"You were dead. I wasn't doing it for you. I wanted something to hold onto. Even after Fred and I—"

"Okay."

"How could your name be on that list?" she whispered. "Joe—how? I would have waited. You know I'd have waited."

"Molly."

"I've got it in my car. The box. I'll give it to you."

He got up and went to the stove. He lit the burner beneath the iron kettle. He watched the flame a while. He could feel her watching him, so he turned around.

"When did you finish at the university? You must be Dr. Molly Radcliffe now."

She shook her head. She'd twined the towel around her hands.

"I left the program. No degree. I'm just Mrs. Molly Ball. I stay at home with Joe."

"Where's he now? Your boy."

"His grandmother's house. So I could come here. Fred thinks I went to get aspirin and scotch. I better not forget it."

He couldn't believe it. She had been on a trajectory. She wasn't supposed to have landed where she was. He turned off the stove.

"I was going to make tea," he said. "I guess I don't want it after all."

"Don't you have anything stronger?"

"Whiskey."

"Will you have one too?"

"It sounds about right."

"Then pour for us," Molly said. "I'll get your box. I'll be right back. I'll pull myself together. I promise."

She dabbed her face one more time with the towel, and showed herself out. He got a couple of glasses from the cupboard and a bottle of bourbon from under the sink. He poured two fingers' worth into each glass and brought them over to the table. She came back in a minute, and let herself in. She was carrying a round box. She set it on the table and pushed it across to him. They picked up their drinks and raised them to each other.

He took a sip. She downed hers in one go.

"Open it up," she said.

He pulled the lid off, and looked inside.

There was his Army-issue .45. He touched the muzzle and then looked at his fingertip. It hadn't been cleaned since he'd used it in '41. There was still powder residue on it. He set it aside. She'd saved one of his white shirts, and one of his ties.

There was a cloth bag. He picked it up and knew from its weight she'd put his service medals in it.

Then there was a three-by-five photograph. It was McGrady and his kid brother. They were standing in front of a lake. No shirts, no shoes. He had to be about twelve. He set the photograph on the table and tapped it.

"That's my brother."

"I guessed that."

"I forgot—you never saw this when we were together. You never came up to my room."

"Not that I didn't try," she said. "Anyway—it was the only picture I could find of you."

"It's funny," McGrady said. He picked up the photograph and looked at it. "I remember I wanted to tell you something about him. Right before I left. But I don't remember what it was."

"Maybe it'll come to you."

He shook his head.

"It doesn't matter now. It probably didn't matter then."

He looked in the box. There was only one thing left. A telegram card from the Commercial Pacific Cable Company. It didn't look familiar. He turned it over. It was his next to last message to Molly. He'd sent it from Guam.

I HAVE NOT FORGOTTEN A SINGLE THING AND NEVER WILL I HAVE A SURPRISE AS WELL BUT YOU HAVE TO WAIT UNTIL THE TWENTY FOURTH

He set everything back in the box and put the lid on it. The bourbon was numbing his throat. He needed that. He sipped some more of it.

"It was raining so hard the night I sent that," he said. "It rained the whole time I was there."

He got up and went to the kitchen. He brought the bottle

back and poured her another drink. She gulped it down.

"What was the surprise?" she asked. "What would I have gotten on the twenty-fourth?"

He shook his head. He wasn't about to tell her. It wouldn't do her any good to know, or him any good to think about it.

"I don't even know if you'd have liked it."

"I guess we'll never find out."

"We won't. We shouldn't."

"It's a shame."

"A lot of things are."

They finished their drinks. They sat and listened to the night birds and the surf. Then he stood up and walked her to the front door. She put on her shoes and looked at him. She was waiting to see what he'd do. Waiting to see if he'd meant it four years ago when he'd cabled to say he would never forget a single thing. Or if he meant it just now when he'd told her he wouldn't take her back.

The truth was that he meant both.

He nodded goodbye. He shut the door. He waited until he heard the garden gate open and close. Then he locked the front door. Never in his life had he done that while he was inside a house.

He tried to stick to his routine. He was aware what it was doing to him. The routine kept him quiet. The quiet was growing inside him. A deep black space. It was easier to let it grow than to look at it. If it spread far enough, it would erase him. That was okay. Today, especially, that was okay.

So in the morning, he made tea. He sat for a while with his newspapers and read.

The papers were a genuine windfall. He'd gotten them from a vacant house in Kaimuki. A patrolman had tipped him off about it. The house was packed, floor to ceiling. The former occupant had hoarded every kind of trash, but it was the papers McGrady had wanted. He'd excavated through the stacked rubbish. He'd pulled December 1941 to August 1945. He kept them in boxes in the carport. He'd only read them outside. They reeked of cat piss. Some of the pages were black with mold. He wasn't about to throw them away. They were his link back to the time he'd missed.

He was going in order. He was up to July, 1943.

Which meant that today he came across this headline: DANIEL 'DANNY BOY' O'BRIAN STABBED. It was July 17, 1943. The paper carefully avoided the word pimp. O'Brian was a real estate speculator. Fred Ball had been the detective assigned to the case. He'd made an arrest the next day. The perp was an eighteen-year-old Marine from Minnesota. He confessed. So it was a dead end.

But there was a picture.

Ball, hauling the guy into the station. The perp looked scared.

He probably spilled everything inside five minutes. Ball would have gone on another half hour, just for the pleasure of good work well done. McGrady wondered what else he'd done that night, after he'd punched out. He folded the paper and dropped it in the box.

He stood up and went inside.

Their whiskey glasses were still on the table. He picked them up and washed them. He took the hatbox upstairs to his room and set it on a shelf in the mostly empty closet. Last night, he'd told Molly she hadn't done anything wrong. He'd meant it.

He couldn't say the same about himself.

He'd told Molly there were no what ifs. Of course there were. There always would be. There were so many things he'd never know and so many ways he'd never stop asking the questions. What if. What if he'd done it better?

That first night in Yokohama, he could have listened to Takahashi's pitch. Then he could've walked away. Back down the steel stairs, back to his place in the line of naked prisoners. None of the other men from the ship had been given any kind of choice. They had to take whatever the Japs decided to dish out. He could have taken it, too. Maybe he'd have survived. Or maybe not. But in either case his name wouldn't have been on the wrong Red Cross list. If people asked him what had happened in Japan, he'd be able to answer with some kind of dignity.

And everything would be different.

The Kenpeitai boy would be alive. Sachi would have spent the war in the mountains. Her heart would be intact. Fred Ball would be alone somewhere, feeding on his grievances. Molly Radcliffe would have her PhD. They'd each have waited for the other. She'd be asleep in his bed this very moment. That could have been his life. But he'd chosen to leave the commandant's office by the wrong door.

He cleaned the kitchen. He thought about taking a drive. Cooking breakfast. Going for a swim. It wasn't enough. He needed a regimen that meant something. Not just an empty routine. He needed to work, and get somewhere. If he didn't do it fast, he was going to end up parked on a barstool until his funeral. So he sat at the table and read the files he'd stolen. There was nothing he didn't already know. Ball and Kondo worked the case after McGrady left town, but Beamer shut them down after the Japs hit Pearl. McGrady shut the murder file.

Some things might be unknowable, sure. Most everything else was easy to find out. He went over to his telephone and picked it up. He dialed the operator. She came on the line fast.

"Help you?"

"I need a number and an address."

"Yes, sir," she said. "What's the name?"

"Kumi Henderson."

She lived up above the city, off Pali Road. He knew the area. She and her new husband must have been doing all right. There were big houses up there. Plenty of land around them. Cool winds blew down from the Nuuanu Pali pass. The winds and the views were like a magnet for money.

He shaved and put on a suit. He got in his Jeep and drove.

The house had a long driveway. There were five cars parked along its length. He nosed the Jeep into the last position and got out. The house was low-slung and modern. Its roof was nearly flat. He went up to the front door and rang the bell. A little dog started barking inside. He could hear it dancing in circles. Throwing itself at the door. He waited for a few minutes and then rang the bell again.

He started to leave. When the dog finally quieted, he heard laughter from the back. There was a gravel footpath that led around. He followed it and found himself in a well-maintained backyard. There was a swimming pool. There was a wrought iron table in the grass, with an umbrella above it. Four ladies were sitting around the table. They were holding cards. One of them was Japanese, and the other three were white. He'd stumbled into Kumi Henderson's Saturday morning bridge club.

He was standing next to the corner of the house. They hadn't seen him yet, and it gave him a chance to look at her. Kumi Henderson. Formerly Kumi Takahashi. Vanished wife, absent mother.

He reached up and knocked on the wood siding and waited for them to look up.

"Mrs. Henderson?"

"That's me," she said. She set her hand of cards face down on the table. The other ladies followed suit. "Can I help you?"

He'd known she would remind him in some way of Sachi. He hadn't realized how much they'd look alike. What he did next was unintentional. It was a reflex. It was what he would have done with Sachi. He switched to Japanese.

I need to speak to you about your niece, Takahashi Miyako. It would be better if we could do it alone.

The other ladies were looking from McGrady to their friend. Kumi's mouth had dropped open. It took her a second to shake the surprise and remember her guests.

"Excuse me—I need to talk to this gentleman. Would you mind waiting?"

Kumi didn't wait for an answer. She stood up and came across the yard. She whispered.

Who are you, and who sent you?

My name is Joe McGrady. I was a policeman. I met Takahashi

Kansei during the war. No one sent me. He told me you were
here and I decided to come on my own.

She looked at him. He saw the snap of recognition hit her
face.

You were the detective. I remember you from the newspaper.
The last one I sent to Kansei.

That's right.

What happened? It was as if the case just disappeared.

Not for me. Can we talk inside?

Certainly.

They went back around the path to the front of the house.
The door was unlocked. The dog sniffed around McGrady's
feet for a moment and then disappeared. Kumi led him over to
a sitting room. They took upholstered chairs facing each other
in front of a bay window.

"Your Japanese is very good."

"Sachi taught me."

"You've seen Sachi?"

He told her. Not everything, but most of it. Enough that she
could probably guess the rest. She'd left Japan when Sachi and
Miyako were five years old. She'd never contacted them again.
So he didn't think there was any reason to dance around the
facts. She stopped him halfway through. The bridge ladies
were looking antsy out back. He could see them through the
dining room doors. She went out. He watched their body language. She'd asked them to go home. They'd reschedule. When
they were gone, she made tea. She brought the pot and the
cups into the sitting room on a tray. He picked up again where
he'd left off.

When he was finished, she went away again. He heard a
door close. He heard water running. Then she came back. Her
face was damp.

You must think ill of me for leaving her.

I don't think anything either way. Sachi never talked about it. To her, it's just a fact.

Yet I feel I must excuse myself. Takahashi-san is a good man. But he was engaged in very bad things. I wanted no part in it.

He told me the same thing.

He'll be arrested. He'll be tried as a war criminal. They've already arrested his teacher, Togo Shigenori.

I saw that in the paper. But Takahashi-san didn't want the war.

He didn't do anything to stop it, either. Miyako was braver.

She was brave. But so was he. They crossed a line when they killed her. He decided to break the rules. I admire him for it.

Of course you would. He broke the rules to help you. And how can I help you, McGrady-san?

He looked around the room. There was a piano. There was a hand-woven carpet on the koa wood floor. A silver frame above the fireplace had the Hendersons' wedding photograph. Next to her, Bob Henderson looked like he'd just pulled a lever and hit the jackpot.

"Where was Miyako living?"

"There was a building in Nuuanu. It was like a dormitory. All the single girls who worked in the consulate lived there."

"Can you get me the address?"

"Yes—but you won't find anything there. The day the war started, the Army took it over. They turned it into offices."

"I'll take the address anyway. Just so I know."

She went away again and came back with the address written on a piece of paper. He pocketed it.

You must have known before you came that I don't know much.

I had to see you anyway.

Because of Sachi.

I needed to tell somebody. I needed to tell someone that I'm not giving up.

Then I'll tell you something. I don't know if it's true now, but it was true when she was five. If Sachi said she would do something, then she would do it. There was never any question about it.

She took his teacup and put it on the tray. McGrady stood up. He'd been here too long. He'd said too much, and had gotten little in return. He thanked her, and showed himself out.

It was true. There was nothing to see at the old dormitory. It was a two-story wooden building, surrounded by a metal fence. There was a sign in front. It was a supply logistics office. Guards watched the entrances. McGrady drove around it. It was at the edge of Kalihi. A five-minute walk to the consulate. A ten-minute walk to Danny Boy's Chinatown hangouts. The geography told him nothing. The buildings around it were no more helpful. Lunch counters and dry cleaners and seamstresses. It wasn't the right kind of block. You couldn't knock on doors until you found the neighborhood gossip who'd tell you everything she remembered about any given day. It wasn't going to happen.

He drove until it was dark, and went home.

Two pieces of mail were waiting in the box, but there wasn't enough light on the street to see what they were. An envelope, and a cardboard tube. He carried them inside. He set his briefcase on the table, and went to the wall switch.

Except for his name, the envelope was blank. Same for the tube. There were no stamps and no addresses. He got a knife from the drawer, slit the envelope open, and pulled out a single handwritten page.

Dear Detective McGrady,

I would have gotten this to you months ago, when the war ended, but I couldn't figure out how to send it. Simply mailing it to the Honolulu Police Station didn't seem wise. I wasn't sure it would find you. And I hated to think it should end up in a dead letter bin after all we've each endured in the simple effort to get a piece of paper from my hand to yours.

When I last saw you, in 1941, you were in a cage on the ferry dock. You'd just given me all your money. I left you there, and walked up the footpath to the top of the Peak. I had to give something back to you. I had to get the drawing. The same soldiers who'd killed my father were quartered in our house. So you were right. I shouldn't have gone. But after midnight, I broke in. What happened inside — I still haven't the words to explain.

But I got out with the drawing. I hope it helps you catch John Smith. I hope that when you get him, he pays as dearly as I have. I hope he knows I had a hand in it.

In any event, today one of my father's old friends hap-
pened to stop by the house. He mentioned he'd be traveling
from Hong Kong to San Francisco. Naturally, his ship calls in
Honolulu. He agreed to use his time in Hawaii to deliver this
if he could. He's resourceful, as my father's friends tended to
be. I imagine if you are alive and in Honolulu, then he will
find you.

Yours,
Emily

He poured a glass of bourbon and sat down at the table. Then
he pulled the tin cap from the end of the cardboard tube, and
brought out three pages from Emily's sketchbook. He remembered flipping through the book at the café on Victoria Peak.
She'd been masterful in capturing frames from her memory.
But the first drawing still surprised him. He was looking at
himself. He was standing behind a tangle of barbed wire. He
was holding out his left hand, something hidden inside his
loosely closed fist. He remembered the moment, remembered
the way her hand had squeezed his.

The second drawing was a man lying dead on a bed. A
Japanese officer. His uniform shirt was slashed open. His throat
was cut. Blood was spattered on the sheets and the wall. He'd
been savaged with a blade.

He turned to the last sheet. He finished his glass of bourbon
and held it on his tongue. She'd drawn John Smith as he sat in the
Clipper's cocktail lounge. He had a *Time* magazine tied around
his right forearm. The magazine looked tiny. The whiskey tum-
bler in Smith's hand might have been a shot glass. She'd drawn
him leaning forward, head cocked. Ready to pounce off the page.
McGrady studied John Smith's face. He studied it long and hard.

✻

He started early the next morning. He drove to the house where Henry Kimmel Willard had briefly lived. It was on Pamoa Street, in Manoa. The route took him past Molly's old house, and he slowed down to look at it. The trashcans across the street were still dented. Fred Ball had hit them on Thanksgiving, back in '41. It was amazing what things were allowed to endure, while others evaporated. He drove on, to get away.

He couldn't remember the exact street number. It wasn't a problem. He recognized the bungalow when he saw it. He parked and got out. If he'd still been a detective, and if he'd been allowed to work the case, he'd have gotten Emily's drawing photographed and published in the *Advertiser*. Tips would have poured in. That wasn't possible now. He didn't have a private investigator's license. If he published the drawing on his own, it would lead to trouble. He'd rather Beamer left him alone. So it was time for gumshoe work. Door-knocking and canvassing. Have you ever seen this man?

It was a Sunday, and early enough in the morning that most people would be home. They wouldn't have left for church yet. He started with the house across the street from Henry's old bungalow.

Most of the doors he knocked on were opened. Nobody he talked to had seen the man. He got in his Jeep and drove.

It wouldn't make sense to try the neighborhood around Miyako's dormitory. Everything around it had been a business. They'd be closed today. So he went instead to Nuuanu. There were houses and small apartment buildings near the Japanese consulate. The consulate itself was still shut down. But maybe in '41 John Smith had lurked around it to look for Miyako. Maybe he'd gone inside, to meet with his collaborators.

And he might well have done either or both, but after hours of knocking and talking, McGrady couldn't find anyone to back it up.

He went wandering in the Jeep.

He found a take-out stand and bought a plate lunch, then went up toward the top of the Pali. He pulled off at the overlook and ate. It was raining in Kaneohe, but clear where he was. He was nearly as high up as the clouds. He watched their shadows move over the water as they approached. A Packard rolled up beside him. Not a coupe but a big four-door. It was packed full of girls. They were carrying on and smoking cigarettes. They were passing a flask back and forth. They waved at him. They blew kisses. He hit the ignition, backed out, and headed toward Chinatown.

The girls had given him an idea.

He parked off Hotel Street and then walked to the Bowsprit. It was early afternoon. The bar wasn't crowded. A few sailors were nursing their hangovers in the corner. The Wurlitzer was silent. He went up to the bar and pulled a stool. He laid a five dollar bill in front of him and waited for the barman to come over. Tip was the same as ever. Shaved head, scars on his cheeks. Eyes that looked like he'd just been punched. He made as much money selling information as he made pulling beers. McGrady hadn't been a regular because he especially liked the place.

"Joe?" he said. "Joe McGrady?"

"That's me. How you been, Tip?"

"The same. You haven't been around."

"Not for a while."

Not since November 26, 1941. He'd been sitting on this stool, about to drink a glass of scotch, and Beamer called. Everybody

knew McGrady went to the Bowsprit to talk to Tip. He should have picked a different bar that night.

"I saw the papers. I heard the chatter. What're you having?"

"I'm having problems," McGrady said.

"You always looked like you needed help."

"I do. I need help."

"I got all kinds of solutions."

"Okay, first thing—you know this guy?"

He unrolled Emily's drawing and held it flat on the bar top. Tip leaned down and looked at it.

"Nope. Never seen him. Big guy, though."

"Okay. Then I need to know about Danny Boy."

"He's dead."

"I know that," McGrady said. "But not much else. I never worked vice."

"He was a pimp."

"I know that, too," McGrady said. "I saw him in here a couple times. I could figure that much just from his hat."

"Then you got him pegged. Dead pimp. What else could you need?"

"What kind of operation was he running?"

"Way I heard it, he had a couple things going," Tip said. "He'd rent houses and set up girls. This was all off the books."

"When you say off the books—"

"They weren't licensed whores. And even a licensed whore wasn't supposed to be whoring outside Chinatown. They weren't going to the clinics to get their—"

"I get it," McGrady said. "What was the other thing he had going?"

"A call service. Dial-a-whore. He'd send them in taxis, or deliver them himself."

"After he got himself stabbed, what happened to them?"

"The girls? A lot of them stayed where they were. Why leave? They were all set up."

"You know any of them?"

"He used to go around with this blonde. Kate. She's still in town."

"Where?"

"No idea."

"Come on," McGrady said.

"You going to buy anything?"

"I'll buy Kate's number."

"If I had it."

"Work the phone. Call in some favors."

"How much?"

"Ten dollars."

Tip looked at the five dollars already in front of McGrady.

"Fifteen," he said. "Put a ten on top, and come back in a couple hours."

"Okay," McGrady said. "But look—I'm not a cop anymore."

"You're serious?"

"I'm freelancing something. I'm laying out my own cash. So don't call some blonde you know. Don't tell her for five dollars her name's Kate if I come knocking. I'd figure it out. And it'd make me mad."

He walked down Hotel Street. It had changed since '41. In the last eighteen months of the war, Gabrielson and the Army pulled out of the brothel business. They yanked licenses. They shut everything down. No more clinics. No more girls locked in the Territorial Hospital's whore ward until their flare-ups died down. The madams and their girls were free. They could swim on Waikiki beach. They could leave Chinatown, set themselves up anywhere they pleased, and conduct their business any way

they wanted. The only catch was Chief Gabrielson and the vice squad had better not find them.

Kate and her companions were ahead of the game. They'd been in the black market when they could have operated in broad daylight. They knew how to stay out of sight. How to draw clients without chasing lights and neon. They knew which bent cops were dangerous and which ones could lend a girl a hand. So he imagined they were doing pretty well for themselves.

He sat on his old stool. Tip was with a group of men on the other end of the bar. He was sliding beers to them and talking under his breath. One of the drinkers handed Tip a bill. He pocketed it, and came over to McGrady.

"What'll you have?"

"A Primo and the number."

"Good deal."

Tip went to get the Primo. He brought the glass mug back and set it down. Foam was sliding down the side. He took a piece of paper from his shirt pocket and set it next to the beer.

"Here's the thing," Tip said. "You gotta call between six and six-thirty. If it's busy, keep trying till she answers."

"Okay."

"She'll ask where you got the number. You tell her you got it from Mr. Michaels, at the Moana Hotel. She and her friends only service high-end. He screens for them."

"Got it."

McGrady got out his wallet. He took a ten out, and slid it to Tip.

"She's fifty dollars," Tip said. "You put it in an envelope, and you don't say anything about it. But for that and a tip, you get all night. If you want it. Mr. Michaels would've told you about the money, so don't ask her or she'll figure you for a cop and hang up."

∘

He went home after that. It was four o'clock in the afternoon. He took a swim, and then had a shower outside. He made a sandwich and ate it while he read the papers. It was starting to get dark. He waited until ten after six, and then he went inside and dialed.

She picked up on the fifth ring.

"Hello?"

"Is this Kate?"

"It is, and what's your name?"

"Joe."

"Where are you calling from?"

"My house."

"Where's that?"

"On the beach, by Diamond Head."

"You're whispering. I can just about picture it. Your wife's cooking dinner. You pulled the phone into the closet."

She had a nice voice. Her accent was a blend of everything, and that washed it out to nothing. It was all light and fun. The way the girls talked in the movies. Like she'd been born in London and raised in L.A. He couldn't tell if it was natural or something she put on for her clients.

"I'm alone. I'm not married."

"It's fine either way, Joe," she said. "Where'd you get my number?"

"Mr. Michaels, at the Moana."

"Tell me you're not a cop."

"I'm not a cop."

"What do you do?"

"I'm retired—"

"You sound about forty."

"Close enough. I used to travel for A&B. I got caught overseas by the war. I've been at loose ends since I got back."

"What are you looking for, Joe?"

"Tonight, or in general?"

"Tonight."

"Some company."

"I'm free," she said. "Well—not free. But I'm available. I think we might get along."

"I don't know where you are."

"Tantalus Drive."

"You're high up."

"You can't even imagine the view. But I could show you."

"I'd like that."

"If you're coming in a taxi, have the driver come up Round Top and let you out at the last overlook. Tell him you want to look at the lights. Your friends are picking you up. After he's gone, you'll have to walk a bit."

"I've got my own wheels."

"Then it's easier. You can come straight in. It's the third driveway on the left, after the overlook."

"When should I come?"

"Any time. I'm here waiting for you, Joe."

43

He drove out of Waikiki on McCully Street, crossed in front of the Punahou School, and then began the switchback climb up Mount Tantalus. The road was narrow and unlit. Nearer the top, it disappeared into a dark tunnel of trees. He kept an eye out for the overlook, and started counting driveways when he passed it. Hers was steep, curving down the slope. There was a forest of bamboo on one side, and a tangled grove of banyans on the other. The house was all lit up. It was cantilevered over the slope on enormous wooden beams. A broad redwood deck stretched out even farther.

On the way, he'd stopped in Waikiki for a bottle of champagne. He needed a good reason not to go to bed with her the moment he walked in. Without one, he'd have to start asking his questions right away. And he wanted her comfortable before she figured out what he'd really come for.

He rang the bell and waited. Clipped footsteps approached. She was wearing heels. She opened the door and leaned around it. Shoulder-length blonde hair spilled to the side. She was wearing a dusky red dress that fit her so well it might have been sewn in place. A diamond pendant glittered just beneath the low neckline.

"You were fast."

"Kate?"

"The one and only," she said. She looked at the champagne. "And you're a gentleman, aren't you?"

"I try."

She opened the door all the way, so that he could see the rest

of her. A man could go broke. A man could sink into debt. Plenty probably had.

"If you have an envelope, you can just set it on that stand."

He reached into his jacket and got the envelope. He put it on the mail stand by the door. He raised the champagne bottle.

"You mentioned the view, and so I thought—"

"I'd love that."

"I'm sorry I didn't think to bring glasses."

"I have glasses."

He followed her to the kitchen. She took a pair of champagne flutes from a cabinet. He glanced around the living room. She had nice hardwood furniture. Built-in bookshelves held rows of novels. There was a Persian carpet on the floor. There was a wet bar. Stocked and ready. He heard footsteps upstairs. He turned back to Kate.

"I have a roommate," Kate said. "She's off a few nights. She'll stay out of our way."

"That's fine."

She came up to him. She was holding the glasses upside down in one hand. She touched the side of his face, then slid her hand down to the back of his neck.

"You don't have to be nervous, Joe."

"I was hoping you couldn't tell."

"You're an easy read," she said. "But I don't bite. Although—"

He stepped back.

"I'd like to know you a little better before we get to biting."

"Let's go outside," she said. "You can open that up. We'll get to know each other."

"All right."

They crossed the living room. She opened the door and led him out onto the deck. Honolulu was far down beneath them. Lights twinkled from Diamond Head all the way to Pearl Harbor.

He peeled the foil off the bottle's neck and untwisted the wire harness. He pulled the cork and let the little bit of foam spill out past the deck and into the treetops beneath them. She held the glasses while he poured. He set the bottle on the rail and they touched their glasses together. She stood alongside him, her hip brushing his. They leaned on the rail and looked out.

"You were caught up overseas in the war?"

"Yeah."

"Want to tell me about it?"

"It was just a run of bad luck," McGrady said. "I was in Hong Kong on business when the war broke out. The Japs took me to Tokyo. I sat it out until it was over."

She took a sip of her champagne and set the glass on the rail. She turned him toward her. She reached up and traced a fingertip across his lips.

"You know what a friend told me?"

"What?"

"The best way to lie is to start with the truth. It's easier to keep your story straight," she said. Now she was brushing her fingers along his throat. "Now, I don't know a lot about lying. My job's pretty honest. But you're a good liar, aren't you, Joe?"

"I don't understand."

"You didn't really come here to sleep with me, did you, detective?"

She watched his expression and then she laughed. It was a true and happy sound. She leaned up on her tiptoes and kissed him before he knew it was coming. Her lips were cool from the champagne.

"Oh come on," she said. "I spend more time alone than you think. What else have I got to do but read? You made the front page."

"You—"

He stepped back from her. She picked up the bottle and poured more champagne into both their glasses.

"I thought you looked like him," she said. "I wasn't sure. But then—Hong Kong and Tokyo? What other man in this town has that story to tell?"

It was good to be outside, in the dark. He'd never been made into such a fool in so short a time. It was burning on his face. At least she was being nice about it. He leaned on the rail and looked out at the lights. He drank half the champagne in his glass.

"I'm not a cop anymore. I got fired. And I wasn't going to take advantage of you."

"If you put fifty dollars in the envelope, you wouldn't be taking advantage. Why'd they fire you?"

"I put my partner in the hospital," he said. "I'd watched him do it to too many other people."

"So why are you really here?"

"I'm still working the case. The same one I was working before the war."

"That was a murder."

"A double."

"I'm sure you don't think I did it."

"Of course not."

"But I'm connected?"

He turned to look at her.

"You remember in '41, when Danny Boy's car got stolen?"

She set down her glass and took a couple steps away from him. All the good fun had fallen out of her face.

"I never called him Danny Boy. He hated that. He'd gotten so he hated a lot of things."

"Okay."

"Things got better after he died. I don't know why that kid stabbed him, but he did the world a favor."

"I bet."

"I remember about the car. He was angry."

"But he didn't report it."

"He didn't usually report anything to the police."

"That's what I figured," McGrady said. "The killer stole Danny Boy's car and used it. He pulled its plates. He tossed its registration. It took us a long while to figure out whose it was. It would've been faster if someone reported it missing."

"And so?"

"Maybe he picked a pimp's car because he knew it wouldn't get reported. Which means he must have known Danny Boy."

"I see where you're heading."

"I'd like to show you something," he said. "I've got a sketch."

She took a last sip of her champagne and put the glass down. She touched his shoulder.

"I bet any other cop would've taken me to bed first. Then he'd pull a badge. Show me the sketch and ask questions while I was hiding under a sheet. He'd take off and the envelope would be empty."

"That's not me."

"I see that."

They were back in her kitchen, where there was enough light for her to get a good look. He'd unrolled Emily Kam's drawing and spread it flat on her countertop. She was taking her time, studying it carefully. He supposed she'd seen a lot of men up close since 1941.

"I'm not sure," she said. "Back then, we were in a different house. There were more girls. And so more men in and out."

"Does he look at all familiar?"

"A little," she said. "He's a big one, isn't he? He hardly fits the chair he's sitting in."

"The people I've talked to—he was big. A head taller than me."

"I wasn't with him. I'd remember a man that size. But he might have been in the house."

"Are you saying yes? He's familiar?"

"I'm saying maybe."

He felt a little flare of excitement. The same way he'd felt when he'd gotten Emily Kam's letter. Any kind of momentum was a thrill.

"Who else might remember?"

"Let me go upstairs. I'll get Michelle. She was with us back then."

"Okay."

"It could take a minute," Kate said. "If you think I'm jaded about cops, you haven't met her. She's not going to like this."

It took closer to ten minutes.

He watched Kate go upstairs. Then he could hear her footsteps up there, but not her voice. He looked around the kitchen and living room. It was a perfectly normal house. Nicer than most houses, certainly. There wasn't any overt sign that it was a business. He went over to the bookshelves and tilted his head sideways to read the spines of her novels. He pulled a volume of Fitzgerald off the shelf and thumbed through it.

He turned around when he heard them coming.

Michelle was a slender brunette. She looked like she might dart off at a sudden noise. She was wearing a robe. Her hair was wet. There were bruises on her throat.

"Kate said you're okay."

"I'm not looking to give you trouble. I probably hate the HPD more than you do."

"You don't want to have that contest," Kate said. "Not with her. Not tonight. Let her see it."

He went back to the kitchen and got the drawing from the counter. He brought it to her and let her hold it. She leaned against the wall and looked. She was biting her lower lip.

"Yeah," she said. "I've seen him."

"Where? When?"

"I don't remember," she said. "It was while Danny Boy was still around. It must've been before the war. Danny Boy had us in a house in Waikiki. Close to Kapiolani Park. After the war started, he moved us near Pearl. But I saw your guy in Waikiki."

"Was he a client, or did you just see him in the house?"

"I just saw him," Michelle said. "He was with Dorothy. He must've liked her, because later on he used the call service. Danny Boy drove Dorothy and two other girls out to him. His house, I guess."

"This was a while back. How come you remember?"

"Because it scared Dorothy half to death. She'd never done call service. It's different. It puts you in the man's house. They act different. You're inside their walls. They lock the door. You haven't got a clue what's going to happen next."

"Wait," Kate said. She touched the sketch. "It was him? He's the one who did it to Dorothy?"

"What happened?" McGrady asked. "What'd he do?"

"He pulled a knife," Michelle said. "He started playing with it. On her."

"He cut her?"

"He held it to her stomach while he did her. He said he could unzip her. She couldn't work for a week, and Danny Boy took it out other ways."

He looked at Kate.

"You heard about this?"

"We all heard it," Kate said. "The night it happened. But I didn't know it was him."

"What kind of knife?"

"She didn't say," Michelle said.

"There were two other girls watching him, and he did that?"

"He didn't have them all to himself," Michelle said. "It wasn't like that. He just had Dorothy. He had two friends in the house. The other girls were for his friends. They were in different rooms."

"Two friends?"

"That's what Dorothy said."

"Do you know where his house was?"

"No idea."

"What about Dorothy?" McGrady asked. "Where's she?"

Kate had come over closer to Michelle. They were both looking at the drawing.

"She's still around," Kate said. "Sort of."

"What do you mean?"

"Danny Boy tossed her out," Kate said. "About a year into the war."

Michelle handed the drawing back to McGrady.

"With Danny Boy, we had to give all the money to him," Michelle said. "Even tips. He decided if we got to keep any. He figured Dorothy was skimming. So it's like Kate said—he beat her up and kicked her out. He took all her things and threw them in the canal."

"She went to Hotel Street. She found a madam and got a room," Kate said. "There was nowhere else. Not for a girl like her."

"This was the war," Michelle said. "Even when Danny Boy was still around, Kate and I had it pretty easy. We got officers. One a night. It wasn't so bad. Most of them were married. They

knew how to be with a girl. You could have some fun with them."

She looked down and pulled her robe tight.

"But it wasn't like that for Dorothy," she said. "A girl in a boogie house had to do a hundred men a day. Six days a week. There was no kind of screening. If a man had a uniform and three dollars—"

"It broke a lot of the girls to pieces," Kate said. "It broke them in half."

"She's in the Territorial Hospital," Michelle said. "She put herself there with gin and dope, but it was really Hotel Street that did it. She didn't make it five months."

"She's there now?"

Kate looked at Michelle. Michelle spoke first.

"We go see her sometimes. See how she's doing. Kate's the one who can talk to her. She's figured it out."

"What's her last name?"

"Warwick," Kate said. "Dorothy Warwick. She came from L.A. I don't think she's ever going back."

"Is she coherent?"

"She has moments."

"Would she talk to me? I don't want to scare her off."

"You're going tomorrow?" Kate asked. "Pick me up. I'll come along."

"You mean it?"

"We should get there between nine and ten."

"Visiting hours start after lunch. Last time I checked."

"Not for Dorothy. She's in the shock ward, so they—"

"Electro, or insulin?"

"Insulin. She starts coming out of it around nine. At ten they take her to eat, and at half past they shoot her full of the stuff. After that, she's gone again."

"All right," McGrady said. "I'll pick you up."

Kate walked with him to the door. She put her hand on it before he could open it. She was looking at his envelope on the mail stand.

"We could finish the champagne. I bet you've got stories."

"I bet we both do."

"You don't have to leave."

"I ought to get going."

"This is where I'm supposed to go doe-eyed. Blink a couple times and say something like, don't you want me, Joe? Aren't I pretty enough?"

"Kate—"

She stopped him with laughter.

"It doesn't matter. I'm not asking. I know what you think, even if you wouldn't say it. I know what's stopping you, too."

He didn't answer.

"But can I ask a real question? One that isn't a game?"

"Okay."

"If you catch him, you can't arrest him. So what are you going to do?"

She'd let go of the door. Now she was holding his arm.

"It depends on what he does. And who's watching."

"Say no one's there to see. And he doesn't want to come with you."

He thought of Takahashi, standing in the wastelands.

"Then it'll be easy."

"You wouldn't be in the wrong. It'd be a good thing."

"I don't know."

"I do."

"Then you're lucky."

44

He got to Kate's house at a quarter to nine the next morning. She came outside, dressed and ready to go. She was wearing green slacks and a white blouse. She'd covered her hair with a silk scarf. She was holding a bouquet of ginger and heliconia tied together with a piece of pink ribbon. She looked past him, to his open-topped Jeep.

"I'll drive," she said. "It's always raining over there."

"All right."

There was a standalone garage. He pulled the door up for her, and waited while she backed her car out. It was a maroon DeSoto Custom. An old model, but it looked new. She must not have used it much. He got in on the passenger side and she drove out.

"It's nice of you," he said. "You didn't have to."

"I was thinking about something I said last night."

"What's that?"

"I poked fun at you for lying."

"I'm almost over it."

"It's not that. I said my job's honest."

"It is."

"As long as everyone understands the rules. If someone doesn't, then it's all a sham."

"Okay."

"But most men get it. They know when I'm acting. It's part of the deal. It's what they're paying for. And I always know I'm acting. But then that gets confusing for me. Because if I were to truly like somebody—if I wanted to see him again, and soon—it

might take a while to sort out. The acting, and what's real."

"It sounds complicated."

"It is," Kate said. "But I've sorted it out. And so I just wanted you to know it. That it isn't an act right now and it wasn't completely last night, either."

He was looking at her. He was trying to think of what to say. It must have shown on his face. She cut him off.

"You don't have to respond to any of that. In fact—don't."

"Okay."

"And it's not going to be much of a date. You've been to the hospital?"

"More than I'd like. Maybe not as often as you."

"But you know how it is."

"I wouldn't want to be a patient," McGrady said. "I can think of some people I wouldn't mind sending."

"Your old partner, for one."

"And our captain. The whole vice squad. The man from the drawing."

"Those are all men."

"Yeah."

"Aren't there any women? Some girl who crossed you? Who could use a lobotomy and a good electric shock?"

"There's no one like that. No women on my list."

The police and the courts had women on their lists. McGrady and Kate were walking across the grounds from the parking lot to the main building, and they saw at least five times as many women as men. There were women in white gowns wandering in circles on the grounds, and women drooling into their laps on the hospital's columned front porch, and women lying on the lobby floor screaming at their clenched fists while nurses walked past them.

They went to the front desk. Kate told the orderly she was there to see her half-sister. She gave the name. The man drew on his cigarette and then tamped it in the ashtray next to him.

"You know the way?"

"Of course."

"You know the rules?"

"Yeah."

"Have a ball."

Kate led the way. The floors were sticky. The air smelled of urine and cigarette smoke. She took him along a corridor that led to the back of the hospital. She pushed through a metal door, and then they were outside again. A paved pathway led to a temporary plywood building. The green curtain wall of the Nuuanu Pali cliffs rose behind it. Kate paused before she went up the steps. She looked around, and so did he. It should have been pretty. It was the last place on the island anyone would want to be.

They went inside. There was a nurse's desk, but it was empty. Twenty beds were staged in two rows down the middle of the room. Every bed was occupied. Women lay asleep, or in states of dazed stupor. No one was watching them.

Kate brought him up to a bed in the middle. There was a dark-haired girl sleeping face down. Kate touched her shoulder. She gave it a shake, then helped roll the girl over. She was *hapa*. Half Japanese, half Caucasian. And she couldn't have been a month over twenty-one. Which meant that back in '41, she should have been in high school somewhere. Not being loaded into Danny Boy's Packard. Not working out of a Hotel Street brothel.

She looked around. Her face was slack and her eyes were cloudy. Her thin arms were tracked wrists to elbows with fresh injection marks and older scars.

"Dorothy?"

The girl sat up a little. She rubbed her eyes. She looked around blankly.

"It's Kate. I came to see you."

"Kate."

Her voice was a dry whisper. Her lips were cracked.

"You want a cup of water, dear?" Kate asked.

"Yeah."

"I'll get it," McGrady said.

There was a sink up front. He found a tin cup on a shelf. He washed it, then filled it. He took his time. Better to let Kate be the one to wake Dorothy, to do the talking. He walked back to the bed. A few of the other women had stirred, but Dorothy was the only one with her eyes following anything. He checked his watch. They had half an hour before the nurses dragged Dorothy off for a feeding and her next insulin injection.

He gave the cup to Kate. She passed it to Dorothy.

"How are you feeling?" Kate asked.

Dorothy drank some of the water. Kate had to help her hold the cup.

"Betty stole my only underpants."

"I'll bring you some, next time."

"I'm going to kill her."

"Now then," Kate said. She touched Dorothy's cheek. She used her sleeve to dab water from Dorothy's chin. "We'll have to see about that."

"Unless they get me first. They send me out and pull me in. Throw me down and yank me up. Maybe one time, I won't come back."

"We'll watch out for you," Kate said. "You see my friend Joe right here? Joe will watch out for you."

"Okay."

"You see what a good job he's doing?"

"He's doing it right now?"

"Sure he is, hon," Kate said. "He can see them. Now look—I need to ask you something important. But I don't want to upset you. So if I ask you, and you don't get upset, then Joe and I will go and give Carolina these flowers."

Kate was kneeling next to the bed. She'd been rubbing Dorothy's shoulders while she talked. Now she reached down and brought the flowers up and let Dorothy see them. The girl's eyes softened.

"She'd really like them. They're so pretty."

"Aren't they?" Kate said. "Do you want to smell them?"

"I can't smell anything," Dorothy whispered. "Betty took my nose. She put it in a box. She sent it airmail to Shanghai."

"All right. That's okay. Now—can I ask you the important thing?"

"Okay."

"You won't get upset?"

"I won't."

"It's about a time with Danny Boy."

"Okay."

"You remember one night, he took you and a couple of the other girls out to a house, and the man gave you a bad time? He had a knife, and he scared you."

Dorothy sat perfectly still. It was like looking at a wax statue. Then she pulled the covers aside. She lifted her gown up past her hips, past her pale ribcage. She was bared in front of them. She put her hands on her stomach. She looked at Kate.

"He was going to unzip me. He was as bad as Betty. But she uses scissors."

Kate gently pulled the gown back. She resettled the covers.

"We need to know where the house was."

"It was in the dark."

"I know it was, hon. You went there at night. Do you remember where we were living then?"

"No."

"We were in the Waikiki house. Do you remember it?"

"It was yellow."

"That's right."

Kate smoothed Dorothy's hair back. Dorothy started to close her eyes. Kate tapped her cheek.

"How'd Danny Boy drive out of Waikiki?"

"In the yellow car."

"But which way?"

"We went over the bridge."

"And then what?"

"We turned left."

"How long after the bridge before you turned?"

"I don't know. Kind of long."

"Then what?"

"Danny Boy told us to go in."

"What'd it look like—the house?"

"It was dark."

"What was the last thing you saw on the drive—the last thing you remember?"

Dorothy put her hands together. Her fingernails were torn up. There were scars on her knuckles.

"The Makiki Drive-In."

"You're sure?"

"Danny Boy said I shouldn't look at it. Just looking at it would make me fatter."

Kate was still smoothing Dorothy's hair. She was doing every-thing she could to keep her awake and unafraid.

"The house was close to the Makiki Drive-In?"

"I could hear the music when we got out."

"What else do you remember?"

"It was dark. Under the trees. We got mud on our shoes, walking up to it. The house was dark, and— Oh. Oh no." Dorothy was looking down at her blanketed lap. "I shouldn't have had any water. I shouldn't have. Betty will be so mad."

She looked up at Kate. Her eyes were wide and afraid.

"She'll snip something," Dorothy said.

"That's all right. We'll take care of it."

"Will you?"

"I will."

"And did I do okay? Can Carolina have the flowers now?"

Kate glanced back at McGrady. He gave her a nod. She'd gotten as much as anyone could get.

"Sure, sweetie," Kate said. She lifted the blankets enough to look under them. "We'll give them to her. Now let's have a kiss. Joe's going to go outside a minute."

Kate leaned down and kissed both of Dorothy's cheeks. McGrady went. He waited outside on the lawn while Kate changed Dorothy's linens and cleaned her up. She was quick about it. She came out and down the steps in just a few minutes. She turned away from him and leaned one-handed against the side of the building. She had her head down. Her shoulders moved as she breathed. After a while she turned around.

"But for the grace of God, right?"

"I don't know."

"I do," she said. "I know."

"You know what?"

"That we were all skimming. That it could've been any of us. It could be me in there, right now," she said. She held up the bouquet. "Anyway—Carolina gets her flowers. We promised."

She walked him to the other side of the hospital's grounds.

There was a picket fence enclosing a weedy patch of never-mown grass. She went through the gate and then over to one of the corners of the enclosed space. She started digging at the weeds and fallen banyan leaves with her foot until she'd uncovered a gray rectangle of stone. McGrady got down to look at the engraving.

CAROLINA WARWICK

DECEMBER 1, 1943 – DECEMBER 2, 1943

He stood up and stepped back. Kate placed the flowers on the grave. She brushed the rest of the stone off with her hand. Then they walked out of the little cemetery and back toward Kate's car.

"She delivered here?" McGrady asked.

"She was a couple months along when the judge signed the commitment papers."

"Who's Betty?"

"I don't think she exists," Kate said. "Or at least, I hope not. She sounds like a goddamned nightmare with those scissors. And I'm awfully sorry I couldn't get more."

"I never would've gotten half that far. You were wonderful."

"Now you're the one being nice."

"I'm serious," McGrady said. "It's more than I had. It gives me something to work with."

They got back into her car. She started it, and backed out of her parking space.

"Is that what you're going to do now—work?"

"It's all I've got," he said.

"But you've really got to start right now?"

"Not this second."

She pulled to the side of the road and stopped the car. She was looking at him.

"Then would you do something for me?"

"If I can."

"I'm not asking much," Kate said. "Or—I don't know. Maybe I am. Nobody ever does it with me. Not in years and years."

"Does what?"

She pointed through the windshield.

"It's pretty today, isn't it?"

"It is."

It was gorgeous. They were looking at the cliffs. The Pali Road went up in switchbacks. The sky was mostly blue. The few clouds blowing past were catching on the cliffs' sharp teeth.

"Let's take a walk somewhere," she said. "We could go to Kapiolani Park. We could walk through it, and down into Waikiki. We could have lunch and get a drink. We could catch a cab downtown, and see a movie."

He turned away from her. He called up Sachi's face. He held onto it. He knew how well that worked. He couldn't bear to let her fade. He didn't know how to stop it.

"That'd be great," he said. "I'd like that."

"You don't have to say the rest," she said. "I already know."

"Because I'm an easy read."

"You are. And you're waiting for someone."

He looked at her. He didn't answer.

"But we could still have the day," she said. "Couldn't we?"

He reached across the seat and touched her wrist. She took his hand in hers. She was right. They could spend the day together. They could be together as innocently as she'd described. And afterward, they could go back to their own homes. They could each pick up where they'd left off. They could take up the routines and the habits that drove their isolation.

"It sounds like a plan," McGrady said.

They walked through Kapiolani Park, and then along the beach. They cabbed downtown and had lunch and wine at the Alexander Young Hotel. Afterward, they walked a few blocks down Hotel Street, and checked the marquee above the entrance to the Hawaii Theatre. The movie was *Spellbound*. It was the one thing on offer. It had Gregory Peck and Ingrid Bergman. McGrady didn't know who they were, but Kate did. So they stood in the box office line and bought tickets. They went in through the lobby and past the statue gallery, and entered the theatre as the curtain was rising. An usher led them to their seats. The lights went down as they were walking. The opening overture began. The usher clicked on a flashlight so they could read the seat numbers.

They sat close up against each other. Kate took McGrady's arm and put her cheek against his shoulder. She stayed right there until the film was done.

After the credits had rolled, they walked out of the theater and blinked at the afternoon sunlight. It had rained. The sun was reflecting from the water-filled potholes on Bethel Street. She pointed to a taxi. He hailed it, and they went back to her car in Kapiolani Park. Then she drove him up Tantalus. They arrived at sunset. His Jeep was parked to the side. Rainwater was pooled on the seats. Wet bamboo leaves were plastered all over the hood. He walked her to the door. They stood facing each other.

"I'll make it easy on us both," she said. "I won't invite you in. That way, you won't have to turn me down."

"Kate, you've—"

"No, wait—hear me out. Are you in the telephone directory?"

"I haven't been back long enough."

"Then I'll call the operator, and ask for Joe McGrady. We could do this again."

"I'd like that."

"We'll take it however you want it."

She got up on her tiptoes. She laced her fingers behind his neck. She kissed him goodnight. He knew he'd beat himself up about it later. But while it was happening, he was grateful for every second they were connected.

He went to work.

He used the side of his hand to sweep the water off the Jeep's driver's seat. He fired up the engine and drove down Round Top Drive. That put him in the right neighborhood. He remembered the Makiki Drive-In. It was gone now. It had been razed to the ground while he was in Japan. An apartment building had popped up in its place. He drove there and parked.

He got out and leaned against the Jeep. He looked at the drab gray new building. He saw the drive-in's pink and green neon. He saw the carhops in their short skirts and high heels, bussing burgers and shakes out to the cars. The cars would have been full of kids. Juniors and seniors from Punahou and Mid-Pac. Soldiers and their dates. They would've all had their windows down. Every car's radio would be going full blast. The drive-in would have been bopping to the static fuzz of three different stations. Dorothy would have been able to hear the music for at least a couple of blocks.

He pictured her, riding in the back of Danny Boy's coupe. Looking out the window. She'd have been scared. She was

probably doped up. Most of all, she was hungry. She probably wasn't allowed to eat unless Danny Boy let her.

McGrady stood and watched the street. The house had to be somewhere close. A dark house. John Smith had been waiting for her inside, with his knife. Everywhere McGrady looked, he was finding Smith's victims. He was going to lose count.

He walked to the corner and put his hands in his pockets.

There was just enough light to see the street sign. He was at the intersection of Wilder and Liholiho. Of the two, Wilder was the busier road. It carried traffic out of Manoa toward Punchbowl and downtown. It was no kind of major thoroughfare. But there were a few streetlights. There were businesses. It wasn't dark. Liholiho was dark. He started walking down it. There were new apartments. They already looked shabby. Washing hung to dry out the windows. The side lots were crowded with junk. Maybe the dark house had been torn down. Maybe something new had been built up in its place. The world hadn't been waiting around for him to get here.

But there were still houses squeezed between the new construction. Little bungalows. Boxy, two-room cottages with sagging roofs. There were worn-out picket fences. There were dogs barking at him. He saw houses with porch lights on, and houses with light shining through open windows.

Then he stopped. Across the street was a house that lived beneath the deep shadows of mango trees. He walked over. The trees had thick canopies. Grass wouldn't grow beneath them. There wasn't enough light. The yard was just dirt. Fruit had rotted into the mud. There was a smell like wine. The house was buried in there. Covered in fallen leaves and fallen fruit.

And it was perfectly dark. No porch lights, no lit up windows. It was a craftsman bungalow. Maybe three bedrooms. Two down, and one up. There was a garage to the side. McGrady

stood looking at it. He glanced at the mailbox. It was 1547 Liholiho. It matched everything Dorothy had said. It was a dark house. It would have been within earshot of the drive-in. But that was nothing to go on. Even if he'd still been a cop he couldn't kick in the door and search the place on facts so thin. He walked.

He made it five paces.

He'd seen what you could buy with caution. He didn't want any more of it. Back in Hong Kong, he could have ended it in the Empire Hotel. But he'd decided to follow the protocols. He'd had plenty of time to think about what might have been.

There was no percentage in waiting.

He checked up and down the street, then walked across the dark house's yard to the back. There was a brick patio. The back door was locked, but that didn't matter. It was flanked by jalousie windows. The burglar's best friend. Nothing but old caulk held the glass slats in their frames. He yanked them out one at a time and set them on the windowsill. He climbed into the house and then put the slats back. Then he turned around, his back to the wall. He stood silently while he took in the house. The place reeked of cigarette smoke. Years and decades of it. He could see just well enough to feel his way down the hall. He found the kitchen. There was a faint glow coming from the stove's pilot light. He turned on two of the burners. Now he had a diffuse blue light. It was enough to search the counter-tops until he found a Zippo lighter.

He turned off the stove. He snapped the Zippo open and got his bearings.

From the kitchen, he could see into the living room. There were stairs going up. Best to start high, then work low. The longer he was here, the more likely the owner would return. If that happened, he'd rather not be stuck on the second floor.

He went to the stairs, then closed the Zippo to save its fuel. He climbed up in the dark and flicked the flame alight again when he reached the top. There was just one room. Windows faced front and back. There was a pair of narrow beds, with a bureau between them. A rug on the floor. He went to the bureau and opened the top drawer. It was full of pamphlets. He read the block letter headlines.

JEW BANKS BACK ROOSEVELT

L.A. MEX SPREE – WHITE VIRGINS RAVAGED!

WORLD JEWRY ON THE RUN!

There were plenty more. The bureau was stuffed with shoddily printed tracts. He saw cartoon Jews and cartoon Negroes. He saw Hitler standing proud at the top of the globe. There was a map of the United States with a black swastika branded across the plains. At the bottom of the drawer, he found something made of silver. It was about the size of a policeman's badge. He plucked it out. He was turning it to the flame to see what it was when the front window lit up.

Headlights. Someone had turned into the driveway.

He snapped the Zippo closed and shut the drawer.

Outside, old springs bounced and creaked. The car had braked to a stop. The engine cut. The headlights died. McGrady went to the back window. This one wasn't a jalousie, but a sliding double pane. He unlocked it and lifted it open. He was climbing through it when he heard the front door open. Now he was kneeling outside on the soft asphalt shingles of the lower roof. He closed the window. He crawled to the corner of the roof. It wasn't high. Nine or ten feet above the ground. He could jump it. But there was an overhanging branch of the mango tree. Climbing down would be quieter. He swung onto the branch and then went hand over hand toward the tree's

trunk. He eased himself down from there and crouched behind the tree.

Lights were coming on in the house. He was in the side yard. He crawled up to the house, then moved along the wall toward the front. He stayed beneath the windows. There was more cover in the front. Another mango tree. He got behind it, and looked back.

The man who'd just come in was standing in the kitchen. He was framed by the window. He looked up, maybe catching his own reflection in the glass. He was lighting a cigarette. McGrady was holding onto the tree, gripping it tight. For years he'd assumed he'd never get all the answers. That he'd have to learn to live around the blank spaces. But that had just changed. He was going to get everything. Things he hadn't understood for four years were suddenly making sense. And he was going to get more. He was going to make the man answer for all of it.

The skinny old bastard in the kitchen set down his cigarette. He reached into the breast pocket of his uniform shirt and brought out a Benzedrine inhaler. He shoved the tube up his nose and took a snort. Then he turned away from the window and disappeared.

McGrady took the opportunity. He trotted out of the front yard. He crossed the street. He walked fast, hands in his pockets. He was going back up toward Wilder. Back to his Jeep. He still had Captain Beamer's Zippo. He still had the silver badge he'd taken from upstairs. That was okay. He wasn't worried about stealing them. He could return them later on. He'd be back here soon enough.

46

He was on Merchant Street, leaning against the back of a parked car. The car had city plates. It was two blocks down from the station. The western sky was going purple and orange. He'd gone home last night. He'd slept on it. He'd woken up and known what to do. Even if he didn't like it, it was the only way. He'd spent the day checking up on things and getting ready.

A group of men came out of the station. They stood on the corner and talked a while, and then they split up. Four of them headed up toward the Royal for a drink. The fifth walked the other direction. No surprise there. He was a married man now. A father. Home was waiting. A wife and son were waiting.

McGrady tilted his hat back. He wanted to be seen. He put his hands behind him, between his back and the car's trunk. He could feel the .45 tucked into his waistband. The last time he'd pulled the trigger, he'd killed a man. The next time he pulled it, he'd probably kill another.

Fred Ball stopped on the sidewalk, ten feet back. He and McGrady stared at each other. The bruises around Ball's eyes were fading from black to dark purple. The whites of his eyes were shot full of broken vessels. There was a scab on his forehead and a piece of white tape across the bridge of his nose.

"You ought to get some dark glasses," McGrady said.

Ball laced his fingers together and cracked his knuckles. He shook his hands to loosen up his elbows.

"I didn't think I'd get a rematch."

"If you want to go around again, we can go around again. I just wanted to talk to you. But I'm fine either way."

"Everyone knows if that'd been a fair fight, you'd be dead."
McGrady laughed.

"You don't believe in fair fights any more than I do."

"What do you want?"

"I want to buy you a beer and tell you a story. And then I want to help you take a man down. It'll be the biggest thing you've ever done."

"I don't owe you any favors, McGrady."

"You don't. I know someone who does. He owes us both."

"If this is about Molly you'll be picking your teeth out of your toilet."

"It's not about Molly," McGrady said. "Come on—let's go for a ride. We ought to talk someplace else."

"I've seen smarter setups."

"Fred, look—you were my partner when this got started. You should get a chance to be there for the end."

"Jesus, McGrady. It's that case? You're still stuck on that?"

"It's not a case. It's my goddamn life. And yours, too. You go home, she meets you at the door—it comes back to this. Neither of us is going to feel all right about anything until we finish it."

Ball just stood there staring at him. His jaw muscles were bulging out. He looked like he was trying to bite through a padlock.

"I feel just fine."

"Sure you do," McGrady said. He pushed off the car and walked around to the passenger door. He opened it and climbed in. "Get in and let's go."

They went to a dive on South King. There was a card game in the back. Loud voices, three or four languages. The front was empty. Ball got a booth by the window and sat. McGrady went up to the bar. He slapped at the countertop until a man came

through the batwing kitchen doors. Then McGrady was carrying a couple of beers back to the window booth. He gave one to Ball and sat down across from him. He slid the .45 around, so he could get it in a hurry. Shoot from underneath the table, right into Ball's lap. He hoped it didn't go that way.

"You want me to take it from the top?"

"Fine."

He told him the whole thing, from landing at Wake Island to stepping off the *Missouri*. He left out Sachi. Ball didn't need to know about her. Then he told Ball about the drawing from Emily Kam. He skipped over Kate. Ball didn't need to know about her, either. He jumped straight to Dorothy. He told Ball how he'd followed Dorothy's memory, and found the house.

"So what, you just broke in?"

"Are you going to arrest me?"

"Whose house is it? John Smith's?"

McGrady reached into his pocket. He pulled out the silver badge. A spread-winged eagle was perched atop a shield. There were stars and stripes on the shield. It was utterly American except for the symbol on the raised seal and the German writing around it. He passed it across the table.

"Someone who's into stuff like this."

Ball looked at it. His eyebrows went up.

"That's a goddamned Nazi swastika."

"I'd never seen a badge like it. I had to ask around. I took it up to Schofield this afternoon. I figured someone there would know this kind of stuff."

"So?"

"It's from the German–American Bund. The guy who owns this is a high-ranking member."

"Which guy?"

"Your boss."

"What?"

"I always knew there was something wrong with him," McGrady said. "The way he handled the case was rotten from the get-go. I thought it was just because he couldn't hack it. But it's worse than that."

"You're talking about Beamer. Captain Beamer's the guy. That's what you're telling me."

"Yeah."

"He doesn't live at Liholiho. He lives a couple blocks down the road from me. I've been to his house."

"He may not live there, but it's his," McGrady said. "I went to the Bureau of Conveyances this morning, when it opened. I pulled the records. He got that house in '35. No mortgage. No liens. He bought it with cash. Headquarters, for his other life."

Ball turned the badge around in his giant hands. He put his thumb over the raised swastika.

"Just for this, he's off the force," Ball said. "Inside the house, there's more like this?"

"Plenty."

"Then it doesn't matter if the rest is true. The Bund's illegal."

"It's not just the Bund. The rest is true, too. He was in on it."

"Spell it out."

"Nazis and Japs, working together. Common cause. They killed those kids to keep Yamamoto's secret. What's good for the Japs was good for Germany."

"Jesus Christ."

"You can sit up nights, thinking how things could've been."

Ball looked at the silver badge one more time. He hefted it in his hand, then gave it back to McGrady. They were on their second round of beers. Ball took his glass and lifted it.

"I got to say—I'm glad it's Beamer," Ball said. "That little fascist fuck. And you know what else?"

"What else?"

"I'm going to enjoy it. Every second of it."

"It's why I brought you in. I wanted you to show me how it's done."

Ball drank his beer down to the bottom. He pointed at his blackened eyes.

"I thought we were supposed to be better than this."

"I guess we're not."

"So you're gonna apologize?"

"No."

"Tell you the truth, I'd think even less of you if you did."

They found a hardware store that was still open. City Mill, near Pier 38. They got in just before it closed. They bought twenty feet of half-inch hemp rope. Ball had his switchblade. If they needed to, they could cut the rope into shorter lengths. Back in the car, Ball opened his glove box. He had a lead sap. A pair of brass knuckles. A banged up single-shot .22—probably his throw-down gun.

"What was he doing there last night?" Ball asked. "Checking the mail?"

"Probably. He wouldn't want it to stack up. Not the kind of letters that go to that house."

They drove to 1547 Liholiho. Beamer's car was in the drive-way, but there were too many witnesses. There was a gathering in the house across the way. Ten or fifteen people were crowded on the porch. It was no good.

"Let's drive a bit," Ball said. "They'll wrap it up, and then we'll make our move."

"And if he's gone?"

"We'll get him at his other place."

"I'd rather do it here."

Ball drove. They went down Wilder and around Punchbowl. McGrady could see Tantalus. Kate's house was all lit up. It was a single bright spot in the midst of a thousand acres of jungle. She'd left the door about as wide open for him as it could get. He looked away. Ball was pulling to the curb. There was a pay-phone on the corner.

"Hang on a sec," Ball said. "I need to check in. Tell her I'll be late."

"Yeah."

Ball got out. He went to the phone and dropped a coin. McGrady watched him talking. He opened the glove box and got the brass knuckles. Just something to hang on to. Something to squeeze. Ball came back, and they kept driving. They killed fifteen minutes, and then they came back.

Liholiho Street was the way it was supposed to be. It was dark. It was empty. The people from the porch had either gone inside or gone to their cars. Beamer's car was still there. Ball parked two doors down, and they both got out. They walked up to the house. There were lights on. They could hear a radio. They came to the door and Ball rang the bell. McGrady stood off to the side.

McGrady heard Beamer walking to the door. He was turning the locks. He was opening it.

A pause while he reacted to seeing Ball at the door. At this door. "What are you doing here, detective?"

"Something came up on the Lake case. I needed to get your thoughts."

"Lake—what're you talking about? And how'd you—"

"Veronica Lake. She's in town. There's some trouble."

He heard Beamer open the door the rest of the way.

"Veron—"

The punch cut Beamer short. McGrady came around the

door and helped Ball shove the captain back into his house
before he collapsed onto the front stoop. They spun him around
and pressed his face against the wall. McGrady got Beamer's
hands pinned behind his back. Ball slammed the door with his
foot.

"Where'd you hit him?" McGrady asked.

"Just a tap on the stomach."

"He didn't like it."

"I guess not."

Beamer had gone limp. He was gasping for breath. His chest
sounded like a leaky bellows. He was in his uniform, but he'd
taken off his Sam Browne belt. They'd torn his shirt open spinning him around. Ball was holding him up, one hand on the
back of his neck. McGrady spotted a lit cigarette on the floor. It
was burning a black scar into the hardwood. He crushed it out
with his heel. Then they took Beamer under the shoulders and
dragged him to the kitchen.

Ball tilted his chin at a wooden chair.

"That'll do."

The chair had armrests. It'd be perfect. They turned Beamer
around and dropped him onto the seat. McGrady held the old
man's arms down. Ball had two pairs of cuffs. He used one on each
wrist, so that Beamer was chained to the armrests. Then McGrady
held Beamer's feet while Ball tied his ankles to the chair legs.

Ball came around behind the chair. He tipped it backwards,
spun it around, and dragged it across the kitchen. The chair's
back legs left parallel scratches along the floor. He pivoted the
chair again, and then Beamer was facing his dinner table. Beamer
was catching his breath. He was getting his strength back. It
didn't matter. He was fixed tight to the chair.

"Sit down and have a talk with him," Ball said. "I want to
look around. I want to see his Nazi shit."

"Try upstairs."

Ball looked around. He spotted the stairs and headed that way. McGrady pulled out a chair and sat. He put his elbows on the table. Beamer was trying to look stern and confident. His lips were curled into a sneer.

"I don't buy it," McGrady said. "You're scared shitless. I can smell it."

Beamer didn't answer. McGrady reached into his pocket. He brought out the Bund badge, but didn't show it. He held it inside his loose fist.

"I know just about everything now," McGrady said. "Help me fill in the gaps, and I won't sic Ball on you."

Beamer's nostrils flared. His sneer bent back far enough that McGrady could see his yellow teeth. Fred Ball shouted down from upstairs.

"Holy shit, Joe," he said. "This guy's gonna hang."

McGrady spoke quietly.

"What I was saying—late November, 1941, you called up Danny Boy O'Brian. You had three girls delivered here. You had some houseguests to entertain. You're a great host, aren't you?"

Beamer only stared, so McGrady went on.

"We were at the autopsy. The Colonel and I stretched out Miyako Takahashi so he could cut her open. You fainted. It wasn't just because you're weak in the knees, was it? It was because you were getting a good look at what you'd helped do."

McGrady wasn't expecting an answer. He didn't get one. Instead, he heard footsteps coming down the stairs. Ball came in carrying a piece of folded red cloth.

"Hey Joe," he said. "Look what I found."

He unfurled the cloth and held it up. It was a Nazi flag. Beamer wouldn't look at it. He wouldn't look at McGrady.

"You know what this means?" Ball asked.

"I've got a guess."

They were looking at each other while they spoke. They were ignoring Beamer. But they were talking to him. All three of them knew how it worked.

"From here on, anything goes," Ball said. "When they see what's up there, no one's going to give a rat's ass what we do to him. Is he talking yet?"

"Hasn't said a thing."

"Let me try."

"Sure."

He'd been ignoring the sounds coming out of the dining room for half an hour. He was tearing the house apart. Now he was in the bedroom. He found more tracts. There was a copy of *Mein Kampf*. A stack of newspaper clippings. Beamer's taste was clear. He liked Jewish massacres. German victories. Photographs of people starving behind barbed wire.

Somehow, it got worse. There was a collection of smut books in the closet. He flipped through them. Homemade. Beamer must have put them together when he'd worked vice. He and his pals had been busy. Round up girls, bring them to the station. Nude mug shots. Poses. Sex acts. Beamer was in a lot of the shots. He was having fun.

Beamer wasn't having so much fun right now. He was down the hall, keening like a hurt dog. Ball wasn't saying anything at all. He was using his hands. He could hammer home any point. Beamer was getting the message. It didn't bother McGrady one bit.

McGrady went to the bed. There was a .38 under the pillow. A .44 on the nightstand. Before these, he'd found a German Luger in the kitchen, and a little .22 caliber ankle gun at the

bottom of a box of magazines next to the toilet. All that prepa-
ration for someone showing up, and Ball had put him down
with a tap to the stomach.

McGrady flipped the mattress off the bed. He lifted the box
spring. There was a slit in the thin fabric backing. He tore it
wide open and searched between the springs. He pulled out a
pocket-sized notebook. It was filled front to back with Beamer's
jittery handwriting.

In the dining room, Ball said something. McGrady couldn't
catch it. Beamer must have. He started screaming. It didn't last
long. Ball had cut it short somehow. McGrady closed the door.
He sat down on the floor to read the notebook.

There were names. There were telephone numbers. He
didn't see anything clearly related to John Smith. Special Agent
Shivers could go crazy for a year. It might take that long to sort
the good leads from the dead ends.

There was a knock on the bedroom door. McGrady stood up.
He put the notebook in his pocket. He crossed the room and
opened the door. Ball was standing there. He'd taken his jacket
off. He'd rolled up his shirtsleeves and was rubbing his knuckles
with a damp hand towel.

"He's ready to talk."

"Yeah?"

"I'm pretty sure."

They walked back to the dining room. Beamer was in his
chair. The flag was stuffed in his mouth. Ball had gotten most
of it in. The part hanging out was about the size of a handkerchief.

"I told him, look, if you're not going to talk, you could do
something useful. You could get rid of this Nazi flag."

Beamer's face was purple and his eyes were bulging. His
cheeks were puffed out like a balloon. His neck was engorged.

"But he couldn't get it all the way down," Ball said. "So I asked him—are you ready to talk to Joe?"

"And?"

"It was hard to tell," Ball said. "Maybe he nodded."

"Could be."

Ball took the bit of flag hanging from Beamer's mouth. He pulled it out. It was like watching a magic trick. Six inches of red cloth became a foot. Then two feet, and then three. The last bit unleashed a gout of vomit. It landed in Beamer's lap. The old man doubled over, choking for air.

"This is good for him," Ball said. "See? It's probably the longest he's ever gone without a cigarette."

McGrady sat down again. He watched Beamer gasp for breath. He waited. He was in no hurry. He had nowhere else to be. No one was waiting for him at home.

"Yes or no," McGrady said. "You had a mainland contact in the German–American Bund. Time to time, he gave you instructions."

Beamer tried to swallow. It made him gag. He coughed up some more bile.

"I said yes or no," McGrady said.

Beamer nodded.

"November '41, your contact reached out to you. He told you to expect a couple of friends. He told you to help them out. This isn't just your little personal playhouse. It's a safe house. A Bund meeting house. They fronted you the money to buy it. Yes or no?"

Beamer hesitated. Ball backhanded him in the teeth. McGrady waited for him to recover.

"Was that true, what I just said?"

Beamer mouthed something, but there was no sound. He began crying. Pain or humiliation. He raised his right hand as

far as it would go. The cuff pulled tight. He pointed to his throat and shook his head. Then he mimed writing.

"He wants a pen," Ball said. "He's going to write it down for us."

Beamer nodded. He dropped his imaginary pen. Now he was extending his index and middle finger, his yellow fingernails a centimeter apart. At first McGrady thought he was asking for a pair of scissors. Then he got it. The old bastard wanted to smoke. Ball understood, too.

"See if you can find some paper and a pen," Ball said. "Get him that pack of Luckies in the kitchen. If he's got any cold beer, grab it. I could use one. And we could be here a while."

Ball fished in his pocket for the handcuff key. He knelt down next to Beamer. McGrady walked out. He went down to the kitchen. He found a notepad next to the telephone. There were pens and pencils in a jelly jar. He grabbed the pack of Luckies and checked the Frigidaire. There was beer but he didn't take it.

He walked back into the dining room. Beamer was up close to the table. His right hand was uncuffed. McGrady shook a cigarette loose from the pack. He stuck it in his own lips and lit it with Beamer's Zippo, and then gave the cigarette to the man. He put the notepad in front of Beamer. He put a pen there. Beamer sucked on the cigarette. He tried to inhale and gagged on the smoke. The cigarette fell into his lap, then rolled between his thighs. Before Beamer could grab it, Ball caught his free hand.

"You sold me out, didn't you?" McGrady said. "You couldn't risk letting me catch John Smith. So you cabled him. You told him I was coming. And you let him know I had a witness. A girl named Emily Kam."

Beamer was squirming in the chair, trying to get the cigarette out.

"You cabled him," McGrady said.

Beamer nodded, and Ball let go of his hand. Beamer reached between his legs and grabbed the cigarette out. He set it on the corner of the table.

"So here's what I want," McGrady said. "Start with John Smith's name."

Beamer's hand was shaking. He began to write. His letters were slanted and small. McGrady had to lean in to see what he'd put on the page.

They never told me his real name.

No surprise there, but it had been worth a try.

"Was he a German?" Ball asked.

Beamer didn't bother writing. He just nodded. Outside, a dog started barking. Ball walked over to the window. He hooked a finger inside the curtain and bent to look out.

"He left you a forwarding address," McGrady said. "Some place you could reach him."

Beamer nodded again.

"Write it down."

Beamer took the pen and held it to the paper. But he wasn't writing. Maybe he was thinking. Trying to remember.

"Is it in this book?" McGrady asked. He set the black book on the table. Beamer's face gave up the game. The book was bad news. It would sink him. But he shook his head. He was still holding the pen to the paper. He scrawled something on the page.

Not in there. I need to think.

"Think fast," McGrady said.

"McGrady," Ball said. "Come here a minute."

McGrady stepped around behind Beamer and then crossed to the window. Ball made room for McGrady and they looked

outside together. There was an HPD patrol car parked on the street opposite Beamer's house. Its headlights were on. There was no one inside it. The dog was still barking.

"What do you think?" Ball whispered.

"Maybe it's just—"

McGrady heard a click. Spring steel sliding off a metal surface. He whipped around.

By the time he finished turning, he'd drawn his .45. Beamer was lifting a revolver from underneath the table. He was raising it toward Ball's back. McGrady saw the angles. He saw his chance. He pulled the trigger. So far, every bullet in this clip had found its mark. This one was no different.

He plugged Beamer in the forehead.

Ball spun. He wasn't holding his gun. He wasn't reaching for it. His eyes were doing fast takes. Shutter clicks. He snapped Beamer, who was slumped forward. He was missing most of the back of his head. The exit wound. He got a look at the china cabinet splattered with blood and gray matter. He took in Beamer's dangling hand. It was still holding the pistol. A .38.

Ball's lips were moving. McGrady couldn't hear him at first.

"He must have had it on a clip," McGrady said. "Under the table. He had guns all over the house."

"Fuck."

Ball was digging in his ears. The dining room was small. No carpet. Hard walls. The gun blast had been as loud as a stick of dynamite.

"He was going to shoot you in the back."

Ball swallowed that. He wasn't steady on his feet. He stepped around and looked at Beamer. He had to hold onto the corner of the table. As they watched, the .38 fell out of Beamer's fingers and hit the floor. McGrady knelt down and looked under the table. There was a spring clip screwed underneath.

"You see how this looks," Ball said.

McGrady stood up. He saw. There was an old man cuffed and tied to a chair. He'd been beaten up. He'd had his pinkies broken. He'd been choked. Then he'd been executed. It was going to be hard to explain. They might have to explain it in the next thirty seconds if the cop across the street had heard the shot.

"What's going on out there?" McGrady asked.

Ball went to the window and parted the curtain again. He cupped his hands and looked outside. There were more dogs barking now. There were always dogs barking somewhere.

"I don't see anything. Wait—"

McGrady came over and looked out. They watched a uniformed cop come out of the house across the street. He went down the walkway and got in his patrol car. He sat for a while, writing something. Then he put the car in gear and drove off.

"Okay," McGrady said.

"I need to sit down."

There was a chair right beside him. But sitting at the table and looking at Beamer wasn't going to make Ball feel any better. They went into the kitchen. Ball leaned against the counter. Then he sat on the floor.

"Fuck," he said.

"Don't worry about it."

"I turned my back on him."

"So did I. It's what he was waiting for. He was probably faking it, not being able to talk. He just wanted us to uncuff him and put him a little closer to the table."

"I need to think."

Ball put his thumbs on his temples. McGrady went over to the kitchen sink. He opened the refrigerator and grabbed two of Beamer's beers. He came back and handed one to Ball.

"Jesus, McGrady."

"Like you said."

"I said what?"

"You could use one."

Ball drank. He winced at the taste. He finished the bottle and set it on the floor. He looked up again, at McGrady.

"Okay," he said. "I'm fine. We're good."

"What's your call?"

"You clear out. You disappear. Are your prints in here?"

"I wiped everything I touched."

"You better hope so," Ball said. "I'll wait here an hour. Then I'll call Gabrielson at home. I'll say I dropped by to ask Beamer about a case. The door was open. I went in to see if he was okay. It looks like he got in a fight with his Nazi friends."

"They'll want to know how you know about this house. You better come up with something."

"A couple years ago, he called me from here. His car had broken down and he wanted a lift to the station."

"Guess that'll do. It keeps you out of the house at least."

"You know if that notebook doesn't have what you need, it's over. We're not getting anything else."

"We'll see."

"Get out of here," Ball said. "Walk two miles before you call a cab. They'll hit up the taxi stands to chase down the pickups around Makiki."

"They might," McGrady said. "Or maybe it'll be like you said. They'll find all the Nazi shit and figure it'd be better if the whole thing never happened."

Ball stood up. They walked through the house to the front door. McGrady was about to go through it and Ball stopped him. He put his hand on McGrady's shoulder and turned him around.

"Joe."

"Yeah?"

"Once you knew about Beamer, you must've wondered why he sent you to work with me," Ball said. "How'd you know I wasn't in his pocket?"

"I didn't."

"What?"

"But I figured if I brought you here, I'd find out pretty quick. And I was guessing I could outdraw either of you."

Ball ran his fingers through his graying buzz cut.

"You didn't bring me because you needed me."

"No, and I'll tell you what," McGrady said. "You're lucky he was pointing the gun at you. If he'd gone for me first, I'd probably have just shot you both."

Ball took his time thinking that through.

"You're a mean sonofabitch, Joe."

"Not half as mean as you."

"We'd have been good partners. I wish everything had turned out different."

"Me too."

Ball held out his hand. They shook. Then McGrady walked.

He didn't sleep. He sat in an all-night tea shop in Chinatown and read Beamer's black book. There were too many names. Too many numbers. It would take squads of detectives to run it all down. He was just one man. He had no authority. Lies and bribes would only carry him so far. He gave up on the book. He pictured Beamer. The first week of December, 1941. The old man would have gone to meetings in Kincaid's office. Admiral Kimmel would have been there. Chief Gabrielson and Bob Shivers. They got McGrady's cable from Guam, asking for Emily Kam's address. At which point Beamer would have started to worry. McGrady must have found something. A handhold. Maybe he'd use it to force the door open. If that happened, if he grabbed John Smith and didn't kill him on the spot, certain names might come up. So he had to act.

McGrady closed his eyes. He pictured Beamer, walking out of the Alexander & Baldwin building. Standing on Bishop Street, patting at his pockets. Jittery until he got a hit of Benzedrine. The closest place to send a wire was the Commercial Pacific Cable office, in the Alexander Young building. That was just a few blocks up Bishop Street. Beamer wouldn't have wanted to do it there. He was committing treason and he knew it. Off-duty detectives and businessmen packed the bar and restaurant in the hotel. People who'd know Beamer. Who'd remember seeing him. But time was running short. He had hours, not days. McGrady was going to hit Hong Kong, and then anything could happen. He'd have to weigh his risks. He'd have told himself to keep the message vague. There was nothing private about a cable. Clerks read them on both ends of the line. They kept copies.

McGrady paid his tab and walked. He wandered Chinatown in the early dawn. It was empty. As the sun came up, he only had the rats to keep him company.

At eight o'clock, he walked into the Commercial Pacific office. He'd sent plenty of cables in his time. He knew the drill. You stood at the counter and took a message slip. You took a pen on a chain, and filled out the form. You took it to the clerk and she counted the words and calculated the charge. She'd rip off the carbon copy and stick it in a file, and put the top copy on a tray that went to the wire room.

He went up to the desk and looked across at the woman. He was the first customer of the day. She'd been doing her makeup when he walked in. They had the place to themselves, and that was just fine with him.

"I'm working an old case and wondered if you could point me in the right direction," he said.

"And you are?"

"Detective McGrady, HPD."

He'd found a handful of gold HPD stars in Beamer's bureau. There were no good reasons for Beamer to have hoarded them. Just as there was no legal excuse for McGrady to take one and flash it around. He showed it to the woman and then put it back in his jacket pocket.

"How can I help you, Detective?"

He pointed at the metal cabinet beside her.

"You take the carbon copies from the message slips and put them in there, right?"

"That's right."

"Then what happens to them?"

"When the drawer fills up, we dump it in a box. We send the boxes down to storage."

"For how long?"

"Officially?"

"Sure."

"Two years, and then we pulp them."

"But unofficially?"

"We haven't pulped in a while. The war started, and then a man came around from the F.B.I. He was worried about spies, you see. He told us what to look for—so we could tip him off. Like secret agents. And he wanted us to hang onto everything. No more pulping. In case they had to go back later, and look for evidence."

"You haven't purged the files since before the war?"

"No sir."

"I guess that's off site somewhere? The storage?"

"No, that's here. In the basement. Under lock and key."

"But you'd have a key to that, wouldn't you?"

He was in his element. A dim basement full of rotting files. It was all fine and good to tie a man to a chair and beat him for answers, but cases got solved in rooms like this. The message cards were stored in pressboard boxes. Each box had a range of dates penned on the front. The space was so overcrowded he had to walk sideways to get through the stacks. All but the newest boxes were dotted with black mold. His eyes were watering before he made it to the back.

He could recite the dates without checking notes. He'd landed in Guam on the night of December 5th. He'd cabled Kincaid that night, asking assistance in running down Emily Kam's address. Guam was a day ahead, so Beamer might have learned about the cable that same morning. December 5th. He'd have fired off his warning the first chance he got.

McGrady picked his way to the back of the room. The boxes were stacked more or less in order. He found the one he was looking for and carried it off so that he could sit on the floor beneath the nearest light bulb. He opened it up and began reading.

Half the messages were handwritten, probably on the counter in the office upstairs. The rest were typewritten. He ignored those. Beamer didn't type, and he wouldn't have given that task to a girl in the station's secretarial pool. He'd have come in, and written it himself.

McGrady read love notes. He read business cables and bulk purchase orders. He saw a woman break up with her lover and then retract it two hours later. He saw mothers worrying that war was coming. He saw sons pretending that nothing was wrong. And then, halfway through the box, he found it. Beamer's handwriting was as shaky as ever. He'd written the message itself in block letters.

TO: JOHN SMITH
C/O GOLDEN PHOENIX TRANSSHIPPING
SHEUNG WAN, CPDB5 SSS HONG KONG EXPEDITE

JOE MCGRADY FROM MY OFFICE EN ROUTE TO KOWLOON
PENINSULA HOTEL STOP ARRIVES DECEMBER 7 STOP
CABLED FROM GUAM TO INQUIRE ABOUT CLIPPER
PASSENGER EMILY KAM STOP TREAT HIM TO A SHOW
BUT BE ADVISED HE HAS AN INSTRUMENT LIKE YOURS
AND PLAYS IT JUST AS WELL

McGrady pocketed the message slip. He put the box back where he'd found it. He clicked off the lights, locked the door, and ran the keys back upstairs to the woman.

Before he left downtown, he stopped at his bank. He paid his January mortgage installment and withdrew enough to last a month. He hoped it would be enough, anyway. Then he went home and started making calls. Pan Am wasn't flying across the Pacific anymore. Air Transport Command was the only game in

town. He called the ATC logistics office at Hickam Field, identified himself as a retired captain, and started dropping every name he could think of. Admiral Kimmel. Major Devereux. Bob Shivers. If there were any empty seats heading to the Orient, he'd take one. The lieutenant on the other end of the line said he'd look into it. He told McGrady to call back in an hour.

He'd only just set down the receiver when the telephone rang. He picked it back up.

"Joe McGrady?"

He'd thought it might be Kate. But it was a man. He didn't recognize the voice.

"Who's this?"

"John Carroll, with the *Advertiser*."

"I remember you."

"I'm writing the piece. I'm reaching out to whoever might have a comment."

"A comment on what?"

"You didn't hear?"

"Didn't hear what?"

"Beamer got clipped last night."

"No one told me," McGrady said. Which was perfectly true. No one needed to tell him anything. "Last time I was in the station was December 7."

"You quit?"

"I've got no comment."

"What about Beamer?" Carroll asked.

"What about him? You should ask someone who knows something. Maybe Chief Gabrielson."

"How about Fred Ball?"

"You could ask Fred anything you want," McGrady said. "If I were you, I'd do it on the phone. Then all he can do is yell at you."

"I saw him a couple days ago."

"Good for you."

"Any idea what happened to him?"

"I've got no comment on that, either."

"It looked like someone broke a baseball bat on his face."

"That's no way to treat a bat."

"What kinds of cases were he and Beamer working on?"

"No idea."

"Is it true Beamer was a member of the German–American Bund?"

"I haven't got a clue."

"If it's true, would that be a problem for the department?"

"You tell me, Mr. Carroll," McGrady said. "You know more about it than I do."

"You're really not going to comment?"

"I'm not."

"What I heard is, he was tied to a chair and tortured. Maybe for a couple hours. Then they executed him. Did he have enemies?"

"Doesn't sound like something his friends would do."

"Did he fire you, or was it Gabrielson?"

"It's been nice talking, John."

He hung up. He looked at his watch. It seemed like a good time to be leaving town.

48

A journey that took five days in 1941 took only two in 1945, but it wasn't nearly as comfortable. Instead of short hops in a Pan Am Clipper's bridal suite, he was wedged on the floor behind the flight deck of an unheated C-54. The rest of the plane was loaded with penicillin. The direct flight to Guam took twenty hours. When it arrived, he walked stiff-legged around the tarmac for the time it took to refuel, then climbed in again with a replacement crew for the eight-hour flight to Manila. That was as far as Air Transport Command had been able to get him.

He'd guessed that to cover the last seven hundred miles to Hong Kong, he'd have to book passage on a ship. But the flight engineer on the second leg steered McGrady instead to a hangar on the far end of Nielson Field, which served as the Manila base of a nascent air mail service. He was able to negotiate a spot on a mail plane that made a run to Shanghai by way of Hong Kong and Taipei. The ticket was cheap; they charged him by weight. He came the final distance the next morning as a parcel of air mail.

The customs inspectors were more thorough this time. They made him put his suitcase on a table and open it up. An officer picked through it, lifting his clothes and his files with a small black baton. There was nothing special to see. He'd tucked his .45 into the back of his pants. The trench knife was sheathed and in his inside breast pocket when the immigration man stamped his new passport and let him into the Crown territory.

He walked from the Kai Tak Airport to the Peninsula, following the Kowloon waterfront. Rickshaw pullers flocked around him. Touts for brothels and girlie shows pushed hand-stamped flyers into his hands. The harbor was crowded. Steamships and junks and water taxis. Fast British gunboats. There were Union Jacks everywhere. The Brits were back. They wanted everyone to know it.

He stood across Salisbury Road from the Peninsula and looked up at it. Two lines of bullet holes went across the top floor. They'd replaced the window glass and painted over the holes. The patchwork couldn't hide the history. The hotel had been strafed. He crossed the road and went up the steps. Doormen in top hats and coattails ushered him into the lobby.

He had no reservation, but that was no hindrance. He paid cash and wrote his name into the registration book. He changed a hundred U.S. dollars into Hong Kong dollars. The clerk handed him his keys and money, and wished him a nice stay.

"Do you have a telephone directory?"

"Yes, sir."

"Can you check something for me?"

"Of course."

"It's a company. It's called Golden Phoenix Transshipping. It's supposed to be in Sheung Wan."

"Very good, sir."

The man went away for the telephone directory. He flipped through it, tracing his finger down the newsprint page. He brought the book over and turned it around for McGrady to see.

"It would be right here," the man said.

"Maybe it's unlisted."

"Would you like me to try the operator?"

"Please."

The man picked up the phone and dialed. He spoke in Cantonese. He said the name of the company in English, and then

again in Cantonese. He waited. He shook his head, and then he
hung up.

"I'm sorry sir. Perhaps the company doesn't have telephone
service."

"Or maybe it didn't make it through the war."

"A lot of things didn't."

He waved off the porter who wanted to carry his suitcase to
the elevator. He rode up to the fourth floor and went down the
hall toward his suite. If Golden Phoenix was gone, this trip was
going to be even more pointless than his last visit. At least it
would be shorter.

He unlocked his door and walked into the room. It was the
same setup as before. An entry hall led into the main sitting
room. There were Chinese vases. Lacquered woodwork. There
was a desk in front of the main window. He pulled back the curtains. The window faced the harbor, and Hong Kong Island.
The city hadn't grown the way Honolulu had. It had been
blighted by the war. But the mountain still looked good. Green,
and dotted with mansions. He wondered which one was Emily
Kam's. He hadn't cabled her to say he was coming. Just as he
hadn't let anyone in Honolulu know he was leaving.

He looked through the supply of stationery on the desk. The
telegraph forms were decorated with a galleon ship under full
sail. The local company was called Cable & Wireless. The address
of its central cable office was on the form. He set off right then.

He was four years behind. He was done with waiting.

The Cable & Wireless office was on the Hong Kong side of the
harbor. He took the Star Ferry across, then walked. He went
past the pier where his ship had departed on its journey to
Yokohama. Ferries were there now, loading passengers for the
run to Macau. The telegraph office was opposite.

He crossed the road and went into the building through the

double set of brass doors. There was a central lobby, and a reception-tionist. The guts of the operation lay on the floors above.

"Yes, sir?"

"I'd like to see the shift manager," McGrady said. "Or operations supervisor. Or whatever you call the man in charge."

"If you're a vendor representative—"

"I'm not selling anything. This is personal."

"Personal?"

He came a little closer to the desk. He leaned down and lowered his voice.

"I lost track of a good friend back in the war. I'm hoping he's all right. It's a long shot, but last thing I could find was a cable that came through this office."

"Is it—"

"And it won't take but a minute of anyone's time."

He had his hands on the desk. He hadn't reached for his cash yet, but he was ready to. Most receptionists were susceptible to a dollar or two. But she picked up her telephone and dialed, speaking with her hand cupped over the receiver. She listened, head cocked to the side. She looked up at him.

"Your name please?"

"Joe McGrady."

She repeated that in the phone, and then hung up.

"You can take the elevator to three," she said.

There was a woman waiting at the elevator doors when he stepped out.

"Mr. McGrady?"

"Yes, ma'am."

"Mr. Renders is free at the moment, but I hope you won't need too much of his time."

"I'll be quick."

They were walking through the cable room. Hundreds of clerks were stationed at tables. They were taking incoming messages off the teleprinters, snipping the tapes with scissors and gluing them onto Cable & Wireless greeting cards. A woman circulated, pushing a wheeled cart. She was collecting the messages from each clerk's tray. The room was hot and loud. There was so much electricity flowing into the building that the air smelled of ozone.

"His office is just back here."

The office had a mahogany door and a frosted glass window. The floor boss's name was stenciled in gold. John Renders.

The woman tapped on the door and opened it.

"I have Mr. McGrady."

"Come in."

He went in and closed the door. It dampened the noise a little bit. The office was crowded with machine parts and coils of wire. Renders looked about sixty. He was thin and wore a tan suit. The windowless office was thick with pipe smoke.

"What can I do for you, sir?"

McGrady reached across the desk and shook hands with Renders. Then he pulled out the visitor's chair and sat.

"I'm trying to trace a company. It's called Golden Phoenix Transshipping. It's supposed to be in Sheung Wan."

Renders looked at him blankly. He didn't move, except to glance at the telephone on his desk.

"I thought you were looking for a friend. Someone you'd lost in the war."

"I am," McGrady said. He wondered how Kate would rate his performance so far. He was starting from the truth. "I got word he could be reached there. Just before the war, it's where he was working. But the place doesn't have a telephone. I know it's gotten cables. So I was wondering—"

"If it's a shipping company it would send a lot of cables, wouldn't it?"

"You'd think."

"So it ought to have an account with us. I could look that up."

"That's what I was hoping."

"I'll check with our billing department," Renders said. He got up, but motioned for McGrady to stay put. "Can you wait a moment?"

"I don't mind."

Renders left the office door open. McGrady stood and went to the doorway, watching the rattling machines spit out tape. One of them had hammered out Beamer's message in 1941. A lady—maybe one of these—had snipped the tape and glued it to a card. Another had collected it from a basket and routed it to the messenger department. Someone had gotten on a bicycle and set out across the city, pedaling to Golden Phoenix Trans-shipping to deliver a message that had darkened every day since.

Now he was here to retrace that path, but surely John Smith wouldn't be waiting at the end of it. He would have moved on. His bosses in Berlin would have ordered him off for other duties. If he'd truly been a sworn soldier of the German Reich, the odds were better than good that he was dead. Which is all McGrady would have asked of him were they to meet in person. But if he'd died from anyone else's bullet, there'd be no justice to it. McGrady watched the machines unspool their messages. Thousands of letters a minute. So many voices. So many connections across the world. And yet he stood here alone.

And then Renders was back, a folded slip of paper between his index and middle fingers.

"Mr. McGrady, it seems you're a lucky man."

"You got an address?"

"Of course, but that was a given," Renders said. "When you

said you could reach him there before the war, I supposed—
well, a lot could happen in a few years, couldn't it?"

"There's something besides the address?"

"Yes, sir. It's an active account. It pays monthly—a fair amount,
I should say—so it's as we said. A good bit of traffic going back
and forth on the wires. Up to today."

Renders held out his hand and McGrady took the slip of
paper. He unfolded it, and read what the man had written:

> *Lord Nelson House, Flat 1C*
> *Connaught Road*
> *Klara Weber / D. Richter*

"What are these names?"

"The two signatories on the account," Renders said. "Maybe
one of them is your friend?"

"No luck there," McGrady said. "But maybe I can ask them.
Do you know the Lord Nelson House?"

"Not far from here. Down by the Western Market."

"I've been to the market."

"It's two or three doors down from there."

McGrady considered asking for more. He had the cash to
pay for whatever Renders was willing to sell. Carbons of the
last month of cables would be worth all the money he had on
him. But it was too much risk to push. He'd been arrested in
Hong Kong once before, and that was enough.

"I appreciate it, Mr. Renders," McGrady said. "You really
helped me out."

He shook hands with Renders once more, and left.

By the time he reached the Western Market, it was getting
dark. The last time he'd been here, he'd stood in the shadows
to watch the entrance to the Empire Hotel, across the street. It

was still there. The block was scarred with war damage. Hastily covered shell-holes had been patched with off-colored brick. The intersections were pocked with rough gravel where barricades of cars had burned. But otherwise the area was intact. The Empire Hotel was open. Touts beckoned men to the walk-up brothels. And things were beginning to make sense.

Smith had stepped off the Pan Am Clipper after killing three people on his way across the Pacific. Then he holed up in the hotel nearest Golden Phoenix Transshipping. He'd told Beamer how to reach him there. The place was important. It was Smith's foothold into Hong Kong, and would be McGrady's stepping stone to Smith.

He began walking along Connaught Road. He passed a narrow alley and studied the front of the first building he came to. Letters carved into its stone façade declared it the Yardley House. He moved on, and got lucky on the third building. A brass plate mounted on the bricks above the cornerstone announced the place.

THE LORD NELSON HOUSE
1895

It was a one-story pile of bricks. It didn't live up to its namesake. The climate was going to finish what the war hadn't. Ferns and vines were growing from cracks in the slipshod masonry. A tailor's shop occupied Flat 1A. Past that, Flat 1B was under refurbishment. The front wall had been knocked out, and the space behind it was empty brick and concrete. Bamboo scaffolding held up the ceiling. McGrady walked on. He could see the door to Flat 1C. The office behind it had to be tiny. About half the space of a one-car garage. The door itself was black-painted steel. It was marked with the flat number, and nothing else. A padlock secured it from the outside. A big brass job that

held tight to a hasp bolted through the bricks. There was a door buzzer, and a mail slot. McGrady kept walking.

Another narrow alley cut between the Lord Nelson House and the next building. He followed it. There were no windows on the side of the Lord Nelson. He came down the alley until he saw that this building backed up against the one behind it, only inches of space between them. Which meant Flat 1C didn't have a back door, and there'd been no side entrance leading into the torn-open Flat 1B. Of course there might be tunnels, but he couldn't do anything about that. What he could do was watch the front door.

He turned around and went back to Connaught Road. He dodged rickshaws and Rolls Royces and walked into the Empire Hotel. The desk clerk was new. He had all ten fingers and no rings, but he was as susceptible to five dollars as the last man had been. McGrady scanned the registration book and didn't see John Smith's name. But that didn't concern him. If he'd stayed in Hong Kong through the war, he would have found better lodgings. The Japanese owed him a favor.

McGrady handed the book back, and got out his wad of cash again.

"I want a room facing the street."

"How many nights?"

"One, to start with."

"If you have company, you've got to pay for her, too."

"It's just me."

He went outside again before he went up to the room. He hadn't eaten since Manila. A street vendor's cart took care of that. At the corner tobacconist, he bought a can of lager and a church key to open it.

Then he brought his things upstairs. The mattress was caved-in

and the light bulbs had burned out, but none of that mattered. What mattered was the window. It overlooked Connaught Road and had a view on Golden Phoenix Transshipping's front door. Whenever headlights of passing traffic swept the building, he could see the padlock. He moved the wooden chair to the windowsill and ate his meal while he watched the street. He didn't care how long he had to wait. There was nowhere else he needed to be, and he could afford to sit here for however many nights it took.

By midnight the traffic had thinned out to nothing but a stray rickshaw every few minutes. The trolleys had stopped coming. An hour after that, when his neighbors quieted down, McGrady was wishing he could make a pot of coffee. He sipped at his can of warm lager, and eventually the travel caught up to him. He fell asleep with the beer balanced on his knee, his hand around it.

It was a car horn that woke him, startling him up from sleep. He fumbled the can, but came to his senses quickly enough to catch it before it hit the floor. The curtain had fallen back across the window. He pulled it away. A truck was blocking his view of the Golden Phoenix's door. He waited for it to move. The lock was in place. There was no way to know whether he'd missed something in the night. Someone could have come and gone. But he had to be reasonable about this. He was just one man. He couldn't keep watch around the clock, unless he decided to sleep in the Golden Phoenix's doorway.

There was a shared washroom down the hall. He used the toilet, then came back to his room with a basin of water. He sat at the window and brushed his teeth, then bathed with a wash-cloth and shaved. No one on the street stopped at Flat 1C. No one even gave it a second look. It was a plain black door that had disappeared into its anonymity.

✿

Around eight, he went out to the street. He stayed within sight of the Golden Phoenix and bought supplies for the day. Bottles of soda, steaming hot *xiaolongbao* in a woven bamboo basket.

Back in his perch, he waited and watched.

The room reeked of sweat, and cigarette smoke, and desperate couplings. He supposed it had quartered soldiers during the war. Or perhaps the Japanese had turned it into one of their comfort stations. He didn't need to be doing this. There was no reason he had to be here, carrying on this fight. The war was over. What was lost was lost. He didn't take his eyes off the Golden Phoenix, but reached behind his back and drew his knife from its leather sheath.

It was the second trench knife he'd owned. The first had been taken from him just across the harbor, at the Peninsula Hotel. He'd sent for this one from a mail-order catalog at the end of October. A double-edged dagger. A spiked knuckleduster. He took off his belt and flipped it around backwards, then used the hard leather grain to polish the blade until it was sharp enough to shave with.

There was a knock on his door. He held the blade at his side and crossed the room. Three steps. No peephole in the door. No chain. He opened it and found a twelve-year-old girl passing out handbills for a brothel. In another year she'd be working there.

Now he was standing at the window. He'd propped the chair under the doorknob. The girl had unnerved him. The last time, Smith had been tipped off by Beamer. This time no one knew he was here. Well—not quite no one. Probably four people at Air Transport Command. A couple of four-man flight crews who'd brought him across the Pacific. A clerk and two pilots at

the air mail hangar. The Peninsula knew he checked in. Then there was Renders, at the cable company. That was seventeen people and he'd only been considering it for a minute.

The problem was that he didn't know how far Smith's web stretched. Far enough, if it had entangled Beamer. It was hard to look for a man without talking to people. You couldn't do this sort of thing without taking risk. But that was true of everything.

There were footsteps on the stairs. He turned to look at the door. He saw shadows beneath the crack. They moved on, continuing up to the fifth floor. It was getting warm again, now that the sun was up. He slipped off his jacket and tossed it on the bed.

When he looked out again, there was a bicycle parked in front of Flat 1C. A young man in a khaki Cable & Wireless uniform was leaning down to slide a message card through the mail slot. Then he reached out and pushed the door buzzer, and was pedaling away. It was over in five seconds. McGrady would have missed the whole thing if he'd so much as bent down to tie his shoe.

But now he had to decide what to do about it. If no one came to get the message, he could wait until nightfall. Go over there with a coat hanger and a piece of chewing gum and fish the message card out of the slot. Maybe then he'd—

The door to the tailor's shop swung open. A kid came out, walking purposefully. Fourteen, fifteen years old. Chinese, with short-cropped hair. He wore a nice linen shirt and new trousers. He was sorting through a key ring as he walked. He stopped in front of Flat 1C, unlocked the door, and opened it. He didn't go inside. He just took the message card from the floor. By the time he'd stood up, and before he'd locked the door, McGrady was already out of his room.

He pounded down the stairs. Four flights in twenty seconds.

The lobby and the entry hall took three seconds. He should have asked for a room on the second floor. Paid the guy to kick someone out if that's what it took.

He burst through the door and came out onto the sidewalk under the Empire Hotel's ratty canvas awning. The kid wasn't walking back to the tailor's shop. He was crossing the street. He was coming straight at McGrady, paying attention to nothing but the traffic. McGrady took a sudden interest in the brothel handbill. He pulled it from his pocket and studied it, pretending to parse out the Chinese.

The kid reached the sidewalk and turned right. He passed a foot from McGrady. He smelled like pressing starch. The shirt he was wearing was still a work in progress. Its sleeves were held on with pins. Whatever his orders were, they were important. He'd dropped everything to do this.

The kid went into the tobacconist's. McGrady wandered along the sidewalk, still reading the handbill, until he could see through the window. Between the cigar boxes and the bottles of *baijiu*, he had an eye on the kid. He was standing at the counter. The tobacconist had passed him the telephone, and the kid was waiting while the operator connected the line. Then the kid took out the card, and motioned to the tobacconist, who ducked away into the back room. The kid put the message card on the counter and leaned down close to it while he read it out.

McGrady had to hand it to John Smith. It was a pretty good system. Someone might trace the cables coming in, but the Golden Phoenix Transshipping office was nothing but a drop box. A tailor's kid read the messages into a tobacco shop telephone, and who the hell knew what happened after that. If there was any weak point in the system, it was right here, in about ten seconds.

Inside, the kid set the receiver onto its cradle. He pushed the message card into his right pocket, and came out of the store. McGrady was up against the wall, still absorbed in the handbill when the kid passed. He took what looked like a careless step forward. But it was carefully timed. He tripped up the kid and gave him an extra push in the back to make sure he went sprawling.

"Sorry!" McGrady said. The kid was rolling over to sit up. "I didn't see you. Shit. I'm sorry. You okay?"

The kid was just looking at him. He'd been blindsided. McGrady couldn't tell if he'd understood his words or not. He reached down and took hold of the kid's biceps. He pulled him up and set him on his feet and then swept his hands down the kid's sides to straighten out his shirt.

"I'm really sorry about that," McGrady said.

The kid pulled away from McGrady. He darted across Connaught Road, and McGrady waited until he was behind a bus before he went into the lobby of the Empire Hotel.

He didn't take the message card out of his pocket until he was back in his room.

Two hours later, he was back in the Peninsula, sitting at the bar in the lobby. He was watching the foam slide down the side of a schooner of beer. The message card was in his pocket. He'd have made a Manila pickpocket proud, the way he'd lifted it from the kid's pocket and sent him packing. But it'd been no use. John Smith hadn't gone to all this trouble so that whoever was cabling him could do so in plain English, or Chinese, or German.

The message on the card was encrypted. Nothing but X's and O's. No wonder the kid had leaned down so close to read it into the telephone. McGrady was no cryptographer. He'd studied Morse in the Army. It was rusty, but it only took him a few seconds to see the card wasn't written in Morse code. And so now he was back to nowhere. What could he do? Go back to the tailor and brace the kid? That would blow up in his face like 1941 all over again. As soon as he left, the kid would find a telephone. In fact, he could be doing that now—once he got back to his parents' shop, surely he'd noticed the message card was missing.

McGrady looked at the stepped shelves of bottles behind the bar. Gin. Vodka. Whiskey. If the road ended here, he wasn't sure what he would do. As long as he was working, he could keep himself in order. But when he finally admitted he'd reached a dead end, he'd have nothing else to go on. And no reason to stay in line. He ordered a shot of whiskey, to go with his beer. He didn't particularly like it. But it was strong. It helped keep the walls in place.

These gilded walls. Class and power. He looked around.

There were wing-backed chairs and low marble tables where waiters were running an afternoon tea service. He was supposed to have met Emily Kam over there. They were going to have a pot of Darjeeling tea. She'd give him the drawing. Then he'd have gone to the Hong Kong police and nailed John Smith to the wall. A perfect plan, except that John Smith and the Imperial Japanese Army had been ahead of them.

He thought about Emily Kam. She'd been wrecked by this every bit as much as he had, and she had John Smith to thank too. One more person for him to let down. One more to fail to deliver justice for. He was raising his beer to his lips when he remembered something she'd told him, about when John Smith had come to her house with the soldiers who'd murdered her father. Hiding in the woods, she heard him.

He was speaking Japanese.

McGrady took the message card out of his pocket. He unfolded it on the wet bar top. Since stepping off the *Missouri* in Honolulu, he'd been struggling to keep Sachi's face alive in his memory. But now he was back with her. It was the night of March 9, 1945. The hearth fire was burning low. Sachi had moved their cushions close together. She was leaning her head on his shoulder. He could smell the chrysanthemums. The book of photographs was spread between their laps. She'd slid the tip of her index finger up his wrist until she'd found the most tender place. She was brushing and tapping.

Tap brush, tap tap.

Dot dash, dot dot.

He looked at the Cable & Wireless message card. He was half in Tokyo, half on a Hong Kong barstool. Sachi's finger was on his wrist. *Tap, brush.* He sounded out the *katakana* syllables. Sachi could have decoded this in ten seconds flat. Then she could have translated it into four other languages.

McGrady took ten minutes, and transcribed it into English.

He sat for a while, staring at what he'd written. Then he pushed his unfinished beer away and signaled to the barman.

"Let me have a cup of coffee," he said. "And bring me the telephone."

At three o'clock, he was sober, bathed, and in his clean suit. He was sitting on a teak bench at the bow of the Star Ferry, crossing from Kowloon to Hong Kong Island. Up ahead, his destination was easy to spot. The U.S. consulate was on the second floor of the headquarters of the Hong Kong and Shanghai Bank. The only thing higher was Victoria Peak.

When he stepped off the ferry, he walked across the city, umbrella in hand courtesy of the Peninsula's doorman. Rain squalls blew past on a warm wind. Every few blocks, another rolling squall drove him into a covered alleyway. He edged sideways through crowds more cosmopolitan than any he'd ever seen. Chinese apothecaries and Indian merchants hawked their wares alongside African shipping agents. Solemn-faced Russians stood guard in front of red-lit doors.

Finally, McGrady made it to the bank building. He climbed the stone steps, pushed through the brass doors, and stepped into the lobby. It was his first time in an air-conditioned building. He didn't pause at the bracingly cool wonder of it. He crossed to the main stairs and trotted up to the second floor, spotting the oak-and-brass entry to the General Consulate as he reached the landing.

He let himself in. He'd been expecting security, but there was none. Just a young brunette who looked up from her magazine when she heard him.

"Was there something?" she asked.

"We talked on the telephone," McGrady said. He set the

umbrella in a stand, crossed the lobby to her high desk and leaned on it. "You said Nathan De Vries is in today?"

"You rang off pretty fast," she said. "You've got an appointment?"

"Old business," McGrady said. "Something he and I were discussing when the war broke out."

"Is he expecting you?"

"Not in the slightest."

"Why don't you sit down a minute?"

"I'm fine right here."

She looked at him. He had on his best suit. He'd touched up his shave with the trench knife. Not a nick on him. He'd splashed himself with the Peninsula's complimentary bay rum. He backed up a few steps, to give the woman some reassurance. The last time he'd seen Nathan De Vries, he'd wanted to rip his throat out. Now he needed a favor.

"Just a moment."

He thought she'd put a call through the office switchboard, but instead she got up and let herself past a secured door. It wasn't a long wait. The door opened, and the woman came back with De Vries behind her. His hair was shorter than the last time McGrady had seen him. A bit of gray at the temples.

"Mr. McGrady?" De Vries said, with no sign of recognition at all. "I've got a packed schedule this afternoon, but we always make time to meet a citizen. I'm Nathan De Vries, the Acting Consul General."

They shook hands, and De Vries stepped back to let McGrady through the open door. Then they were walking along an oak-paneled hallway.

"We've actually met," McGrady said.

"Have we?"

"It was a while back. I'm not sure you'd remember. Strange circumstance."

"The last few years have been a tumble. Was it in the service?"

De Vries took McGrady's elbow and ushered him into an office. A pair of tall windows looked toward City Hall and the harbor. The ceiling was high and paneled with a lighter wood than the walls, which made it seem higher still. His desk sat in the room's center, and was long, wide, and empty on top. McGrady took a seat.

"The first day of the war. At the corner of Hollywood Road and Old Bailey."

De Vries was patting his pockets for his cigarette case, but stopped. He studied McGrady anew.

"You're the detective. From Honolulu."

"That's right."

"They had you in for rape."

"It was a setup."

"That's what you told me back then."

"It was true in '41, and it's true now."

"You offered me money," he said, and looked away. He found his cigarettes and pulled one out. He lit it with a match from his desk drawer. "I was too frightened to take it. How'd you get out?"

"I waited for the war to end, and then I got a ride home on the *Missouri*."

"From Tokyo Bay."

"That's right," McGrady said. "You were supposed to evacuate. How'd that go?"

"Not according to plan," De Vries said. He leaned back and pulled on his cigarette. "The Japs shot down our plane before it even arrived to take us out. We couldn't organize another one. So we were still here when the city fell. The Consul handed the keys to this office to General Sakai, and then we were his prisoners."

"For the whole war?"

De Vries tapped ash from his cigarette and shook his head.

"The boys back home worked out a swap—they had the whole Japanese delegation in the U.S. to trade. They did the exchange in Maputo, in Portuguese East Africa."

"So you were home when—by '42?"

"Late '42, yeah."

"You mentioned the service."

"I resigned from State and signed up. I saw a piece of Italy. A lot of France. A bit of Germany. I only got back here two months ago."

"Sounds like you had a good war."

De Vries laughed, but not happily.

"I wouldn't say that," he said. "No one ought to say that. But there's this—I did a lot of things in France that were a hell of a lot harder than it would have been to take your five hundred dollars and get you out of that cell. And I'm sorry I didn't."

It took McGrady by surprise. He hadn't come here looking for an apology.

"It's probably better you didn't," McGrady said. "I gave the money to someone else, and it sounds like the Japanese would've gotten me either way."

"Yes," De Vries said.

He sat back and smoothed out a wrinkle in his jacket, and McGrady let him take his time.

"You didn't come all the way back to Hong Kong just to see me. Patch things up."

"I didn't."

"New case?"

It was McGrady's turn to shake his head.

"What then?"

"When I came here in '41, I was looking for a man. A German. A spy."

"Holy Christ, man. That was four years ago."

"He's still here."

"How the hell do you know that?"

McGrady laid it all out. He only left out the fact that he'd been fired from the Honolulu Police Department. He explained the telegram that had led him back to Hong Kong and his stakeout of the Golden Phoenix. As he was describing the kid from the tailor's shop, De Vries' secretary knocked on the door. She had a tray of tea. She poured for both of them and put two sugar cubes into De Vries' cup. When she was gone, De Vries took a sip and then spoke for the first time in a while.

"Have you gone to the British yet?"

"I'm not going anywhere near the Hong Kong Police. I'm bringing this to you."

De Vries nodded. "Something you said fits in a way you probably don't even know," he said.

"What's that?"

"Klara Weber," De Vries said. "The first signer on the Golden Phoenix account."

"Do you know her?"

"The Brits who arrested you never told you anything, did they? But I got the police report. And the complaining witness —that woman who fingered you in the lineup? Her name was Klara."

McGrady didn't answer at first. He was remembering that night. She'd come in through a side door. Blonde, shapely. Battered all to hell and wearing a policeman's jacket over her shoulders.

"You're sure about that?"

De Vries nodded. "If you'd asked me an hour ago, I wouldn't have remembered. But when you said the name, it came back. Klara, with a *K*."

"I guess that police report's gone," McGrady said. "It would've had an address. Something to follow up on."

"Everything's gone."

McGrady set his cup on its saucer and put it on the side table. He pulled the Cable & Wireless message card from his pocket and slid it across the desk. De Vries opened a drawer and took out a pair of reading glasses. He put them on, then leaned close to look at the card.

"It's not Morse," he said after a moment. "I don't know what it is."

"I didn't either," McGrady said. "Not at first. But then I tried *Wabun*."

It seemed to McGrady that De Vries' eyes held a measure of respect they hadn't before. Maybe he was imagining it.

"This is Japanese?"

"A telegraphic *katakana*."

"You can read it?"

"Not quickly."

"You weren't wasting your time in Tokyo," De Vries said. "What's it say?"

On his walk over, he'd worked out how to play this. He wasn't going to just feed the message to De Vries. The man would have to take the last step on his own. Then he'd be invested. Once he was committed, he'd take risks. God knows there were risks to take.

"It's bigger than John Smith," McGrady said.

"I don't understand. What's in this message?"

"He's organizing escapes," McGrady said. "Setting up the routes, getting the documents together. He's got some big names coming in. Wouldn't you like to take one more shot at them?"

De Vries was silent. He was tracing his finger along the lines of code pasted to the card.

"This is the Consul's office, for god's sake. The war's over. We're not spies."

"Of course not." McGrady let it hang there.

"What is it you want?"

"I'm only here for Smith. The rest of them are yours. You can let them go. Maybe they'll live good lives. Or maybe not."

De Vries lifted the card again and studied it.

"And what do you want from me?"

"You've got resources I don't. If I were in Honolulu, I could find out who owns that building, the Lord Nelson House. Then I'd find out who's renting Flat 1C. If I had to roust the landlord out of bed at midnight, that's what I'd do."

"The landlord might well be in London."

"You've got men in London. You've got men everywhere."

De Vries put the card into his pocket. He stood up.

"I'll see what I can do," he said. He went for the door and McGrady got up to follow. "No promises. We've got a man on staff. A Dutchman, I think, but he's got a British mother— anyway, he's been in Hong Kong forever. He's not with State. We brought him on as local staff a couple months ago. He came knocking for work. Now he's our jack of all trades."

They were going back down the oaken hallway.

"I'll give him the address," De Vries said. "He can run it down. As far as I can tell, the only language he doesn't speak is Japanese, so you've got him there. But he can get records. That'll be no problem."

"All right," McGrady said. "But that's all you give him." He stopped walking, and pulled De Vries around by the shoulder to look at him. "The address. We don't tell him why we're asking. He doesn't talk to the landlord. He doesn't talk to anybody. If it gets out, we're done. These people are being hunted, and they know it. They've got their ears to the ground."

"It won't get out," De Vries said. "Anyway, let's see if Jan's still here or if he's knocked off for the day."

They reached the end of the hall. There was a tall door. De Vries reached out and opened it.

It was a records room. Because of the air conditioning, there was no mold. Still, McGrady could smell old paper. The chemical trace of disintegrating typewriter ribbon. The overhead lights were off. A green tinted lamp was lit somewhere in the back. McGrady could see metal shelves lined up in rows down the middle of the long room. He felt that twinge of excitement. This was the kind of room where cases got closed. Where scores were settled.

"You in here, Jan?"

"In the back."

The man's voice was deep. There was an accent, but it was bland and vague. The same as any Dutchman. They went down a narrow aisle between the stacks. McGrady could see a shadow moving. A heavy book snapped shut. Files fell into a bag.

"I've got a project for you," De Vries said.

"A good one, I hope."

"We'll see."

They hit the end of the stacks. To the right was a small desk. The lamp was there. Behind it was a mountain of a man. He stood up, and his face was tinted green by the glass shade.

"This is my friend Joe," De Vries said. "A citizen in good standing. And we always help our citizens."

McGrady didn't back up. Didn't grab De Vries and hustle him out of the room. He wanted to do those things, and didn't. He could feel the .45 in his waistband. It might as well have been back in Honolulu, in Molly's hatbox. Here was the moment, and he was frozen. He knew the face behind the green light.

He'd studied it for hours. Emily Kam had nailed him. She'd drawn John Smith to perfection.

John Smith stepped around the desk. He reached across the space, hand outstretched. If he'd made it into a fist, it would have been the size of a melon. But he was extending an open palm. McGrady watched his own hand come up, take Smith's, and shake it.

"Good to meet you," Smith said. He glanced at De Vries. He hadn't let go of McGrady's hand. "You said Joe?"

"McGrady," De Vries said. "And this is Jan Van Dijk. We need you to run down the owner of a certain building."

The man calling himself Jan Van Dijk hadn't reacted at all to McGrady's name. He let go of his hand. He patted De Vries on the shoulder. A friendly giant. A Dutchman in Hong Kong, happy to have a paying job to help his American friends. He went back to his desk and took his seat. Sitting didn't make him any smaller.

McGrady was thinking: *He never saw my face. He thinks I'm dead.*

And he was thinking: *I could be wrong.*

He'd been wrong about so many things. Wrong to go to the Bowsprit on the night before Thanksgiving for a glass of whiskey. Wrong to take Beamer's call. Wrong to agree, without a second thought, to board an airplane to Hong Kong. He'd known damned well a storm was coming, even if no one could have guessed just how bad it would be.

"What's the address, then?" Van Dijk asked. He'd gotten a pen. A piece of paper.

McGrady cleared his throat. There was no backing out now. If he tried to shut this down, and if Jan Van Dijk was John Smith, then Smith would know anyway.

"The Lord Nelson House," McGrady said. "Flat 1C. It's a little rundown brick pile on Connaught Road, a couple doors down from the Western Market. You know it?"

"Not offhand."

"Connaught Road has its share of rundown piles," De Vries said.

"What's in Flat 1C?" Van Dijk asked. He was writing on his

sheet of paper. McGrady could read it, upside down. Lord Nelson House. Connaught Road. He wasn't giving off any signals. He was made of stone.

"Not sure," De Vries said. He was sticking to the script. They were just going to give him the address. McGrady had been clear on that.

"I know a little," McGrady said. "It's supposed to be some kind of shipping office. Golden Phoenix Transshipping."

If De Vries looked askance at him, McGrady didn't see. He watched as Van Dijk jotted down the new information. Still nothing. No reaction. He put the pen back in its holder. He folded the piece of paper into a square, and pocketed it. He pulled out a watch and checked the time. An innocent act, maybe. It would look that way to De Vries. But he wasn't doing it for De Vries. This was a show for McGrady. A test. He snapped it closed and set it on the desk.

"The records offices are closed by now," Van Dijk said. "Can you come back in the morning?"

"The morning's fine."

"Eleven o'clock should do it," Van Dijk said. "Or I could bring it to your hotel?"

He picked up the watch and ran it through his fingers like a gambler with a gold coin. Now McGrady could see the front and back of the case, and there was no doubt. It was a Waltham trench watch. There were probably a couple million of them still ticking. The company had made them by the truckload to equip the boys on their way to France. You could buy one for two dollars from the same catalog McGrady had used to send for his knife.

"I'll come here," McGrady said. "I'll need to meet with Nathan anyway."

"Then we'll do it here."

"Thanks, Jan," De Vries said.

McGrady hated to turn his back. But there was no other way to walk out. He let De Vries go first. It would do no good to put De Vries in between them. And it'd be a shame if they both got shot in the back. This wasn't De Vries' fight. They went down the narrow aisle. Away from the lamp's circle, and into the dark. De Vries reached the door and opened it. A crack of light, then a giant rectangle of it. McGrady fought the urge to run. He stepped out, and followed De Vries back to the consulate's front door.

"Eleven o'clock tomorrow, then?" De Vries said.

"Sure."

He took the stairs down to the bank's main lobby, hand on the rail so his knees wouldn't buckle. It was cold, but he was sweating. Hours had gone by since he'd had the drinks at the Peninsula, but now he could feel the whiskey working its way back up. He kept it down, and looked around. The building was shutting down for the evening. All the doors were locked from the inside but one, and that one had a guard on it.

The guard said good night as McGrady passed, and McGrady said nothing.

Outside it was near dark. The warm evening felt sweltering after the air conditioning. The air was thick and languid and so weighted with moisture that it seemed like it might burst into a thunderstorm on a moment's notice. A wide plaza spread out in front of the bank. Marble steps led down to it. He took them one at a time, then got his pace up to weave into the crowd. Fifty feet in, there was a stone planter. Benches built into either side. A banyan tree grew in the middle, dangling its air-borne roots. He sat down, facing the bank.

He should have a newspaper. A straw hat, pulled low.

He had nothing. He'd always had nothing, but he'd gotten this far. He'd found his man. It didn't matter that he'd walked right up to John Smith and practically tripped over his feet before recognizing him. He'd gotten out of the building alive. Now he could think. If his heart would stop trying to jump out of his chest, he could put something together. He breathed in and held it. He closed his eyes for a moment. He'd expected he'd die holding tight to promises he hadn't kept. That could still happen. Call it a fifty-fifty chance Smith would beat him to a pulp and unzip his guts in an alley. One of them was going to win, and one of them was going to lose. If the worst happened, then at least he'd have come close. At least there'd be no uncertainty.

He let out his breath. His stomach had settled, his heart had slowed.

Maybe it wasn't such a surprise for Smith to reinvent himself as Jan Van Dijk and come knocking at the Consul General's office. McGrady didn't know everything Smith had been up to before the war, or what he'd done during it. But he'd read the coded cable, so he had a good idea of what Smith was doing now. A job in the consulate would be a gold mine for one simple reason. A Consul General had the blanket authority to issue a temporary passport, and the equipment to print one. Not as good as the real thing, but good enough for a man to get home. Or to cross a dozen borders and disappear.

And John Smith would know a lot of men who needed to disappear. Men who were working hard to bury their real names and their old ranks and the deeds they had done in service of the Reich. The hunt for them was on. The gallows stood ready. The trapdoors would start dropping open any day. The Army had plenty of rope, and no shortage of men willing to climb the thirteen steps and pull the lever.

John Smith wasn't going to take that drop.

*

It was full dark before Smith emerged from the bank's front door. McGrady had moved to the other side of the plaza, where he could mix with the crowd at the Des Voeux Road trolley stop. McGrady was too far away to see Smith's face, but he didn't need it. No other man that size was going to come out of the building.

Smith stood at the top of the stairs for a moment, looking at something he'd drawn from his pocket. The Waltham watch, maybe. He was wearing a hat and carrying a briefcase, a closed umbrella in the same hand. He started down the steps at an angle, and turned left when he reached the bottom.

McGrady stepped out of the crowd and followed. There was no need to stay close. He couldn't lose Smith in a crowd. Not when he stood an easy foot and a half taller than everyone else. Smith led them around the side of the bank and then across Queen's Road. He wasn't going fast, but wasn't idling at shop windows. A normal pace. There were trolleys on Queen's Road. A few taxis mixed in with the ubiquitous rickshaws. A rickshaw wouldn't be a problem. If he got into taxi or a trolley, McGrady would have to make some fast decisions.

But Smith just plowed ahead, without sidestepping or pausing. The crowd parted ahead of him and came together again behind him. McGrady followed along in his wake. Then Smith turned onto Ice House Street, a narrower lane. The buildings were close. Five- and six-floor tenements. Laundry hung from lines above the street. Shops and restaurants occupied the ground floors, and pedestrians shared the street with the rest of the traffic. McGrady stepped around a woman washing vegetables above a sewer grate. He lost sight of Smith briefly when a handcart loaded with caged chickens came between them. But Smith was still there when McGrady pushed his way clear.

Just walking up the hill. Not looking sideways, not looking back. A steady ship in a turbulent sea.

At the top of the hill, Ice House merged with some larger street. McGrady didn't see a sign. He'd lost his bearings. They were going up. Away from the harbor, and into the maze of roads that followed the lower slopes of the Peak. A higher class of buildings. Ornate brick and stonework. Glittering chandeliers behind leaded glass windows.

They went higher still. The pedestrians thinned out, and now there was space between the buildings. McGrady had to hang far back. Banyans loomed from the roadside and stretched overhead. Underfoot, the pavement was carpeted with crushed figs. The air was fragrant with their peculiar, dry scent.

Up ahead, John Smith was going slower against the slope. Then he turned through an open gate in a stone wall and disappeared.

McGrady paused. Smith was out of sight now, but that didn't mean he was still walking. He could be setting up an ambush, or doubling back along some unseen path. Which left McGrady with nothing but bad choices, and therefore no reason to stop. He drew his gun and kept it out of sight beneath his jacket, and walked the rest of the way to the gate.

He was looking down a white gravel path. It ran alongside a darkened villa. Stately white columns. Marble-clad walls. But no roof, and no glass in the windows. Probably a bomb crater ten feet wide in the living room floor.

Yet there was light coming from the back yard, where the path led. McGrady held the gun out in front of him. He went down the path, staying in the unclipped grass so that his smooth-soled shoes wouldn't crunch on the gravel. Now he was in the shadows along the side of the house. There was a flurry of motion above him. He swung around and nearly squeezed off a shot

before he realized it was nothing. The wrecked villa was full of nesting pigeons.

He went on, toward the light, then stood behind a tree and cautiously looked around its trunk. At the back end of the walled-off yard was a little cottage. A caretaker's house or a maid's quarters. All its lights were on. The front door was open. John Smith had taken off his shoes before going inside. They were on a shelf by the door.

And John Smith was sitting in an upholstered chair. He'd moved it, so that it was at the back of the room and framed by the door. He sat with his right ankle on his left knee, and his hands folded on his lap. There was a side table next to him. A bottle and two glasses.

McGrady couldn't tell if Smith had seen him or not. But when Smith poured an inch from the bottle into the first glass, and then poured another inch into the second, McGrady supposed he probably had. Smith set down the bottle and picked up the second glass, then rose from his chair. He stepped out of sight for a moment, then returned. The glass was no longer in his hand. McGrady didn't think he'd handed it to a guest. McGrady was the guest.

He stood shielded by the tree for another moment. He breathed the night air. He smelled the night flowers. He thought: savor it. Because one man will win everything, and the other will lose everything. There's no such thing as a draw. And however it goes you'll wish you held onto this moment. It won't be long now. Just a few minutes more to go.

He put the gun back into his waistband. If he came through the front door with a .45 in his hand, John Smith might feel like the contest had to be decided then and there. And at the moment, sitting again with his legs crossed and his hands folded, Smith looked like he wanted to talk.

So McGrady stepped out from behind the tree and followed the path the last fifty feet. He came up the three wooden steps to the small porch. He paused a moment at the threshold, and then he stepped inside.

Smith had set the scene. There was a matching upholstered chair. A matching side table, to the right. The glass sat waiting for him. McGrady scanned the room. There was nothing behind the chair Smith had arranged for him. And sitting there, he'd be out of sight of the windows, while having a full view of the rest of the house. So he sat down. He kept his back straight, his body leaning slightly forward. Nothing could obstruct his hand's path to the gun.

He was keenly aware that eight feet away, John Smith's posture was identical. At the consulate, Smith had held the pen with his right hand. Which was now resting under his left hand, just above his belt buckle. Smith's side table was on the left. It was all very nicely staged. He could distract McGrady by reaching for the glass with his left hand, while he drew his gun out with the right. He'd had a long, steady stroll from the consulate to work it all out.

"Do we keep pretending, or no?" Smith said.

"No need."

"You were very collected in front of De Vries."

"I was going to tell you the same thing."

"You wanted to shoot me then, but you couldn't be sure what De Vries would do. Of course, I had the same dilemma."

McGrady could smell the apricot spirits in the glass next to him. Schnapps. Sweet and sharp. The room was nicely kept, and well appointed. A rug on the floor. A whitewashed fireplace. Bookshelves.

"No," McGrady said. "Your dilemma was different. Because

you wouldn't have minded killing De Vries. Except that if you'd done it there, it would make it hard to go back to the consulate. And you have people coming in three days. They'll expect certain documents from you. I think you stayed late tonight to finish them."

Smith smiled. His teeth were as white as sugar, and as wide as spoon handles.

"I'm afraid you wasted yourself at the Honolulu Police Department," Smith said. "What a talent you could have been, in a better field."

"Like yours."

"Like mine, yes."

"Which was what, exactly?"

Smith's eyes shifted to his glass. His left hand moved to pick it up. Testing McGrady, again, but McGrady didn't bite. Smith picked up the glass. He took a sip and set it back down.

"Ah—so close. You didn't shoot me when my hand was full. You wanted to hear my answer."

"Who says I have a gun?"

"Please."

"So tell me the answer."

"The *Abwehr*—do you know it?"

"German intelligence."

"German *military* intelligence. Not some political branch."

"So you were an officer."

"Was. Am. Whichever way you'd like to frame it," Smith said. "Admiral Canaris sent me to New York in 1936. Before the Duquesne mess, and well ahead of the incompetents tasked with Pastorius. I suppose you were out of circulation for a bit. These are familiar references?"

"I caught up. And the Duquesne ring got broken up before I left."

"So it did. And now I've answered your question, so you can answer mine. It's fair?"

"It depends on the question."

"Everything depends on something," Smith said. "I knew who you were when De Vries told me your name. And if he hadn't done that, I'd have known when he gave me the address. But you knew me when I stood up. How did you know my face, when I didn't know yours?"

Smith's hands were perfectly still. Which meant nothing. Snakes could hold perfectly still.

"I'm just wasted on HPD. By the way, Beamer fired me, so good riddance. It didn't stop me from figuring out what he was. And then I killed him."

"Very well, but you didn't answer my question," Smith said. Another smile, the wide teeth gleaming. "But your stall tells me you're protecting someone. Which makes sense. A reasonable man—and I'm sure you are a reasonable man—would be worried he might not leave this house alive."

"I answered your question."

"But you wouldn't bother protecting someone unless it was someone I could reach," Smith said. "So it's obvious. It was the girl. Wait—her name will come to me."

He drummed the fingers of his left hand atop the back of his right hand while he feigned deep thought. Every move a distraction. A game to raise McGrady's tension until something broke.

"That's it!" Smith said, lifting his left hand to snap his fingers. "It was Emily! Emily Kam, who lived a little higher on the hill than I ever will. She was quite the sketch artist, was she not?"

"It doesn't matter."

"Either way, the stakes are higher if you lose."

"I didn't come here to lose."

"Neither did I, Detective McGrady." Again, his left hand crept toward the drink. He reached out and picked it up. Another small sip. His right hand stayed in place as he set the glass down. "Which leads me to my point, and the reason we're having this quiet conversation."

"You can stop there. The answer's no."

"But indulge me, Joe. Neither of us wants to lose. We can't both win. Unless we reach a deal."

"I didn't come here to make a deal, either."

"I was afraid you were going to say that," Smith said. "And I'll give you a chance to change your mind. Just think—you're an intelligent man. We're both intelligent men. Resourceful. We move freely around the world."

"You're a Nazi."

"That's only a word," Smith said. "Politics. A way to divide people."

"It's a big divide."

Smith shook his head. He looked at his lap. A second ticked by when his eyes weren't on McGrady. Then he looked up. McGrady had lost the moment, and Smith knew it. Another test.

"Admiral Canaris was a mentor of mine," Smith said. "A close friend. Herr Hitler hanged him in a concentration camp after marching him naked in front of his staff. They say he was one of the July 20 plotters. Who knows if that's true? But if it is, I applaud Canaris. And if I'd been there, I'd have hanged alongside him."

"Easy to say that now," McGrady said. "And hard to believe. Not a minute ago, you threatened to kill Emily Kam."

Smith picked up his glass again.

"And when I do, it'll be like gutting a fish."

When he launched the glass, McGrady was ready. He dove off his chair, bringing his gun up. Smith's right hand emerged.

A black blur and a flash. They might have pulled their triggers simultaneously. It was hard to say, because Smith's pistol worked and McGrady's jammed.

McGrady rolled away. The air was full of white cotton. Padding from inside the chair. Smith had blown a hole through its back.

McGrady got to his knees. He threw his .45 overhand at Smith. The man caught it on the fly, left handed. He tossed it aside and raised his own pistol. He was laughing as he took aim at McGrady down the iron sights. McGrady was still on his knees. His hands were up. Smith was out of reach.

"I'll pass your regards to her," Smith said. "To Emily."

Once again McGrady was watching a stop motion film. A cheap thrill in the penny arcade. Smith's finger flexing. The grin widening. Quick bursts of thought flashed through McGrady's mind like flares on the battlefield. The night flowers. Sachi in his arms.

A scream brought him out of it. Not his own. Not Smith's.

"Jan!"

Smith pivoted away from McGrady, firing as he moved. McGrady jerked around in time to see Nathan De Vries sprinting through the open door. The bullet caught him somewhere on the left side. He spun and fell behind a coffee table. Smith would have to step around it to get his next shot. It wasn't much of an opening. But it was the only one he was going to get. McGrady drew his knife, left handed, and grabbed Smith's wrist to keep the gun high. Smith put two shots in the ceiling, and then went dead still.

McGrady had hammered his trench knife hilt-deep into Smith's abdomen.

Warm blood flowed across McGrady's hand. He walked Smith backwards until he had him pinned up against the wall of the cottage. The gun fell out of his hand and hit the floor.

McGrady had stuck him well below his navel. But he hadn't left the blade there. He was working it up, and it was sharp as a new razor. All Smith could do about it was watch.

McGrady whispered, his mouth close to Smith's ear as the man slid to the ground.

"This isn't about Emily. Takahashi Kansei sent me here. If that doesn't ring a bell, you murdered his niece. He didn't forget it. He lived for this day. So did Admiral Kimmel. The boy you killed was his nephew." He shoved hard with the knife, drawing a hoarse grunt from the dying man. "But when I see Emily, I promise, I'll tell her what you said—and that I gutted *you* like a fish, with your favorite blade."

He'd sliced all the way up to Smith's sternum now. He was saving the autopsy boys a lot of work. The man's eyes were opening and closing. His mouth was agape, smaller sounds emerging. If he had something to say, he couldn't get it out. It didn't make any difference to McGrady.

He withdrew the blade and let Smith go. He spilled to the floor. Half in the fireplace, half out. A mountain of flesh. Lifeless or soon to be.

McGrady picked up both guns and then crossed the room to De Vries. He'd managed to crawl backwards. Now he was sitting up against the wall. There was plenty of blood. On the floor, on the wall. All over De Vries. But McGrady couldn't tell where he'd been hit.

"You all right?"

De Vries shook his head. He blinked. Then he nodded. McGrady set the guns down and peeled his jacket back, exposing the hole in De Vries' white shirt.

"It's in your shoulder. You'll be okay."

"I know. I've done this."

"Done what?"

"I got shot in France," De Vries said. Smith's gun was next to him on the floor. De Vries was looking at it. "Same fucking German Walther. But that time was in the other shoulder."

"Let me help you up."

McGrady lifted him to his feet and brought him to the chair.

"I'll find some towels, get a press on this. And then we should get out of here. There's a phone. You got someone you trust with a car?"

They needed a car. No way could they walk on the street. McGrady was even bloodier than De Vries.

"There's someone."

McGrady went to the bathroom. He found a couple of clean white towels and came back. He ripped the sleeve off De Vries' shirt, then tore the shoulder seam up to the collar. He used the sleeve to wipe away the blood.

"In the front, out the back," McGrady said. He pressed the towels down. "How long were you standing out there?"

"Long enough."

"Why'd you come?"

De Vries coughed hard for a moment, then answered through clenched teeth. McGrady was pressing hard now to staunch the wound. It had to hurt.

"Fire in the office. Trash can, in a broom closet. Full of papers. No idea what got burned. So I checked the place. Van Dijk, whatever his name is—fuck, that hurts—he'd cleared out his desk."

"So you came looking."

"I came."

"You came in without a gun, after he'd started shooting."

"So you want to tell me what that cable says?"

"Later," McGrady said. "Let's get you on the phone. We better do it now, before you pass out."

52

McGrady walked out of the American consulate. It was an hour past sunset. Christmas Day. Smith had been dead for nineteen hours.

McGrady didn't know where he was going tonight. He knew where he was going in the morning. There was a mail plane that left at seven A.M. It stopped in Taipei and left the next morning for Shanghai. He had a letter from the consulate that would get him onto an Air Transport Command C-47 that left Shanghai on December 28th. De Vries had taken care of that from his hospital bed.

He went past the Central Police Station. He went past the bank where he'd been imprisoned. He went down Pottinger Street and then back up it. He wandered in search of a drink. Near the Garden Street Station he spotted a pub that was open. He put his suitcase on an empty stool and sat next to it. He ordered a two-finger pour of scotch. The good stuff, from the Isle of Skye. The cost had gone up since the last time he'd ordered it. But now he couldn't peg its price to the number of hours it took him to earn it. He didn't make anything an hour. He didn't need anything, either. The bartender set the scotch in front of him. McGrady had asked for a single piece of ice. He watched it melt. No one came to interrupt him. No one in the world knew he was here.

He drank the scotch, put coins on the bar, and left.

He walked up to the tram station, carrying his suitcase. He bought a seat in the third class car and crossed the platform to

board the waiting funicular tram. The doors closed, and the car began its ascent. He watched out the window. He saw the city's gas lamps and the running lights of boats in the harbor. A little higher, and he saw Kowloon glittering. He got out at the final stop and walked out of the station. He saw the café where he'd once sat with Emily Kam and had a bottle of cold mineral water.

She lived at Number 8, Old Peak Road. He'd never had to find the place because she'd met him at the station. This time, she didn't know he was coming. It was dark. It was cool, and cloudy. Everything had changed since that day. But here he was again.

He found the house after half an hour of false starts up the wrong unmarked roads. He went around the vehicle gate and walked up the steep driveway. There was a turn circle. There was a fountain gurgling. He saw upper terraces and grooved stone columns.

He went to the front door. He found the bell and rang it. He didn't expect her to answer. It would be a servant. Or her mother.

But the door opened, and it was Emily Kam. Her dark hair was a little bit longer. She was wearing a printed silk robe, and slippers. She looked at him. He wasn't surprised that she recognized him. She had an artist's eyes. She remembered faces well enough to draw them from memory after the fact.

He spoke before she did.

"I know it's rude, dropping in out of nowhere. Especially on Christmas."

"It's all right—of course it's all right."

"I thought you'd want to know."

"You've done it, haven't you?"

"Last night. Here in Hong Kong."

"He was here all along? Did you arrest him?"

"He's gone."

"He escaped?"

"He didn't get away."

"Would you like to come in?"

"For a little bit. Sure."

They were upstairs, on the terrace. They were leaning on the balustrade and looking at the city lights down below. Her mother was in Macau, with a man she'd met there. Her grandmother had passed on. The servants had the day off. She had the house to herself. She was still wearing her robe.

They'd talked about some of the things that had happened after they'd last seen each other. Now they were just looking at the lights. McGrady turned to her.

"If Vincent Russo hadn't come knocking on your window that night, he wouldn't have met up with Smith—"

"His name was really John Smith?"

"I've got no idea," McGrady said. "And I doubt I ever will. But what I meant was, it's funny. How things work out. All the little turning points."

She nodded. She stood up from the rail and used the backs of her fingers to wipe her eyes.

"A lot of things are funny," she said. "I thought I'd cried all the tears I had. You wouldn't think I'd have any left for Vincent. But I suppose I do."

"It's okay."

"Don't you ever?"

"More than I'd like to admit."

"Here—wait a moment. One of my father's friends dropped something off this morning, for Christmas. I didn't open it. Let's have it. Is that alright?"

"Sure."

"And I want to show you something."

She went away. He leaned on the rail and looked at the lights. He'd become very good at thinking about nothing. Leaning on a rail and looking at lights was good for that. She came back in a few moments. She had a bottle of champagne and a couple of glasses. She had a sheathed Japanese sword tucked under her arm. She put the bottle and the glasses on the rail. She handed him the sword. He unsheathed it, and looked at the blade. It was more like a gemstone than a piece of steel. He tested its edge with his fingertip.

"You sent me a drawing. The dead officer."

"I wanted to tell you. I wanted to tell somebody. But I couldn't write it down."

"Is this what you used?"

"It was his."

"It happened when you went to get the drawing."

She nodded. She put her back against the rail, so that she was looking at him.

"The sketchbook was in my bedroom. I slipped in, barefooted. I was very quiet. He was asleep in my bed. I could have taken what I wanted and gotten out without waking him. But I recognized him. He was the one talking to John Smith while his men bayonetted my father."

He looked down at the blade. The lights of Kowloon shone on its edge. It was a heavy sword. Yasukuni steel. It had been made by an artist. But its beauty was an illusion. It was made to take lives.

"It was next to him," Emily said, looking at the sword. "I picked it up and unsheathed it. I held the tip right at his neck. I could have cut his throat in his sleep, and he'd have never known it."

"But you couldn't do it."

"I couldn't. You're right. I was relieved. And also ashamed. I watched him give the order to kill my father. Here I was, with the chance to avenge him, and I couldn't do it. I was stepping away when he woke up. He sat up and turned toward me. There was something in his hand. Small and black. A pistol, I was sure. And I couldn't let him yell."

"The house was full of soldiers—you didn't have a choice."

"I wasn't thinking at all. I killed him and I wasn't thinking about my father, or what they did to my mother, or anything else. It was just fear. Like an animal. I was trying to save myself. He could have been anybody. It wasn't for my father."

She had her arms wrapped around herself. She was rocking lightly back and forth. He remembered the first time he'd spoken to her. She'd just turned twenty-two. Life was a game to be played. She'd been playing to win. That was only four years ago. Now she had her house and her money back, but nothing else would ever be the same.

"It was a prayer book," she said.

"What?"

"In his hand," she said. "Not a gun. A prayer book."

"You wanted the drawing to mean something," he said. "For it to have been worthwhile."

She looked up at him. She stopped rocking.

"Was it?"

"I'd have never gotten him without it," McGrady said. "Not a chance. And he paid for what he did. I can promise you that."

He sheathed the blade. He was handing it back to her, but she wouldn't take it.

"Look at the cloth tied under the guard," she said. "Can you read it? I've always wondered. But I didn't want to go around asking. But since you were in Tokyo all that time—but maybe that's presumptuous."

She began opening the champagne. He spread the strip of crimson fabric out on the balustrade and bent to look at the calligraphy. He'd expected a poem. Maybe something in classical Japanese. The language the Emperor had used at the moment of surrender. But what was written was very simple.

Father—do your duty, and come home to us.
We will hold the world still, until you return.

The man's daughters had signed it, four of them. McGrady stood up. He looked at Emily. She was holding a glass of champagne out for him. He took it.

"I can't make it out," he said. "I think it's about glory. Empire, conquest. That kind of thing."

She touched her glass to his.

"You don't have to make up stories," she said. "I can read enough to know that's not what it says."

"All right."

"I just want to know. If you know, then tell me."

He told her what it really said. She listened. She drank a bit of her champagne. He told her about the teenaged boy he'd killed. He told her the fear that still woke him up—that the boy had gone into the privy hole alive. She took his hand and held it tight. He squeezed back. They let go of each other. She refilled their glasses.

"Let's do this over," she said. "We need a new toast."

"Okay."

"This is the same sort Vincent brought to my window," she said, holding the bottle. "Brut Imperial. I didn't want to share it with someone who didn't understand."

She touched her glass to his a second time.

"But you understand, don't you, Joe?"

"I hope so."

"Then this one's for everything we haven't lost."

They both turned back to the view. They drank their champagne. They were on a balance point as fine as the edge of the sword that lay on the balustrade between them. They slid along it a long time before Emily finally spoke.

"You brought a suitcase."

"I'm catching a plane in the morning."

"You're going home."

"There's something I've got to do first."

He finished his glass and set it on the rail. He'd finally understood it yesterday, as he'd been sounding out the *katakana* syllables of Smith's code, tapping and brushing his wrist. He'd understood a lot more than just Smith's message. He couldn't go home. There was no such thing as home.

She touched his shoulder.

"What's that? That you need to do?"

"Walk. I need to think."

"You'll walk all night?"

"It wouldn't be the first time."

53

The mail plane out of Hong Kong was a repurposed Mitsubishi twin-prop. Its Manchuria Aviation Company markings were still visible beneath a thin coat of new gray paint. McGrady sat in the co-pilot's seat. The pilot climbed in beside him. His hands were black with engine grease and his coveralls smelled of gasoline. He took off and circled the city and headed to the northwest before he said anything.

"McGrady, right?"

"That's right."

"Anders."

"Okay."

"You bring lunch?"

"No."

"Oh well."

Anders had nothing else to say to McGrady. He spoke English, Cantonese and Mandarin over the radio, an unlit cigarette bouncing between his lips. When he patted at his shirt pocket looking for a lighter, he pulled out a wad of currency as thick as the New Testament. Behind their seats, the plane was loaded with cargo. McGrady wasn't sure any of it was mail. When they hit turbulence, he could hear bottles rattling against each other. He could smell gun oil. There was some kind of live animal scratching at the inside of a wooden box. They landed outside of Taipei. There were rice paddies on both sides of the landing strip, December-brown and muddy. No one had yet bothered to fill in the bomb craters.

Anders taxied to a hangar and killed the engines. He pointed through the windshield to the hangar door.

"Tomorrow," he said. "Sunrise."

"I'll be here."

"You might try around the Lungshan Temple. You can get one for the price of a bowl of soup."

"Get what?"

"A girl."

"I'm not looking for that."

They pressed through the cargo to the plane's rear door, and climbed out to the dusty tarmac. The pilot disappeared into the hangar. McGrady walked until he found his way off the airfield and onto a street. He found a taxi and talked to the driver. He said what he was after and the driver brought him to Hsimenting. He walked through narrow alleys. The neighborhood was close to the banks of the Danshui River. The breeze stank of raw sewage. He bought what he could. De Vries had warned him. In the occupied zone, he'd need to bring his own food. So he bought canned goods. Eel and sardines. Rice and dried noodles. He found a lightweight canvas jacket. He found a pair of heavy khaki pants.

At dawn, he was back at the hangar. Anders was already in the plane. The engines were turning. McGrady ran to the plane and climbed through the open rear door. The cargo compartment was empty, but for a single box. He shut the door and then went up front to take his seat. They flew to Shanghai without speaking.

He stayed on the Bund. He called at the consulate, and showed his letter. Then he walked out looking for provisions and warm clothes. He found a pair of worn-out wool socks. He found a white cotton scarf. There hadn't been any gloves for sale. There'd been no hats. He was going to have to wear his street shoes.

The next morning, he was on another Air Transport Command flight. A C-47, this time. He was surrounded by men in uniform. Army brass. A handful of diplomats and newspapermen. There was an enlisted kid who handed out hot coffee and sandwiches. By three in the afternoon, he was in Tokyo again. American M.P.s met the plane. They were checking passports. They were checking credentials and press passes. McGrady got out his letter from the Hong Kong consul. He expected trouble but didn't get any. He looked like he knew what he was doing. That was good enough for them.

There were no clothes to buy in Tokyo. In fact, there was almost nothing to buy in Tokyo. Instead, there were lines at the Methodist tent camps around Haneda Field. Missionaries were handing out condensed milk. They were giving out tinned fish. He walked past them. It was a degree above freezing, and it was raining. He hitched a ride with an Army doctor who'd been on the Shanghai flight. The man took him all the way into the city. He jumped out at Tokyo Station.

The Nagano train wasn't leaving until the next morning. The station hotel was booked solid with American brass. He spent half the night on the railway platform. When he couldn't take the cold anymore, he paced.

In the morning he went to Nagano. It was a journey of a hundred and fifty miles. It took all day. The locomotive broke down twice. They had to wait hours on sidetracks so freight trains hauling American military equipment could pass. When he finally reached Nagano, the last northbound train to Togari had already left. He went walking around the station in search of an inn. He found a room in a family's house. He paid for it with a can of sardines and a bag of raw peanuts from Taipei. He spent the night huddled under a wool blanket. In the morning, he walked back to the station. A train with frost-whitened windows was waiting on the platform.

It pulled him north into a snowscape.

He had a sagging wicker bench in the second-class car, up against the window. The seat next to him was empty. The train was struggling up a steep section of track. The window glass was frozen. Feathery fingers of ice had grown from the edges to the middle of the pane. He kept one spot clear by breathing on it. He could wipe it with his sleeve and see outside.

Snow-covered trees. Snow-covered rock berms. Villages buried in snow. They passed frozen waterfalls. They passed a troupe of snow-covered macaques huddled at the mouth of a railway tunnel.

His clothes were inadequate. He'd known they would be, but there was nothing to do about it.

Togari Station was just a little wooden hut next to the train platform. Its steeply pitched roof was covered in three feet of snow. Icicles dangled. He went inside. He stood shivering by the coal stove for a moment, and then he went to the ticket office.

Can you tell me the way to Nozawaonsen?

The station agent looked at him. This big underdressed American speaking Japanese. The man got over his surprise. He stepped out of his booth. He was wearing a fur-lined hat and leather gloves. He went out onto the platform and pointed.

That way. You have to cross the river. It's six or seven kilometers.

Is there a bus? A taxi?

No bus — no taxi. Cross the river on the bridge, and go straight.

Are there inns?

They'll be full. Why do you want to go there?

I'm looking for someone.

You must really want to find him. Maybe someone will give you a ride.

✿

No one gave him a ride. He stumbled along the icy road, leaning into the wind. He found the bridge. The river was frozen. Greenish black ice, crusted in places with newer snow. He could see the current flowing down beneath the surface. He went on, through a snow-covered field. There were houses ahead. A little farming village. By the time he reached the houses, he couldn't feel his feet. He'd only gone half a kilometer from the station. He switched his suitcase back and forth, warming one hand in his pocket while the other one froze into an aching claw.

He went onward, and up. His cheeks stung. His ears felt like they might freeze and break off. He jogged the last three kilometers. His breath hung in frozen clouds in the air behind him.

The village of Nozawaonsen was tiny. Buildings were made of unpainted cedar. Their roofs were buried in snow. There was a smell of brimstone mixed with the wood smoke. He looked up into the surrounding ring of mountains. The trees were pure white. There were tendrils of fog winding through the snow-covered trunks. Every time the wind gusted, he could hear ice shattering. It sounded like someone walking across a field of broken glass.

He found a teashop that was open. Even with no customers, it was cramped. Like two phone booths stuck together. He went in and dropped his suitcase on the floor. He stood at the counter shivering. The owner came through a curtain.

Welcome—

The man stopped when he saw him.

Hot tea, please. I can pay in American dollars. Or with rice. Whichever you prefer.

Are you all right?

I will be, once I have some tea.

The man went to get the tea. He came back with a pot of it. He poured a cup. When McGrady touched it, it burned his frozen fingers. He picked it up anyway. He drank it. He could feel ice melting in his eyebrows.

You are American?

I am. But not in the Army.

Are you looking for a place to stay? I have one room.

I am looking for a family. They are friends of mine. They live here.

They are Japanese? This family?

Takahashi Kansei. Takahashi Sachi. They live in Tokyo. In Yanaka. But Nozawaonsen is their true home.

The old man nodded. He poured more tea into McGrady's cup.

You must have met them overseas. Deputy Minister Takahashi traveled so much.

You know them?

I grew up with the Deputy Minister. I saw Sachi-san last week. I have not seen her father since before the war.

McGrady squeezed his hands around the teacup. She was here. She was within walking distance. That didn't mean she wouldn't bolt her door at the sight of him. Which was her decision to make. All he could do was give her the choice.

How do I find their house?

Did the Americans send you? Are you a policeman?

I am here for myself. I would never hurt them. I would never hurt Sachi. I swore that, to her father.

The innkeeper looked at him. He considered that for a long while. McGrady finished the tea in his cup.

You keep going up this road. When you pass the hot spring, you turn left. You follow that road all the way to the end. The Takahashi house is the only one up there.

Is it far?

At least fifteen kilometers. But there was a storm last night. A heavy, deep snowfall. I don't know about that road right now.

He didn't know if he could do another fifteen kilometers. The last six had been hard enough. The innkeeper read it on his face.

You should have some more tea. You should have something to eat, if you have anything. Then you should wait until you have different clothes, and boots. Or you should wait until there's a thaw. It's no road for casual mistakes. And it's too late, anyway.

That decided it.

He drank the rest of the tea in the pot. He paid the man, and then he left. He wasn't going to wait for anything. Not when he was this close. But it was more than that. He wouldn't prove anything if he waited for everything to be easier. He needed to be able to look her in the eyes.

It was already beginning to get dark. The sun was going down at such a steep angle, the dusk would linger a long time. He hurried up the road. He passed houses and small shops. He saw a few people on the street. They bowed to him. He set his suitcase down, and bowed back.

The public hot spring was the town's central square. It flowed from one stone-lined pool to another. Stairs and wooden railings led down to it. Steam rose up from the water and from cracks in the street. He found the left turn. The road went up into the trees. It was narrow. It hadn't been plowed all winter. If Sachi had been coming up and down it, she must have been using skis or snowshoes. He had neither. But he also had no choice.

He started up the road. The first kilometer was all right. The snow was compact. He only sank as far as his ankles. The trees blocked most of the wind. But as the road curved higher, the

snow became deeper. He was up to his knees. Some of the fresh powder drifts were as high as his waist. His pants weren't waterproof. Neither were his shoes or his socks. He kept going. He tried to run through the deepest drifts. It was almost like swimming. In places, where the road was steep, he had to grapple at the snow with his fingers. He had to throw the suitcase in front of him and then climb up to it.

He was making progress, but it was slow. It was full dark. There were stars above the ice-laced branches. The night was getting colder by the minute. He was barely an hour in, and he was already getting strange ideas. Deadly ideas. He pictured crawling inside a snow bank to sleep. The snow was thick and fluffy. It would be so warm underneath it. A while later, he imagined the road was bent into a tight curve. That he could cut the distance by leaving the road and breaking through the woods.

He forced himself forward. He focused on the road. She was at the end of the road. That was the only thing that mattered.

The first time he fell, he was on a downward slope. He landed face first and skidded downhill. He hit a soft patch and disappeared into it. He had to fight his way up. He'd lost the suitcase. It was either up above him somewhere or it was buried with him. Five days of food. His service sidearm. The rest of his money.

He went on without it.

Now he had snow down his collar and up his sleeves. Some of it melted. It froze onto his skin. He was clad in ice. It felt like someone was hitting his toes with an axe. He pressed his lips together to keep from screaming. They froze in place. It hurt so much, he couldn't balance. Which meant that after the first fall, he fell all the time. Onto his knees and onto his back.

He was freezing. He was losing control. He understood what could happen. What was probably going to happen. But he was sure he'd come more than halfway. It would make more sense to go forward than to go back. And at any rate, going forward was the only choice. If going back were an option, he would have gone back a long time ago.

When he saw the light, he figured he was dreaming it. He didn't get his hopes up.

It looked enough like a dream. It was blurry. It was split by a hundred prisms. Ice had stuck to his eyelashes. He pressed through the last hundred yards. He went beneath a tall wooden gate and stumbled into the yard. The house was up ahead. It was the one he'd seen in the photographs. There were lights coming from inside. Chimney smoke. He fell on his knees at the front door. He was arriving at her doorstep exactly as he had the first time he'd come to her. Empty handed. Desperate. There was no bell. He didn't know if he'd have the strength to knock. He tapped his bare knuckles on the wood. The door was frozen solid. It was like hitting a rock. He tapped again. He waited. He flailed at the door. He was making as much noise as a foraging mouse.

At last the door cracked open. He could feel the ribbon of heat slipping out. Then she was there. She was wearing a heavy white kimono. Her hair was pinned up with black sticks. He tried to say her name. His lips were sealed. His tongue was swollen and stuck to the roof of his mouth. He couldn't speak.

He wasn't sure she'd even know him. But her eyes went wide. There was recognition. Then fear. But she wasn't scared of him. She came out of the house. She shut the door behind her.

Joe—Joe—

She put her hands on him. She pulled him up. He thought she'd bring him inside. She didn't. She was leading him around the side of the house. There was a shoveled path. They went down it. The way was lined with stone lanterns. They were still lit. She was hurrying him. They were going into the trees again. He would have fallen five times already if she hadn't been holding him up. If he didn't get inside soon, he was going to die. He was going to collapse in front of her, and die at her feet. He tried to pull away from her, tried to bolt back to the house. But she led him on. She was stronger than him now. He couldn't shake her loose.

Trust me, Joe. You have to trust me.

They went through another gate. They went down a set of wooden steps. The steps had been scraped clean. They'd been salted. There was a bench beneath a wooden pergola. Black stone steps led down from there to a pool of opalescent water. Clouds of steam rose from its surface. The stairs went to the edge and then disappeared.

She took his army jacket off and put it on the bench. She unbuttoned his shirt. She knelt and took off his shoes. To remove his socks, she had to crack blocks of ice. Then she got him out of his pants. He couldn't help her. His fingers were useless. He was so frozen that he wasn't any colder with his clothes off than with them on. He stood naked and trembling. She untied her kimono's sash. She let both of her robes fall onto the bench. Her entire body blushed at the sudden cold. She stepped out of her house slippers. She pulled off her split-toed socks. She held his arm and helped him down the steps and into the steaming water.

It burned his toes and his ankles. It was scalding hot. She saw him hesitate, saw him try to pull back. She put her hands on his shoulders.

It's all right. You just need to get in. It will hurt. And then it will be all right.

She went with him down the steps and into the pool. She got him all the way in. There were needles pushing into his skin. They flipped from ice-cold to branding-iron hot. She sat down on a stone bench beneath the surface. The water came to her shoulders. She drew him to her and held him to her chest. She held him tight through his spasms.

All the blood was draining from his head. It was like someone had pulled a plug at the base of his skull. His pain blinked out. The stars switched on. They were too bright to look at. They were searchlights. They were spinning and switching positions. New constellations came into focus. He was going to faint. He was struggling against it. He knew he'd lose.

He wasn't scared. She was here. She hadn't turned him away. She would hold him through it. She wouldn't let him drown. She scooped water up in her hand and used it to wash the ice out of his hair.

He closed his eyes. Time slipped.

He startled awake. She held him down. She shushed him. She pulled him close until he slept again. He could feel the world spinning. He could hear the vortex of arctic wind cycling down from the pole.

He opened his eyes. He was facing the sky.

It was clear overhead. The wind was carrying in snow from somewhere else. It was coming down through the trees. Big flakes, swirling. Blinking in and out between the starlight and the shadows. A snowflake landed on his face. Another landed in Sachi's hair. He brought his hand up from the water and touched it. She took hold of his fingers. She brought both their hands back into the water's heat.

He wasn't sure he could speak. He didn't want to try. He couldn't get this wrong. He found her forearm under the water. He slid his finger along her inner wrist and found the most delicate patch of skin. He began to tap and brush the small bones leading up to her palm.

There was so much he wanted her to know. But he began with the most important thing. He started with the first principle. The foundation. The bedrock on which they would build everything else if she let them go forward.

Acknowledgments

My grandfather, John Grundmann, and my great uncle, Henry Grundmann, were like so many other men of their generation: humble, reserved, quiet. They were Oklahoma farmers. They raised cattle, and mowed hay, and planted pecan orchards. They didn't boast about what they had done between December 7, 1941 and September 2, 1945, because every man they'd grown up with had done the same things. But if you could pin them down and draw them out, they would tell stories. I wish that I could give this story back to them. The best I can do now is dedicate it to their memories.

This book would also never have come together without the support of many other friends. In Hawaii, some of the most generous and well-connected men in the state let me sit at their table and drink on their tab while they told stories. Bert Kobayashi, Alan Goda, Walter Dods, and Warren Luke brought bygone Honolulu to life from the lounge at the Waialae Country Club. They looked the other way while I spilled martinis, and told me about the Pan Am Clippers, and the manapua men who used to walk the neighborhoods, and what life was like behind the wire of Japanese–American internment camps.

Likewise, Yasuki Takano, Shoji Fukuta, Yoshiko Saito, Shimpei Ogata, Kazuto Uzuhashi, and Yuichiro Nishi hosted me in Japan on five separate trips, opening doors I wouldn't have even known to knock on had I just been a foreigner bumbling around Tokyo with a guidebook. The Tokyo that existed before the firebombing of March 9–10, 1945 is all but gone. It burned to ash and blew

away. But there are pockets of memory, and they showed me where to look.

Ian Childs, formerly of the Royal Hong Kong Police Force, helped me skirt street protests and tear gas, on a nighttime run to see the horse races at Happy Valley. I was writing about one dark turning point in Hong Kong's history while looking at it through the lens of another. I hope to visit Ian and his city again, though I worry that may be a long time coming.

Steve Silver, the preeminent Japanese translator in Hawaii, helped me immensely—and blessedly without sending me an invoice. On one particular point—the correct, 1940's era military order to fix bayonets—Steve also put together a brain trust including Yuko Funaki and Glen Melchinger. Yuichiro Nishi also deserves additional thanks for reading the manuscript a second time and walking me through the particulars of Japanese etiquette. Under his guidance, I learned to read *hiragana* and *katakana*, and together with what Mandarin I have leftover from four years of living in Taiwan, I can now at least stumble through a Japanese menu. The upshot of this study is that I can say, without a doubt, that any man locked in a house for four years with a beautiful woman who spoke Japanese would surely emerge a fluent speaker.

For help with military matters, I must thank Dallan Reese and Russell Reese, of the U.S. Air Force, and Navy veterans Ray Waid and Mike Wright. Dr. Nathaniel Boyer has for years answered questions about injuries and autopsies that would drive a normal person to report me to the FBI. The same is true of Tom Yee, who has told me so much about firearms over the course of seven novels that I should probably report him.

My deepest thanks go to early readers of this manuscript, which initially weighed in at a scale-breaking seven hundred pages. Bruce Nakamura, Thomas Cooney, Elizabeth Moore,

and J Strother Moore all took the plunge and helped me to rethink some of the early drafts.

Finally, two people deserve the most credit for bringing this story to the world. My agent, Alice Martell, read every draft. She stood behind the story even as she urged me to cut out nearly sixty thousand words, and this story would simply not exist on a printed page without her hard work and encouragement. Charles Ardai, the force behind Hard Case Crime, went to bat for this book in every possible way, and at a point in history when I didn't think anyone would have the guts to take a risk on a work of fiction. Being published by Hard Case Crime is a great honor, and one I'll never forget.

The LOST Detective Novel
From the Creator of PERRY MASON

The KNIFE SLIPPED

by ERLE STANLEY GARDNER

Lost for more than 75 years, *The Knife Slipped* was meant to be the second book in the Cool & Lam series but got shelved when Gardner's publisher objected to (among other things) Bertha Cool's tendency to "talk tough, swear, smoke cigarettes, and try to gyp people." But this tale of adultery and corruption, of double-crosses and triple identities—however shocking for 1939—shines today as a glorious present from the past, a return to the heyday of private eyes and shady dames, of powerful criminals, crooked cops, blazing dialogue and wild plot twists.

RAVES FOR THE KNIFE SLIPPED:

"A remarkable discovery…fans will rejoice at another dose of Gardner's unexcelled mastery of pace and an unexpected new taste of his duo's cyanide chemistry."
— Kirkus Reviews

"A treasure that's not to be missed."
— Book Reporter

"A gift to aficionados of the Cool and Lam series."
— New York Journal of Books

"A time machine back to an exuberant era of snappy patter, stakeouts and double-crosses."
— Publishers Weekly

SONGS of INNOCENCE

by **RICHARD ALEAS**

Three years ago, detective John Blake solved a mystery that changed his life forever—and left a woman he loved dead. Now Blake is back, to investigate the apparent suicide of Dorothy Louise Burke, a beautiful college student with a double life. The secrets Blake uncovers could blow the lid off New York City's sex trade…if they don't kill him first.

Richard Aleas' first novel, LITTLE GIRL LOST, was among the most celebrated crime novels of the year, nominated for both the Edgar and Shamus Awards. *But nothing in John Blake's first case could prepare you for the shocking conclusion of his second…*

PRAISE FOR SONGS OF INNOCENCE:

"An instant classic."
— Washington Post

"The best thing Hard Case is publishing right now."
— San Francisco Chronicle

"His powerful conclusion will drop jaws."
— Publishers Weekly

"So sharp [it'll] slice your finger as you flip the pages."
— Playboy